WESTERN

Rugged men looking for love...

Sweet-Talkin' Maverick

Christy Jeffries

The Cowboy's Second Chance

Cheryl Harper

MILLS & BOON

Christy Jeffries is acknowledged as the author of this work
SWEET-TALKIN' MAVERICK

First Published 2024
First Australian Paperback Edition 2024
ISBN 978 1 867 29967 7

THE COWBOY'S SECOND CHANCE

First Published 2024
First Australian Paperback Edition 2024
ISBN 978 1 867 29967 7

Published by
Harlequin Mills & Boon
An imprint of Harlequin Enterprises (Australia) Pty Limited
(ABN 47 001 180 918), a subsidiary of HarperCollins
Publishers Australia Pty Limited
(ABN 36 009 913 517)
Level 19, 201 Elizabeth Street
SYDNEY NSW 2000 AUSTRALIA

Printed and bound in Australia by McPherson's Printing Group

Sweet-Talkin' Maverick

Christy Jeffries

MILLS & BOON

Christy Jeffries graduated from the University of California, Irvine, with a degree in criminology and received her Juris Doctor from California Western School of Law. But drafting court documents and working in law enforcement was merely an apprenticeship for her current career in the dynamic field of mummyhood and romance writing. Christy lives in Southern California with her patient husband, two sarcastic sons and a sweet husky who sheds appreciation all over her car and house.

Visit the Author Profile page
at millsandboon.com.au for more titles.

Dear Reader,

When I was a young romantic with stars in my eyes and I read a story about a confirmed bachelor, it was so difficult for me to relate to the concept. Who *wouldn't* want to fall in love and get married?

And then twenty-one years ago, I met my then fiancé's uncle Tommy.

Now, Uncle Tommy is the definition of the term *fun uncle*. My sons even bought him a T-shirt that says FUNCLE. He's the life of the party and people naturally gravitate toward him...especially the ladies. He's also a very successful sales broker without giving off that stereotypical salesman vibe. Sure, someone out there will come along one day and capture Uncle Tommy's heart, but it'll definitely take the right woman.

In *Sweet-Talkin' Maverick*, salesman Dylan Sanchez reminded me so much of Uncle Tommy. He adores his family, yet also enjoys his role as the last single Sanchez sibling. His relatives, though, have a different plan and convince him to host a Valentine's Day–themed bakeoff.

Horsewoman and business owner Robin Abernathy is more comfortable outdoors on a ranch than she is inside a kitchen. But that doesn't stop her from entering the contest in an effort to spend more time with her crush. Will it be Robin's secret cookie recipe or her skills at ranching that will eventually capture Dylan's heart?

For more information on my other books, visit my website at christyjeffries.com, or chat with me on Twitter at @ChristyJeffries. You can also find me on Facebook (authorchristyjeffries) and Instagram (@christy_jeffries). I'd love to hear from you.

Enjoy,
Christy Jeffries

DEDICATION

To Tommy Thompson, everyone's favourite uncle. The first time I met you, you got a business call and told the person on the other end of the line that you couldn't talk right that second because you were about to do a shot of Cabo Wabo with your niece. Since that day, anytime you've introduced me to someone (and you seem to know *everyone*), the phrase *niece-in-law* has never been in your vocabulary. It's no wonder everyone in your family—especially your "grand-nephews"—adore you. You have the biggest heart and you make life more fun...

PROLOGUE

NEARLY EVERYONE IN our small Montana town had attended some sort of event in the newly renovated Bronco Convention Center. But only one other couple had thrown an actual party inside of it. Of course, the last weekend in January wasn't exactly the time of year for a large outdoor gathering, and the crowd tonight was definitely a large one.

Everyone knows that when the beloved mayor invites the whole town to celebrate his thirtieth wedding anniversary, it's not a question of *if* you'll go. It's a question of what you should wear and who else is going to be sitting at your table. Sure, you could miss the annual Christmas tree lighting or a rodeo on occasion. Those types of events brought in enough tourists that your absence might go unnoticed. However, tonight's party celebrating Rafferty and Penny Smith was strictly for the locals. And anyone who was anyone in Bronco, Montana, had RSVP'd yes before the invitations were even printed.

"Thank you all for coming out to join me and Penny on this momentous occasion," Mayor Rafferty Smith began his speech welcoming everyone. The man was a great speaker and an even better storyteller. It was no wonder he kept getting reelected. "You know, when I first asked Penny to marry me, I wasn't sure she'd say yes. In fact, I don't think *she* even knew she was going to say yes. But we were just a couple of young kids in love back then, flying by the seats of our pants. We had no big plans other than making it through each day and having as much fun as we could. Nobody tells you how much work a marriage takes… I mean, nobody except all the boring adults who know better than you. But you ignore them because you've got too many stars in your eyes. Then, as time goes by and you begin to look back on all the ups and downs, all the good times and the bad, you begin to realize what you've actually accomplished. Personally, my biggest achievement is sharing the past thirty years with the woman I love."

Everyone oohed and aww'd as the mayor pulled his wife onto the stage beside him. "Penny, you've stuck by my side all this time and there is nothing I could give you that would even come close to everything you've given me these past years. But I couldn't show up here completely empty-handed." The crowd chuckled politely, then applauded as Rafferty presented his wife with a black velvet jewelry case. "They say pearls are traditional for the thirtieth anniversary, but if you ask me, there is nothing traditional about you, Penny Smith. Like this necklace, you are one of a kind and I can't wait to see what the next thirty years have in store for us."

Rafferty made a big show of fastening the stunning heirloom pearl necklace around Penny's neck, causing the guests to cheer uproariously when he hauled his wife into his arms for an over-the-top kiss.

Everyone in the crowd agreed—the party was already off to a fabulous start.

CHAPTER ONE

DYLAN SANCHEZ FORCED himself to come tonight because he didn't want to be the only business owner in Bronco who refused the mayor's invitation. Oh, and because his parents and siblings would've never let him hear the end of it if he'd skipped.

At the rate the Sanchez family was growing, though, it wasn't just the opinions of Dylan's two brothers and two sisters he had to contend with, either. He'd assumed that when his sisters got married and his brothers got engaged, they would find better things to do with their time than remind him that he was now the odd man out.

Clearly, he'd been wrong about that.

Not that Dylan wasn't proud to be the last Sanchez standing. Growing up in a competitive family, if he wasn't going to be the first one to do something, then he sure as hell was going to outlast everyone else. It was just that being surrounded by so many happy couples, talking about anniversaries and upcoming weddings, could start to wear on a happily single guy.

Plus, he hated crowded events.

"Aren't these tables only supposed to seat ten people?" Dylan muttered to his father. "How did we manage to get thirteen chairs crammed around one tiny space?"

"Thirteen chairs *and* a stroller," his brother Dante said as he rocked his and his fiancée Eloise's daughter back to sleep in her little buggy. Merry, Dylan's eight-week-old niece, was officially his favorite family member, and not just because she kept her opinions to herself.

A few minutes later, when Dylan mentioned the lack of elbow room, his sister Sofia replied, "Boone and I are going to sit with the rest of the Daltons once they pass out the cake. You can put up with being squished for that long, Dylan."

"Yeah, but I don't know how long I can put up with Felix stealing my beer." Dylan snatched the pint glass from his older brother's hand. "The bar's right over there if you want to go get your own."

Felix had the nerve to smile unapologetically. "Shari and I are going to head that way for another round as soon as she and Mom get done talking about bridal shower themes. In the meantime, you can share."

Uncle Stanley returned from the buffet line with two full plates and his fiancée, Winona Cobbs. As the older couple took their seats, there was even less space to move.

Dylan turned toward his sister Camilla. "I think your in-laws are looking for you."

"No they're not," Jordan Taylor, Camilla's husband, replied. "My dad and uncles are busy holding court with the mayor."

"If you need to get away from us, Dylan," Camilla said as she nodded discreetly at a table with several young women, "there's room over there."

"Stop trying to set me up. Between the car dealership and the new ranch, I don't have time for a girlfriend right now."

"When have you ever had time, Dyl?" Sofia asked. "Aren't you getting tired of the dating scene? You're not getting any younger."

"Uncle Stanley is eighty-seven and *he* just got engaged. So there's not exactly an age limit for someone getting married. In fact, I don't have to get married at all." Dylan knew he sounded defiant, possibly even stubborn. But the more his family talked about weddings, the more determined he became to stay single.

"Don't forget, kiddo, that I was already married once and there's nothing better than sharing your life with someone." Uncle Stanley, who'd been a widower for some time, turned to Winona. "Speaking of which, we should probably be setting our own wedding date soon."

Winona, a ninetysomething-year-old psychic who was prone to mystical statements, shrugged noncommittally. "We will when the time is right."

"You're not having second thoughts, are you?" Uncle Stanley asked, concern causing the wrinkles around his eyes to deepen.

Winona shook her head, her messy white bun tipping to one side. "Of course not. But love cannot be rushed. It *will* not be rushed." Then she pointed an age-spotted hand covered with several rings at Dylan. "But it cannot be avoided, either. Love always finds a way."

Dylan opened and closed his mouth several times, unsure of how to respond. Or if he should. He reclaimed his beer once again from his brother and drained the glass before changing the subject.

"Anyway, the ranch has me so busy lately, I hired two new salespeople for the dealership to cover for me. But January is normally a slow month for car sales. I need to think of something to get business moving again."

"You could try not spending so much time at Broken Down Ranch," one of his sisters suggested.

"It's called Broken *Road* Ranch," he corrected. His family had always been supportive of his dream to own land, but several of them had recently questioned his decision to own *this* particular property. The place was a bit of a fixer-upper and most of the buildings had seen better days. But it sat in one of the best spots in the valley and, hopefully, the grass would return this spring and make it look not so…well…run-down.

"What about a car wash?" Dante, the elementary school teacher, suggested. "My school did one before summer break last year and made a decent amount."

Dylan frowned. "I don't need a onetime fundraiser. I need to get more people on my lot. But without being one of those cheesy salespeople who resort to gimmicks or corny commercials just to make a buck. You know how I hate public speaking."

"What about a game of hoops?" Their father had raised his children with a passion for sports. "We could do a tournament, like we do with the rec league. I'll be the referee."

Several people at their table groaned, including Dylan's mom, who had attended more than her share of basketball tournaments over the years.

"That would take an awful lot of time for people to form teams and have practices," their mom said. "You need to put something together sooner and you need a theme."

"Valentine's Day is coming up," Sofia said a bit too casually and all the women were very quick to agree. Suspicion caused the back of Dylan's neck to tingle.

"You guys want me to do something on a commercialized holiday created for the sole purpose of selling romance to people? What am I going to do? Have a Valentine's dance?" Dylan snorted at the absurdity. "No wait, maybe I should send everyone who wants to test-drive a car on a ride through a tunnel of love."

Uncle Stanley raised his hand. "I vote for the tunnel of love idea."

Dylan needed another drink. "Buying a vehicle is a big decision, you guys. When someone comes to my dealership, it's to make a practical purchase. They're not there for all that mushy stuff."

And neither was Dylan. He didn't do mushy. He certainly didn't do grand gestures like Mayor Smith had done up on the stage a few minutes ago when he'd given his wife that necklace in front of the whole town.

"Valentine's Day is one of the biggest nights of the year in the service industry," Camilla, who owned her own restaurant, pointed out. "Trust me, when it comes to gifts, some people want more than flowers and chocolates."

Dylan grimaced. "So I just get some big red bows and hoist up a new banner? Maybe dress up as Cupid and shoot arrows at the potential customers?"

Winona lifted her wineglass. "Lots of gals in this town wouldn't mind seeing the Sanchez brothers dressed up like Cupid and wearing nothing but a tiny white toga."

Thankfully, that suggestion got a resounding set of *noes* from Felix and Dante. Several more ideas were offered and rejected before Dylan excused himself to go to the bar while his family wore themselves out discussing the most absurd concepts that would never come to fruition. He told himself that he'd grab another beer, maybe a plate of food, and by the time he got back to the table, his family would have moved on to another subject.

However, Dylan got sidetracked talking with a few buddies about the upcoming baseball season, speaking to one of the city council members about a permit application for some electric vehicle charging stations and checking the score on the college basketball game. When he returned to the party, he ran into Mrs. Coss, the older lady who owned the antiques mall next door to his dealership.

"I think it's a great idea, Dylan. I'll even be willing to lend you a few pieces from my 1920s rolling pin collection as long as they're just used for display purposes."

He smiled politely despite his confusion. "What's a great idea, Mrs. Coss?"

"The bake-off. Maybe I'll put out a shelf of my older cookbooks and a rack of mid-century aprons to do a little sidewalk sale." The band began playing their rendition of the "Cha Cha Slide," and before Dylan could ask her what she meant, Mrs. Coss said, "This is my song. We'll talk more about cross-promotion tomorrow." She patted him on the arm and dashed onto the dance floor before he could say another word.

Dylan heard the word *bake-off* several more times on his way back to the table. By the time he arrived at his seat, most of his siblings and his mom were already gone, blending into the crowd. His dad was still there, though, holding baby Merry and serenading her with the off-key lyrics of the line dancing song.

"Where'd everyone go?" Dylan asked his dad.

"They're spreading the word about the bake-off."

Dylan's temples began pounding. "Please tell me that this doesn't have anything to do with my dealership."

"Hey, Dylan," LuLu, the owner of his favorite BBQ joint, called out from two tables over. "What's the prize for the bake-off?"

His dad responded before Dylan could. "A year's worth of free mechanical service. Oil changes, new brakes, tire rotations, that sort of thing."

All the color drained from Dylan's face as he stared at his dad in shock. "I was gone for thirty minutes."

Apparently, thirty minutes was all it had taken for Dylan's entire family to come up with a harebrained idea to hold a Valentine's Day–themed bake-off at his place of business. Oh, *and* promise the winner a prize valued at potentially thousands of dollars. But it was too late to call the thing off. Gossip spread like wildfire in Bronco and Dylan was officially on the hook for a contest he hadn't authorized.

"Nobody even asked my permission," he told Dante, the first sibling who returned to the table.

"Have you met Mom and our sisters? You walked away midconversation. That's practically giving them your blessing to proceed however they see fit."

Dylan rolled his eyes. "It's a car dealership, not the set of some cooking show. You've seen my break room. I have an old microwave and a toaster that sets off the smoke alarm anytime I want a bagel. How do they think they're going to hold a bake-off there?"

"I don't know. Something about a giant party tent and one of Camilla's suppliers who rents out restaurant-grade ovens." Dante took his baby from their dad. "I wasn't really paying attention, man."

Could this evening get any worse? The pounding at Dylan's temples revved into a full headache and he was about to call it a night. But if he left the party now, what other crazy schemes would his family come up with in his absence? Needing to ward off the gossip and do damage control, he rose from the table.

Unfortunately, he didn't get more than two feet when the mayor thwarted his plans.

"Dylan!" Rafferty Smith reached out to enthusiastically shake Dylan's hand. "I hear we're holding an exciting town event at the dealership next month. Penny loves that British baking show, by the way. Obviously, I'd be honored to help judge the contest. I'll tell my assistant to clear my schedule for that day."

Okay, so having the mayor make an appearance at his dealership could actually be good for business. Plus, Dylan was in the middle of working on a bid proposal to supply the city officials with a fleet of vehicles. Since he didn't want to risk losing that contract, he had no choice but to clench his jaw, smile and act as though this ridiculous bake-off plan could actually work. That it wouldn't be nearly as embarrassing as him running around dressed like Cupid. "Great. It should be a lot of fun. I look forward to having you join us."

Mayor Smith then took a step closer and lowered his voice. "Just between us, any chance you happened to see a pearl necklace around here?"

"You mean like the one you gave your wife less than an hour ago?"

"Shh. Keep your voice down. Penny had it on when we were on the dance floor, but it must've fallen off somewhere. I'm trying to ask around discreetly because I don't want to cause a—"

"Attention, ladies and gentlemen," the lead singer of the band interrupted as he spoke into the microphone. "We have an announcement to make. If anyone finds a pearl necklace, please bring it up to the stage so we can reunite it with its owner."

The crowd's hushed murmurs quickly grew louder as everyone realized whose necklace had gone missing. Rafferty Smith muttered, "So much for doing anything discreetly in this town," before striding away.

Dylan couldn't agree more.

Surely someone would find Penny's necklace soon. Dylan doubted his own reputation as a serious businessman would be recovered as easily.

ROBIN ABERNATHY WAS better on the back of a horse than she was in front of an oven. But she'd been known to have a few tricks up her sleeve when it came to the kitchen. Or at least a few recipes.

Okay. Two recipes. One of which, fortunately, was a

batch of cookies. Besides, she didn't want to actually win the Valentine's Day bake-off. She just wanted to get one of the judges to notice her.

She parked one of the ranch trucks at the curb in front of Bronco Motors, then stared at her reflection in the rearview mirror. Her summer tan had long faded, and her complexion could benefit from a swipe of blusher. Too bad she didn't own any makeup. She dug around in her purse and came up with a tube of colorless lip balm. Oh well. She yanked the elastic band out of her hair, ditching her usual ponytail. Maybe she'd look more feminine with her hair down.

For the first time in thirty-one years, Robin asked herself why she couldn't be better at the whole flirtation thing. Probably because she spent too much time with her brothers and the other cowboys out on her family's ranch. If she couldn't find the time to go out on many dates, then she certainly didn't have the time to put much effort into her appearance. If a guy didn't appreciate her for being herself, what was the point in bothering with a second date?

But that was before Dylan Sanchez had smiled at her during Bronco's annual Christmas tree lighting event. She hadn't been able to stop thinking of the man since then.

She'd planned to casually run into him at the Smiths' anniversary party, but a last-minute emergency with one of her client's horses had kept her away. Maybe it was better this way since his recently announced bake-off might prove to be a better opportunity to talk to the man without such a huge crush of people around.

As if on cue, she saw him striding across the dealership lot and heading into the office. Robin wasn't used to the feeling of butterflies in her stomach because it was rare that her nerves got the best of her. Before she could overthink what she was about to do, she exited the truck and slammed the driver's door, closing off any doubt and leaving it behind her.

You can do this. Gripping the printed flyer tighter in her fist, she entered the building that served as a couple of offices and a showroom for a brand-new 4x4 truck. She'd purposely picked a time when she thought the dealership wouldn't be busy and, from what she could see, it appeared she'd planned well. Nobody else was around.

Dylan's voice made its way through an open door and then a second voice responded from what sounded like a speakerphone. Not wanting to interrupt his call, she casually walked around the vehicle on display, reading the information on the back window sticker.

It wasn't that she was trying to eavesdrop, but it was hard not to hear him in his office ten feet away. It only took her a few moments to figure out the extent of the conversation. His small herd had been overgrazing in the same spot for years and he couldn't move them until he had time to repair some fences. The other voice clearly belonged to a fertilizer salesman trying to convince Dylan to invest in an untested anti-erosion soil product. The last phrase sent a warning bell to Robin's brain and she found herself inching closer to the office.

Dylan was pacing back and forth in the small space, the lines on his forehead deeply grooved. When he caught sight of her, she immediately took a step back, but not before she saw his face transform from concern to a veneer of charm and grace.

"Let me call you back, Tony," he said as Robin pretended to be absorbed in reading about all the off-road features listed on the truck's sticker price.

"Welcome to Bronco Motors," Dylan told her with that same smile and those same cheek dimples that she'd been seeing in her dreams the past several weeks. "Are you interested in trying this out?"

She almost said yes, then realized he was talking about the car between them. "Oh, um, not today. I came to sign up for the bake-off."

She held up the flyer, as if to prove that was her sole intention in coming here.

If Dylan was disappointed that she wasn't there to buy a car, he covered it well. "Right. So full disclosure, my mom and sisters did the flyers this past week and posted them all over social media before I even got a chance to create any sort of official sign-up or even come up with contest rules. I wasn't really prepared for the amount of interest I've already gotten." He walked over to an empty reception desk and retrieved a clipboard. "So I've just been having people put their contact information on this sheet. We'll reach out when we have all the details finalized."

Whoa. Up close, the man smelled even better than he looked. Trying not to let the scent of his cologne go to her head, Robin took the clipboard from him and it only took a quick glimpse at the other names on the list to see that it was all women. Apparently, she wasn't the only one in town who wanted an excuse to get up close and personal with the last single Sanchez brother.

She paused with the pen in her hand. This was so foolish. What was she even doing here? Someone like her wouldn't have a chance of winning a baking contest or attracting a guy like Dylan. But as he stood there watching, another thought occurred to her. He'd just asked her if she wanted to go for a test-drive. Her parents bought all their ranch vehicles from this dealership, including several of this exact same model. If Dylan knew who she was, then he would know that Robin wouldn't need to test-drive a car she often used at work.

Which meant he had no idea who she was.

Robin wasn't sure if she should be relieved or offended. Until he added, "I should probably warn you that the bake-off is on Valentine's Day. In case you're already busy that day. Or, you know, have plans."

She looked up quickly and was rewarded with the sexiest smile and the most smoldering pair of brown eyes she'd ever seen. At least this close. Was he suggesting that she might have some sort of date for the most romantic day of the year? Her sister, Stacy, teased her about being oblivious to men flirting with her. Was this one of those times?

Since Robin couldn't just stand there staring at him in confusion, she mumbled what she hoped sounded like, "No, I'm available." Or at least it would've sounded like that if her tongue wasn't all tied up in knots.

She scribbled her name on the list, along with her cell number and email address. Her face was flushed with heat by the time she returned the clipboard to him, but he didn't give it so much as a glance before tucking it under his arm.

His phone rang from his pocket and he pulled it out long enough to glance at the screen and then silence it.

"I should probably let you get back to work," she said, jumping on the excuse to get away before she did or said something else that made her seem like a lovesick fool.

"Only if you're sure I can't interest you in a test-drive."

No, Robin wasn't sure at all. But her whole goal in coming here today was to meet the man in person and see if this crush she'd developed on him from afar was just as foolhardy as she'd been telling herself. And the answer was yes.

"Nope, I'm all set," she said, pivoting to leave. Before she executed a full turn, though, she stopped in her tracks. "Actually. I know this is none of my business, but someone needs to stop you from making a huge mistake."

CHAPTER TWO

DYLAN'S HEAD JERKED in response to her words and his skin bristled. He was already sensitive to his family's teasing about not knowing the first thing when it came to ranching. He didn't need some stranger offering him unsolicited advice, as well.

"I have a feeling this mistake you're referring to has nothing to do with the bake-off." Although, Dylan was pretty sure that this silly contest was already proving to be more trouble than it was worth.

"No. It's about the untested fertilizer product that you really shouldn't be using."

"Thank you for your concern, but I assure you I have it well under control. Tony, the salesman I was talking to, has advanced degrees in chemistry and geology and knows quite a bit about soil erosion. I doubt he'd steer me wrong."

"Come on." The blonde woman put her hands on her hips, the bake-off flyer now crumpled in her fist. "It doesn't take a degree to know what works for a herd of cattle and what doesn't. But, hey, what do I know about ranching?"

She said it with such confidence, as though she was accustomed to people eagerly taking her advice. She also said it with enough sarcasm to suggest that he should know who she was. Dylan blinked several times as he tried to place her, but he was pretty sure he'd remember meeting someone with a face like that. A face that was almost more enhanced by the lack of makeup.

Hoping for a clue, he glanced at the clipboard. Robin *Abernathy.*

Hell. How had he missed that? She must be one of the younger sisters that graduated high school after he did.

The Abernathys were the second richest ranching family in Bronco, right after the Taylors, his brother-in-law's family. Dylan didn't like the trail of unease making its way through his body. Although he'd grown up in a ranching town and thought of himself as being familiar with horses and cattle all his life, his dad was a postal worker and his mom was a hairdresser. Besides the occasional sleepover with friends when he was in high school, Dylan never really spent any significant amount of time on a ranch. Until he found himself owning one.

Curiosity, though, outweighed his embarrassment and he couldn't stop himself from asking, "Why would it be a mistake?"

Robin sighed, as though she had to explain something to a child. "I've heard of his product and even though it's a hot new trend, what your salesman isn't telling you is that one of the main chemicals they add to the fertilizer has proven to be harmful to some breeds of cattle. Especially maternal cattle."

She said the last part as though she was already aware that the previous owner of the Broken Road Ranch had left Dylan with a herd primarily consisting of female cows. It was something Dylan was still kicking himself for overlooking.

"Plus, that brand of fertilizer is way overpriced. You'd be better off spending your money and time on repairing your fences or even using a feedlot until the land has time to be properly restored."

The problem was that he was getting low on time. He needed a quick fix.

"There's no quick fix," Robin said as though she was reading his mind. "Ranching is time-consuming."

"I'm aware of that," he said a bit too quickly. A bit too defensively. Deep down, he knew that she was only trying to offer some friendly advice. However, he was already sensitive to the fact that he was in way over his head. It didn't help that someone from the successful Abernathy family was the one pointing it out.

Admitting that he needed help was a tough pill to swallow. The only thing worse would be admitting defeat and losing the ranch completely. Dylan was going to have to suck it up and take whatever advice he could get at this point. But that didn't mean he had to like it.

He crossed his arms in front of his chest. "So then why would Tony give me the exact opposite advice?"

Robin bit her lower lip, as if considering her words. After a weighty pause, she finally said, "Not everyone in this world is truthful if their paycheck depends on making a commission."

"That's certainly a polite way of saying you can't trust a salesperson." He'd always enjoyed making deals, but sometimes the used car salesmen jokes hit a little too close to home. "Not all of us are liars looking to make a quick buck."

The way Robin scrunched her nose would've been adorable if her doubtful expression wasn't directed at him. "Nobody called *you* a liar or said *you* were untrustworthy. But tell me again why you're having a Valentine's Day bake-off at a car dealership. Is it because you have so much free time on your hands running two businesses that you decided to throw in hosting a community event just for a fun little challenge?"

If her words were intended as a blow to his ego, she definitely hit the mark. The building tension in his shoulders and neck, as well as her know-it-all smirk, made him more defensive. Or at least competitive enough to play along with her sarcastic comment. "Maybe it's because I simply enjoy having a pretty woman like you cook for me."

She gasped and her high cheekbones turned a rosy shade of pink.

Realizing how sexist his words sounded, he immediately held up his palms. "I didn't mean it like that!"

She shifted on her feet. Her formfitting jeans were tucked into tan cowboy boots, making her long legs seem even longer. "H-how did you mean it?"

"Not that I expect a pretty woman, or any woman, to cook for me. You can ask my mom and my sisters, I'm actually a pretty decent cook. In my family, we take turns making Sunday dinner and I can hold my own."

"I know. Eloise Taylor told me about your flaming fajita incident." Robin pointed at his eyebrows. "They grew back nicely, by the way."

He rubbed the bridge of his nose, which probably only drew more attention to his brows. "It was a little fire and it only happened that one time… Wait. You're friends with my brother's fiancée?"

His question was unnecessary, though. Of course the Abernathys knew the Taylors. The wealthy families of Bronco Heights all tended to run in the same circles. But he hadn't recognized Robin when she first walked in, and he was pretty sure he would've remembered if Eloise had a hot friend who was also an experienced rancher. Or at least Dylan's mom and sisters would've mentioned it. They were always trying to set him up with someone.

"I'm actually one of her clients. She's working on a marketing campaign for my company."

"You have a company?" Why was he repeating everything she said? "I mean, I assumed you worked for your family since you act like you know so much about ranching."

"I know a lot about ranching because I grew up working on my family's ranch. But I also own my own business. Rein Rejuvenation. It's a line of horse therapeutics I created..." Robin trailed off as a young woman walked into the dealership office. The newcomer's high heels clacked against the tile floors despite the fact that it definitely wasn't high heel weather outside.

"Hi, I'm here to enter the bake-off," the woman said excitedly.

"Of course. Here you go." Dylan handed her the clipboard he was still holding. When he turned back to Robin she was already walking toward the exit.

"Robin, hold up," he called across the small showroom floor as he took long strides to catch her. She paused, her head tilted as though she was confused about why he was running after her. Or maybe she was just insulted and eager to get away.

"Before you leave, I wanted to say thanks for your advice about the fertilizer and...everything. I think I'm going to reach out to some of my neighbors and see who they use for fence repairs."

If Dylan was being honest, the reason he hadn't reached out to them before now was the same reason he'd gotten all defensive with Robin earlier. He didn't want people thinking that he had no idea what he was doing. Plus, he wanted to do the work himself. Not hire someone to do it for him.

"I'm sure they'd be willing to make some suggestions. There's a lot to learn about the ins and outs of ranching, but you have to be open to asking for help."

Again, Robin seemed to be reading his mind. Or else issuing a challenge.

It was a challenge he knew better than to accept. In spite of that, Dylan fired back, "Are you offering to teach me?"

"If you're willing to learn," she replied cheekily.

Dylan found Robin attractive before, but her self-assurance now had him fully intrigued.

"Cool truck." The young woman he'd left with the clipboard made her way over to them. "I'd love to take it for a test-drive."

When his family had concocted this ridiculous bake-off scheme, they'd insisted on people signing up in person instead of online. He'd agreed thinking it would get more people stopping by the dealership, which ultimately was the goal. But at this exact second, Dylan wished one of the other salespeople was here to help.

"Don't let me keep you from your customer." The way Robin said the word *customer* sounded as though she wanted to use air quotes. But maybe that was just Dylan's imagination because her smile toward the woman looked genuine.

As Robin turned toward the door, he reminded himself that he was a professional at his place of business. Now wasn't the time to be admiring the view of her rear end in those jeans. Clearing his throat, he forced himself to give a polite wave and simply say, "I'll be in touch about the bake-off."

Dylan suddenly had the urge to taste anything Robin Abernathy put in front of him.

"So, HE HAD no idea who you were?" Stacy Abernathy practically shouted the question inside Bronco Java and Juice, causing the other customers to turn in their direction.

Wincing, Robin immediately shushed her sister. "Once

he saw my name, he knew who I was. But no, he didn't recognize me."

Despite the fact that Robin wanted to saddle her favorite horse and go for a long ride to forget about all the awkward moments at the dealership earlier today, she and her sister had a standing coffee date every Monday after school let out.

Stacy took a sip of her triple espresso—she always got a triple when her first graders had an especially rough day. "Didn't you two go to high school together?"

"No, I graduated the same year as Dante Sanchez. Dylan was a couple years ahead of me."

"So when he smiled at you during the tree lighting, he had no idea who you were?"

Robin shrugged. At the beginning of December, the entire town—along with plenty of tourists—attended the holiday celebration at the park in the center of Bronco Heights. "It was crowded and there was a lot going on that night. He's a charming guy with a reputation for being a huge flirt. I guess he smiles that way at everyone."

"But that was the night you fell for him."

"I didn't *fall* for him, Stacy. I just developed a tiny little crush." Robin used her thumb and forefinger to indicate the smallest amount possible. "Very tiny. Barely even a crush. More like he merely caught my interest. From afar. We've never even had a conversation up until two hours ago."

"Now I feel stupid for talking you into approaching him at all."

"Don't blame yourself." Robin made a swatting gesture at the air. "When has anyone ever talked me into doing anything? I'm a big girl and I make my own decisions."

"Yeah, but I was the one who told you that Dante and Dylan Sanchez aren't as big of flirts as people make them out to be." Stacy and Dante were both teachers at Bronco

Elementary and Robin had, in fact, slightly relied on her sister's assessment of the brothers.

In order for Robin to feel as though she were in control, though, she also needed to shoulder some of the responsibility. "But I was the one who convinced myself that Dylan noticed me that night and that he could possibly be interested."

"That's because I might have made the suggestion in the first place," Stacy argued. "However, in my defense, Dante seemed to be easily snatched off the market by Eloise when she unexpectedly returned to town a few months ago. It was fair to assume that Dylan wouldn't be so hard to get, either."

"Speaking of Dante, here comes Eloise," Robin said as soon as she caught sight of her friend pushing a stroller past the window outside. "Don't mention anything about this to her."

"Hey, ladies, thanks for letting me crash your coffee date," Eloise Taylor said a few moments later when she parked the stroller by their table. "I'm technically still on maternity leave, but I got the proofs back from the photo shoot of that magnetic horse blanket and I couldn't wait to show you, Robin. Also, don't ever fall in love with the fixer-upper your Realtor shows you and move in the second you close escrow. The construction crew remodeling our downstairs bathroom is currently jackhammering the tile. Merry can sleep right through the noise, but I can't hear myself think let alone do a conference call. I desperately needed a latte. So what's going on with you two?"

"Well, I'm currently questioning my poor decision to take my first graders on a field trip to the wildlife center during birthing season and Robin is trying to make me feel better by telling me about how she made a fool of herself in front of your future brother-in-law."

Robin shot Stacy a scathing look.

Eloise made a dismissive motion with her hand. "Felix is a veterinarian, Robin. I'm sure he knows the difference between dog flatulence and human flatulence."

"Not *that* brother-in-law," Stacy corrected with a chuckle. "But now I don't have to ask how Bandit did at his deworming treatment."

"Oh, were you guys talking about Dylan, then?" Eloise dropped into the empty chair, sitting on the edge. "What happened?"

Silently cursing Stacy for bringing it up, Robin resisted the urge to drop her forehead into the palm of her hand. "On a whim, I stopped by the dealership to sign up for the bake-off."

"Really?" Eloise asked. "I didn't know you baked."

"She doesn't," Stacy replied.

"Yes, I do," Robin corrected. "Sometimes. Once in a while. Stop looking at me like that, Stacy, and drink your coffee."

A teenage barista with purple dyed hair came over to the table and asked Eloise if she wanted her usual. When the girl left, Robin hoped to change the subject, but Eloise was too fast.

"Was it crowded at the dealership when you went?"

Okay, Robin could at least answer this question easily enough. "Not when I was there, but there were already quite a few names on the list. And another woman came in when I was leaving. Why? Is everyone expecting a big turnout?"

If there were too many contestants, Robin could bow out gracefully and still save face.

"Nobody knows what to expect yet. Although, there's been some speculation on how many legitimate bakers will sign up and how many young single women will go in just to offer Dylan their phone number and..." Eloise's eyes widened with realization. "Oh my gosh, Robin, is that why you entered the contest?"

"No!" Robin said at the exact same time Stacy said, "Yep!"

Eloise looked between the two sisters.

Robin wanted to sink lower in her chair, but she forced herself to sit up straighter. "Okay, fine. Maybe I just wanted to test the waters and see what would happen if we talked in person. But he didn't know who I was."

Eloise frowned. "How does he not know who you are? Everyone knows the Abernathys. Didn't your family just buy a bunch of work trucks for the ranch? I remember Dante going in one weekend back in November to help Dylan with all the paperwork."

"Except Robin doesn't leave the ranch as much as the rest of us," Stacy pointed out. "Or at least she hasn't these past couple of years when she's been too busy working on her products."

"It's not like I'm a hermit," Robin corrected her sister. "I go to the feedstore and to other ranches. And I travel for some conferences and rodeos. I just don't have a lot of extra time for the Bronco social scene."

"Bronco has a social scene?" The barista set Eloise's latte on the table. She was wearing a nose ring and an I <3 NY pin on her apron. Her name tag said Solar. "Could've fooled me. My college acceptance letters can't come soon enough."

The three women all smiled indulgently at the teen. "We all thought the same thing when we were your age," Eloise told her. "But somehow we all ended up back here after college."

Actually, Robin had never wanted to escape Bronco. This was her home. Even when she'd gone off to get her degree, she'd picked the closest university so she could drive home every weekend to spend time with her horses. Which probably explained her lack of a social life.

When Solar left, Stacy asked, "So I'm still waiting to hear what happened after Dylan didn't recognize you. Did you at least correct him?"

"Sort of. When I walked in, I overheard him on the phone getting some bad advice. So before I left, I mentioned that he might want to reconsider taking that advice."

Stacy rolled her eyes.

Robin scowled. "What's that for?"

"Because you're a know-it-all and sometimes your so-called advice can come off a little condescending."

"There's nothing condescending about telling a man who has never owned a ranch that a fertilizer pumped up with all sorts of lab chemicals is going to have a negative effect on his breeders. I was saving him from an expensive and, frankly, potentially deadly mistake."

"If that's the tone you used," Stacy said as she nodded her head, "then I'd say it definitely came across as condescending. Possibly even bossy. Even if you were right."

"Of course I'm right."

Her sister pointed a finger. "See?"

Eloise drank some coffee and then sighed dramatically. "Man, I missed caffeine when I was pregnant. I feel like I'm making up for lost time. Anyway, regardless of how you presented the advice, I hope he took it."

"I hope so, too," Robin said, then tried to soften her tone so that it didn't sound quite so righteous. "Do you think he won't?"

"I'm still new to the Sanchez family and not really in a position to divulge their personal business. So I'm going to try to phrase this as delicately as I can because I only want what's best for my soon-to-be brother-in-law." Eloise looked up to the ceiling for several seconds as though she was trying to carefully choose her words. Then she blurted out, "Dylan has no idea what he's doing on that ranch and can use all the help he can get. But he's too damn stubborn and insists on doing everything himself. It's driving my cousin Jordan nuts and he's threatened to bring over the foreman and some ranch hands from the Triple T to help fix things. But Dylan won't hear of it. Dante says he's refusing everyone's advice, but maybe he'll listen to you."

Robin understood a person's need for independence. But she wasn't sure how she could make a difference when he wouldn't even listen to Jordan Taylor, who like her, was born into a cattle dynasty.

Stacy's drink was already halfway gone. "So did Dylan at least seem receptive to you?"

"Maybe?" Robin shrugged. "I guess we'll see."

She didn't want to tell them that he'd referred to her as "a pretty woman" or that she'd blushed like a fool when he'd said it. Nor did she want to tell them that she'd offered to teach him a few things if he was willing to learn. She'd already made the mistake of going to see the guy based solely on a smile he gave her in the park two months ago. She wasn't going to make the mistake of thinking he was flirting with her when he probably said the same thing to everyone who'd signed their names on his little clipboard.

All Robin knew was that she definitely wasn't going to follow through on the bake-off. She wasn't about to be lumped in with all the other women angling for his attention. In fact, she had every intention of trying to forget the entire incident.

Until her phone rang later that night.

She didn't have the number in her contacts and almost let it go to voice mail before realizing it might be someone at the rodeo arena calling about a horse. Despite the late hour and the fact that she was already in her pajamas, she answered professionally. "This is Robin."

"Hi, Robin, it's Dylan Sanchez." His voice sounded just as smooth and silky over the phone as it had in person. When it took her more than a few seconds to form a response, he added, "From Bronco Motors?"

As though she didn't know exactly who he was.

Robin grabbed her TV remote to mute the reality dating show she was watching. "Of course. Hi, how are you?"

"Busy. And I'm about to become a lot busier."

When he didn't elaborate, she made an assumption. "Too many bake-off contestants wanting to go for a test-drive today?"

"What? Oh. No. I mean, yes, there was a lot more traffic at the dealership than we usually get on a Monday in February. But I was actually referring to my ranch."

Wait. So he *wasn't* calling to update her on the bake-off rules?

As if he knew what she was thinking, he said, "I hope you don't mind that I got your number off the sign-up sheet. But I was hoping I could pick your brain about the best types of feedlots."

"Um..." She stared at the frozen image on her TV, wishing she hadn't paused the show at the exact moment when the couple was sharing their first kiss. She scrambled to push the off button and clear the visual from her mind. "Go for it."

"So I was trying to research how much they cost. But then I read about this option involving fostering a herd with a neighboring ranch. I haven't started asking around yet, but I'll probably need to move the cattle myself and, uh, I've never really done that before. How many hands do you think I'll need to hire?"

"How many cattle are we talking about?"

"Thirty-five."

"You can probably get away with only using two riders."

"Right." He chuckled and she could almost imagine him on the other end of the line, running a hand through his thick, short-cropped dark hair. Was he standing in his office this late at night? Or was he home, in bed like she was? "But what if one of us isn't all that experienced?"

Robin gulped, then shook her head to clear the intimate image.

"At riding?" she asked. Because there was no way Dylan Sanchez wasn't experienced at things in the bedroom.

"At riding…" He paused a few more beats then finally said, "And at asking for help when I need it."

Whoa. So this was really happening. As much as Robin wished his motive for reaching out was to ask her out on a date, she knew better than to expect immediate results. Like training a horse, the first step was to get him to trust her. Not that she should be making that comparison.

Still.

The supposedly stubborn Dylan Sanchez was actually calling *her* for advice. Before she could consider her sister's earlier comments about sounding too arrogant, Robin said, "You've definitely come to the right person."

CHAPTER THREE

DYLAN THOUGHT ABOUT the best way to respond to Robin's confident statement. His first impression of her today was that she was gorgeous. His second impression was that she was gorgeous *and* she was a know-it-all.

By the time she'd left his dealership, though, he was convinced that women who were gorgeous know-it-alls likely had egos to match. But he'd spent the afternoon researching her advice and came to the conclusion that maybe it wouldn't hurt him to at least listen to her.

"Well, you did offer to teach me a thing or two," he finally replied to Robin.

"I did. But it also depends on what kind of help you're looking for." Robin's voice was raspy, but feminine, and Dylan liked the sound of it a bit more than he should. He'd noticed it earlier today when she'd introduced herself. Over the phone, though, it had an even stronger pull. Probably because he couldn't see her in person, forcing him to use his imagination to envision her full pink lips pronouncing each word. "If you're looking for a ranch hand, then you should know that I don't work for free. But if you're hoping for some neighborly advice, then I don't mind giving you my experienced opinion."

"I would never dream of asking you for free help. I'd obviously buy you lunch." Either Dylan's joke fell flat, or Robin Abernathy was really going to make him earn it. When she didn't reply, he added, "To be honest, what I really need is for someone who knows a lot more about ranching than I do to come out and make an overall assessment for me. I started a to-do list, but every time I turn around, I have to add another chore to it. Now I'm at the point where I don't even know which task I should tackle first. I guess, more than anything, I need someone to steer me in the right direction."

"If there's one thing I know how to do, it's steer something, or in your case *someone*, in the right direction. At least according to my brothers. But I have to ask, Dylan..." Robin paused as though she was trying to figure out how to phrase her question. "Why haven't you talked to Jordan Taylor or Boone Dalton about helping you with any of this?"

Jordan's family owned Taylor Beef and their ranch, the Triple T, was the biggest cattle operation in Montana. Boone worked with his family on Dalton's Grange, which was also an impressive ranch, even if some of Bronco's elite still considered the Daltons to be "new money."

Dylan exhaled, hoping it didn't sound like a sigh. "Trust me, they've talked to me about it plenty. My brothers-in-law, as well as everyone else in my family, have felt free to give me their opinions. At length. And while Jordan and Boone might have questionable skills on the basketball court, I'd never doubt their ranching abilities. However... my family hasn't exactly been optimistic of my recent endeavor."

"Really? Because Eloise gave me the impression that the entire Sanchez family is ultra supportive."

"Supportive, yes. In fact, sometimes they're a little *too* supportive." Dylan was now holding a bake-off contest, thanks to them. "But that's different than being optimistic. Long story short, nobody in my family thought acquiring Broken Road Ranch was a good idea. Obviously, they don't want me to fail at it and know how I get when I make up my mind to do something. But if they can throw in a few *I-told-you-so*'s along the way, they're going to. I guess you can say that I don't want to give them the opportunity."

"How did you acquire the ranch anyway? I heard a rumor about some sort of trade you made with the previous owner."

If Dylan could keep Robin's curiosity piqued, then he might have a shot. "I'll tell you what. Why don't you come by the ranch tomorrow and I'll fill you in on the entire history, as well as anything else you may want to know."

"Fine." Robin's tone was hard to gauge until she added, "But remember that I was promised a free lunch if I help."

DYLAN ENDED UP buying her breakfast.

"Thanks for stopping by so early," he told Robin the following morning when she got out of a newer model truck with the Bonnie B logo on the side. Yep, he'd definitely sold this same vehicle to her family just last November. All the more reason why he felt foolish for not recognizing her yesterday. "I have to leave by nine to get back to the dealership, but I picked up some muffins from Bean & Biscotti."

"I'm not going to say no to anything from Bean & Biscotti," Robin said as she scanned the barn and the broken fencing he hadn't had time to fix yet. "But just based on my first impressions driving up, I might need to raise my consulting fees."

Great. Dylan normally avoided asking for input because he was getting pretty tired of people telling him exactly what he didn't want to hear. He couldn't stop himself from sounding like a petulant child when he said, "It's really not that bad."

"I didn't say it was bad." Robin shoved her hands in

the back pockets of her jeans, which caused her small, but round breasts to push out of her sheepskin coat. "It's just going to require a lot of time and energy."

"I've got the energy, but I'm a little short on time at the moment. Or at least, I am until I hire an office manager for the dealership." He glanced at his watch. "That's why I need to be back by nine. I have someone coming in for an interview. So do you want the full tour?"

"No need. I pulled up some land reports online and already made a couple of phone calls to your neighbors."

Dylan took a step back. "You did what?"

If he had wanted someone else coming in to usurp him and calling all the shots, he could've just asked one of his brothers-in-law to do it.

"I called the people who own the neighboring ranches." She pointed to the white bakery box balanced on a log fence post. "Are those the muffins?"

"No, I understood what you said. I guess I'm trying to understand *why* you did that."

"To get a better understanding of what we're dealing with. Are you telling me that you never called them when you bought the property?" Robin walked toward the fence post and Dylan found himself following.

"I mean, I didn't make a formal call because I've met them before around town at council meetings and business events. I even danced with Mildred Epson at the mayor's anniversary party."

"Yes, she told me. She said you asked about the hatchback you sold her great-grandson before he went off to college and informed me that you can two-step like nobody's business. But she also said you never brought up the disputed acres adjacent to Hardy's Creek."

"What dispute? It's on my property. At least according to the parcel maps."

"So that's your first lesson from me," Robin said as she helped herself to the box of baked goods. "Learn about the land's history and the people who owned it before you."

"How's this supposed to be a lesson? I'm still completely confused." He tilted his head as he watched her angle the top of the muffin into her mouth and take a bite right out of the center. "And who eats a muffin like that?"

"Did you ask Hank Hardy anything about the property before you bought it?" Robin asked, looking down at the baked good in her hand. "Also, the center is the best part. Why wouldn't I eat it?"

"You're supposed to peel back the paper first, like this." He took the muffin out of her hand and gently unwrapped it so the entire thing was exposed. When he passed it back to her, his fingers slightly brushed hers, sending a current of electricity through him. He cleared his throat. "Besides, I didn't exactly buy the ranch. It was signed over to me."

"Why would Hank Hardy just give you a ranch?"

"He didn't give it to me outright. But, according to him, he wasn't getting any younger and didn't think he'd be able to stand another snowy winter. His plan was to retire and drive across the country with a travel trailer, but he wanted to do it in a new truck. We made a bargain. He deeded the property to me, and I gave him the title to one of my trucks."

She finished off the muffin before asking, "Did you ever get an appraisal done?"

"Sort of. One of my buddies from college is a property agent with the state and ran some comps."

"So then you know that two hundred acres with outbuildings and a herd of thirty-five cows is still worth significantly more than that top-of-the-line 4x4 on your showroom floor. Even with all the bells and whistles."

"Thank you," Dylan exclaimed. "Could you please explain to everyone else in town that I got a smoking deal for my beef ranch?"

"No." She shook her head, her blond ponytail bouncing in the breeze.

"Why not?"

"Because you got a horrible deal for a beef ranch. Why do you think the herd that came with it was primarily female?"

"I figured ol' Hank was too kind to slaughter them."

"Maybe. But he also wasn't legally allowed to. The land is designated as a conservation easement."

"I'm not a total idiot, Robin. My friend informed me of that. I can only use the land for agricultural purposes. With the exception of rebuilding the main house and the outbuildings, I can never turn the property into something else or sell it to developers."

"In a normal conservation easement, that'd be correct. But this particular property is actually part of an agreement with several other ranches in the area limiting how the land can be used. Think of it as a no-competition clause put in place by all the neighbors. Or at least their ancestors. It's rare, but it happens. It used to happen a lot more a hundred years ago when ranchers were fighting over the grazing rights of their cattle and sheep herds."

"Sheep?" Dylan felt the blood drain from his face. Sure, the fluffy animals were cute and he loved the wool one of them had likely provided for the jacket he was currently wearing. But that didn't mean he wanted to raise them himself.

Robin must've been able to read the panic on his face because she giggled, which was exactly how his siblings would've responded if they were here.

"Don't worry." Robin had to pause to smother another bubble of laughter. "It doesn't have to be sheep. You can have any type of livestock you want on the land. There's just a slight catch. Your easement restriction is that any livestock over the age of nine months can't be sold for food. That means no beef or dairy cattle."

All of the air seemed to whoosh out of Dylan's lungs, taking his big plans and dreams right along with it. "But those are the kinds of cattle that make money."

"You're really going to make me earn this free breakfast, aren't you?" The smile Robin had been trying to hold back was now a full-fledged smirk. She reached for another muffin then said, "*Nine months* is the key term. You can still have an active breeding program, which can also be quite lucrative given the cows I see out on that pasture are maternal breeds. That means they're moderately sized and genetically predisposed to birthing calves. There are plenty of smaller ranches around here that don't have the resources to both breed *and* raise young calves. There's a steady market for herd replacements once a calf is weaned. You can also supply cattle to be used at nearby rodeos and charge rental fees. When I spoke with Mrs. Epson, she said that's what Hank's family used to do before he inherited the land. They made a pretty good living at it, too."

"Hank never disclosed any of that to me."

"Would you have taken the deal if he had?"

"Probably." Dylan cupped his hands against his forehead to block out the sun now blasting through the twin peaks of the snowcapped mountains in the distance. "I mean, it's pretty hard to top that view."

Robin paused with the center of the muffin halfway to her mouth and Dylan felt the weight of her stare. It reminded him of the weight of a different woman's judgment from the past that he still carried with him today. He dropped his arms to his sides and shrugged.

"I suppose *you* might be able to top it. Obviously, the

Broken Road Ranch would never compare to something as vast and valuable as the Bonnie B. Yet, for a middle-class boy raised in a tract home in the Valley, there are times I have to pinch myself at the realization that this is all mine." Dylan pointed beyond the pastures toward a rising grove of trees. "See the creek that winds down from the mountain? When spring comes and the snowpacks start melting, it'll flow like a river all the way down here, passing only a few hundred yards behind the barn. Even on my most profitable days at the dealership, I've never felt as fulfilled as I do when I'm standing in this exact spot. Nobody dreams of becoming a car salesman, Robin. At least, I didn't. Luckily, I've been good at it. Growing up in Bronco, though, you know as well as I do that success is often judged by the size of one's ranch. One of my biggest goals in life—other than playing in the NBA—has been to own my own spread. The dealership has always been the means to that end. The truth is that I probably would've traded all the cars on my lot if Hank had asked me to. I can't seem to explain it, and trust me, I've tried. All I know is that this land is already a part of me. And that's why I'm damn well going to learn to run this place myself."

ROBIN'S HALF-EATEN MUFFIN sat forgotten in her palm as she studied Dylan. Initially, his smile had charmed her and drawn her interest. His request for advice had only made her more curious. But the man's passion for his ranch had just rendered her downright speechless.

Something her siblings and favorite ranch hands claimed didn't happen very often.

"I think you just explained it perfectly," Robin said when she finally found her voice. She blinked several times to focus her thoughts. "Now that I know why you love the land, tell me what you want to see happen with it."

"Ultimately, I'd like to see it turn enough of a profit that I can justify spending more time out here than I do at Bronco Motors. In the meantime, I wouldn't mind getting the house fixed up a little more so I could start sleeping out here regularly."

Robin tilted her head. "I thought when Eloise and Dante were dating, you used to spend the night here all the time."

"Only a few nights, and I was miserable. But I'm sure Dante would've done the same thing for me."

"What do you mean?"

"I mean bringing a woman home is a lot less romantic when you share an apartment with your brother. So I took one for the team and pretended like I needed to be out here more than I did. Thank God those two finally stopped caring about the gossip and eventually settled in at the Heights Hotel before buying their house."

If Dylan's love for the land hadn't convinced her that he was a good guy, then the fact that he'd been willing to sacrifice his comfort for his brother and Eloise's relationship would've proved it. She glanced at the main house that looked as if the roof might collapse at any minute and knew that she wouldn't have slept a single night inside it.

But she was also stuck on Dylan's statement that Dante would've done the same for him. Not *had* done the same. *Would* have. Was Dylan implying he'd never brought a woman back to his apartment? With his reputation, the idea was hard to believe.

Not wanting to be too obvious, Robin asked, "Has it been an adjustment, living on your own now that your brother's moved out?"

"Only to my wallet. I haven't won as many bets now that we aren't watching any games together in the evenings. That reminds me, I need to look into getting cable service out here. Or at least a solid internet provider. My apartment lease is up in six weeks and I'll be living out here full time. I need to be able to live stream March Madness."

He pulled his cell phone out of his pocket and began tapping on the screen.

"What are you doing?" Robin asked.

He didn't look up as he kept typing. "Adding to my growing list of things that need to get done."

"Don't you think taking care of that roof might be a little more important than some college basketball tournament?" she asked.

Dylan squinted at her. "Can't they be equally important?"

Robin sighed. Either she was going to fully commit to helping him or she wasn't. He was a successful business owner in town and his family was well respected and well-liked. Dylan Sanchez also struck her as a very determined individual. There was no way he couldn't learn enough about ranching to at least get some things fixed up around here.

But twenty minutes into their tour of the outbuildings, Robin was rethinking that assessment.

He jerked his thumb toward several rows of metal bars and frowned. "I'm not sure who designed that corral or whatever it is, but it's too long and takes up way too much space on this end of the barn."

"That's a breeding chute," Robin explained. "The heifer is pinned up in this area with her head facing away. Then the bull comes in from that gate over there and...well... you can use your imagination."

Dylan shuddered. "I don't want to use my imagination."

Robin laughed at his obvious discomfort. "If you're going to have a working ranch, Dylan, you have to know how the mating mechanics work."

"I know how it works. Sort of. I just don't need the

image seared in my brain. Can't the bull take the heifer out to nice pasture somewhere and maybe they eat some grass together and moo at each other before…you know… he shows her a good time?"

"He could. But that way might take a little longer. You're not squeamish about such matters, are you?"

"No. At least I don't think I will be. My brother Felix is a veterinarian so it's not like I've never seen a litter of puppies being born."

"Okay, the second thing you're going to learn from me is that birthing a calf is a bit more complicated."

Dylan's face was full of doubt. "Tell that to the mom dog who just delivered six puppies."

Robin didn't know whether to laugh at his naivete or to throw her hands up in the air and give up on this plan entirely.

Except she'd never been a quitter.

"You said you have to be at your office by nine. What's the rest of your day looking like?"

"It looks like I'm chasing my own tail." Dylan glanced at his watch. "After that interview and a conference call with the distribution plant, I have to be back here at noon to meet with a plumber. If you think this barn is in need of a complete overhaul, wait until you find out about the plumbing in the main house. Later on, Camilla wants me to stop by her restaurant to check out some plans she and Sofia came up with for that bake-off thing they're making me do. I'll stop by the dealership again to work on a sales forecast report and check in with the salespeople and the service tech. Then I'll try to be back out here before dark for the evening feeding."

The bake-off they're *making* him do? Robin tucked that nugget of information away to think about later. "Would you mind if I stayed here and showed myself around the rest of the property? Maybe take some notes and figure out a game plan?"

"Are you kidding? I would love that. I found an old golf cart in the barn. And when I say old, I mean it's ancient. But Hank put some off-road tires on it and the battery can hold a charge for at least an hour." Dylan's phone pinged and he took it out of his pocket to look at the screen. "Sorry to run like this, but I really need to take off. Maybe you can call me later tonight and let me know what ends up on your to-do list."

Her heart did a little fluttering dance at the thought of another late-night conversation with him. But then reality settled in as her eyes landed on one of the broken grain silos inside the barn. "I'll probably still be working on it when you get back."

"It's going to be that long, huh?" His charming smile had finally returned, but it didn't quite meet his eyes. She could see that he was still overwhelmed but trying to play it off.

"No." She returned his grin, trying to offer him a little reassurance. "But it is going to be that detailed."

He lifted only one brow. "Detailed sounds expensive."

"It doesn't have to be if you know where and how to get a good deal."

The gleam of excitement finally returned to his eyes as his shoulders visibly relaxed. "You sound like a woman after my own heart."

His words hit a little too close to home and heat rose along her neck. Before it could spread to her cheeks, Robin said, "Let me just grab a notebook and my coffee out of my truck and I'll get started."

She took long, fast strides to get outside, the cool winter air a welcome to her overheightened senses. At least it was until she realized he was right behind her. His voice was like warm honey when he said, “Hey, Robin?”

Hearing her name on his lips caused her to stop in her tracks. But she didn’t turn around. “Yeah?”

“Do you think we should talk about my overall budget before you get too invested in this?”

Her family was a little old-fashioned when it came to talking about money, which meant that they didn’t. But he’d already brought the subject up vaguely when he’d mentioned his upbringing and how he relied on bets with his brother to make extra cash. She would definitely need to be sensitive to his financial concerns.

Clearing her throat, she said, “Of course.”

He named a sum that was surprisingly higher than what she’d anticipated. Her eyes widened for a brief second before her mind started calculating all the best ways to reinvest it into the ranch.

However, Dylan must’ve read her expression differently because he jerked his chin a little higher. “What? You didn’t think a boy from the Valley could have that much saved up?”

“No.” She reached up to straighten her ponytail, as though she could regain her composure. “But I do think with that kind of money to throw around, you can definitely afford to buy me lunch.”

CHAPTER FOUR

DYLAN FELT LIKE a champion when he somehow managed to eke out enough time to return to the ranch with takeout from Bronco Burgers. But he hesitated when he saw the plumber's truck parked next to Robin's. She was standing on the weathered front porch with the plumber, her mouth moving nonstop as the poor man furiously scribbled notes onto his clipboard.

Dylan looked upward in silent prayer. *Please save me from determined women who like to plan things on my behalf.* Grabbing the sack of food and a flimsy cardboard carrier holding cups of sweet tea, he tried not to think of how much this was going to cost him. Not in terms of money so much—although he didn't want to blow through his entire budget just yet—but in terms of pride. He was still annoyed with himself for not realizing that the property he'd acquired had a restricted covenant.

"Hey, Brad," Dylan said as he cautiously avoided the missing board on the second porch step. The middle-aged plumber was the power forward on Dylan's recreational basketball team and had done some remodel work on the restrooms at Bronco Motors last year. He also had a daughter graduating from high school in a few months and was hoping to get a good deal on a used car for her.

"There better be some extra French fries in there." Brad's pen paused long enough to point at the bag in Dylan's hand. Then he explained to Robin, "My wife is on a health kick, which means we're all on a health kick since all carbs are currently forbidden from entering our house."

"I've got extra fries, onion rings and a patty melt with your name on it. But you better not tell Monique that I'm the reason you didn't finish that kale salad she keeps packing you for lunch." Dylan set the food on the porch railing and noticed Robin's eyes eagerly follow the bag. She was tall and lean, but after seeing her dig into the bakery box this morning, it was clear she enjoyed eating. He had a feeling his gamble was about to pay off. "I probably should've called to ask your order, but I was in such a rush to get back here, I made an executive decision and got you the double bacon cheeseburger."

Robin lifted one perfectly arched brow. "With extra bacon?"

Dylan resisted the urge to pump his fist in the air, his confidence restored. He might not be the most knowledgeable about cattle, but he still knew how to read people.

"I figured anyone who eats the top of the muffin first isn't going to want to scrimp on the bacon," Dylan said before turning to Brad. "You want to finish doing your walk-through or do you want to eat first?"

Brad cleared his throat. "Actually, Robin already showed me around and gave me an idea of what you guys were thinking."

You guys? That was a bit presumptuous considering that Dylan and Robin hadn't even talked about the plumbing yet. Not to mention that it was Dylan's property and ultimately his decision, not hers.

"Is that right?" Dylan put his hands on his hips. "Remind me of what *we* were thinking, Robin."

"One of the first things *we* noticed was the newer, county-issued water meter outside the barn. Which means Dylan is already tied into their sewer system." She opened the bag and began passing out the burgers before adding, "Technically."

"Yeah, technically." Dylan nodded in agreement despite the fact that he most definitely had not noticed the water meter outside the barn. But he appreciated her including him in the discovery. Or at least covering for him by making him sound less clueless than he clearly was.

Robin continued, "But the house still uses that old septic tank over there, which probably explains the weird smell coming from the kitchen faucet. So Dylan can either replace the forty-year-old septic system or he can convert to sewer, which might be cheaper at this point and require less maintenance."

Damn. There was another thing he'd completely missed. Granted, he'd grown up in town and had never dealt with a septic system. Dylan's frustration quickly gave way to relief, though, at the realization that he might not have to totally replumb the house to fix that funky stench. That might be a big time-saver.

He took the fries Robin handed to him and asked, "Any chance you talked to Brad about the irrigation system for the pastures, too?"

"As a matter of fact, I did." A corner of her mouth tilted into a smirk and she actually winked at him. Dylan didn't know whether to be aroused or annoyed at her boldness. But there was no doubt in his mind that Robin knew full well that he was reliant on her expert opinion.

"Robin thinks the system is tied into several wells that are fed by Hardy's Creek," Brad said before biting into his sandwich.

Of course she does. Dylan silently asked himself why he bothered having the plumber come out since Robin was apparently the expert on everything.

"You'll eventually want to have those checked out,

Dylan." Robin reached for one of the cups of sweet tea. "But with how much rain we usually get in March, you won't need to worry about that until the end of spring. We'll put that further down on your to-do list." She hesitated a moment and assessed him. "Why aren't you eating?"

Dylan glanced at the uneaten food in his hands. Normally, he would've made quick work of the burger, especially since he thought better when his belly was full. But something made him pause. "Because I'm still trying to figure something out. If all I need to do is convert the house to the already existing sewer system, then why was Brad taking so many notes when I pulled up?"

His friend had just shoved an entire onion ring into his mouth and had to finish chewing before he could respond. "We were working on an estimate?"

Again with the *we*. Wait. Why had Brad phrased it as a question?

"An estimate for what?"

"The roof. And some of the electrical wiring that's pretty shoddy."

"But you're a plumber," Dylan reminded him.

"Technically." There was that word again, making Dylan see dollar signs. Brad continued, "But I was just telling Robin about how I recently got my general contractor's license and I'm thinking of expanding my business to work with a few subcontractors."

Sure, Dylan had been rather cocky when he'd told Robin earlier this morning that he had the budget for making the improvements. But just because he had the money didn't mean he wanted to waste it. Even if he had no need to worry about the financial side of things, there was still an emotional investment he'd been looking forward to creating.

"I was actually planning to do some of that work myself," Dylan said as though it should have been obvious. "I mean, isn't that part of owning land? To build it with your own two hands?"

"If you were a homesteader from the eighteen hundreds and had limited resources and an abundance of time, then sure." Robin once again seemed to be studying him, sizing him up. "But nobody goes it alone anymore, Dylan. Doing everything by yourself would be too time-consuming and it's not always economically feasible."

He knew her words were practical, but he still had to swallow a lump of disappointment that his dream might not happen the way he'd hoped. There'd been a tug-of-war raging inside him these past few months and it felt as though reality was about to win.

Robin put her palm on his shoulder and something about her touch sent a wave of peace through him. "Just because your two hands aren't doing the actual work doesn't mean you won't be putting in plenty of blood, sweat and tears. If Brad is taking care of the house, that gives you more freedom to focus on everything else that needs your attention. Both on the ranch and at your dealership."

"Yeah, I heard about that bake-off you're holding." Brad's reminder of the upcoming competition made Dylan wince. "Monique wants to enter, but she's yet to master a carb-free recipe that wouldn't earn her last place. Like this lunch, though, that's another thing we're going to keep between us."

Robin used her fingers to make a zipper motion across her lips.

Since Dylan would rather talk about sky-high construction estimates than that ridiculous contest his family was organizing, he brought the conversation back to the chaos he could at least control. "Knock 20 percent off your labor costs and I won't say a word to Monique about anything you eat on the jobsite. Now walk me through what you guys have in mind."

WHEN THE PLUMBER drove off, Robin was still slightly in shock. She'd never really dealt with the repair side of things on her family's ranch, but she'd watched enough home renovation shows to know how much a full kitchen remodel would cost.

Granted, Brad was slowly expanding his business and it would benefit the man to lower his prices in an effort to build his clientele. But clearly, Dylan Sanchez's smooth-talking skills were not limited to just women.

"Do you always get what you want, Dylan?" she asked as he browsed the plumbing fixtures catalog Brad had left him.

He lifted his head, a crease between his brows. "What do you mean?"

"I mean that you somehow managed to get Brad to agree to an amount that's nearly a third lower than the going rate. Plus, he's adding a complete teardown and rebuild of both the front and back porches to the roofing contract."

"No. What I *wanted* was to do the repairs myself. Hiring Brad to do it was actually a compromise."

Robin chuckled as she shook her head. "There's certainly nothing wrong with your work ethic, I'll give you that. But they were right about your stubbornness."

His brown eyes widened. "Who said I was stubborn?"

She bit her lower lip, wishing she could take back her words. Eloise had simply given her some insight into the Sanchez family, but Robin worried that if she admitted as much, it'd seem like they'd been gossiping. Or that she'd been fishing for information about him. Which she sort of had been doing.

"I've heard it mentioned around town," she said quickly, then changed the subject. "So how did the interview go?"

Dylan's smile was immediate and caused his whole face to relax. "Better than I could've hoped. I hired her right on the spot. She's starting tomorrow."

Her? Robin remembered the pretty young woman from yesterday and wasn't accustomed to the split second of jealousy that flashed through her. "She must be quite impressive."

"She is. I don't know if you've ever met Mac, Jordan Taylor's assistant. It's her older sister. They look so much alike, right down to the steel gray curls and penchant for bright colored sneakers. Mickie is just as feisty as her sister and twice as organized."

Robin let out the breath she didn't realize she'd been holding. She had no claim to Dylan, and it was silly of her to even allow a single possessive thought to cross her mind.

"I know you have to get back for a meeting," she told him. "But I made some other notes before Brad got here. Maybe we can touch base tomorrow and go over those?"

"Just bring your list tomorrow afternoon when we go to that wholesale home improvement store Brad recommended."

Robin looked behind her to see if he was speaking to someone else. Nope. She was the only one there. "When did we decide I was going with you?"

"When you told Brad that *we* needed to demo all that ugly brown tile in the shower before replacing the drain pan. You didn't think I was going to go pick out all the bathroom materials by myself, did you?"

Alarm bells went off inside her head. "But I don't know anything about color schemes and decorating and making things look pretty."

His eyes dropped to her feet and then took their time

traveling up her body to her face. "You seem to be well-equipped to me."

An unfamiliar tingle raced along the back of her spine. But that only caused her earlier panic to spread, which made her stiffen in defiance. "Why? Because I'm a woman?"

"No, because you're hot as hell, yet you make it seem effortless."

Her defensiveness vanished and she was only left with the tingling sensation as she tried to explain. "It's effortless because I literally put zero effort into being this…oh."

"You're even hotter when your cheeks get all pink like that." One side of his mouth rose in a slight smile and she wondered how she could be so warm when there was still snow on parts of the ground.

"I guess I'm not accustomed to people giving me compliments about…about something that doesn't involve my horses or my business."

"Probably because they're too afraid to get shot down."

"Why?"

Dylan shrugged, but his expression remained confident. "I guess some men get intimidated by a smart and beautiful woman."

Okay, he needed to stop with all this talk about her appearance. It was getting her all flustered and she was having a hard time concentrating on the conversation. "No, I meant why would I shoot them down?"

"Do you?"

"Do I what?" Her lips parted in confusion.

"Shoot a guy down when he asks you out?"

Robin snapped her mouth shut. She couldn't very well admit that she didn't get asked out very often. Focusing on a spot behind him, she asked, "Are we talking about my dating life or about your house remodel?"

He crossed his arms as he leaned back to give her a full appraisal. "I'd like to talk about both, but I suppose one of those topics isn't any of my business."

If she were good at flirting, this would be the time to tell him that she wanted to make her dating life his business. But what if it came out sounding desperate? Or worse, what if he told her that he already had more business than he could handle? Instead of humiliating herself any further, she drew in a long breath. "Listen, Dylan, I'm not the type of woman you consult for decorating tips. I'm more the type that you would ask to accompany you to the feedstore. Or a livestock auction."

He narrowed only one eye, almost giving him the appearance of winking. "How are you in a tractor supply setting?"

She extended her arm in a wide arc as though to say, *There you go. Now you're getting it.* "I can hold my own."

"Perfect. There's a tractor supply place on the way to the home improvement warehouse in Wonderstone Ridge. On Thursday, we can swing by the feedstore and then hit that livestock auction at the Bronco Convention Center on Saturday."

"Wait. What?" Robin scratched her head, knocking her ponytail off-center. Although, now it matched the rest of her, which was feeling equally off-center.

"Assuming that would work with your schedule." Dylan pulled out his phone and swiped until he opened the calendar app. "I can't leave until two tomorrow since Mickie is coming in for her first day and I'll need to walk her through some things."

Robin lost all ability to protest, or even respond with much more than a nod of her head as she pulled out her own phone to accept his calendar invite. It all happened so fast. Before she knew it, Dylan was telling her he had to get going to his next meeting and thanking her for all her help today.

If Robin had been slightly in awe when the plumber had driven away earlier, she was in complete shock by the time she got inside her own truck to leave. Dylan Sanchez was truly a smooth talker. How had a simple offer of advice yesterday turned into several hours and two meals with the man today, and then the promise of at least three dates later this week?

No, they weren't dates, she told herself as she pulled onto the long dirt driveway better known as Broken Road. They were shopping trips. Shopping trips that would benefit his ranch. That would benefit him.

Although, if she was being honest, they would also benefit her because it meant she'd get to spend more time with Dylan. And wasn't that her goal? Why she'd even considered entering the bake-off in the first place? If she was going to use her feminine wiles—or lack thereof—to get close to a man, she was going to have better luck if she was on familiar territory. She'd definitely be more comfortable inside a feedstore rather than baking cookies in the kitchen.

Still. None of this was going quite how she'd envisioned. Her plan had taken an unexpected turn, and something wasn't sitting right. Maybe it was the fact that Robin had formulated a plan in the first place instead of allowing nature to take its course. In her defense, though, her entire business model for her line of horse therapeutic products was based on the premise that sometimes nature needed a little help moving things along.

Except her products were designed to benefit the horse in the long run. When it came to her crush on Dylan Sanchez, Robin wasn't sure who was benefiting from her plan. Was she using his ranch as an excuse to get close to him?

Or was he using her to get closer to his goal of having a successful ranch?

An unease settled over her as she drove to Cimarron Rose to check on a capsule collection of mane products she'd developed for the Rein Rejuvenation's grooming line. For years she'd dedicated herself to growing her business, and throwing herself into her work was always a default when she wanted to avoid anything uncomfortable.

But the discomforting doubt didn't go away at the boutique owned by Evy, her cousin Wes's wife, and only grew stronger by the time she returned home. That evening, Robin reached for her phone multiple times to call Dylan and tell him that she couldn't go to the home improvement store. However, as soon as her finger would hover over the screen, she couldn't make herself tap that green button. She needed just a few more hours with him before she could convince herself that she was wasting her time. Plus, there was a small part of her that was flattered he'd wanted her opinion. She went back and forth in her head until right before eleven o'clock on Wednesday morning when her phone pinged with a text notification.

When she saw Dylan's name, Robin's heart picked up speed. Her brain quickly shut down any excitement. He was probably sending her a message to cancel. Feeling foolish for not canceling first, she sighed as she opened the text.

Mickie has already made herself comfortable and politely suggested I "get lost" so she can set things up the way she wants. Dylan included a photo of a no-nonsense-looking older woman sorting papers behind the reception area desk. A second message popped up below. *I know we agreed on 2:00, but is there any chance you can slip away sooner? I can pick you up.*

Robin's pulse skyrocketed again, and she took three

breaths in quick succession to get ahold of herself. This was *not* a date. At least not in his mind. He was simply asking her to tag along with him and give him some advice.

If she was going to help Dylan, then she should really help him by giving him a sneak peek into what he was getting himself into. A sudden idea occurred to her, and she quickly typed a response.

If you can make it to the Bonnie B in the next hour, you'll find me in the cowshed on the south side of the property.

Smiling to herself, she shoved her phone into her back pocket. Then she told the cow in the stall with her, "Let's see how Mr. Smooth Talker does on an actual working ranch."

CHAPTER FIVE

DYLAN KNEW A setup when he walked straight into one.

Because if Robin would've told him that he was going to find her inside a stall with another ranch hand and a bleating cow about to give birth, there was no way Dylan would have raced across town to get to the Bonnie B.

"You ready to witness something incredible?" she asked, her eyes radiating the same excitement in her tone. She looked so wholesome and completely in her element, the same attraction he'd experienced yesterday returned like a swift kick to his gut.

"Can I witness it from this side of the stall?" Dylan asked. He'd owned his own ranch for a couple of months now and was used to the smell of manure. But the scent of amniotic fluid spilled on fresh straw hit the nostrils differently. "I don't want to make the mother-to-be nervous."

"This is Becky's fourth birth. A pro like her doesn't get nervous anymore." In response, Becky made a whimpering moo. "But she's definitely in pain, aren't you, girl?"

Robin remained by the cow's head, murmuring words of encouragement as the ranch hand knelt behind Becky, ready to help guide the calf out. Yep, this was definitely different than when Princess had her litter of puppies. And despite his initial hesitation, Dylan was so completely mesmerized by the process that he didn't look away once.

"You got this, girl." Dylan followed Robin's lead, wanting to offer the cow some verbal motivation. Although, perhaps he wasn't quite as calm as the labor progressed and he continued to cheer from the sidelines. "There are the front hooves, and the head. It's time to bring it on home, Becky. Okay, that last contraction was a swing and a miss, but you're going to get it on the next one."

A burst of adrenaline pumped through his body when the calf was safely delivered, making him feel as though he'd just hit a home run, scored a touchdown and made a three-pointer all in one. Dylan whooped and lifted his arms in victory. "Way to knock it out of the park, Becky!"

The ranch hand paused his examination of the newborn to tilt his head in Dylan's direction. Dylan immediately lowered his voice. "Sorry, I'm used to coaching youth sports and got a little excited there for a second."

Robin bit her lower lip as she came out of the stall, leaving the exhausted cow to bond with her calf. Dylan caught the twinkle of something in the woman's eyes.

"That was incredible," he said, then looked around at the surrounding pens holding very pregnant cows. "You have any other ones in labor we can watch?"

Robin let loose with the laugh she'd apparently been holding back. When she finished, she shook her head. "It's still early in the birthing season, but if you come back in March, we average about two or three a day. I have to admit, this isn't exactly the response I was expecting from you."

"I wasn't expecting it from myself, either. I had my doubts at first, but then something came over me and the whole experience seemed so natural, so right. I think I can actually do this, Robin."

"They're not always this easy," Robin warned. "The heifers are first timers and not all of them are as calm as Becky. They might not respond as well to your shouts about sticking with the hard-court press and staying loose."

"They will if I install some TVs in the barn so they can watch the sports channels."

"So you're really committing to this, huh?" Robin's smile was wide. "You're going to breed cattle?"

"Why? Was this some sort of test?" Dylan looked at the cow, who was already back on her feet and licking her calf clean. "Were you in on this, too, Becky?"

"Yes, Becky was the mastermind." The cow mooed her agreement and Robin gave Dylan's arm a playful shove. "See. She says you passed. I need to go wash up and change before we go. Do you want to stay here or follow me over to the main house?"

Dylan had passed the massive home on his way to the barn area. He was curious if the inside was just as spectacular as the wood beam and river rock architecture outside suggested. He'd once gone to Jordan Taylor's equally impressive family home for his sister's rehearsal dinner and had been disappointed to discover that something so beautiful could also be utterly devoid of warmth. At the time, his curiosity about how the other half lived had only made him feel more like an outsider.

Dylan wasn't ready to feel that way with Robin. Yet.

"Actually, I'll just cruise around the maternity ward here and see if any of the ladies need me to give them a pep talk."

"Okay, Coach," Robin said. "I'll meet you outside in ten minutes."

There were several employees hard at work and he didn't want to bother them with questions. Although he did have plenty of questions. Instead, Dylan walked around the pens taking mental notes before heading outside. It would require a lot more people and a hell of a lot more money to get his operation up to this level. After his rec league game last night, he'd buried himself in research about the pros and cons of breeding cattle as well as the expected profit margins. He'd learned that bigger ranches, like the Bonnie B, had the resources to both breed and raise their own cattle. But a ranch the size of his was better suited to doing one or the other. He'd been a little late to the party figuring out the differences, but at least he had a better sense of direction now, thanks to Robin.

As he stood outside one of several cowsheds, comparing the size of the structure to his own barn, a man in his sixties called out to him. "Hey, Dylan, what brings you out to the Bonnie B? Is there a problem with one of the new trucks?"

"Hi, Mr. Abernathy." Dylan lifted his hand in greeting. Robin must've gotten her height and blond hair from her father, but that was where the resemblance ended. No wonder he hadn't recognized her that day at the dealership. "I'm not here on business. Or at least not on car business. I'm waiting for Robin. She's helping me with a project out at my ranch."

Just saying the words *my ranch* to such a respected member of the Bronco community gave Dylan a thrill of satisfaction.

"Right. I heard you and Hank Hardy worked out a pretty sweet deal for Broken Road Ranch."

Sweet deal. See? Even Asa Abernathy saw that Dylan had made a smart investment. His chest swelled with pride. "We did."

"Also heard he left the place a mess. Old Hank was never cut out for the ranching life."

Some of Dylan's confidence took a slight dip. The last thing he wanted was for anyone to say those same words about him. Many of the people in this town possibly thought it, and might even talk about it amongst themselves. They wouldn't for long, though. Dylan would prove all the doubters wrong, but not by comparing himself to Hank. And definitely not by complaining that his ranch was anything less than what he hoped it would be. He recovered by pushing his shoulders back and smiling anyway. Sometimes, a guy had to hard-sell himself. Other times, the best response was no response.

Asa Abernathy seemed like the type of person who could tell when someone was feeding him a line. Dylan's gamble to wait it out worked because the man continued. "Anyway, if Robin's getting you squared away then you shouldn't have any problems."

"That's what I'm hoping, sir." Dylan appreciated the man's faith in his daughter. After all, his own parents weren't shy about singing their children's praises. The Abernathys might be wealthy, but at least they weren't as stuffy as the Taylor patriarchs.

"Although, if I'm being honest." Mr. Abernathy leaned in closer but didn't bother to lower his voice. "I wish my little girl would stop getting caught up in all these hobbies and start thinking more about her future."

"I think about my future all the time, Dad." Robin joined the conversation before Dylan had even noticed her walk up. And before he had time to wonder if Mr. Abernathy was referring to him and the Broken Road Ranch as one of his daughter's hobbies. "For the record, Rein Rejuvenation isn't a hobby. The CPA said my income last year was almost on pace to match my trust dividends."

Dylan tried not to wince. Of course Robin had a trust account. It was another reminder that unlike him, she didn't have anything to prove financially.

"What happened to your mouth?" her father asked, drawing Dylan's attention from Robin's snug jeans to her lips, which were much redder than they'd been when she'd left the barn. "Did Becky whip you with her tail again?

Or is that from the dye you've been using in those practice cookies?"

"No, Dad." Robin's cheeks were getting close to matching the shade of her lips. "It's just lipstick."

"Since when do you wear—" Mr. Abernathy must have read something in his daughter's glare because he wisely stopped talking and faced Dylan. "Anyway, where are you two off to?"

"I have to go to a home improvement wholesaler in Wonderstone Ridge and we're going to stop by Turner's Tractor Supply either on the way there or on the way back."

"On the way there," Robin corrected. "They close at five and we probably won't be done looking at bathroom vanities by then."

"Whoa." Dylan held up both palms. "Nobody mentioned anything about vanities. I thought it was just the toilets and shower tile getting redone."

Robin pushed a loose strand of hair away from her face. "That makes no sense. Why would you update most of the room, yet leave those old rotting cabinets in there?"

Dylan started to respond, but Mr. Abernathy made a tsking sound. "Son, it's better to just follow along when she gets going in a certain direction. Did she tell you that her brothers call her Trail Boss?"

Robin rolled her eyes. "I'm not bossy. I'm practical."

"Sure, honey. Let's go with that. When you're at the tractor supply store, will you ask Johnny Lee when they're expecting their next shipment of electric cultivators? Your mother is talking about replanting her garden."

"Not the gardening idea again. Remember when she forgot about those tomato plants a few years ago and we had that rabbit infestation?"

"You know how your mother is. She needs a project just like—" Her father stopped, making Dylan think the man knew better than to refer to Robin's penchant for projects again.

"But she has baby Frankie to dote on now," Robin pointed out. Dylan knew firefighter Jace Abernathy had adopted a baby boy after assisting with the birth during an emergency call. In fact, Robin's brother had also helped deliver Dylan's niece Merry. He was pretty sure that Jace and his fiancée, Tamara, now lived in their own house out here on the Bonnie B with their baby.

"Speaking of grandchildren," her father continued as he hooked his thumbs through his belt loops, "now that Billy's kids are getting older, your mom thinks Frankie needs some cousins his own age. So unless you want her focusing on which one of our children is going to provide the next baby, I suggest you let her run with her gardening project."

"That sounds familiar," Dylan mumbled to himself, but apparently his words were louder than he'd meant them to be.

"What's that?" Mr. Abernathy asked.

Dylan cleared his throat. "Mrs. Abernathy sounds like my parents. My niece is only two months old and already my mom and dad are dropping hints about more grandchildren."

"Is that right?" Mr. Abernathy studied Dylan rather intently, looking him over from head to toe.

Dylan's eyes shot to Robin, hoping she could explain why her dad was suddenly sizing him up like a prized bull. But Robin's expression looked equally confused. Or mortified. He couldn't tell which.

"Okay, Dad, we have to get going." Robin grabbed Dylan's arm and tugged him toward the truck. Although, she didn't have to use too much force because he was eager to get away from what had suddenly become a tricky conversation.

"You two have fun," Mr. Abernathy called. Dylan could feel the man staring at their retreating backs, so he only turned around long enough to give a quick wave goodbye. Something inspired Mr. Abernathy to give another parting comment. "And take your time. Maybe grab a bite to eat while you're there. Robin is less bossy when she's eating."

Robin gasped as her head pivoted to give her dad another warning look, reminding Dylan of the same expression his sisters used whenever someone in their family embarrassed them. He would've laughed, but since Robin was too busy silently communicating her displeasure at her father behind them, she didn't see the icy patch in front of her. The hand she'd been using to propel Dylan forward was still on his arm when she slipped, making her close enough for him to catch before she stumbled.

Even though she'd quickly regained her footing, he slid his arm around her, allowing his palm to curve along her small waist. Surprised brown eyes locked onto his, her thick lashes fluttering at him several times. "S-sorry. I wasn't watching where I was going."

"Good catch, Dylan." Mr. Abernathy was apparently still keeping tabs on them, which for some reason made Dylan want to prove that he was more than capable of continuing to protect her.

Hauling her against his side, Dylan steered Robin toward a melted spot on the road and kept his arm firmly in place as he walked her to his truck. Man, she fit so perfectly beside him, he was reluctant to let her go. If her dad hadn't been there, Dylan might not have.

"Please ignore everything my father just said and did," Robin said under her breath when Dylan opened the passenger door for her. "And for the record, I'm not that bossy."

"You kind of are," Dylan replied. When she opened her mouth to object, he added, "I do like your red lips, though."

ROBIN THOUGHT SHE'D been subtle borrowing her sister Stacy's lipstick. And then her dad had gone and pointed it out right in front of Dylan.

If that hadn't been embarrassing enough, her father had taken things one step further by mentioning grandchildren and then suggesting Robin and Dylan have dinner together. When it came to playing matchmaker, Asa Abernathy clearly had more experience pairing livestock than humans.

Robin had been in such a hurry to get away from her father's mortifying comments that she would have fallen flat on her face if Dylan hadn't been there to catch her. Then she'd been so stunned by the feel of his hand above her hip that she'd allowed herself to believe that his gentlemanly attention made this outing almost seem like a date.

Even though she knew it wasn't.

When Dylan made that comment about liking her lipstick, though, Robin couldn't think of anything but the way he was staring at her mouth as he said it. Not knowing how to respond, especially with her father still a few yards away and pretending like he wasn't watching them, Robin panicked and launched herself inside his truck. Hastily, she reached for the interior handle and almost caught Dylan's elbow with the edge of the door when she slammed it shut in his face.

She took several deep breaths as he made his way to the driver's side, warning herself not to look in the sideview mirror for fear of seeing exactly how red her face was. In fact, she took her time pretending to be absorbed in the process of securing her seat belt so that she wouldn't have to make eye contact with him.

However, she didn't have to be looking in his direction to see that he was removing an item of clothing. She inhaled the passing scent of his cologne as he tossed his jacket over the armrest and into the back seat.

Oh boy. Now she had to risk taking a peek. Her mouth went dry. Unlike the normal button-up shirts she'd seen him wear for work, he had on a snug-fitting Henley that showed every ridge of his athletic muscles underneath.

Great. How was she supposed to keep her cool when the man looked and smelled this good?

Luckily, Dylan got a phone call just as he started the truck. "Do you mind if I take this?"

"By all means," she said, relieved to have a few more moments to regain her composure.

He answered before shifting into gear. As much as Robin tried not to pay attention, it was hard to ignore since he was using the speakerphone and the caller's voice was broadcast throughout the cab of the truck.

"Dylan, it's Keith Monk from the Helena dealership. I have a customer here who is interested in the crossover SUV sport but only if she can get it in Carefree Crimson. I don't have one in that color, but was looking at the inventory database online and saw that you might. I called your office hoping you still have yours in stock, but some woman answered the phone."

"Yes, that's Mickie." Dylan looked both ways before pulling out onto the highway. "She's my new office manager."

"Well, she said that you guys have to hold on to all your red inventory for some sort of baking contest you're having. Something about a Valentine's Day color scheme. What's that all about?"

Dylan muttered a curse under his breath. "You have any sisters, Keith?"

"Can't say that I do."

"Then it'll be too hard for me to explain." Without going into any more detail, Dylan went on to negotiate a swap with Keith, telling the salesman he could send the red SUV and a blue sedan in exchange for a pair of red convertibles and a white minivan.

Even though they were using several acronyms and other terms Robin didn't understand, Dylan's voice was confident and leisurely and almost soothing. It wasn't long before the tension in her muscles had completely vanished, and she relaxed into the heated leather seat.

When the deal was made and delivery coordinated, Keith again asked, "So what's going on with the cooking show?"

"It's a bake-off. I'll email you the flyer if you're interested in signing up." Dylan said goodbye and disconnected before apologizing to Robin. "Sorry about that."

"Business comes first," Robin said, reminding herself, as well. It wasn't like he'd taken a call while they were on an actual date. "So you're going to decorate your entire parking lot with red and white cars for Valentine's Day?"

"I have no idea. Obviously, Camilla and Sofia already told Mickie their plans before they bothered to fill me in. Probably because they knew I would've put my foot down."

"I've met both of your sisters and I think it's cute that you're under the impression you could actually put your foot down with them."

"I put my foot down all the time."

"Like when?" Robin asked. "Give me an example."

"Like the time Sofia wanted me to wear a pink shirt in some fundraiser fashion show at the boutique where she works."

"You were in a fashion show at BH Couture? Like as a model?"

"Yes." He pointed one finger. "But not in that shirt. Why? You don't think I could be a model?"

"On the contrary. I think a lot of women—and men—would buy whatever you were selling." But mostly women. Dylan had a reputation for being a carefree and charismatic bachelor and Robin had a feeling it was well-earned. "So you draw the line at wearing pink. What else?"

"Oh, I'm fine with wearing pink. It was more the cut of the shirt and how it felt on my arms. I hate constricting fabric. I need to be able to move." He extended and retracted his forearm in a way that caused his bicep to flex under the soft material of his current shirt. Suddenly Robin needed to take off her own jacket. "I also put my foot down when it comes to my turn to cook Sunday dinner. Nobody ever wants to do appetizer night except Dante, so my family always tries to get me to try something besides buffalo wings and nachos. You want me to let you in on a little secret?"

Robin got butterflies in her tummy every time Dylan lowered his voice that way. "Sure."

"You know the flaming fajitas incident everybody in town seems to have heard about?"

Robin recalled mentioning it to him the day they met. "Of course."

"It was totally worth singeing off my eyebrows and being the subject of everyone's jokes for three whole weeks because now my family lets me cook whatever I want. As long as open flames aren't involved."

Was there anything sexier than a man who could laugh at himself? Robin didn't think so. Unless it was the matching dimples in Dylan's cheeks when he did laugh.

Before she could fall completely under his spell, Robin challenged, "I don't know if a cooking mishap that you didn't plan counts as putting your foot down."

"Fair enough. Then how about the time Camilla and Jordan tried to pay for my parents' kitchen remodel. I insisted on matching whatever amount they were contributing. Which is a good thing because now I know what I'm getting into with the cost of materials and the labor delays. Although, it's also a bad thing because now Camilla expects me to know how great of a deal her restaurant equipment supplier is getting me for the rental of a bunch of commercial-grade ovens. Which reminds me, I need to figure out which part of the lot she plans to use for them."

"The ovens are for the bake-off?" Robin no longer had to worry about being too flushed because her blood went cold.

"Yeah." Dylan pulled ahead of an 18-wheeler and picked up speed.

"You're holding the bake-off at the dealership? As in contestants are going to make their recipes all together? In the middle of an open parking lot?"

"Someone mentioned some heated party tents, but the idea was to generate some extra money and every time I turn around, it seems like my family is spending more of it."

Crap. Robin hadn't realized that she would actually have to bake her cookies in front of witnesses. She needed to figure out a way to back out of this contest, but without seeming like she was afraid of coming in last place. Was it too much to hope for a blizzard to cancel the entire thing?

"So if you don't want to do the bake-off and you don't like the idea of having red and white cars on your lot during it, then why aren't you putting your foot down for this?" Robin asked. "I mean, as far as risks go, I'd be more concerned about having control over a business promotion than I'd be about a tight shirt making my biceps look amazing."

Unfortunately, they were on a long stretch of road with no oncoming traffic and he felt safe enough to tilt his head as he looked directly at her. “You think my biceps look amazing?”

“Keep your eyes on the road,” she said, refusing to answer a question he surely knew the answer to already. “And tell me why you’re letting your sisters have free rein when you clearly want nothing to do with this contest.”

“Because I love my family and it makes my mom and sisters happy to feel like they’re helping me. Plus, as much as I hate the entire concept, I also trust them to pull it off. I have no idea how they’ll manage it, but if anyone can make something work, it’s them.”

Robin looked out the window, blinking several times to clear the dampness from her eyes. If she thought it was attractive that Dylan could poke fun at himself, she was absolutely impressed—and touched—by his ability to speak so highly of the women in his life. Her dad always said that it would take a confident man to not be intimidated by his strong-willed daughter.

And Dylan Sanchez was definitely not intimidated by strong women.

But then again, he’d never been to a tractor supply store with Robin Abernathy.

She’d learned to drive a John Deere 6 Series before she’d been allowed to drive a car and was usually the first person to hop in the cab when a row of alfalfa needed to be tilled or an irrigation channel needed to be cleared. If only she could be as confident about her expertise in baking cookies as she was with horses and farm equipment.

When they pulled into the lot of Turner’s, a place she’d been coming to since before she could walk, Robin realized that she’d never asked him why they were going there in the first place. They’d talked about his barn layout, his fencing, even his fertilizer needs. But they'd never talked about heavy machinery.

"Do you know what you're looking for here?" she asked.

"I think so," Dylan replied. "But I'm sure you'll let me know if I get something wrong."

He winked at her, just like she'd winked at him the other day to let him know that she wouldn't tell Brad she'd figured out the plumbing issue before he had. Was this going to be another instance of her having to jump in to explain something to Dylan? Because no matter how confident he was around strong women, she wasn't looking forward to living up to her Trail Boss nickname. Again.

But it turned out that Dylan knew exactly what he wanted. And it wasn't a brand-new tractor. Robin's jaw nearly fell open when he told the man who greeted them, "I've got an International Harvester 856 that needs a new clutch, water pump gasket and a set of brake piston O-rings."

Johnny Lee Turner, the owner, asked about the year and horsepower and Dylan easily rattled off details that helped the older man locate the parts that would fit. Robin was left to follow behind as she silently stared in amazement at Dylan's knowledge about something ranch related.

"What about tires?" Johnny Lee asked as they passed a display of wheels.

"I already had my service tech order some from my wholesale dealer. Speaking of which, how's your wife liking her new wagon? Has she noticed a difference having the all-wheel drive with the snow?"

Of course. Robin nearly slapped her forehead at the late realization. No wonder Dylan was so comfortable talking shop about tractors. He was a car guy and engines were engines. When Johnny Lee finished gushing about how much his wife was enjoying her new car from, not surprisingly, Bronco Motors, Robin finally spoke up.

"Wait, how much are the tires from your wholesale person, Dylan?"

Dylan relayed an amount that was significantly cheaper than the price tag above the display in front of them.

"Hmm..." Robin tapped her chin. "So then why does the Bonnie B pay so much for tires?"

Johnny Lee squinted, then pushed his glasses higher on his bulbous nose. "Is that you, Lil' Robin Abernathy? I didn't recognize you with your hair down like that and all that makeup."

Her fingers flew to her mouth. Why was everyone acting like she'd just undergone some drastic makeover? Was she normally so hideous looking that a simple swipe of lipstick made that much of a difference? Refusing to be distracted, though, she squared her shoulders and lifted an eyebrow, waiting for him to answer her original question.

"Now I know what you're thinking, Lil' Robin," Johnny Lee said. For some reason, his tone sounded a bit more condescending. Probably because he referred to her by the same name he'd been calling her since she was three years old. "But the markup is on account of me having to pay added delivery fees plus the cost of keeping so many tires in stock. That way, they're readily available as soon as you need them."

"Yeah, I know how retail prices work, Johnny Lee, and the concept of supply and demand." After all, Robin was a business owner, as well. "But our ranch goes through a lot of tires and I'm wondering if it would be more cost-efficient for us to just deal directly with Dylan's wholesaler."

"I don't know if Mario will give you the same prices he gives me," Dylan said, then shrugged. "But I guess it wouldn't hurt to ask him."

"Why wouldn't he give me the same price?" Robin asked. Was he part of some good ol' boy network that only did business with men? She was certainly starting to get that impression from Johnny Lee.

"Because you didn't help him with his econ homework in college, and you don't volunteer to coach his son's Little League team with him."

"Humph." She crossed her arms in front of her chest, somewhat defeated. "I could comp him some horse therapeutic products."

"He doesn't have a horse."

Robin tried to think of something else she could bargain with. "What about a few hundred pounds of grass fed beef?"

"He's vegan."

Johnny Lee gasped. "And this tire friend of yours lives here in Montana?"

"Born and raised," Dylan confirmed, clearly holding back a smirk.

Robin's friend Daphne Taylor had caused quite a stir within her family when she'd announced to her ranching father that she no longer ate meat and was opening an animal sanctuary. Some of the old-timers in town were still adapting to the current century.

"I don't know that your daddy would want to buy tires from some granola-eating type, Lil' Robin. Best you just keep getting them here at Turner's. I got me a big freezer at home that could fit a whole rack of beef if you wanted to work out some sort of trade."

Robin frowned at the older man's offer, which frankly, was a little late considering they'd been paying full price all these years.

"Actually, Johnny Lee," Dylan said as he flashed that same smile he'd used yesterday with Brad the plumber,

"Mrs. Abernathy was hoping to get a top-of-the-line electric cultivator for her garden. Why don't you let Robin take that one home with her today. I think it would go a long way in sweetening the pot when she tells her father about your generous offer to discount the Bonnie B's tires by 20 percent."

Robin's eyes widened at Dylan's audacity, but she kept her mouth closed as the owner seemed to actually be considering his suggestion. She'd also completely forgotten about her mom's cultivator, so she was amazed Dylan had remembered. But more than that, she was both impressed and slightly aroused by his negotiation skills.

When Dylan loaded the cultivator into the bed of his truck ten minutes later, Robin realized that this little crush she'd developed was going to turn out to be a bigger problem if she ended up like everyone else in this town and couldn't resist his charm.

CHAPTER SIX

ROBIN STARED RELUCTANTLY at the entrance to the home improvement warehouse and asked, "Are you sure we should be doing this before we eat?"

Dylan looked at his watch. "Maybe you're right. It's already five o'clock and I only had a protein bar for lunch. There's a taco shop across the street, unless you had your mind set on eating somewhere fancier?"

Was she expecting him to take her to a five-star restaurant while they were out running errands? No. Did she hope they could possibly go somewhere a little more romantic than a fluorescent-lit fast-food joint in a strip mall? Maybe.

Unfortunately, her dad was right and Robin was more feisty when she was hungry. Or overwhelmed with cabinet choices. She didn't want to scare off Dylan by having their first major argument in front of a display of toilets. Still, she was a little defensive when she asked, "Why would I expect fancier? Did you think I was the prissy type?"

"Not when I watched you chow down that double bacon cheeseburger yesterday. But then today I saw the house where you grew up and realized that you may be accustomed to something a little more formal."

His comment gave her pause. As a kid, she'd been aware that her home was bigger than some of the others in town. By the time she was in high school, the financial disparity between her and her classmates became more noticeable and she realized that some people treated her differently when they found out her last name was Abernathy. It wasn't until her second date with an ambitious rodeo cowboy when she was twenty-two that she realized there were men out there who were only interested in her because of her family's bank account. She really hoped Dylan wasn't the same way.

"Formal?" She pushed her hair back, still not used to having it down around her shoulders. "Did I look formal when I was covered with straw and amniotic fluid back in the cowshed?"

"No, but then you got all dressed up."

Her arms dropped quickly to her sides, causing her palms to slap her hips. "I'm wearing lipstick. That's the only difference. Why is everyone acting as though I transformed into some sort of alien from outer space?"

"It's not that. It's just that those jeans are a lot tighter and the sweater under your jacket is…uh…the neckline is just a little more…" His hands made a V symbol in front of his own chest.

She glanced down and saw that the wide opening of her sweater dipped low enough to expose the curve of her breasts. She jerked the lapels of her jacket closed. "I borrowed this from my sister's closet. I guess I should've worn a shirt underneath it."

"I think it looks great exactly the way you have it." Dylan's dimples were now in full effect.

Her legs trembled slightly, and she didn't think it was from the new knee-high boots her mom had just bought her.

"So tacos sound good, yeah?" Robin said a bit too quickly before starting out across the parking lot. Luckily, Dylan caught up to her and didn't say anything else until after they'd ordered their food.

"I don't think the cashier was expecting you to speak such perfect Spanish," Dylan said as Robin filled a plastic cup with hot carrots and jalapeños from the salsa bar.

"I did a semester abroad in Argentina with my equestrian studies program and nobody down there seemed to think anything of a blonde American speaking Spanish. But here in Montana, it always catches people off guard."

"Probably because your accent is almost as good as mine. And my dad and Uncle Stanley are originally from Mexico, so I grew up speaking it."

"*Almost* as good?" Robin lifted her chin and challenged, "Let me hear it."

If she thought Dylan's voice had been soothing when he'd been on the phone earlier talking about mundane things such as factory incentives and cruise control options, it was absolute magic when he spoke to her in Spanish. She hadn't realized she'd closed her eyes listening to him until he said, *"Tu comprende?"*

"What?" She blinked several times. "Yes, of course I understand. You said that you know white marble countertops are classy and expensive, but you always wanted butcher-block countertops because your aunt Celia, Uncle Stanley's late wife, had them in her kitchen and used to make the best tortillas on them. So they remind you of home-cooked food."

"For a second there, I thought I might be boring you. Any other languages you speak?"

Robin shook her head. "Nope. But we did have a ranch hand once from Germany who taught me and my siblings some bad words."

Dylan repeated the same curses, making Robin laugh. "Wait. What other languages do *you* speak?"

"French, Mandarin and Arabic. And one of the salespeople at the dealership is really into K-pop, so I can sing a few verses in Korean, but I have no idea what they mean."

Robin's jaw went slack, again taken by surprise. He must've been accustomed to the response—or at least expected it—because he shrugged. "I was an international business major in college. At one time, I planned to make my fortune in the global stock exchanges, but it turns out I liked living in Bronco too much to ever move overseas."

"So you became a car salesman instead?" she asked.

Dylan shrugged. "It was supposed to be a summer job, but one commission led to another and before I knew it, I got the opportunity to open my own dealership. I like cars almost as much as sports and since there isn't a high demand for a professional basketball franchise in Bronco, I found something I could do that I was decent at."

The person behind the counter called their order number. Robin watched with a new sense of wonder as Dylan walked across the restaurant to retrieve their food. He was a great salesman and obviously well educated. But like her, he also had a close family and deep roots in their small town. He'd even mentioned before that his desire to make money was more of a means to an end. His real dream was to own his own land.

Leaning back comfortably in her chair, she was more certain than ever that she'd made the right decision to assist him in making his dream a reality.

At least she was until they finished eating and were crossing the street heading back toward the home improvement warehouse again.

Robin's pace slowed. "I was just thinking that your sister Sofia is in the fashion industry. Camilla owns a restaurant and is probably an expert on kitchen layouts. And Eloise has impeccable taste. Don't you think you should've brought one of them to help you pick stuff out for your new home?"

"Maybe. But you volunteered." He continued walking toward the entrance.

"I didn't exactly volunteer for this part," she pointed out. Her words failed to slow him down.

In fact, it felt as though he was now moving faster. "Except you kind of did."

"But, Dylan, home improvement is such a personal thing. You're going to have to live in the house once it's done. Not me. What if you don't like something I pick out?"

"Then I'll tell you that I don't like it. I'm not afraid to put my foot down with you, too, Robin. Just like I'm currently refusing to let you talk your way out of this."

He must've realized that she wasn't following him, because he turned around and grasped her hand to pull her along. His grip was firm but gentle and radiated heat all the way up her arm and into her chest. For someone whose nickname was Trail Boss, she certainly had no problem allowing him to lead her. This was the second time today he'd physically taken control of a situation and somehow it made her feel more secure.

He didn't let go of her hand, even when they stepped inside. The vastness of the store caused her to inch closer to him. As if staying glued to his side wouldn't make the shopping trip quite so overwhelming. "There's certainly a lot more options here than at the hardware store in town."

"I know. I hate not buying locally, but Brad said he could get everything for a much lower price here with his contractor's license. He also said we only need to take pictures of what we want and send them to him. He'll come back and pick up the items."

"Do we have a list of everything we'll...*you'll* need?"

Robin knew she'd been guilty of using the *we* word yesterday. But that was back when she'd been trying to get Dylan to agree to her ideas by appealing to his sports team mentality. Now, she was questioning if that had been the best approach since her original plan seemed to be moving so quickly.

"Brad emailed it to me this morning." Dylan paused in front of a row of bathtubs. "Mickie was working on a spreadsheet with all the contact info for the bake-off contestants, so I asked if she had your email address on there. She found it and said she'd forward you the list. Check your inbox."

Robin reluctantly released his hand to pull out her phone. Sure enough, there was an email from Dylan's new office manager. But a thought popped into Robin's mind before she could read it. "So Mickie knows we're here together?"

"Yeah, why wouldn't she?"

"Does anyone else know?"

"Besides your dad, my brother Dante, who is in the middle of his own remodel project with Eloise, and probably my sisters and parents. Oh, and also Brad and everyone else on our rec basketball team since we all went to Doug's bar together last night after the game. I'm not sure who else might know. Why? Is it supposed to be a secret that we're hanging out?"

Okay. Keep breathing normally and don't freak out. This was no big deal. So what if Dylan just told a bunch of people at the town bar that he was "hanging out" with her? He hung out with a lot of women, from the sounds of things. There'd always been the risk that people would eventually figure out Robin had a crush on him. She just wasn't ready yet for the public humiliation if he ended up rejecting her.

"Nope. No secret on my end." Robin made her voice sound as casual as possible, trying to focus her attention on the emailed list. Although she couldn't help but ask, "Um, did anyone say anything about it?"

Dylan pulled out a tape measure she didn't know he had and stretched it out across one of the bathtubs. "About us hanging out?"

"Yeah." Robin continued to pretend as though she were completely engrossed in reading the words floating around the screen in front of her.

"What would they say?"

Oh, what *wouldn't* they say? But Robin didn't voice that thought aloud, probably because she didn't want to really hear the answer. Bronco was a small town and small towns meant big gossip. And gossip wasn't always complimentary. But then again, she was merely helping Dylan on his ranch. It wasn't as though people would immediately jump to the conclusion that they were dating. Because they clearly weren't.

"This is a nice tub," Robin said, changing the subject and hoping he didn't notice her internal distress about their nonrelationship. "I like the gold claw feet on the bottom. It makes it look like an antique, but it's much bigger than the old-fashioned ones."

"I was thinking the same thing," he said. "I'm not really a bath guy, but if I'm going to buy one, I want to at least fit in it."

Robin drew in a ragged breath at the mental image of Dylan Sanchez soaking in the tub, his hair wet and his chest bare… She cleared her throat. "What about the faucet? Would you do something in a gold color to match the feet?"

And that's how it went for the next hour. Sinks, mirrors, vanities, it was like something clicked between them and they both liked the exact same things because they were making quick work of their list. He'd pick a tile for the backsplash, and she'd suggest a lighting fixture. Then they'd both nod their heads and move on to the next item. She'd stop to look at a hardwood floor sample and he'd take a picture and type in the item number and price. Check. The kitchen was a no-brainer because she already knew what kind of countertops he wanted and they both loved the blue cabinets, even though they'd have to be custom ordered. They even pointed to the same drawer pulls at the same moment. The only time they weren't in complete agreement was when he thought the window shutters were the next aisle over and she thought they'd already passed them. They'd both been wrong.

Before Robin knew it, they were done. She shoved her phone in her back pocket. "That was way easier than I thought it would be."

"I know." Dylan looked around the store at several other people, including three couples, who seemed to be in the same sections they'd started in. "It feels like we should get some sort of prize for finishing so quickly."

"Like a double fudge brownie sundae?"

"From Cubby's?"

"I mean, it is on the way home," Robin said, wishing it wasn't already time for them to leave.

But Rome—and Broken Road Ranch—wasn't be built in a day. For the first time in Robin Abernathy's life, she would just have to be patient.

"WHY HAVEN'T YOU responded to any messages in the group chat yet?" Brad asked when he stopped by the dealership the following morning to pick up a deposit from Dylan. "The guys all want to know how things went with Robin last night."

So Dylan hadn't exactly been honest with her about the response he'd gotten at Doug's when it slipped out that Robin was helping him on his ranch. A few of the guys were a little more than curious. After all, it wasn't like the woman was making the social rounds in Bronco. Someone speculated that it was because she might think she was too good to hang out with people from the Valley. But so far, nothing about Robin—other than the size of her house and ranch—made Dylan think she was stuck up.

He rubbed the back of his neck, not really knowing how to answer any personal questions if they came up. "Things went great. Mickie turned your list into a spreadsheet for me and downloaded all the photos we took last night and matched them by item number."

Mickie shoved a binder at Brad. "It went from three pages to twenty-six, so I put it all in here to keep things organized."

"Twenty-six pages?" Brad opened the binder, quickly flipped through the contents then whistled. "You managed to pick out everything on my entire list? In one night? With Robin Abernathy?"

Dylan was already feeling rather accomplished today. Probably because Mickie had also organized the schedule so that he only needed to be in the dealership in the mornings with the other salespeople taking the later shifts. Now he would have the afternoons to work with Robin on the ranch and could dedicate his evenings to sports—both watching and playing. The spirit of competition flowed through him. "Yes. Why? Is that some sort of record?"

Brad gave him a look of disbelief. "It's unheard of. When we redid my bathroom at home, it took Monique an entire week just to decide between two different towel bars. You know that most couples don't normally agree on everything like this."

"Oh, Robin and I aren't a couple," he replied. At Brad's raised eyebrow, Dylan added, "We're just friends."

"You could do a lot worse than Robin Abernathy," Mickie, who'd only moved to town last week, said rather confidently.

"I wasn't aware that you two knew each other," Dylan told his assistant.

"I don't. But Jordan Taylor knows her and he told my sister, Mac."

And this was how rumors spread. While Dylan might be Mickie's employer, her sister had once done his sister a big favor by backing Camilla's restaurant as a silent partner. The overlapping connection between their families was sure to blur some boundaries. But if it meant his office would be this well organized, Dylan was willing to deal with the occasional unsolicited opinion. Especially because the woman was right about Robin.

"Nobody heard anything from me, though," Mickie clarified by making a key locking gesture in front of her mouth. "Because I'm a vault. I don't go around talking about your personal business in front of people."

Brad raised his hand but didn't bother looking up from the binder he was still thumbing through. "I'm a person and you're talking about it in front of me."

Mickie shrugged. "Yeah, but you brought it up first."

Dylan held up his palms. "It doesn't matter who brought it up. Robin Abernathy and I barely know each other."

"I thought you said you were friends," Mickie said, then answered the ringing phone before Dylan could explain. "Good morning. Bronco Motors."

He wasn't quite sure if he and Robin were friends actually. More like associates. Although, he wouldn't mind being her friend. Possibly even something more. Unfortunately, girls like Robin didn't go for guys like him. Dylan had found that out the hard way a long time ago and wasn't going to make that mistake again.

"You working through a play?" Brad asked, apparently done with the list and pictures since he'd closed the binder.

Dylan shook his head. "What do you mean?"

"Your expression. It's the same one you get when you're playing point guard and trying to calculate how to break down the defense."

If only it were that simple. Dylan had no chance of scoring any points with Robin if she found out people were already pairing them up as a couple. Last night when she'd asked if his teammates had said anything about them, Dylan had tried to change the subject. Mr. Abernathy had already acted super weird when he found out his daughter was going somewhere with Dylan. And Robin had responded by getting defensive. Or embarrassed. It was hard to tell yet since he was still getting used to her personality. Suffice it to say, she was visibly flustered by her dad's comments. Just like she seemed to be flustered anytime Dylan tried to flirt with her.

Which was weird because the woman was so confident about everything else.

Brad waved a hand in front of Dylan's face. "Wow, you're really in the zone, man."

"Sorry." Dylan shook his head to clear it. "I guess I have a lot going on in my head right now."

"I bet. So I'm going to go order all of this." Brad held up the binder. "And once I confirm everything's in stock, I'll schedule a demo crew to get started on the house. Do you think the cows are going to be affected by the noise?"

"I don't know," Dylan admitted. "Let me call Robin and ask her."

"Before you do that," Mickie said as she held her hand over the mouthpiece of the phone receiver, "this is the second news station to call this morning asking about the Valentine's Day bake-off. It's that anchorwoman with the big red hair and the even bigger you-know-whats. She said she wants an exclusive interview with, and I quote, 'That sexy car salesman who's running the contest.' She also asked if the winner would get a date with you. What do you want me to tell her?"

Dylan grimaced but hesitated at refusing the free publicity. "Tell her no dates, but I will agree to an interview if it's not live and if she does it here on the lot. Oh, and only if Eloise makes the arrangements."

Up until now, Dylan had refused to make a single commercial for Bronco Motors because he hated the thought of being in the spotlight. But a one-on-one interview for thirty seconds during some late-night news program that nobody watched shouldn't generate too much attention. And since Eloise and her successful marketing firm had taken over the Bronco Motors social media account, he hoped she wouldn't mind dealing with the press, as well. Although, he might need to reciprocate with some babysitting shifts.

Instead of asking Eloise separately, he fired off a quick text in his family group chat because there were so many cooks in this particular kitchen, it helped when they all were going off the same menu. Okay, so maybe that was a bad bake-off analogy. The other benefit to communicating via family chat was that it might save time and give everyone the opportunity to ask about Robin so he'd only have to respond to their nosy questions once.

After he sent that text, he dialed Robin's number.

She answered on the third ring, and he could hear what sounded like a horse neighing in the background.

"Am I interrupting something?" he asked.

"Not really. I'm trying to fit Sparkler with a custom-made magnetic pulse blanket, but her arthritis must be flaring because she's having none of it. What's up?"

"Poor Sparkler. It's tough for an aged athlete to deal with being past her prime. Anyway, Brad wants to know if the noise from the demo crew is going to bother the cattle."

"I'm not going to tell Sparkler that you just called her old. How long is the demo going to take?" Dylan relayed her question to Brad who held up a couple of fingers. "Brad says two days. But I tried to get some of that ugly mushroom print wallpaper off the dining room wall and I'm thinking they'll need at least twelve hours for that alone."

"Yeah, but that won't make much noise. How's the fence looking for the east pasture? I didn't make it that far out when I was there the other day."

"You didn't take the golf cart?" he asked with surprise because that was the first thing he'd tried out when he took over the ranch.

"No, I was embarrassed someone might see me driving it."

"That's not nice," he said, holding back a laugh. "But the east fence is looking the same as the others. Although, it does have that built-in shade structure, which can provide some protection in case the weather gets nasty."

"Okay, so if we can get that fence fixed by this weekend and then get the herd moved over there, Brad's crew could probably start demo next Monday and make all the noise they want."

Now he just needed to find the time—and a crew—to fix the fence. "Does Monday work for you, Brad?"

The contractor gave him a thumbs-up and started typing into his own phone. Mickie was on another call, but Dylan sensed that they were still paying attention to him. He turned his back and lowered his voice. "Are we still on for going to the feedstore this afternoon?"

"Yes," she responded, sounding almost breathless. Then she added, "Why are we whispering?"

Because Dylan was making a big deal out of nothing and acting like they were planning some sort of secret rendezvous. And because he didn't want to contribute to any more gossip about them spending time together. Because gossip led to opinions and opinions led to someone saying that Robin Abernathy was out of his league and he had no chance with someone like her.

Obviously, Dylan knew it. But he wasn't quite yet ready to admit it.

CHAPTER SEVEN

INSTEAD OF PICKING her up at the Bonnie B this time, Dylan met Robin at Bronco Feed and Ranch Supply. One of the things he was starting to like most about her, other than her willingness to share her expertise with him, was that she didn't need to flaunt her family's wealth and success. She didn't drive a flashy car and her clothes were simple, yet fit her perfectly. In the parking lot, Robin walked toward him with the type of confidence that comes from knowing what you're doing and not how good you look. Although, she did look pretty good in those jeans and that fitted wool jacket with her long blond hair blowing loosely around her beautiful face.

How had he only known this gorgeous woman for a few days?

He'd told Brad and Mickie that they weren't a couple and barely friends. *Associates* was the word he'd stupidly used. The problem was that he now didn't know whether to shake her hand or give her a hug hello.

Apparently, Robin didn't feel the need to waste time with a greeting because she launched right into the purpose of their errand. "I think the stainless steel feeding troughs you have in the barn will last for another few years, but the ones in the outside enclosures I saw have been exposed to the elements for too long and the damage is only going to get worse this winter and spring."

"Right," Dylan said, shoving his hands in his coat pockets. It was supposed to snow again tonight and the temperature was already dropping. But he also wasn't sure what he should be doing with his hands considering the last time he'd entered a store with Robin, he'd been holding hers.

It wasn't like him to be this uncertain around a woman before. Of course, it also wasn't like him to be so uncertain about purchasing so much feed and hay at once, so maybe his uncertainty was stemming more from that.

"Out of curiosity, how have you been getting the cows from pasture to pasture?" Robin's question broke into his thoughts.

"What do you mean?"

"I mean, most ranchers ride alongside the cattle to herd them, but you don't have any horses."

"That should probably be added to your to-do list for me. Both getting a horse and moving the cows to another pasture. Until now, I was doing what Hank said he did, which is to keep the barn doors open so they could come and go from the corral. I knew I'd have to get them out to pasture eventually so that was why I was looking for a good fertilizer to get the grass ready for them to graze. I figured that once I had a spot ready, then I'd figure out how to move them. Probably with the golf cart."

Robin scrunched her face in the most adorable way. Too bad Dylan couldn't enjoy the expression because he knew she was about to deliver an opinion he wasn't going to want to hear.

"Don't hold back now," he told her. "I asked you to help me because I knew you'd be honest and tell me when I was making a mistake."

Just like she had within the first few minutes of him meeting her.

"I'm thinking we shouldn't have picked those custom-ordered cabinets last night. That's money you could be using to buy a trained working horse. You're going to need that more this spring than a remodeled kitchen."

"Not if you ask my sister Camilla. She said that if I move into that house without a proper kitchen, then she and the rest of the family will set up one of those meal trains where people sign up to bring a casserole on a designated day of the week. They did that to my uncle Stanley after my aunt died and his house was crawling with well-meaning divorcées and widows looking for their next husband. People are already trying to couple me up with any single women they can think of. There are only so many ways that I can politely refuse."

"So it's true what people say about you?" Robin's facial expression was hard to read. "You're relationship averse?"

"I wouldn't say that. I'm just not falling for that whole soulmate thing. You of all people should understand. You're beautiful and a total catch, but you're still single..." Dylan trailed off, realizing he never actually asked her about her relationship status before. His buddies from Doug's hadn't warned him that she was already taken and her father had made it seem like he was eager to see her settled with children, so Dylan had simply assumed—or at least selfishly hoped—that there wasn't someone else. He gulped before he continued. "Right?"

"Uh..." She started to answer but an older woman was exiting the building right that second.

"Look who it is," Mrs. Epson, the woman owned the property neighboring the Broken Road Ranch, said. "What are you doing here, Dylan Sanchez?"

He double-checked the lettering on the sign above the door to make sure they were in fact at the feedstore. Yep. "I'm guessing the same thing you are, Mrs. Epson."

"Buying new wiring for your chicken coop?" she asked,

and he realized she was pulling a shopping cart behind her containing two small rolls of metal fencing.

His eyes shot to Robin, silently asking, *Do I even have a chicken coop?*

Robin bit back a smile and said, "The supply of pellet feed Hank Hardy left Dylan is almost gone and I wanted to show him a couple different brands that might work better for his herd."

Mrs. Epson leaned forward and squinted. "Is that you, Robin Abernathy?"

"Yes, I spoke to you on the phone the other day about Dylan taking over the Broken Road Ranch. Remember?"

"Of course I remember, dear. I just didn't recognize you with your hair down like that."

How did Robin normally wear it? Because this was now the second person from Bronco who hadn't realized it was her.

Robin ran a hand through the loose blond waves and Dylan found himself imagining what her hair would feel like draped across his chest. "Yep, it's me."

"Thank goodness." Mrs. Epson chortled. "For a second there, I thought Dylan had brought some cute little thing to the feedstore on a date."

Dylan didn't like the implication that he couldn't get someone like Robin to go out on a date with him, so he replied by wrapping an arm around her waist and pulling her closer to him. "Who says I didn't?"

Robin made a squeaking sound but didn't pull away. In fact, he felt her body relax against his side, and when Mrs. Epson glanced down to Dylan's hand, he boldly dropped it lower to cup Robin's hip.

"Back in my day, a date usually involved a nice meal." It was hard to tell, but it sounded like Mrs. Epson was making a tsking sound as she maneuvered her cart in front of her. "But you kids do things differently, I guess."

As they watched the older woman depart, Dylan lowered his voice. "Can I ask you a question?"

"I guess?" Robin glanced down at his fingers, which were lightly rubbing along the side seam of her jeans. But Dylan wasn't going to release her when Mrs. Epson might glance back in their direction.

"Do I strike you as the type of guy who wouldn't take you out for a nice meal?"

Robin shrugged, or at least it felt like a shrug the way she was tucked so closely against his side. "It depends on whether you'd describe Bronco Burgers and the taco shop last night as a nice meal."

"Yeah, but that wasn't a real date."

"That's not the impression you just gave to Mrs. Epson."

"I know. Sorry about that, but I didn't like her implying that I couldn't get someone like you to go out with me."

Robin pulled back far enough so that she could stare up at his face. "I'm pretty sure she was implying the exact opposite."

Before he could ask her what she meant, another customer came out of the store and held open the door as though he was waiting for them to enter.

"Thanks, Chuck," Robin told the man as she stepped away from Dylan and headed inside the store.

Dylan had no choice but to nod at the gentleman and follow her.

Knowing he'd need to buy feed eventually, he figured he'd just order the same stuff Hank already had stored in the barn. But having found out that the previous owner of his ranch hadn't always made the best decisions, Dylan had decided to do his own research ahead of time.

So he was relieved when he saw Robin standing in front

of a pallet of bags that matched one of the better rated brands he'd researched. "This is what we use for our pregnant and nursing cattle because there's added nutrients. But this brand behind me is good as an all-purpose. Do you know if any of your herd are expecting?"

"Hank said he sold all the bulls two years ago. But when my brother Felix came out last weekend, he noticed that what I thought was a steer actually still had all of its equipment. It also has a different color ear tag, so I'm thinking it snuck in through one of the broken fences. Anyway, one of Felix's professors from vet school gives students extra credit for pro bono work and found a few volunteers to come out with my brother this weekend to examine the rest of the herd."

"That's a good idea," Robin said, again giving Dylan a sense of relief that he'd made another sound decision.

Felix had told him that ranches the size of the Bonnie B or the Triple T, which Jordan's family owned, usually had a veterinarian or at least a vet tech on staff. Unlike other owners of smaller ranches, Dylan wasn't experienced enough to know when he needed a vet and when he didn't. Luckily, he had a brother who would keep him in check.

"Hey, Dylan, I figured I'd see you in here eventually," Brady Sellers said as he approached them. "How's it going out at the Broken Road Ranch?"

He hadn't greeted Robin, which made Dylan think the owner, like Johnny Lee and Mrs. Epson, hadn't recognized her, either. Instinctively, Dylan reached for Robin and wrapped his arm around her before Brady could act surprised that Robin was with him.

Robin's face whipped around to Dylan's, but again, she didn't pull away. In fact, she fit herself against him just as easily as she'd done outside. Good, because he was starting to become fond of having his hands on her.

"Hi, Brady. You know Robin Abernathy, right?"

Brady's forehead creased in a frown. "Of course I know Robin. I waved at her when she walked in the door before you. I came over as soon as I finished my call."

Robin nodded in confirmation, probably wondering why in the world Dylan had suddenly switched into protective mode. Despite her likely confusion, she remained at his side, though. He didn't hate it.

"So Robin has been helping me out at Broken Road and recommended I buy..." He turned his face toward her. Their noses were inches apart, so he lowered his voice. "How much did you think I should buy?"

"Three pallets of that brand." Robin's voice was raspy, but she pointed at the larger display of all-purpose feed. Then she jutted her thumb at the stacks next to her. "And a dozen bags of the sweet formula."

"You got it," Brady said. "How are you on hay?"

"Hank had a supplier making weekly deliveries," Dylan said. "But I don't love his prices. Especially since I'm hoping to get my pastures back into shape and could be using the extra money there."

Brady and Robin discussed the benefits of alfalfa and sprouts and grass fed pastures and Dylan listened attentively. Then he asked, "So if I go with the hay from Clover's Farm, that's only a few miles down the road from my ranch. I could just buy it from the Clovers directly."

"You could, but Dottie Clover doesn't deliver. Not even locally. I'm one of several distributors she works with who bring their own loaders and trucks to do the transporting and delivery."

"So you're a middleman?" Dylan asked, already knowing the answer.

"You could say that."

"Well, I wouldn't want to cut you out of your share.

But at the same time, my supply needs are much smaller and I'm right along the route so it wouldn't be as though your driver would really be going out of the way. Maybe we could come to some sort of agreement."

Brady lifted his chin. "What are you offering?"

Thirty minutes later, Dylan was pushing his receipt into his wallet as he walked out to the parking lot with Robin.

"How did you do that?" she asked him.

"Do what?"

"My family's been ordering from Brady Sellers for the past fifteen years, and never once has he ever given us free delivery."

Dylan shoved his wallet in his back pocket and slipped his arm into place around Robin's waist. "Did you guys ever ask?"

"No, but we shouldn't have to. We give him enough business, he should be offering *us* the discount. Most ranches the size of ours have land dedicated to growing their own. But we still need to supplement with an outside source."

"Can I grow my own?" Dylan suddenly asked. It would actually save him quite a bit of money. "I mean, do my conservation easements allow it?"

"We can look into it. I parked over there. Why are you walking me toward your truck?"

"Because Mrs. Epson wanted me to take you somewhere nice for dinner."

Robin paused. "I don't think that was what she actually said."

"It was what she meant." He maintained a loose grip as he continued walking.

"You know that she's not out here watching us, right? And there's no ice for me to slip on. You don't have to keep your arm around me like this."

"I know, but it's becoming a habit." He released her so he could open the passenger door for her. "Why? Does it bother you?"

Her cheeks were pink and she bit her lower lip as she slowly shook her head.

"Good," he said, then gestured for her to climb inside the cab before he took things further and kissed her right here in the middle of the feedstore parking lot.

"YOU NEVER ANSWERED my question earlier," Dylan said to Robin after the hostess seated them at the small table for two inside The Library, his sister's restaurant.

"What question?" She'd had a million of them buzzing through her head, but they were all things *she* wanted to ask *him*. Unfortunately, they weren't things she could ask inside the feedstore. Or when he'd been on the phone on the short ride over here answering a question from Mickie when she'd called.

"Whether or not you're single," he said.

"Oh." She didn't know why she felt the need to stall for time, but she wasn't ready to have this conversation. Not here. Not with people pretending like they weren't casting subtle glances their way and wondering to themselves why sexy Dylan Sanchez was at one of the most romantic restaurants in town with plain tomboy Robin Abernathy. Shouldn't he have asked that *before* he'd put his arm around her to pretend they were on a date in front of Mrs. Epson? Robin straightened the perfectly aligned silverware in front of her. "I am not committed to…uh…anyone. Or anything."

Dylan exhaled loudly and nodded. "So, you get it, then."

"Get what?"

"Obviously, you could have your choice of guys, but you're probably like me. You need to be free to do what you want. To not be tied down. Why does everyone think that someone has to be married to be happy? I mean, look at us. We look happy, don't we? Our lives seem perfectly content, don't they?"

She was flattered that he thought she was in high demand when it came to dates. But she was also floored by his suggestion that anyone would possibly compare Robin's lack of a love life to Dylan's reputation as a carefree bachelor.

She didn't want to correct him and admit that men were definitely not beating down her door. But she also wanted to be clear that, unlike him, she wasn't content to remain single.

She twisted the linen napkin in her lap. "I don't know that I'd say I'm opposed to being in a relationship. It just wasn't something I spent much time thinking about when I was younger. I had more important things to work on."

A high school–aged busser brought two ice waters and a basket of chips with queso dip. "Hey, Coach D, did you catch the Bulls game last night?"

Dylan shook his head as he leaned back in his seat. "I only caught the highlights afterward. That dunk right before the buzzer was insane."

The teenage boy's face looked confused. "But they played the Knicks, Coach. You never miss a Bulls-Knicks game."

"I know, Ty, but I had something come up." Dylan shrugged and Robin realized that he hadn't watched the game last night because he'd been with her.

The busser and Dylan exchanged a few opinions about a jump shot and a technical foul in the third quarter before the kid left their table. Robin figured the interruption had distracted Dylan from the topic of her being single, but he picked right back up where they'd left off.

"Yeah, your dad mentioned that you like having projects that take up a lot of your time."

"I did. I do. But I..." She thought of the best way to explain that finding a man was her next project and decided that she couldn't come right out and say that. "Now that my business is off and running, I seem to have more time on my hands."

"For dating?"

If she said yes, would he think she was trying to lay the groundwork for him to potentially ask her out? She didn't want to come across as desperate. Or give off the vibe that she was actively husband hunting. Because that would send him right out the door.

"For socializing." Robin shrugged. "According to my sister, Stacy, I should be going out more in general. In fact, Eloise wanted me to go to the mayor's anniversary party since it was right after she launched the ad campaign for Rein Rejuvenation here in the U.S. But one of my client's horses came down with colic and I was the only one he'd let give him mineral oil."

"I knew I didn't see you there." He pointed his finger at her as though to say *aha*. "I'm actually pretty good with faces."

"Apparently, not everyone in this town is," she murmured, thinking he wouldn't hear over the noise of the other diners around them.

But Dylan heard her and knew exactly what she was referring to. "Yeah, that was weird that Johnny Lee and Mrs. Epson didn't recognize you. I've seen you with your hair both up and down and you look exactly the same to me."

Before Robin could find out if that was a good or bad thing, a server came to take their order.

Dylan didn't even need to look at the menu, which he probably knew by heart. "Let's start with the shrimp spring rolls, the bacon-wrapped brussels sprouts, and the birria torta sliders. Robin, do you want an appetizer?"

"You know that they're meant to be shared, don't you?" Camilla Sanchez Taylor appeared at their table and gave her brother a playful tap on the shoulder.

Robin had been a couple years ahead of Camilla at Bronco High, so they'd never really hung out in the same circles. The Abernathys socialized regularly with the Taylors, but Robin had been too busy working on her latest patent to attend Camilla and Jordan Taylor's wedding. Although, she'd recently gotten to know Camilla a bit more through Jordan's sister, Daphne, who used Robin's products out at the Happy Hearts Animal Sanctuary.

"I was going to share." Dylan rolled his eyes at his sister. "But unlike some people who try to control everything and everyone around them, I wanted to make sure Robin got to choose something, too."

"Are you calling me controlling?" Camilla asked her brother and Robin noticed that they had identical playful smirks.

"I'll take the chicken lettuce wraps," Robin said to the server, who was standing there looking back and forth between her boss and Dylan.

"And a couple of small plates so that we can share because I always share," Dylan told the woman who should retreat to safety before the real fireworks started between the siblings.

Camilla arched a dark brow. "Really? You're not sharing any ideas about how to limit the judges to only five. Both Mrs. Coss, who owns the antiques store, and the mayor said you told them at the anniversary party that they could judge."

Dylan rubbed his temple. "I don't remember it going down like that, but there was a lot going on that night.

Kind of like how you have a lot going on with generating enough electricity to run the twelve industrial-sized ovens you want to use for the bake-off. Do you really think we need twelve ovens?"

"That reminds me that Mickie said we don't need as many generators since you have the electric vehicle charging stations. And yes, we need twelve ovens because we finally narrowed it down to twelve contestants."

"I thought I said that we should only allow local residents to be contestants," Dylan said. "I don't mind drawing customers from other towns but, if there are news crews there, I want to make sure we're properly representing Bronco."

"The twelve *are* local residents," Camilla said, then turned to Robin. "By the way, Robin, congratulations on making the final cut."

Robin nearly jumped out of her chair. "But I never turned in any official paperwork."

"Your name was on the sign-up sheet." Camilla tilted her head as her eyes went back and forth assessing Dylan and Robin. "Although, there might be some complaints about Dylan being a judge if he's openly dating one of the contestants."

"Oh, we're not openly dating," Robin said quickly. A bit too quickly.

Camilla lowered her voice to a near whisper. "Sorry. I didn't realize you guys were keeping it a secret."

"I think what Robin meant was that we're just friends," Dylan told his sister. But he wasn't smiling and there wasn't even a hint of a dimple. Was he mad about the assumption?

"That's not what you told Mrs. Epson. She stopped by here an hour ago to pick up a to-go order and said that you specifically told her that you and Robin were on a date at the feedstore. She was very concerned that you weren't—" Camilla used finger quotes *"—wining and dining your new lady."*

Robin's heart suspended in her chest, bracing for Dylan's explanation that he was only teasing his older neighbor.

"I know she was concerned," Dylan said. "I'm sure she'll be relieved to know that I brought Robin to this fine establishment and didn't just buy her burgers or tacos like I usually do."

Camilla gasped. "Robin, do not lower your expectations for my brother. I know he's been extra busy lately with the ranch, but he can make time for an actual sit-down meal once in a while. Especially on a date."

Instead of correcting his sister, Dylan was looking straight at Robin, his steady gaze practically daring her to deny it. Was this a date? Or was it one of those times she was supposed to know what needed to be done—like the septic plumbing system. All she could do, though, was give him a questioning look.

Finally, he said, "You're probably right, Cam. I won't judge the contest. We don't want to give anyone the notion that I might not be impartial when it comes to Robin."

"Actually, I'm more than happy to withdraw from the contest," Robin said, seizing the opportunity to get out of it before she made a complete fool of herself. "It wouldn't be fair to make him choose between me and this special event that he's been so excited about."

"No." Dylan held up his palms. "We already have the twelve ovens and we wouldn't want our numbers to be off. I insist that I'm more than happy to relinquish all judging duties to whoever else thinks they can do a better job than me."

That's when Robin realized that he was allowing his

sister to think they were dating so that he could get out of judging. Although, Robin had just done the exact same thing. Unfortunately, she'd been too late and now she was stuck baking cookies in front of…

"I'm sorry, can we go back to the part where you guys said news crews would be there," Robin said. "As in more than one?"

The server returned just then and asked if they were ready to place the order for the main course.

Something sparkled in Camilla's eyes as she said, "I'll let you two get back to your date. Teresa, bring them a bottle of the Möet. On the house."

When his sister and the server both left, Dylan's dimples returned. "Why are you looking at me like that?"

Robin lowered her voice. "Everyone is going to see us sharing a bottle of champagne and think we're actually dating."

Dylan shrugged. "Is it so bad if they do?"

"It is if we're only pretending to be dating so that you can get out of judging the bake-off."

"Well, I couldn't very well let you be forced out as a contestant when you're obviously looking forward to it."

When the server returned, she made a big show of popping the cork on the champagne, and anyone in the restaurant who hadn't looked in Dylan and Robin's direction before certainly noticed them now. Teresa filled their glasses and returned the bottle to an ice bucket near their table before telling them she'd be right back with their appetizers.

"Who says I'm looking forward to it?" Robin asked.

"Why else would you have entered the contest?" Dylan tilted his fluted glass toward Robin's and clinked them together.

She couldn't very well admit that she'd only entered it

to get closer to Dylan. Especially when her plan seemed to be working. Instead of replying, Robin gulped nearly half the bubbly contents of her glass at once.

"Besides," he said after swallowing his even, measured sip. "That's not why I told Mrs. Epson we were on a date."

A warm sensation spread through Robin's bloodstream, and she didn't think it was the alcohol taking effect this quickly. "Then why did you?"

But before he could answer, one of his buddies stopped by the table to ask about basketball practice and Dylan introduced him to Robin. One of the ranch foremen from the Bonnie B stopped by next and this time it was Robin who made the introductions. But the man seemed more interested in speaking to Dylan.

"My nephew is discharging from the military next week and moving to Bronco before the end of the month. He says he doesn't want his uncle pulling any strings to get him on at the Bonnie B, but if you're looking for someone for the Broken Road Ranch, I could give him your number."

Dylan's brow rose so slightly in her direction, Robin knew she was probably the only one who noticed it. He was asking for her input.

Robin gave a discreet nod. "If Manuel's nephew is anything like him, then I'd jump at the chance to recruit him."

Dylan pulled out his wallet and handed Manuel a business card just as the server returned with several plates of food. By the time they started eating, the moment was lost and Robin didn't know how to redirect him to the subject of why he'd let Mrs. Epson think they were on a date.

In fact, now that she was on her second glass of champagne, Robin was practically convinced that they *were* on a date. He asked her about her company and she explained how she created and patented a line of horse therapeutic products and was toying with the idea of developing a line of skin care products and shampoos for the horses.

He listened intently, leaning his elbows on the table as she spoke and asking follow-up questions. Especially about the ad campaign, which was proving to be just as successful as Eloise had promised.

"My brother Dante certainly lucked out with her and baby Merry." Their dinner plates had already been cleared and the bottle sitting in the melting ice bucket was nearly empty. "In fact, all of my siblings were pretty fortunate in finding their matches."

Robin smiled across the table at him, the champagne giving her the courage to say, "So then what's stopping you from finding yours?"

CHAPTER EIGHT

DYLAN WAS STILL thinking about Robin's question the next day.

So then what's stopping you from finding yours?

He hadn't had a chance to answer it because Robin's brother Billy and his three kids had chosen that exact moment to walk into the restaurant. Charlotte Taylor, Eloise's sister, came inside only a few minutes after them. Billy and Charlotte had dated in high school and had even planned to get married. Dylan wasn't sure of the details, but they'd broken up and Billy had moved away, gotten married and had kids. Charlotte had moved away, as well, but now both were back in Bronco and both were single. Sort of.

Dylan was pretty sure they were back together, but it was none of his business. Just like what was going on with him and Robin was nobody's business.

"So what's going on between you and Robin?" Dante asked late Friday afternoon when they'd finished coaching the kids in Dante's after-school basketball league.

Dylan sighed, sitting down on the hardwood floor to stretch. His body wasn't as young as it used to be, and he was starting to feel as though he was burning the candles at both ends. "Nothing. Why?"

Dante stacked some basketballs on a rack. "Because you told Camilla that you guys were dating."

"No, I said that I told Mrs. Epson that we were dating."

"So are you and Robin dating or not?"

"I'm not sure," Dylan answered honestly.

"Come on. Your reputation around town as a ladies' man is well-earned. You can't seriously tell me that you don't know how dating works."

"Yes, I know how dating works, little brother." He pulled the whistle off his neck and chucked it at Dante. "And I'm not the only Sanchez who had that reputation. Just because you're getting married and became a daddy doesn't mean that you can rewrite the past."

"*Had* that reputation?" Dante asked. "Or *has* that reputation still?"

"Leave it to the teacher to point out the difference in past and present tense."

"Stop stalling and answer my original question. What's going on between you and Robin?"

Dylan lifted his arms. "I don't know. She's been helping me a lot with ranch stuff. I guess you could say we're becoming friends."

"The ol' *just friends* routine, huh? Eloise and I tried to tell ourselves that, too."

"I don't really see a need to define it," Dylan said defensively.

"Eloise and I said that about our relationship, as well. Keep in mind, though, that if you don't define it, someone else eventually will."

Dylan rose to his feet to do some lunges. "Then let them define it."

"I think they already have. Mrs. Epson was in Mom's salon this morning and said she saw you two at the feedstore and you guys couldn't keep your hands off each other."

"So?" Dylan blew out a noisy breath to let his brother know exactly how annoyed he was with their conversation.

"So you never hold me like this when we're shopping." Dante tried to wrap one of his arms around Dylan's waist.

Dylan responded by elbowing his brother in the rib cage. "That's because you're not my friend."

"Why are you getting so defensive?" Dante asked.

"You know why. I don't like having my baby brother all up in my business like this."

"Come on. We've been up in each other's business for over thirty years. Why can't you just be honest about how you feel?"

"Because I don't know how I feel," Dylan said so loudly, it echoed throughout the gymnasium. Several women who were playing pickleball at the nearby court turned in their direction.

Dante waved at the pickleball players but lowered his voice. "Do you *want* to date her?"

"I want to keep hanging out with her. And I want her to keep helping me on the ranch. I like spending time with her, and Mrs. Epson is halfway right. I can't seem to keep my hands off her. But I can't even tell if she has the slightest interest in me. I try to flirt with her, but maybe I've lost my charm."

A pickleball came flying in Dylan's direction and he easily caught it and jogged it back to the court and asked, "Did you ladies lose something?"

He could hear the giggles as he returned to where Dante was standing.

His brother was holding back a grin. "You definitely haven't lost your charm."

"So then I guess the only logical conclusion is that Robin doesn't appreciate my attempts at flirtation."

"Possibly. But Robin is pretty direct and straightforward. When we were in high school, she was super athletic and lettered in several sports. But I don't remember her hanging out at Cubby's after games or going to any dances. She was a straight A student so I always just assumed she was super focused. I work with her sister, Stacy, at the school and I can ask her about it."

Dylan was about to warn his brother not to do that when his phone rang and he saw Robin's name on the screen. His pulse picked up speed.

"It's her, isn't it?" Dante asked. "I haven't seen you blush like that since—"

Dylan pushed the top row of Dante's carefully stacked basketballs off the cart before walking away to answer the call.

"Hey," he said by way of greeting.

"Are you in a cave?" Robin asked. "There's an echo."

"No, just leaving the gym before my brother chucks a basketball at my head. What's up?"

"Did you ever hear from Manuel's nephew?" she asked.

"Yeah, he called me this morning. He's supposed to fly into Montana next weekend and said he can stop by the ranch sometime. I don't think he has a ton of experience, but at this point, I'll take any reliable help I can get."

"Good," Robin said. "Because I know of a couple of ranch hands here at the Bonnie B who are off duty this weekend and looking to make some extra cash. I told them about your fences."

Dylan looked at his watch. "Do you know what time the lumberyard closes? I better get over there and order some posts. How many do you think I need?"

Robin rattled off a number. "I looked at the property map and did some calculations and while I doubt you'll have to replace every single fence post in the east pasture, it's probably a safe bet to go ahead and order extra since you'll end up using them for the other pastures."

"Any chance you can meet me over there?" he asked, hearing the hopefulness in his own voice.

"Right now?" she asked.

"We can grab dinner afterward," he suggested.

"You have no idea how badly I want to say yes," she said, her throaty voice making him want to groan. "But I'm in Rust Creek Falls with Eloise and her sister Charlotte meeting with a wedding planner. I haven't tried on a bridesmaid dress before and I've got to tell you, I've never been decked out in so much—or should I say so little—satin in my entire life. I think I'm going to need a jacket."

Great, now he would be thinking about Robin's skin barely covered by a swath of silk. He swallowed the growl building in the back of his throat.

"Are we still set for the livestock auction tomorrow evening, though?" she asked, cutting off his inappropriate thoughts.

"Yes," he said. "I was thinking of making reservations at DJ's Deluxe for afterward."

"I'm not sure you need to do that," Robin said, and he could hear the voices of other women in the background.

Dante had made it seem like Robin could be very direct. And Dylan had definitely witnessed it himself. However, it was only when it involved things that had to do with the ranch. Maybe she wasn't as confident when it came to things like bridesmaid dresses and...whatever this was between them. In which case, he'd give her the opportunity to be as direct as possible.

"Because you don't want it to seem like a date?" he asked, then held his breath as he waited for her response.

"No, I meant because I've never left an auction in under five hours. I doubt we'll get out of there in time to make the reservation. But you can buy me a hot dog from the concession stand and hold my—"

He heard a rustling sound and then a thump. "Sorry, my zipper got stuck and I dropped my phone. We can figure out the details tomorrow. Right now, I have to get out of this dress."

The line disconnected and once again, Dylan was left with the image of her in a state of undress. But more importantly, what had she been about to say before she dropped her phone?

He could hold her *hand*?

He could hold her *beer*?

Did they even sell beer at livestock auctions? It was at the Bronco Convention Center, so they must.

All Dylan knew was that he was going to need to hold *something* tomorrow night.

"SO DANTE WAS asking me about you at the school play last night," Stacy said when she came into the kitchen and saw Robin making a test batch of cookies with their niece Jill.

"Why would Eloise's fiancée be asking about me?" Robin couldn't remember where she'd left the pot holder, but Jill was already using it to pull the hot tray out of the oven. She was grateful for the help of her brother's youngest.

"He wasn't asking for himself," Stacy said as she plopped onto one of the counter stools. "He said Dylan was curious to know more about you."

Jill's loud squeal matched the exact same sound of excitement Robin had just made inside her head. "Isn't he the one you've been crushing on, Aunt Robin?"

"Who told you I've been crushing on him?" she asked Jill.

"Seriously? We're making cookies called Heartmelters." Jill held up a faded yellow piece of paper. "Clearly, you're trying to melt someone's heart."

Robin scrunched her nose. “I don’t think that’s why they’re called that.”

“You found Great-Aunt Jackie’s Heartmelters recipe?” Stacy reached out her hand so their niece could pass the paper to her. “Where was it?”

“In a worn-out tin box on a shelf in the cellar. I was looking for that old-fashioned butter churner and came across it. I figured that it seemed simple enough that I couldn’t mess it up. Plus, it’s kind of Valentine’s themed.”

Stacy carefully turned over the sheet of paper. “It says right here, *‘When made with the right ingredients and given to the right person, the Heartmelters will have the desired affect.’*” Stacy read it a second time, then added, “I think Aunt Jackie meant to say *effect*, with an *e*.”

“So is Dylan Sanchez the right person, Aunt Robin?”

“Right now, I can’t even figure out the right ingredients.” Robin blew a strand of hair out of her eye with an exasperated sigh. “Or at least the right measurements. It says three handfuls of flour. But whose handful? Aunt Jackie was barely five feet tall. Jill’s hands are the closest size to that, but the cookies keep coming out too dense. Same thing happened when I had Mom do the measurements. Stacy, let me see how big your hands are.”

Stacy yanked her fist back from Robin’s examination to pick up one of the bright heart-shaped cookies from the cooling rack. “Have you tried using your own hand?”

“They’re obviously way too big.” Robin held up her palm right as her phone timer went off. “I’ll have to try another batch tomorrow. Dylan’s picking me up in thirty minutes for the livestock auction.”

“That sounds like the least romantic date I’ve ever heard of,” Jill said.

Robin took off her apron and Stacy immediately frowned. “You’re not wearing that, are you?”

Robin glanced down at the gold-colored sweater that wasn't as low-cut as the last one she'd mistakenly worn with Dylan. "What's wrong with this?"

"It looks like you got it in the same tin box where you found that recipe," Jill said. "Not gonna lie, but the color totally washes you out."

"Are all teenagers this brutally honest?" Robin asked Stacy.

"Let's just say there's a reason why I work with first graders and not middle schoolers." Stacy grabbed a second cookie. "Come on, let's go upstairs and pick a better outfit. I'll tell you what Dylan wanted to know about you."

Jill pumped a fist in the air. "Makeover time. I call dibs on doing Aunt Robin's hair."

FIFTEEN MINUTES LATER, Robin stared at her reflection in the full-length mirror in her sister's room. "Get that makeup case away from me, Jill. I said you guys could do my hair and pick my outfit. And I'm already not loving the outfit. We're going to a livestock auction, not a fancy dance."

The doorbell rang downstairs.

"Can I just do a swipe of mascara and lip gloss?" Jill pleaded.

"I'll do it myself. You go answer the door please, and, Stacy, you go warn Dad that I'm coming downstairs in a dress so that he doesn't make a big deal like he did a few days ago when I borrowed your lipstick."

"Is that why my bathroom looked like a crime scene?" her sister asked.

"Sorry about that. The red was too dark and no matter how many tissues and cotton swabs I used, I couldn't get it to come off."

"That's because it was lip *stain*, not lip*stick*. Uh-oh. I hear Dad talking to him already." Stacy headed to the door. "I'll run down and try to distract him."

Robin took one last look at her reflection. She was wearing a thick knit dress with a floating hemline around her calves. She'd argued that the pale color looked too summery, but Stacy called it winter white and paired it with a tan, fitted leather jacket that perfectly matched her knee-high boots. Jill had used a heated wand to give Robin's hair something called beach waves. As far as makeovers went, it was fairly subtle and she still felt like herself. Just in a dress. Since she didn't have time to change back into her comfortable jeans, all she could do was brace herself for nobody to recognize her.

"Wow," Dylan said as Robin walked into the formal living room where he was standing with her dad, her sister and her niece. "You look amazing."

"Thanks," both Stacy and Jill said at the same time.

"Robin," her father said, hopefully not about to comment on her appearance, "I was just telling Dylan to be sure he looks at the bulls from Greenacres. They have the best breeds and their life cycles tend to be longer than most."

Dylan nodded at her dad's words, but his eyes remained focused on hers, as though he was waiting for her confirmation. Most men would've been over the moon to get some free advice from a successful rancher like Asa Abernathy, taking his opinion all the way to the bank. But Dylan was still looking to Robin for the final say.

Pride blossomed in her chest and she hoped she could live up to Dylan's expectations.

"We'll see who else is in the crowd with an auction paddle," Robin replied. "Because if Birdsey Jones is there, he's going to drive up the bidding on anything he thinks someone else wants. It's like a sport for him."

"Good point." Her father winked at her, then turned to Dylan. "I'd offer you a drink, son, but you're going to need to be stone-cold sober when those auction paddles start flying in the air."

"And you also don't want him drinking because he's driving your daughter, Grandpa," Jill reminded him. Then she told Dylan, "Make sure to have her home by curfew."

"What time is curfew?" Dylan asked politely without so much as a smirk.

"I don't have one." Robin shifted the borrowed clutch higher under her arm—Jill and Stacy had insisted that her normal tote bag she used as a purse wouldn't go with the outfit—and slipped her free hand into the crook of Dylan's elbow. "We should get going."

He said his goodbyes and as they walked toward the door, Robin could hear her niece asking if someone would talk to *her* dad and tell him that she didn't need a curfew, either.

"You cold?" Dylan asked as they made their way down the front porch.

"A little. I wanted to bring a bigger coat but Stacy and Jill were adamant that it would be warm enough inside the convention center. I think they just hate the jacket I usually wear on snowy nights like tonight."

"Or maybe they know how great you look in that dress and didn't want you covering it up."

The girls had said those exact words, but she'd told them Dylan wouldn't even notice. Heat rose along the back of Robin's neck as she realized she didn't mind being proven wrong.

Dylan opened the door for her, which made her extra aware that she was wearing a dress and couldn't just climb inside. He then walked around the cab to the driver's seat and said, "I'll get the seat warmers going."

If she was hoping for the conversation to sound more date-like, as it had the other night when they were having dinner at The Library, she would've been sorely disappointed. As it was, she knew that the entire reason for their outing tonight was business related. They talked about cattle breeds and market prices and his plan to start slow with only one bull while he dedicated his time and budget toward making improvements to his property first. Then she explained expected progeny differences and how he wanted a sire with a positive EPD number.

Dylan found a parking spot toward the front and Robin hurried out of the truck before he could come around and open the door for her again. She would probably be more graceful exiting in the dress than she had been entering it earlier, but she wasn't going to take that chance.

It was snowing lightly, and the cold would have been enough to force her to walk closer to Dylan and absorb some of his heat. But it was the luxury sedan towing a horse trailer that caused Dylan to shoot his arm across the front of her when the driver took the turn too wide.

Before Robin could think better of it, she reflexively curled her hand around his bicep and hugged his upper arm to her side as he pivoted closer to the parked cars and they resumed walking.

"I like that," Dylan said to nobody in particular as he kept his face forward.

Robin glanced back at the sedan and horse trailer that would never find a double-parking spot in this row. "I guess if you didn't have a truck, you could make it work."

"Not that, although I can appreciate their ingenuity installing a tow hitch on a Mercedes." Dylan used his free hand to cover hers. "I like this. When you're the one grabbing on to me."

"Oh," Robin said lamely because she couldn't come up

with anything more clever. And also because her heartbeat was vibrating in her eardrums and she couldn't hear herself think.

It only got louder as they entered the arena, which wasn't as deafening as it could be when there was a rodeo going on. They registered and picked up their paddles and Robin tried to concentrate on the animals displayed in the holding area, but it was hard not to notice that there were significantly more men in attendance than women. And she was the only one who was wearing a dress.

Although, maybe that could work in their favor.

CHAPTER NINE

"LOOK HOW ADORABLE this one is," Robin cooed to the Red Angus bull on the other side of the metal bars. "I just have to have him."

Dylan frowned at Robin's unexpected use of a baby voice and glanced down at the description card attached to the pen. "But this one is from Rosewood Farms and I thought we were looking for a—"

The soft leather of her jacket sleeve did nothing to soften the sharp jab of Robin's elbow into his rib cage.

"But I love this one, Dyl." She searched his face while batting her eyelashes in the most awkward sequence. Was she trying to seduce him or speak in Morse code? It didn't matter because she had looped her arms around his neck and was pressing her chest against his torso as she spoke. "See how his fur has those supercute patches that are the exact same color as my mom's dog Queenie? They would be adorable together."

Dylan might be a greenhorn, but he knew that you never referred to a cow's coat as "fur." Robin was up to something, but he had no idea what. Her thumbs tickled his hairline, causing him to shiver and pull her closer against him.

Robin whispered through her clenched smile, "Is that guy in the blue shirt watching?"

Half the people in this place were wearing blue, or at least denim, so Dylan couldn't be sure. But there was at least one stockier man furtively glancing in their direction.

"I don't know, babe," Dylan said loudly, hoping that he was playing his part. "I don't think we should be buying a bull just because he matches someone's pet."

"Please, Dylan." She lifted on her tiptoes unexpectedly, which caused his hands to slip lower. Her breathless gasp sent waves of desire spiraling through him and he cupped her rounded behind through the fabric of her dress. Her normally sexy voice was even more sultry as she slowly said, "I have to have him. No matter the cost."

He almost responded that he had to have *her*. But he was pretty sure that wasn't supposed to be in this impromptu script. "Uh…how much is it worth to you?"

She leaned forward, her breasts grazing his chest, as she settled her lips against his ear. "Is he still watching?" she whispered.

"Uh-huh," Dylan mumbled, even though he had no idea who *he* was or whether or not anyone was watching. He was too busy trying to control his breathing and not crush her mouth with his.

"Pretend like I'm saying something super arousing to you," she continued, and Dylan almost laughed because he didn't have to pretend anything. "Then, tell me that you'll spend whatever it takes to buy me this bull. Make sure he can hear you."

When she pulled away, she added a coy giggle that must be fake because he'd never heard her laugh like that. She gave him a pointed look and he said his line a little too loudly.

"You're the best boyfriend ever," she said, a little too believably, then lowered her voice. "Now make sure your paddle is in your back pocket and covered by your jacket as you walk away."

Dylan released her long enough to adjust his clothing,

which also helped to hide his body's physical response to her.

When she faced away from him, she used her own paddle as a fan, holding it up as she resumed her baby voice and told the bull, "You're going to love living with us. We have a big yard with lots of grass and the sweetest Maltipoo for you to play with. But right now, Daddy promised Mommy some nachos before the bidding starts. The next time you see me, I'll be the one in the stands holding up number 985."

Again, Robin clung to Dylan's arm as she pulled him away, although he noticed that she angled herself slightly behind him, possibly to block the view of his back pocket.

Over his shoulder, he heard her say, "Okay, we have fifteen minutes before the bidding starts. Come with me."

Instead of getting nachos, though, she led him to where several rows of vendors had set up booths selling everything from sheep shearers to saddles.

"Here." Robin shoved a cowboy hat at him. "Put this on."

"Black's not really my color," he said, sarcastically. "How about the tan one?"

"Fine." She swapped the hats while keeping her eyes glued down the aisle behind him.

"Robin, do you mind telling me what's going on?"

"We don't really have time for that. You need to buy this hat and then make your way to the most northwest corner of the stands. Find a group of other cowboys and sit as closely to them as you can. Better yet, try to blend in with them. Do *not* look for me and definitely do not wait for me. According to the sale catalog, the third bull they bring out should be number 873 from Greenacre Farms."

"I thought we wanted that one from Rosewood with the

patches that match your dog Queenie. I'm pretty sure you referred to us as its mommy and daddy."

Robin winced, then shook her head. "Our dog is named Bandit and…never mind all the rest. I'll explain later. Remember, you're bidding for 873, the third bull."

Dylan was more than confused, but so far she hadn't steered him wrong. He was going to have to trust her. "How much should I bid?"

She named the amount he shouldn't go over, then added, "I'll meet you at the sales office afterward."

Robin squeezed into a passing crowd of teenagers in their matching 4-H uniforms and Dylan was left to pay for the cowboy hat. He made his way into the arena area and found a seat in the back row behind several young men wearing the standard cowboy attire of jeans, hats and button-up work shirts.

He'd never felt more like a poser, especially because they were all enjoying plastic cups of draft beer, which Asa Abernathy had warned him not to drink. When one of the cowboys offered Dylan a pinch of Copenhagen, he had no choice but to accept and then pretended to insert it in his lower lip before discreetly slipping the unused chewing tobacco in his front pocket.

Robin had told him not to look for her, but it was rather difficult for him not to notice her. She stood out in this crowd. Not only because she was wearing a dress, which clung to her curves in all the right places, but also because she was…well, she was Robin. And Dylan's eyes now instinctively went in search of her anytime he knew she was nearby.

She was sitting several rows from the front, talking to some people around her and pointing toward the entrance to the arena. The stocky man in the blue shirt who'd possibly been watching them back in the pen area was sitting a few feet away, his eyes carefully trained on Robin. There wasn't necessarily anything creepy about the way the man watched Robin, but that didn't stop Dylan from wanting to punch the guy.

The fast-talking auctioneer called for the first animal and Dylan barely had time to blink before the man yelled, "Sold!"

The second bull took a little longer and several paddles throughout the crowd drove the price higher. By the time the auctioneer finished, Dylan didn't dare look Robin's way again.

He had his sales catalog out and, when he saw the bull in the picture and heard them confirm that it was number 873, a blast of adrenaline consumed him. Leaning back in the seat with his new Copenhagen buddy unwittingly blocking him, Dylan gripped his paddle tighter. This was it. Robin better know what she was doing.

He could barely understand a word the auctioneer was saying, but every time he saw a paddle lowering, Dylan would lift his. When the man yelled, "Sold!" several of the cowboys around him turned to offer their congratulations.

"Thanks, guys," Dylan said. Then asked the one next to him, "By any chance, do you know if the sales office is the same place where I registered?"

The man pointed out directions, and just to be safe, Dylan kept his face averted toward the center of the arena as he passed in front of the crowd on his way toward the exit.

He was paying for his new bull and arranging for delivery to Broken Road Ranch when Robin slipped beside him and gave him a side hug. "We did it!"

"*You* did it," he said, returning the squeeze. Man, he could get used to the feel of this woman. "Although, I'm still not exactly sure what it was you did."

"I got Birdsey Jones to think we were buying the Rosewood bull. Then I sat by him and made him think my boyfriend was in the bathroom so he wouldn't see you buying the bull we really wanted."

That's what Dylan had suspected was happening. But Robin had never struck him as the type to use some elaborate farce to get what she wanted.

"Wait. How long was I supposedly in the bathroom?" Dylan asked.

"You're still there." She tsked at him and gently patted his stomach. "Poor guy. It was the nachos. The doctor warned you about all that cheese, but you couldn't help yourself. It was taking so long that I came to check on you."

"That's not embarrassing at all," he mumbled. When the cashier passed him a receipt, Dylan felt compelled to tell the man, "I'm fine with cheese, just for the record. I can eat it all day long."

"I'm happy for you, buddy," the cashier replied. "I just need you to sign here."

Dylan collected his paperwork as Robin laughed, then grabbed her hand to pull her out of the office.

"I thought you said we would be here for at least five hours," he reminded her as they walked toward the parking lot. "We didn't even have time to get a hot dog."

She smiled. "You can use all that money I just saved you to buy me dinner at LuLu's BBQ."

"I'M GLAD ALL that guilt weighing on your conscience hasn't affected your appetite," Dylan told Robin, as she dug into their rib platter for two.

Her stomach dropped. Had he found out that she had no idea how to bake? She scanned the nearby tables to see if anyone had just heard his accusation. LuLu's was usually packed on Saturday nights, but somehow, a table had opened up right when they arrived. Robin was noticing that Dylan knew plenty of people in the restaurant scene. Not only because of his sister's connections, but because he ate out quite a bit. In fact, he actually knew quite a few people from every industry in town, having sold so many of them a car.

When she was convinced nobody was listening, she asked, "What do you mean?"

"You told that Red Angus bull that he would love living with us." Dylan finished a rib and grabbed another.

Robin sagged onto her wooden bench seat with relief, glad he wasn't bringing up everything else causing her guilt.

"He *would* love living with us," Robin insisted. If there was an *us*. "But I don't think he actually heard me."

"I know cows aren't the smartest animals, but that doesn't mean he might not have understood you."

"No, Dylan, I meant that he literally couldn't hear me. That bull had a little marking on his tag indicating a medical condition. According to the sale catalog, which I'd already read in advance, he'd suffered a nonhereditary ear infection that caused long-term damage to his hearing. That's why I went out of my way to talk to him like that. So Birdsey would think I was too naive to consult the catalog."

"That's terrible," Dylan said.

"Terrible that a man would think a woman is naive when it comes to livestock and ranching?" Robin licked a spot of sauce off her thumb. "It actually happens more often than you'd think."

"No, I meant that the bull lost its hearing. Does that mean he won't fetch a good price?"

"Sure he will. He's still pretty valuable as a sire. He comes from good stock and the cause of his infection isn't something that can be passed down. But the Cattlemen's Association requires the disclaimer anyway."

"You could've told me that earlier. Do you know how many times I wanted to turn the truck around and go get him to make good on your promise?"

"You're a softie, Dylan Sanchez."

"Me?" His face was stricken while he looked around as though he thought she might be talking to some else.

"Yes, you." Robin wiped off her hands before picking up a fork to try the coleslaw. "You do know what's going to happen to the calves born on your ranch, right?"

He pointed a rib at her. "As far as I'm concerned, they're going on to a better home on a bigger ranch to live with new friends. That's it. Happily-ever-after."

"Do you mean to tell me that confirmed bachelor Dylan Sanchez actually believes in happily-ever-after?"

"Of course I do. Although, it doesn't always look the same for everyone. My happily is going to be different from your happily. And that's okay." He said the words casually enough, but there was a small trace of defensiveness in his tone.

"Hey there, Robin and Dylan," Phillip Brandt said as he stopped by their table. "Sorry to interrupt, but, Dylan, I need to talk to you about the bake-off and my coconut cream pie. I'm worried that if the weather keeps dropping, my meringue isn't going to hold."

"Camilla said she's watching the weather reports, Mr. Brandt, and is planning to have extra portable heaters if we need them inside the tent."

The man sighed visibly. "That's a relief. But if the weather and the humidity doesn't cooperate, you'll plan to take that into account when it comes time to judge, right?"

Dylan picked up another rib. "Actually, I'm not judging anymore."

"But I heard you love coconut cream pie," Mr. Brandt said. "That's why I'm making it and not my chocolate chip walnut cake. Now I have to rethink my whole strategy. Who's judging?"

"You'll have to check with my sisters. All I know is that I had to recuse myself for—" Dylan gestured across the table at Robin "—obvious reasons."

Robin kicked him underneath the table and he frowned at her.

"Dylan, nobody is going to be worried about you judging in favor of your girlfriend." Mr. Brandt lowered his voice. "No offense, Robin, but I tried the cinnamon rolls you brought to the bake sale at school, and they aren't winning any contests."

Robin would have been insulted if the man's assessment had been completely accurate. "Those weren't *my* cinnamon rolls. My sister made them and when people brought them back for a refund, she blamed it on me."

"Why would Stacy do that?" Dylan's expression didn't appear shocked, though. He looked like he was trying not to laugh. "Not that my brothers wouldn't have probably done the same thing to me."

"Because I'm a horrible—" Robin stopped before she could say the word *cook*. It was bad enough that Phillip Brandt was confirming her lack of culinary skills. "I'm horrible at cinnamon rolls. Or anything else that requires yeast and rising and being patient. Anyway, I'm not even making those for the contest, Mr. Brandt. I'm making something else. And it's going to take first place."

Okay, maybe that was laying it on a little thick, but Robin couldn't very well back down from a challenge. Especially when she knew the risk Mr. Brandt would be taking with that meringue if there was wet weather.

"Nobody stands a chance against my lemon tart," Mrs.

Sellers, the feedstore owner's wife, said from two tables over. "Dylan, you might as well give me those free oil changes now."

And that was how the Valentine's Day Bake-off Trash Talking Tournament started. Solar, the purple-haired teenage barista from Bronco Java and Juice, came over to make a case for her German chocolate brownies, and Gary, the middle school PE teacher, said that any insult to the cheesecake he was making in honor of his late aunt Hildy was an insult to Aunt Hildy herself. May she rest in peace.

Dylan slouched lower in his seat as everyone argued over his and Robin's head. "Maybe I shouldn't have made this a locals-only contest."

Robin wanted to laugh at his obvious discomfort. "If this is how they argue with their neighbors and friends, imagine what would happen if you had a bunch of out-of-towners show up."

"Fair enough," he said before slathering a hunk of corn bread with LuLu's famous honey butter.

Robin reached across the table to help herself to one of his French fries. She was midbite when someone asked, "Robin, what are you making for the bake-off?"

"Hopefully her cinnamon rolls," Mrs. Sellers said under her breath and Robin shot the woman a dirty look.

She opened her mouth to respond, but someone else complained, "Dylan, you can't judge a contest that your girlfriend's in. That wouldn't be fair."

"He's recused himself from judging," Mr. Brandt explained before Dylan could correct the crowd and announce that Robin wasn't his girlfriend. Several heads nodded as though that fixed everything.

She braced herself for public humiliation when Dylan held up his palms. "Mr. Brandt is correct, I won't be judging. If you have any questions about the bake-off, I'd encourage you to stop by Bronco Motors and speak with my office manager, Mickie. She's also posted all the contest rules on our website. Now, if anyone sees LuLu or our server, will you please tell them that we'd like some banana pudding to go and the check. I have to get Robin home before she misses curfew."

"WELL, THAT WAS one way to make an exit," Robin said fifteen minutes later when Dylan was driving her to the Bonnie B.

"I know. I wasn't expecting LuLu to be out of banana pudding."

"That's not what I meant, Dylan."

"I know that, too." He glanced at her across the dimly lit interior of the truck and her muscles tensed. "But when I find myself in awkward situations like that, I tend to make light of the situation and use humor as a distraction."

She knew she shouldn't ask, but she couldn't stop herself. "What was awkward about the situation?"

"You have to ask?" he said.

"I mean, I know which part was awkward for *me*," Robin clarified. "But which part was awkward for you?"

"I don't do crowds very well," Dylan finally admitted and Robin had to do a double take. "I'm better in a one-on-one situation, or in smaller groups."

"You were homecoming king at Bronco High and played college basketball, with several games nationally televised. I've seen you in stores and in groups of people and you don't exactly come across as an introvert."

"Okay, being homecoming king was out of my control. When they announced it at the football game during half-time, I didn't even take off my helmet to be crowned. And when I played college basketball, I was part of the team and didn't draw any more attention than anyone else. I refused to do media interviews because I don't like anything that could potentially cause a scene. What happened inside LuLu's wasn't exactly a scene, but it felt like I needed to make some sort of big announcement and I'm not the type who enjoys making big announcements. I'll leave the speeches to Mayor Rafferty Smith, thank you very much."

Robin studied his profile as he drove. "What sort of big announcement did you think you'd be making inside a barbecue restaurant?"

"You heard them. It was like they were looking for confirmation of some sort, and I didn't exactly know what to say."

Robin pursed her lips, doubting that he was going to say it aloud. But she also didn't want to let him off the hook. "You mean about whether or not I'm your girlfriend?"

"That's part of it," he said, causing her lungs to stop working for a second. "But I've been so on edge about this entire bake-off. I recently hired a couple of new salespeople so that I could spend more time at the ranch. I pay them a salary, but they also work on commission and get factory bonuses for every car they sell. If I want to keep spending time on the ranch, I need to keep my employees happy. And my employees are happy when they're making sales. So as much as I want to increase business, I don't want to be the focal point. I also don't want to do or say anything that's going to scare you away."

Robin shifted in her seat toward him. "You're not going to scare me away, Dylan."

"That's because you've never been to a Sunday dinner with my family."

"Is that an invite?" she challenged.

"I wouldn't do that to you just yet," he said with a chuckle. But what Robin heard was *It's still too soon.* And it was. Maybe she shouldn't be pushing for more.

Reluctantly, she changed the subject. "So we've got three guys lined up tomorrow to come work on the fencing at the Broken Road."

"You're coming with them, right?" Dylan asked as he turned onto the county highway leading to her ranch. "Not to do the actual fence work, but maybe just for an hour or so to help me lay them out. I'll bring breakfast burritos."

Damn him, and his knowledge of food being the way to her heart.

"I can come out for one hour," she said, knowing full well that she'd be giving up valuable time in the kitchen. "When is Felix coming with the interns from the veterinary school?"

"Nine. So you might be gone by the time they get there."

"I really shouldn't miss that, though," she said, already going back on her limit of one hour. "And I guess I should take a second look at your stables and see if I need to do anything before I bring a couple of horses over for Monday when you need to move the herd to that east pasture."

"Robin, you don't need to give me any horses. You've already done so much for me."

He was right about the last part, but not the first. "I'm not giving them to you. I'm only loaning them to you until you can get your own. Also, if I'm going to be the one helping you herd them, I'd prefer a horse I'm comfortable riding rather than that old golf cart Hank Hardy left behind."

Dylan reached across the center console, found her hand in the dark and squeezed it. "I can't even begin to tell you how much I appreciate all your help. I promise that one of these days, I'm going to make it up to you."

Her fingers interlaced with his, but instead of enjoying the comfort of his hand, she wanted to bang her forehead in frustration. If she were trying to play hard to get, she certainly would've lost the game by now. This was why she was a horrible negotiator and paid full price for tractor tires and hay delivery.

She'd gone from just sending over cowboys to probably a full day's work without even giving him time to counteroffer. Could she make herself sound any more available? Or any more eager to be with him?

She should be focusing her energy on figuring out how to make her recipe work, not running out to see Dylan every time he offered her a flash of his dimples and a hot meal. It wasn't as though she had unlimited amounts of open days in her calendar. Her choices were to either spend time with him, or to spend her time baking so that she wouldn't end up a laughingstock when she came in dead last.

It was too bad she couldn't do both.

CHAPTER TEN

THE SECOND SMARTEST thing Dylan had ever done was hire Mickie to run his dealership office and free him up to spend more time on the ranch. The smartest thing he ever did was ask Robin for her advice that day he met her.

As promised, she arrived with three employees from the Bonnie B early the following morning. Dylan had a stack of breakfast burritos and a load of lumber and barbed wire ready and waiting for them. One of the benefits to being a car salesman was access to used cars on the lot and Dylan was able to borrow a trade-in truck to help haul supplies out to the east pasture. After showing the men the property map and reviewing the number of posts they'd need, Robin caught a ride back to the barn with Dylan just in time to meet Felix and the two volunteer vets.

"Nice to see you again, Robin." Dylan's brother reached out to shake her hand. Felix normally saw mostly domestic pets at his practice, but one couldn't live in a ranching town without having some experience treating larger animals. "How's Bandit doing?"

"Better since the treatment," Robin said, smiling. "And the bland diet."

"I have to take a second load of equipment out to the crew," Dylan told her. "Do you guys need anything from me?"

"We've got it covered," Felix said. "Go build your walls."

"Fences," Dylan corrected his brother. "I'm mending fences."

"Oh, that's right. I guess I'm just used to you building emotional walls."

"Robin, don't listen to anything he says about me. He's just jealous that I set a better pick than he does."

"We'll see about that at the next family basketball game," Felix said. "I've been practicing my jump shot and Shari says my calves look better than ever."

"Shari is just being kind because she can't say anything good about your dribbling." Dylan was reluctant to leave Robin, but he was also looking forward to some good physical labor. It was cold, but he needed to sweat. And pound something that wasn't his brother's head.

He spent the rest of the morning pulling out broken fence posts and hammering new ones into place. When they ran out of barbed wire, he and the workers returned to the barn together for lunch and to restock their supplies.

Dylan wasn't surprised to see his dad's car in the driveway, nor was he surprised to find his father in the stables with Robin.

"Hey, Dad, I see you met Robin."

"I didn't need to meet her, son. Robin and I go way back. Her family's ranch is on my mail route." Aaron Sanchez claimed he had more insight into anyone in town based purely on the contents of their mailboxes. "Anyway, Robin was telling me how she was going to bring a couple of her horses over and I was telling her about that time you rode a tame, old mare on the beach in Baja and ended up going for an unexpected swim."

"She wasn't that old," Dylan muttered, making Robin choke back a laugh. "And she definitely wasn't tame."

"All I'm saying, Robin, is if you get my son on a horse, make sure you bring a few ice packs and an Ace bandage."

"You've got it, Mr. Sanchez."

His dad held up a palm. "No, please call me Aaron."

"You know I can't do that, Mr. Sanchez," Robin replied. "My mom and dad would be mortified."

"What your dad should be mortified about is his golf swing," Dylan's father said, then explained, "Asa and I go to the same driving range."

Robin's smile was warm. "I'll be sure to mention it to him the next time we have dinner."

"Speaking of family dinners," his dad said, and Dylan closed his eyes, knowing what was about to come next. "Did Dylan tell you about our family dinners every Sunday?"

"As a matter of fact, he *has* mentioned them," Robin said.

Both Robin and his dad were now staring at him expectantly. But there was no way Dylan was going to invite Robin to his parents' house for a Sunday dinner. He'd only invited one other woman and that had been a mistake he'd never repeat.

"I forgot to tell you and Mom," Dylan said, "but I'm not going to make dinner tonight. I've got too much going on with the fence repair and getting the house ready to start demo tomorrow."

"Well, good luck giving your mom that excuse," his father said. Being absent from Sunday dinner usually required advance notice or a doctor's note. "I'm refereeing a game at the rec center at two and need to get there early to remind the pickleball club to take down their net."

If Robin was disappointed by the lack of invite, her face didn't show it. In fact, after saying goodbye to Dylan's dad, she said, "The stables actually look to be in pretty decent shape, probably because they haven't been subjected to any wear and tear the past twenty years."

"I'm surprised Hank didn't park his golf cart in there," Dylan said.

"Judging by the tire tracks in the old straw, I'm pretty sure he did."

Dylan didn't know whether to laugh or roll his eyes, so he did both. "I'm going to need to sweep out all that muck and lay some fresh straw before you bring the horses."

"I already took care of it."

"When?" Dylan asked.

"While you were out riding the range, cowboy." Robin nodded at his hat. "I see you're making good use of your souvenir from the livestock auction."

He adjusted the felt brim, knowing he was already getting it dirty with his dusty hands. "I should've gone with the black one. Hey, are you staying for lunch? I ordered a tray of sub sandwiches from Bronco Brick Oven Pizza."

"Yeah, the delivery guy just left before your dad got here. I put the rest of them in the kitchen fridge, which is going to need to be moved out to the barn once demo starts."

Dylan was actually thinking the stables would be a better place to move the fridge… "Wait, what do you mean you put *the rest of them* in there?"

Robin wiped the back of her hand across her lower lip, as though she could hide the evidence. "Well, your dad was hungry. And since I only had one breakfast burrito this morning, we sort of helped ourselves."

"You didn't even wait for me?" Not that Dylan blamed her.

"It's after one. I kept thinking you guys were going to break for lunch and show up any minute but I got hungry."

"I should probably take whatever is left to everyone else who is patiently waiting."

"I did patiently wait." Robin playfully shoved his bicep.

Dylan clamped his hand over hers, locking it into place as he spun her around and backed her into his arms. "You waited for maybe ten minutes."

She shrieked with laughter and tried to wiggle away, although it didn't feel as though she were putting that much effort into it. In fact, she seemed to be pushing her backside directly into his—

"There you are, Dylan," Felix said as he came around the corner. His brother's eyes widened briefly before his face broke out in a wide grin. "I didn't mean to interrupt your little wrestling match, but we're about wrapped up here. I was going to see if Dad and Robin left any lunch for us."

Robin gasped, causing her chest to expand directly above Dylan's forearm since he was still hugging her from behind. "We only had one sandwich each, Felix Sanchez. There's at least ten foot-long subs left. Were you planning to eat more than ten?"

Chuckling at the way she'd effortlessly responded to his brother's teasing, Dylan added, "Not if he wants to fit into his wedding tux."

Felix's eyebrows rose at the hint of a challenge. "I bet you twenty bucks I look better in a wedding tux than you, Dyl."

"I'd take that bet, except you know full well you're never going to get me in one of those."

"Yeah, I forgot. You're the Last Sanchez Standing." Felix used his fingers to make air quotes. "Remind me what the prize is for winning that title? Eternal loneliness and regret?"

"I'll go grab the sandwiches from the fridge while you boys argue about tuxes and other manly pursuits." Robin's voice was less playful as she easily stepped out of his embrace. Dylan felt a cool breeze at the empty place where she'd been. "And then I need to take off to get the horses ready."

Dylan watched her walk away, and then he shoved his brother. "Why do you always try to embarrass me like that?"

Felix shrugged. "It's what big brothers do. Don't act like you weren't plenty embarrassing when Shari and I were first dating."

"First of all, I doubt I was. Second of all, Robin and I aren't exactly dating."

"Really? Because that's not what it looked like when I walked around the corner a few minutes ago and caught you guys all cuddled up and giggling."

"I don't giggle. Also, I haven't exactly asked her out on a date. I might be working my way up to that, but I'm certainly not ready to invite her over to our parents' house for dinner."

"I get it." Felix nodded.

Apparently, though, Felix did *not* in fact get it because as the sun began to set, he was in the lead car as several family members pulled into the driveway of the Broken Road Ranch.

Scratch that. It wasn't several members of his family. It was his entire family.

"Dad said you had too much work to do here tonight and couldn't make it to Sunday dinner at our house. So we brought Sunday dinner to you." His mother was carrying a foil-covered casserole dish as she scanned the barn and stable area until her eyes landed on the Bonnie B truck and horse trailer. "Oh, is Robin still here?"

ROBIN HEARD SEVERAL voices coming from outside as she closed Buttermilk's stall door. She thought the demo team wasn't starting until tomorrow morning, but it sounded like a crew of construction workers were shouting orders in the yard.

When she exited the stable, she nearly froze then took a few steps back.

It was the entire Sanchez family. The men were moving several wooden benches in front of a makeshift firepit that Robin could've sworn hadn't been there a couple of hours ago. The women were setting up a table with trays of food and plastic cutlery. Earlier, she'd stood there awkwardly when Mr. Sanchez had brought up Sunday dinner, shifting her feet as she waited to see if Dylan was going to take the bait and actually invite her.

He hadn't.

Then his brother had made that comment about Dylan wanting to stay single and she'd beaten a hasty retreat. Now she was shifting on her feet wondering if she should try to slip into her truck and drive away before anyone noticed her.

Too late.

"Robin," Eloise called across the yard, baby Merry wrapped securely against her chest. "Do you know if there are any napkins or paper towels in the house?"

Was Robin supposed to answer this question? Were they trying to see how "at home" she was on the Broken Road Ranch? Luckily, Dylan answered for her. Or them.

"Actually, I put a lot of that stuff into bins and hauled it out to the stables because they're tearing the roof off tomorrow and starting construction. If we would've known you guys were all going to show up, then maybe we could've had it all set up for you."

She wondered if he even realized he was using the term

we, as in he and Robin. Clearly Sofia and Camilla had caught it because they were looking at each other with raised brows and smirks. But since Dylan seemed to have not known his family was coming, it wasn't like he'd invited her to eat with them.

She wiped her hands on the back of her jeans. She wasn't as dirty as she had been earlier when his dad and Felix had been talking to her; she'd changed when she'd gone home to get the horses. But still, the other women in Dylan's family looked so stylish.

As everyone worked together to light the bonfire and set up the food, she got Dylan's attention and jerked her chin toward the parking area. He shook his head no. Frowning at his refusal to come talk to her, she flicked her wrist to subtly wave him over.

He looked around and when nobody appeared to be watching him, he slowly made his way over to where she was standing and whispered, "You can't leave."

"I can't stay, either," she said through gritted teeth. "It's a family dinner."

"If you don't stay, they'll track you down eventually and drag you to my parents' house some other time. It's best to just let them get it out of their system and then everyone can move on."

She wanted to ask him what they'd be moving on from, but the sound of a horn stopped her.

Stanley Sanchez pulled up with Winona Cobbs in the passenger seat. It took a couple of minutes for the older couple to exit the car.

"Sorry we're late," Uncle Stanley said. "I couldn't take the driveway as fast as I wanted to because I'm not driving my 4x4."

Everything suddenly got very quiet and everyone's eyes turned to Dylan. "Sorry, Uncle Stanley, but I had to sell it. That sedan is just as nice, though. It's safe and reliable and the Gravity Defying Green is an exclusive, hard-to-get color."

"You sold your uncle's truck?" Robin whispered beside him.

Dylan lowered his voice to match hers. "No. It was a truck I'd let him borrow from the dealership anytime he wanted to impress his girlfriend and take her off-roading in the mud. Apparently, my family members, as well as Stanley's doctor, thought it might be a little too dangerous. Not necessarily for my uncle, but for the other drivers who often had to move out of his way."

Robin nearly snorted. Okay, now that was adorable. Totally reckless, but also a bit touching. Clearly Dylan cared about his relatives and tried to help them out when he could.

Denise Sanchez, Dylan's mom, slapped her hands together. "Food's ready. Robin, since you're the guest of honor, you go first."

Initially, she was supposed to know where the paper towels were kept, yet now she was the guest of—

She squeaked when Dylan gave her a light tap on the behind. "Hurry, before it gets cold."

"Why don't you-all start." Robin held up her palms. "I need to go wash up first."

"Don't use the kitchen sink," Sofia warned. "That faucet smells super funky."

Robin smiled. "I learned that lesson the first time I was here."

As she walked toward the temporary wash station she'd set up next to the hose bib protruding from the side of the barn, she could hear Dylan explaining to his family about the septic system.

When she returned, she was relieved to see that people

were already piling their plates with food. She didn't want to be the cause of everyone missing out on a hot meal. Of course, that ship had most likely already sailed. It was February in Montana. Absent a freak heat wave, the temperature was going to make everything outdoors feel pretty frosty. Although, by the time she filled her plate with a thick slice of lasagna, salad and garlic bread and then sat on one of the benches in front of the warm flames, she felt as though she could've been at a beach bonfire during July.

The Sanchez family made her feel right at home, even though she had to remind herself several times not to get too comfortable. Everyone took turns teasing each other and no one was immune from being on the receiving end of a family joke, including the in-laws.

During a story about the previous Tuesday when Dante took his third-grade class on a field trip to the library where Shari worked, Dylan leaned closer to Robin and whispered, "You doing okay?"

She nodded. But when he continued to study her, she asked, "Why wouldn't I be?"

"Because my family can be a lot."

"Dylan, I have siblings, too. Plus, something you don't have yet."

He nodded his chin toward his relatives sitting around the fire. "What do you have that could possibly be any worse than this?"

"Two teenage nephews and a teenage niece. If you think having your brothers tease you about your eyebrows is bad, try having a thirteen-year-old girl list all the reasons why your closet needs a complete makeover. Just wait until baby Merry gets older. Teenagers do wonders for the self-esteem."

"From where I'm sitting, and I have a very good view..." Dylan paused and allowed his eyes to travel up and down the length of her body, causing Robin to shiver. But not from the cold. "I don't see a need for you to change a thing. Although, if she was the one who picked out the dress you wore yesterday, then I can't say that I object to the results."

Robin gulped, hoping that everyone would assume her cheeks were flushed because of the fire. "I'll be sure to pass along your approval."

"Please do that. As a youth basketball coach and the occasional substitute referee when my dad can't make it, I'm all too familiar with that generation's ability to trash-talk. If possible, I'd prefer to be on your niece's good side in advance."

In advance of what? Was he planning on meeting the rest of her family anytime soon?

"Then Dante comes out of the bathroom holding the very wet copy of *Diary of a Wimpy Kid* he just rescued from the toilet and runs straight into Mr. Brandt," Shari said, and everyone laughed. "Thank goodness the man owns a dry-cleaning business."

Robin realized she'd missed the last half of the story because she'd been whispering with Dylan.

"Speaking of Phil Brandt," Denise Sanchez said. "Mallory was in the salon the other day and told me that the bake-off can't come soon enough. She said that if she has to try one more bite of her husband's meringue from the outdoor test kitchen he set up in their backyard, she's going to learn how to change the oil in his car herself."

"She might as well learn anyway," Uncle Stanley said. "Because there's no way Phil is winning the free car service for a year. My Winona and her chocolate torte are going to take first place."

"Miss Winona," Sofia said, "if you don't mind my asking, what are you going to do with the prize if you win the bake-off? You don't have a car, do you?"

"I'm entering the contest to win the gift certificate for dinner at The Library. And for bragging rights. I'm sure everyone has their own reasons for entering, right, Robin?"

The psychic smiled at her knowingly and Robin wanted to slink lower on the bench until she could completely disappear from sight. *Please don't say it out loud*, Robin tried to convey to Winona in the hopes that the psychic could read minds.

"I didn't know you entered the bake-off, Robin," Mr. Sanchez said before taking another bite of food. "Is that why you can't be a judge, Dylan?"

"Of course it's why," Uncle Stanley said. "The man can't very well judge a contest when both his girlfriend and his aunt are contestants. People might think he's biased."

Winona's bracelets jingled as she patted Stanley's hand. "I'm not Dylan's aunt."

Stanley's weathered face looked stricken by the correction. He immediately said, "*Yet*. You mean you aren't his aunt *yet*."

Winona seemed to have not heard her fiancé's attempt to confirm the status of their relationship and continued, "But I do agree that people probably won't think it's fair if Dylan votes for his girlfriend's cookies."

Robin's brows shot up in surprise. "How did you know I was making cookies?"

Everyone turned toward her, their facial expressions clearly suggesting that it was fruitless to even question Winona Cobbs or how she knew things. The woman just did. In reality, the real question Robin should have asked was, *Why do you think I'm Dylan's girlfriend?* But at this point, everyone in town was erroneously assuming that Robin and Dylan were a couple. Especially because neither one of them was doing anything to correct people.

"What kind of cookies are you making, Robin?" Camilla asked.

"I'm just glad to know it's not your cinnamon rolls," Dante said at the same time.

"First of all, the cinnamon rolls weren't mine, Dante. You've worked at the school with my sister long enough to know that Stacy always gets assigned paper plates and utensils when there's a potluck. Second of all, Camilla, I'm making a family recipe I found in my great-aunt's old recipe tin."

"Can't go wrong with a recipe called Heartmelters." Winona nodded and Robin stared at her in amazement. How did the woman sense these things? "It's probably how your great-aunt got your great-uncle. The trick is in the measurements."

Robin exhaled loudly. "You can say that again."

"If you need some help working the recipe and trying different techniques, I'd be happy to help," Camilla offered.

Sofia scrunched her nose. "Mmm, I might not do that if I were you."

"Why not?" Dylan asked. "Robin is going to need all the help she can get."

A chorus of *uh-oh*'s and *oh no*'s came from Jordan, Boone, Felix and Uncle Stanley. Dante laughed out loud at his brother's blunder and Mr. Sanchez dropped his head in his hands. Even baby Merry stirred from her nap and began to fuss.

"I didn't mean it like that, you guys." Dylan glowered at his male relatives. Then he softened his expression when he faced Robin and said, "I promise I didn't mean it like that. I meant I wanted Camilla to help you so that you do well in the contest."

"You're not making it any better, bro." Dante was still chuckling.

Robin crossed her arms. "You don't think I can do well on my own?"

Obviously, she couldn't, but she didn't want Dylan to know that. Yet.

He set down his plate and put his arm over her shoulders. "I think you are great at everything you do. Why else would I want your expertise out here on Broken Road Ranch?"

"Sof, why don't you think it would be a good idea for Camilla to help Robin?" Boone asked his wife. Dylan looked as though he wanted to hug his brother-in-law for getting the conversation back on track.

"Even though Camilla isn't a judge, she's providing one of the prizes and she's helping with the organizing." Sofia stood and started collecting plates for the trash. "It's probably best if we avoid all appearances of favoritism."

Robin wanted to point out that, despite her bragging to Mr. Brandt, she wasn't expecting to win anything. In fact, she wanted to withdraw from the contest entirely. But it was too late to quit without causing more gossip. At least she'd already succeeded in making Dylan notice her, which was the reason she'd signed up in the first place.

"I'm sure Robin will do just fine in the bake-off," Mrs. Sanchez said as she stood to help with the cleanup. "Winona will, too."

"Wait." Mr. Sanchez rose, followed by everyone else in the family. "We can still sample the desserts, even if we're not judging the contest, right?"

"I should hope so," Dante said, patting his stomach before reaching to take Merry from Eloise. "If I have to help set up all those balloon arches and party tents, I should at least be rewarded with my choice of baked goods."

The family continued to joke and tease each other as they made quick work of putting out the flames and packing up the food. The goodbyes were short since the heat from the fire was gone and the cold had settled in. It was rather chaotic as everyone was heading to their cars, especially since Uncle Stanley nearly sideswiped the back bumper of Jordan's SUV as he executed a too-wide U-turn.

Robin thought she'd be able to slip away quickly, but her truck with the empty horse trailer was parked near the stables and the other vehicles were blocking her in.

"So I'll see you tomorrow morning to get the cattle out to the east pasture?" Dylan asked as he caught up to her near the driver's side door.

"Bright and early," Robin replied.

So far, any time they'd ended one of their days or outings together, they hadn't so much as hugged goodbye. But she couldn't stop staring at his mouth, wondering what it would feel like to have his lips on hers, even for a brief moment.

He must have read her mind because he took a step toward her. Just when she thought that he was going to lean down and kiss her, Robin panicked and flung her arms around his neck, averting her face to the side as she went in for the hug.

"Okay, have a good night," she said, giving his back two solid pats. She might as well have been a teammate telling him "good game."

She pulled back from the awkward embrace quickly and hopped into the cab of her truck, needing to get out of there before she embarrassed herself any further.

As she drove away, she peeked in the sideview mirror and saw him standing in the middle of the driveway, his hands tucked in his coat pockets as he watched her taillights.

Yep. She was already a goner.

CHAPTER ELEVEN

"WHY COULDN'T I have used the golf cart, again?" Dylan called out over the sound of mooing.

"Because you wanted to be a real cowboy," Robin yelled back as she easily trotted along in the saddle, keeping her side of the herd in a straight line.

Yeah. Except that was before he realized that riding a horse wasn't any easier as a thirty-four-year-old man than it had been as a fourteen-year-old. It was impossible to grow up in Bronco and not have ridden at least once. Several of Dylan's high school friends had ranches and he'd gone riding with them a handful of times. But when you're competitive and you like to be the best at something, it was easier for him to find other activities he excelled at. Like playing basketball and driving fast cars.

Robin must've seen the grimace on his face as he awkwardly shifted in the saddle because she shouted, "Just trust Buttermilk and do what I do."

The pale horse Robin had brought for him had seemed old and slow at first, but as soon as she had caught sight of the cattle, the mare proved that she knew exactly what to do and was in her element. As much as Dylan wanted to remain in control of the reins, as soon as he relaxed his grip, he realized that he pretty much just needed to hang on and let Buttermilk do her thing.

Besides, his ranch wasn't huge. It wasn't like they were going that far. In fact, within fifteen minutes, they had the herd inside the new fencing of the east pasture and Robin hopped off her horse to shut the gate. Which was probably for the best since Dylan's thighs were already burning. He always thought of himself as being in pretty good shape, but this morning he was using muscles not normally needed on the basketball court.

Robin, on the other hand, had made riding look entirely effortless and fluid. She moved with her horse as though they were one and, unlike him, did not bounce around in the saddle. Dylan could only wish that someday he might have a third of her ability. In the meantime, all he could do was hope that she didn't think less of him for his lack of skill.

Whenever he didn't know how to do something, he found that if he at least acted confident, most people would be none the wiser. So as they turned to head back toward the stables, Dylan asked, "How come I ended up on the horse named Buttermilk and you got the horse named Maze Runner?"

"I think we both know the answer to that," Robin replied with a teasing grin.

So much for his theory of fake it until you make it. "Was it that obvious?"

She reined her horse closer to his. "If it makes you feel better, I've seen worse. One time, my brother Theo brought someone he was dating out to the ranch and she wanted to barrel race. Theo wrongly assumed that since she asked, she had at least some experience, so he put her on one of our fastest mounts. Let's just say there was lots of screaming, plenty of tears and no more dates after that."

"So what you're saying is that I should be proud of the fact that I'm not crying?"

"Well, you haven't cried *yet*," Robin said before making a clicking sound, encouraging her horse to pick up the pace. His mare took that as a sign to follow suit and suddenly Dylan was holding on for dear life.

He would've told Buttermilk to stop succumbing to peer pressure, but he had to keep his jaw firmly clenched so that his teeth wouldn't rattle. Thankfully, the return trip to the stables was much quicker since they didn't have the cows with them this time.

When he was finally able to heave himself out of the saddle, Robin was already walking Maze Runner around the yard, allowing her to cool down.

"At first, I was worried about having to come back for you, Dylan. But you definitely showed signs of improvement. In fact, those last few minutes I completely stopped worrying that you were going to fall and mess up your pretty little face."

"You're lucky I can't let go of Buttermilk's reins as I walk her," Dylan said with a hint of challenge.

Robin's blond ponytail whipped around as she tossed her head back and dared, "Or else what?"

Last night, Dylan got the impression that she'd wanted to kiss him goodbye but had chickened out at the last minute. He'd settled for the hug, not wanting to push her for something she wasn't ready for. But judging by that pretty-face comment and the way the corner of her full lips tilted into a smirk, she was practically begging for it.

"Or else I might find something better for your mouth to do than tease me."

She bit her lower lip as she boldly studied him. "Do you really need both of your hands free to do that?"

Groaning, Dylan took a step toward her to prove that he didn't need any hands at all, but before he could lower his head to hers, they were interrupted by the engine of a loud truck.

They both turned toward the driveway to see Brad arriving with his work crew. For a second, Dylan had completely forgotten that the whole reason they were on the horses this morning in the first place was to move the herd for demo day.

Robin's fingers grazed against his hand as she reached for the reins. "Here, I'll tend to the horses while you go meet with Brad. They need to be watered and rubbed down before I load them onto the trailer."

Warmth spread along his skin at the spot where she'd touched him and, instead of releasing the reins, he used his other hand to clasp her waist. "You're not leaving yet, are you?"

She lifted her face toward him, her voice low and husky as she asked, "Do you need me to stay?"

"I *want* you to stay," he clarified.

"I can stay for a few minutes, but I really need to get the horses out of here before all the construction noise gets going."

"Then you'll come back?" he asked.

She looked at a spot past his shoulder. "For lunch?"

A truck door slammed nearby and Dylan knew that he had only a few more seconds to have her this close.

"And for this," he said before brushing his mouth softly against hers.

It was the barest of kisses and only a promise of what he had planned for the next time he got her alone. Yet, the sound of her indrawn breath would stay with him the rest of the morning.

ROBIN'S LIPS WERE still tingling from where Dylan had kissed her a few hours ago. At least, she was pretty sure it had counted as a kiss. If she had blinked, she would've missed it. That was how quickly it had taken place. By the time she returned from taking the horses back to the Bonnie B, the delivery driver from Bronco Brick Oven Pizza was pulling in behind her.

Since they needed to replace the roof and porch before the next snowfall, the crew was working at a swift pace and took their lunch breaks in shifts. This meant that people were in constant motion on the property, and she didn't get another moment alone with Dylan.

Robin was talking to the service techs from the county and showing them the best spot to install the water line for the house when the younger tech asked her if she was single. Before she could answer, the man's face turned a bright shade of red and his eyes darted to something behind her.

Not something. Some*one*.

Dylan walked up with a clenched grin that didn't quite meet his eyes. Something was wrong. He put his arm around Robin's shoulders as he spoke. "Babe, I need to get back to the dealership and see about a fender bender that happened during a test-drive." He must not have noticed her blinking in confusion over the term of endearment because he kept talking. "Brad has a question about the color scheme we want in the master bedroom so when you get finished here, would you mind going over that with him?"

"Uh, sure," she said, even though they hadn't selected any color scheme, certainly not for something as intimate as his master bedroom. But maybe that was what Brad had wanted to ask her about.

"I hope you're lucky enough to find a woman like this one day," Dylan said to the still-blushing service tech. Then he dipped his head and kissed Robin directly on the mouth. This time, it wasn't simply a brush of the lips. It was searing and hot and almost made Robin forget they had an audience watching them.

Dylan pulled back slowly, his eyes seeming to search hers while his voice confidently said, "Thanks, babe."

Robin was in a complete daze as she stared at Dylan striding away. The last time he'd called her babe was when they'd been putting on an act for Birdsey Jones at the livestock auction. Had his kiss just been another act? Because it had certainly felt real to her.

The older water tech, the one who seemed to be in charge, cleared his throat. "Ma'am, I think we're all good here if you want to let the others know that we'll be running our backhoe on this side of the property for the next hour or so."

"Right," Robin said then walked on wobbly legs toward the house where Brad was supervising a tractor loading rotted roof shingles into a dump truck. Yelling over the noise, she relayed the information about the backhoe then asked, "Did you want to talk to me about a color scheme or something for the master bedroom?"

"Not yet," Brad said as he made a hand motion to the tractor driver, who shut off the engine. Resuming a normal tone, he added, "I told Dylan that we would worry about paint colors later."

"Oh." Robin reached up to touch her lips then realized it would be a dead giveaway so she rubbed the creased line on her forehead instead. "I wonder why he told me to come talk to you about it now."

Brad guffawed. "Probably because he noticed the way that young fella over there was looking at you."

Robin jerked her head up. "What do you mean?"

"That kid from the county water authority was having a tough time taking his eyes off you and, judging by the expression on Dylan's face when he stomped over there, he probably wanted the boy to know that you were already spoken for."

Spoken for? "You make it sound like Dylan was being territorial."

As soon as Robin said the words, all the pieces clicked

together. Calling her babe. Referencing their color scheme for the *master bedroom.* Kissing her so boldly like that while everyone was watching.

Brad must've been able to tell that she'd been slow to pick up on all the signs because he chuckled again. "Growing up on a ranch around a bunch of men, Robin, you've surely had a pair of young bucks fighting over you a time or two."

If she had, she'd been completely oblivious to it. Just like she had been a few moments ago. She wanted to ask Brad if he thought that meant Dylan liked her. But even she knew how naive the question would sound. This wasn't high school when your best friend would ask you to talk to their crush for them.

"Uh-huh," she managed to mumble, then changed the subject to the condition of the roof shingles. "Can any of these be salvaged?"

"Maybe enough to build a little chicken coop later on. But that's going to be way down on the list of things to get done around here." Brad spoke a bit more about the fascia boards and the porch railings, but Robin had difficulty focusing on his words.

She was still thinking about Dylan's kiss and his intent behind it. She wanted him to kiss her because he couldn't not kiss her. Not because he was trying to make someone believe they were a couple. Next time his lips burned against hers, if there ever was a next time, Robin hoped they wouldn't be standing in the middle of a construction zone with at least ten other people buzzing around them.

"We're good here, if you need to take off," Brad said, bringing Robin back to the present moment. Had he noticed that she wasn't paying attention? Probably. But he was likely just as eager to get back to work.

"If you're sure you don't need me, I do have a few errands I need to run." Such as picking up more baking powder at the grocery store because she wanted to practice a few more batches of cookies before the bake-off in two days.

Brad pulled out his phone. "Just leave me your number in case something comes up."

Robin didn't mind the man having her contact information, but surely he should be reaching out to Dylan first. After all, it was his property. But since he might be busy at work, it wouldn't be a bad idea for Brad to have someone to call as a backup.

Robin wasn't gone from the ranch longer than two hours when she received her first text from Brad. Although, technically, it was a group text including Dylan so Robin didn't really need to answer. She set the phone down on the kitchen counter and put on her apron only to hear another notification alert.

It was Dylan's response to Brad.

I think the septic people are coming tomorrow, but you'll have to ask Robin if that will interfere with the county water guys.

And that's how it went for the next couple of hours. Every so often, Brad would have a question and then Dylan would ask her what she thought. But at no point did he text her directly without Brad acting as a chaperone of sorts. He definitely didn't call her to explain why he'd referred to her as babe out of the blue and then publicly kissed her.

Finally, after several more failed attempts at cookies and another episode of the reality dating show she was hooked on, Robin was about to turn out her bedroom light and call it a night when her phone pinged again. It was from Dylan and the first thing she noticed was that Brad was not on the text.

Thank you again for all your help today. I'm still at the dealership dealing with the insurance paperwork.

She typed back a response. Did anyone get hurt in the accident?

Just the sidewalk sign in front of Mrs. Coss's antiques shop. She wasn't happy, understandably.

Robin wanted to ask him about what happened earlier, but maybe he'd already forgotten it. It was Dylan Sanchez, after all. He'd probably kissed plenty of women the same way he'd kissed her.

While she was still deciding what to type, another message appeared on the screen.

I'm not going to make it out to the ranch tomorrow. I'll be knee-deep in bake-off preparations and trying to find a place to hide that ridiculous pink shirt Sofia thinks I should wear for the news interview.

So Robin wouldn't see him at all before the contest. Maybe that was a good thing.

Or maybe it would give her too much time to think.

In that case, try to get some rest. Have a good night. Robin pushed the send button, determined to put the man completely out of her mind.

Except that only left her thinking about the bake-off and how she was going to make a complete fool of herself.

DYLAN LOOKED UP to the sky to send a prayer of thanks that this was the warmest, sunniest Valentine's Day on record in Bronco. They didn't need the heat lamps or the removable walls of the huge party tent, which meant the spectators who came to watch could easily slip off into the lot to look at the cars.

Which was the main reason he was hosting the event at Bronco Motors.

"Your mom and sisters certainly outdid themselves," his dad said as he patted Dylan's back.

"I know," he admitted, even though he'd never really doubted their abilities. Sure, the balloon arches and heart garlands strung across the lot were a tad too much. But having the red and white cars parked in a row facing the street was a brilliant touch. As was the media campaign that Eloise had managed.

"That was quite the news interview you did yesterday," his dad continued. "Did Mom forward you the video clip?"

"Yep." Dylan nodded. So did half of his teammates, Mickie and Mrs. Epson, his new neighbor. But he hadn't watched any of the videos on his phone. In fact, he was keeping his eye out for any sign of the white news van and the redheaded anchor who'd slipped him her number, which he'd passed straight to Mickie since Dylan had no need of it.

Eloise had done a rehearsal of sorts with Dylan beforehand, going through possible interview questions so he wouldn't stumble or mess up during the recording. But when the anchor asked him on camera if any of the contestants would have a chance at winning a date with him, his mind had immediately flashed to Robin. Yet he'd managed to respond, *Well, one of our contestants has been happily married for forty years and I think his wife would rather him win the free oil changes.*

"You ready for this?" Camilla asked as she came over holding a tiny device that was supposed to clip to his shirt.

He took a step back. "Don't you think a wearable microphone is a bit overboard?"

"The DJ said it'll look more natural than having you walk around with a cordless mic in your hand." Camilla batted his hand away as she tried to clip the small wire to him.

"You're pulling on my chest hair!" Dylan's accusation blasted through the speaker system because apparently the microphone was already switched on.

"Then stop pulling away," Camilla said, her voice also serenading the, thankfully, still-empty lot.

Sofia ran over to take the small battery box attached to the wire and turned it off. "Fess up, Dylan, and tell me where you hid the pink shirt. Mickie said she saw it hanging in your office yesterday, but you expect me to believe it's suddenly vanished?"

"It's not like I could wear it anyway, Sof." Dylan grabbed the microphone from Camilla's hand and clipped it to his not pink shirt. "See, I'm already miked up."

The DJ put on the first song, a predictable love ballad, to test the speakers. Dylan grumbled. "Please tell me we're not going to be playing stuff like this the whole time. This song is going to make people want to slow dance, not buy cars."

"Eloise came up with the playlist," his brother Dante said as he joined them. He'd taken the day off work to help and was pushing baby Merry in her stroller. "She said it will inspire romance."

"I need it to inspire sales," Dylan replied.

Both of his sisters groaned in unison. Camilla said, "It's

a wonder you get any female customers at all. You have no idea what a woman wants."

Dylan was inclined to agree, but Sofia took it a step further. "He has no idea what *he* wants, either."

His jaw dropped, then he quickly recovered. "What's that supposed to mean?"

Camilla put her hands on her hips. "It means why haven't you asked Robin out yet?"

"I took her out to your restaurant, Cam. Remember? You made a big deal about it and sent a bottle of champagne to our table."

"What?" Dante turned to their sister. "You never sent me and Eloise a bottle of champagne when we were first dating."

"That's because Eloise was pregnant. And you were eating enough free dessert that I figured the bottle of champagne would be cheaper this time. Stop distracting Dylan, so he can answer my question. Why haven't you asked Robin out on a proper date that doesn't include buying something for your ranch first?"

Dylan lifted his arms in exasperation. "Because I don't know that she wants to."

"There is no way our brother can be this clueless," Sofia said to no one in particular.

"Trust me, he is," Mickie said as she approached with a spray of red roses.

"I thought I was paying you to be loyal," Dylan muttered under his breath.

"No, you're paying me to keep you organized," his office manager with excellent hearing said. "Besides, honesty is a form of loyalty. And if I'm being honest, part of your problem, Dylan, is that you've never had to work for it."

Dante laughed, but Dylan was scratching his head. "What are you talking about? I'm a hard worker."

"With your business and your ranch, sure you are. But from what I've seen, you've never had to work too hard when it comes to women." Mickie stage-whispered to his sisters. "You'd be amazed how many young gals come in here wanting a so-called test-drive with your brother."

Camilla made a gagging sound and Sofia slammed her palms over her ears. "Don't want to hear it."

"She means test-drive the cars!" Dylan used his two fists to make a steering wheel motion, but his thumb caught on the wire twisted around his lapel.

"Do I?" Mickie asked rhetorically. "All I'm saying is that when you have ladies doing the asking all the time, you never really learn how to do it yourself. Anyway, I have to get these flowers to the judges' table."

"I know how to ask women out," Dylan insisted, hearing his words echo in the speakers.

"You really need to stop fidgeting with that microphone," Dante told him before pushing the stroller toward the arriving contestants and guests.

CHAPTER TWELVE

ROBIN TILTED HER head as she squinted at the commercial-grade oven, trying to figure out how to even turn the thing on. This was nothing like her oven at home.

"You turn this knob in the middle to preheat it." The pretty woman at the cooking station next to Robin's pointed at the row of high-tech controls. Gabrielle Hammond. Each contestant had their names custom embroidered across the matching red aprons Camilla had provided.

She'd seen Gabrielle in the grocery store the other day and the checkout clerk, who knew everyone in town, mentioned that the woman was Bronco's newest resident. Then the clerk alluded to some sort of mysterious background that Robin hadn't asked about.

"Thanks," she told Gabrielle with a smile. She could only imagine what it was like moving to a new town and having everyone asking questions that were none of their business.

"I don't think I can work on this stove," Mr. Brandt, who was on the other side of Robin, said to nobody in particular. "The burner is bigger than the one I have at home. Does medium heat mean regular stove medium heat? Or does this stove put out more heat because it's so much bigger?"

Gabrielle left her station to show him the temperature settings. "If you're in doubt, I believe they provided a cooking thermometer, too. You can use mine if you need it."

Thank goodness Robin wasn't making anything in a

saucepan or skillet or she'd have to forfeit right now. She tried to concentrate on her recipe, but she hadn't realized she would need to triple the recipe to make enough for the judges and the spectators. Okay, so that meant three cups of butter. Did she have that much? She should. If not, she'd have to borrow some.

The contest rules had been posted online, but she'd forgotten to read them until this morning when Mickie had sent a last-minute email asking for Robin's signature on some paperwork. One of the rules was that each "kitchen" needed to be set up exactly the same. Everyone had brought their own ingredients, but they were required to use the provided measuring tools. Which meant that Robin couldn't use the antique punch ladle she'd used at home when she'd gotten the best results. It was supposed to be three—make that nine—ladles of flour. She looked down at her cupped hands and tried to gauge the amount in handfuls. She'd never done a practice batch using her own hands for measurement. Was it too risky to try now? Probably. But she had no choice.

There were four rows, with three kitchen stations in each row. There wasn't a ton of space between the rows, which meant the contestants could easily talk to each other if they wanted.

"Now Shep is the one keeping me up at night," she heard Deborah Dalton, the contestant at the station behind Mr. Brandt, say to someone in her row.

"Why would you be worried about Shep?" Bethany McCreery asked. The wedding singer was directly behind Gabrielle with her niece, Molly McCreery, right between them at the station behind Robin. Normally, Robin might find it odd that a ten-year-old could successfully compete in a cooking contest where she was the only person using a step stool to reach the counter. But Molly's mother had died six years ago, and the girl had become like a surrogate mom to her two younger siblings. So she was probably used to helping out in the kitchen at home.

"Because he's almost thirty and shows no sign of finding a significant other," Deborah Dalton responded to Bethany.

"Thirty's not that old," Mr. Brandt said over his shoulder.

"Thirty is ancient," Solar, the purple-haired barista, called out from her row behind Mrs. Dalton.

"Don't fuss at the boy, Deborah," Winona Cobb said from her station in front of Robin. "Shep will settle down."

"Do you know when, Winona?" Mrs. Dalton asked, a hint of desperation in her voice.

But the psychic seemed to be too focused on the contents of her saucepan because she absently replied, "He'll find love when it's his turn."

"My dad already had his turn," Molly said very matter-of-factly.

Robin's heart would've broken for the little girl and Jake McCreery, her widowed father, if Winona hadn't looked up from her pot of chocolate long enough to turn around and thoughtfully say to the girl, "Some people get two turns."

"I know I got two turns," Dylan's uncle Stanley said as he sidled up next to Winona.

"Stanley," Winona scolded her fiancé. "You're not supposed to be over here talking to the contestants."

"I know, but I wanted to come over real quick and tell you that I spoke with Camilla and she said we could have our reception at The Library. I know how much you love the food there."

"I can't talk about that when I'm focused on my ganache," Winona replied. Robin should be focused on her own baking, but she kept getting distracted by everybody else around her. And the heavenly smells.

"You want to have our reception at The Library, though, right?" Stanley asked again, not quite willing to give up. His insistence kind of reminded Robin of another Sanchez man she knew.

"What I want is to make this chocolate torte." Winona used her fingers to sprinkle another pinch of sugar to her pot.

Robin realized this was now the second time she'd heard Winona seem reluctant to give Stanley a definitive answer about their wedding date. Robin, whose brother Billy had once been left at the altar, hoped there wasn't something else going on between the older couple.

"Excuse me, Mr. Sanchez." Robin waved the man over. "Do you know if the rules say anything about us getting access to more ingredients if we run out?"

"I can go check," Stanley offered. When he left, Robin congratulated herself on being able to distract him with an errand.

"Do you need something, Robin?" Gabrielle asked. "I brought way more than I'll need."

Before Robin could answer, Deborah Dalton called out, "Gabrielle, you're new in town, right?"

The woman smiled politely at Mrs. Dalton. "I am."

Oh boy. Robin knew exactly where this was going. Mrs. Dalton was going to try to set up Shep with the first single woman she could find.

"If you have some extra butter," Robin said to Gabrielle before the conversation could become uncomfortable, "I think I'm going to need another cup."

"Is unsalted okay?" Gabrielle asked, but was already walking toward the huge stainless steel refrigerator at the back of the tent.

Wow. Robin was getting pretty good at the whole distraction thing. She'd just successfully diverted two awkward moments. Of course, she hadn't even cracked a single egg yet, or figured out her flour measuring technique. But it wasn't like there was a time limit or anything.

"Ninety minutes, ladies and gentlemen," the DJ announced in between songs. "We have ninety minutes remaining."

Robin's heart sank as she realized she'd missed that information in the contest rules she'd only briefly glanced over this morning. Trying to refocus, she mentally calculated how long it would take to bake nine dozen cookies.

"Here you go." Gabrielle passed her a package of butter right as Dylan made his way into the tent, followed by a news camera.

Robin had seen him thirty minutes—she glanced at the large digital clock she hadn't noticed earlier on the stage—make that thirty-three minutes ago when he'd given a very brief welcome before turning things over to Mayor Smith who was the master of ceremonies. She remembered Dylan saying that he wasn't looking forward to being the center of attention today, but he seemed to be holding his own as he stopped by each station and asked the contestants what they were making. It wasn't until he was talking to Solar, the barista, that Robin realized he wasn't looking in the direction of the camera at all. In fact, he seemed to stay one step ahead of it at all times, as though he was purposely blocking out the fact that he was being recorded.

"I need to go check something," Gabrielle murmured and slipped away from her station right before it was her turn for an interview. Which meant Dylan had to go straight to Robin.

"Robin Abernathy," he said, flashing those irresistible dimples that made her stomach do somersaults. His eyes seemed to fill with relief as he focused on her face. But maybe that was just her imagination. "Tell us what you've got going on here."

Since all she had in front of her was an empty mixing bowl, she held up the package in her hands. "I have this butter."

He glanced down at the package. "Yep, that's butter all right. What do you plan to do with it?"

"I'm making cookies," she said her voice sounding high and squeaky.

"I'm making cookies, too," Molly McCreery said behind her. "Double fudge peanut butter chip cookies."

The cameraperson pivoted toward the child, bypassing Mr. Brandt and causing the boom mic to hit his bald head.

As far as baking contestants went, apparently, there was more news interest in a ten-year-old girl than in a sixty-year-old man.

"Sorry, Mr. Brandt," Dylan murmured as he stepped around the man and followed the camera to the next row. "I guess we'll be coming back to you."

Dylan moved into place behind Robin. They were now back-to-back and if she wanted to reach behind her, she could probably touch him. But she needed to get something in her mixing bowl.

"Miss Molly here is our youngest contestant," Dylan said. "Tell us about the contest so far, Molly."

"Well, Mrs. Dalton is looking for a girlfriend for her son and Ms. Winona said people find love when it's their turn and my daddy might get two turns. Except it's not my turn yet, because I'm only ten and I like making cookies more than I like boys."

"Me, too," Molly's aunt Bethany said, and Robin had to bite back a giggle. She knew that Bethany was likely making it clear to Mrs. Dalton that she wasn't a candidate for still-single Shep.

"I'm making a coconut cream pie with a meringue topping in case anyone's interested," Mr. Brandt said, still waiting for his turn in front of the camera.

"We know, Phil," Gary, the only other man in the contest, called from the back row. Gary, like everyone else in town, had heard his fair share of angst about the meringue and the weather.

The camera moved to Mr. Brandt, who talked at length about his meringue techniques, and Robin heard Dylan whispering to Mrs. Dalton, "They're coming to your station next, and I feel it's only fair to warn you that Shep is going to kill me if I let his mom tell everyone who watches the news that he's single and available."

"He's the only one of my sons not settled down yet and he's almost thirty." She wiped her hands on her apron. "Why you boys do this to us poor mamas is beyond me."

Robin turned on her electric hand mixer so she wouldn't have to listen to Dylan's response. She creamed the butter, wondering what Mrs. Dalton must think of a woman Robin's age still not married, especially since she was older than Shep. And the only man she'd even thought about settling down with was, right this second, probably explaining why he planned to stay single indefinitely.

She switched off the mixer and bent down to grab the sack of sugar from the shelf below right as Dylan was moving out of the way of the camera. When he bumped into her, she dropped the bag.

"Here, let me get that for you," he said, squatting directly beside her to pick up the sugar. Their legs were touching as they both stood at the same time. He reached in front of her to place the container on the counter, letting his arm brush slowly past hers as he retreated.

Robin shivered, but didn't dare look at his face since she had no doubt he'd do something else to make her blush.

"Is anyone else hot under this tent?" Mr. Brandt asked and, for a second, Robin thought he'd witnessed what had just happened between her and Dylan. But then she saw his saucepan boiling over.

The man let out a string of curse words that made Molly and Solar giggle. "Great, now I need to start over with my coconut filling."

Robin glanced at the clock and realized she needed to get moving.

According to the recipe, she was supposed to cream one handful of sugar into the butter. Which meant for this batch, it would need to be three. She looked at the measuring cup with uncertainty. She didn't have enough butter or enough time to do this a second time. Her fingers were tingling and before she knew it, Robin was pouring the sugar directly into her palm.

Robin finally got into a rhythm with her cookies and was using her heart-shaped cutter on the rolled out dough when the DJ announced, "Thirty minutes left."

"You'll see when you have kids one day, Bethany." Deborah Dalton must have already finished because she was back to chatting with everyone around her. "What about you, Gabrielle? Do you want kids?"

Alarm bells went off in Robin's head, because she, too, had been asked that personal question before.

Gabrielle, who had plated her dessert and appeared to be tidying up her station, didn't bother to look at Mrs. Dalton when she replied, "Actually, I already have a daughter."

"Oh," Mrs. Dalton said, disappointment in her tone. "I hadn't realized you were spoken for."

"I'm not." Gabrielle took off her apron and set it on the counter. "Good luck, everyone."

As the woman walked away, Solar turned around holding her tray of German chocolate brownies. “I don’t think she loved your questions, Mrs. D.”

“Oh no.” Mrs. Dalton’s face fell. “Do you think I got a little too personal?”

“Maybe a little.” Robin took the first pan of cookies out of the oven and slid in her second. The woman’s heart was in the right place, but not everyone, especially newcomers to Bronco, wanted to discuss their business in such a public setting.

“You’re right. I better find her and apologize.” Mrs. Dalton hurried after Gabrielle.

Soon, only Robin, Winona, Molly and Bethany were left at the cooking stations. Robin was fanning a pot holder over her last batch of cookies, trying to cool them down quicker.

“Those look lovely,” Winona said as she hefted the enormous cake platter holding her chocolate torte. “You followed your great-aunt’s recipe to a T. I hope you’re prepared.”

“Prepared to be humiliated when I come in last,” Robin muttered under her breath.

But the older psychic must’ve heard her because she replied, “Oh, you’re going to win. And lose. And then win again.”

Robin gaped at the woman as she walked away under the weight of her chocolate torte. What did that even mean?

DYLAN WAS RELIEVED that this event was about to come to an end soon. It was a good thing he hadn’t judged the contest because he, Mickie and the other salespeople had been bombarded with test-drives and sales paperwork. Even his dad and brother Dante, who used to help out in the office on the weekends, had to be called in for reinforcements.

Earlier, he'd been happy to turn over the master of ceremonies duty to Rafferty Smith, who'd thankfully taken over the interviewing, as well. Robin was the last one to get her cookies to the judging table, and even though Dylan had tried to downplay the whole romantic Valentine's Day backdrop, he thought it was pretty cool that she'd matched the theme with her red, heart-shaped cookies.

But now that the judges were conferring behind the table, Dylan knew he was going to be needed soon for the big announcement. Rodeo sweethearts Jack Burris and Audrey Hawkins were comparing notes with Sadie Chamberlin Grainger, who owned the Holiday House gift shop. Dylan expected Kendra Humphrey to be the toughest judge since she owned Kendra's Cupcakes and baked professionally. But DJ Traub, the owner of DJ's Deluxe restaurant in Bronco Heights, seemed to be having a tough time making up his mind.

While they were waiting for Mayor Smith to tabulate the scores, Dylan slipped one of Robin's cookies off the tray and took a nibble. His eyes nearly rolled into the back of his head as he moaned in ecstasy. His second bite was bigger and practically melted in his mouth. This had to be the best thing he'd ever eaten. Who knew Robin was just as good in the kitchen as she was on the ranch?

His eyes scanned the crowd looking for her and spotted her laughing at something her sister was saying. Man, Robin was beautiful. Dylan's family was right. He needed to ask her out. There was no way he could let a woman like her slip past him. He reached for a second cookie and was halfway finished with it when Mayor Smith waved a paper in front of him and said, "We have a winner."

The DJ announced that the results of the contest were in, and the crowd made their way under the enormous tent. Dylan was pleased to see how much more standing room there was outside the tent because so many of the cars on display had already been sold and moved off the lot.

Dylan had ditched the wireless mic a while ago when he'd accidentally asked an older customer if he was buying the convertible for his daughter and it turned out the man was actually there with his much, much younger girlfriend. Whoops.

Taking the handheld mic from the DJ, he said, "Ladies and gentlemen, thank you again for coming out to Bronco Motors and spending your Valentine's Day with us. I'm not as good with the big speeches as our mayor is, so I'll keep this short and sweet. Third place in our bake-off contest goes to Gary Peterson for his Aunt Hildy's Cheesecake."

There was a round of applause as the PE teacher came up on the stage to shake Dylan's hand and claim his prize.

Dylan looked down on his sheet and had to swallow a brief lump of disappointment before he could continue. "Second place goes to Robin Abernathy for her Heartmelters. And I will say that if you get a chance to try one, they're pretty incredible, folks."

More applause and Robin came on stage. Instead of shaking her hand, like he did with Gary, Dylan pulled her in for a tight hug. He inhaled the scent of vanilla lingering in her hair and the mayor tapped him on the back. "That's enough, son. She can't claim her gift certificate with you holding on to her like that."

Dylan, unsure of what had just come over him, quickly released her and cleared his throat. "And the winner of the first annual Bronco Motors Bake-Off and the recipient of a dinner for two at The Library, as well as a year's worth of free car service, is Gabrielle Hammond for her Love Is All Around cake roll."

He scanned the audience for Gabrielle, who he hadn't met yet. Mickie had assured him that the woman was new in town and qualified as a local. But she hadn't been at her station when Dylan had done the interviews with the news camera. Finally, he spotted a brunette making her way toward the stage before pausing to look to her right. She must've seen something or someone she wasn't expecting because instead of coming on stage, she made a beeline to her left and disappeared into the crowd.

That was weird.

When the applause died down, Dylan covered for the winner's absence and said, "We'll keep Gabrielle's trophy and prize in a safe place so that she can claim it later. Thank you everyone for coming out to Bronco Motors and Happy Valentine's Day!"

He turned over the microphone and grabbed another one of Robin's cookies as a reward for getting through that announcement. Then he swore to himself that he was going to stay away from public speaking events for the rest of his life.

The crowd slowly trickled away as the DJ concluded with the song from *Dirty Dancing* about having the time of one's life. If Dylan was being honest, the music playlist had been pretty good and kept people entertained while the baking was going on. Mickie was already directing the tent people and restaurant equipment suppliers to disassemble everything and get the lot back to normal. Contestants were passing out samples of their baked items and Dylan swooped in to take a plateful of Robin's cookies before everyone else descended on them.

Several people stopped him on his way to his office and he smiled and chatted briefly but didn't offer them a single cookie. When he set the plate down on his desk, he thought about locking the door to keep them safe inside. Then realized that he was being absolutely ridiculous. It wasn't like he couldn't ask Robin to make him another batch.

Where was Robin anyway? He needed to see her and make sure she wasn't disappointed at her second place finish. Maybe he could console her if she was. The thought of pulling her into his arms again had him striding out of his office only to find her carrying an arrangement of roses to the reception desk.

She looked up and saw him, her pretty face tilted as she gave him a suspicious look. "What are you doing hiding in here?"

He waved her over to him and when she got close enough, he grabbed her hand and pulled her inside his private office. "It's not that I'm hiding myself, so much as I'm hiding those."

He pointed to the plate of red hearts on his desk and Robin laughed, the musical sound making his chest feel lighter. He sat on the edge of the desk and held one of her hands as she stood before him.

"What did you put in these things?" He used his free hand to offer one to Robin. "They're amazing."

"Thanks." She took a bite and her face softened as she chewed lightly. "Wow. They actually came out better than I expected."

Desire coiled through him like a spring and he couldn't take his eyes off her mouth. "You make everything better than expected."

"Not when it comes to baking or cooking." Robin shook her head. "Although I did get lucky this time, even if Winona's prophecies don't always come true."

"What do you mean?" Dylan asked around another mouthful of cookie.

"She made a comment about me winning and losing. I might not have been first, but I also wasn't last. So I guess I neither won nor lost."

"If you ask me," Dylan said as he swallowed his last

bite, "I don't know how someone could have voted for anyone else."

Robin narrowed her eyes at him. "I guess I must be an acquired taste."

"I seem to have definitely acquired it," he said, then leaned his head to hers and captured her mouth in a kiss. This time, he wasn't testing the waters with a soft kiss goodbye or staking his claim to her in front of some young pup who had no business making eyes at her.

When Dylan hauled her against him, he was telling her in no uncertain terms that they should have done this a while ago. Robin's fingers slid around his neck and he lowered his hands to draw her hips closer so that she was standing between his open knees. When she opened her lips to moan, he took the opportunity to deepen the kiss with his tongue.

She responded just as eagerly and pressed her body against his.

But the phone ringing out at the reception area reminded him of where he was. He quickly pulled his head back, completely dazed.

Her eyelids were still half-closed, her pink lips swollen and her hands resting gently on his shoulders. Dylan growled before pulling her back for a second, longer kiss. His hands moved to her waist and his thumbs grazed the bare spot between her jeans and her sweater. Robin gasped as he slipped his hands higher, his palms on fire against her silky soft skin. She arched toward him, her hardened nipples grazing his chest, and all he could think about was touching her everywhere. And all at once.

His fingers were at the back clasp of her bra when Robin pulled back suddenly.

Had he done something wrong? Was he taking things

too quickly? When he was able to draw a ragged breath he asked, “Are you okay?”

She nodded slowly and whispered, “I’m fine, but I think I heard one of the salespeople out there.”

“Oh wow,” Dylan said, completely releasing her then dragging his fingers through his hair. “I’m so sorry, Robin. I don’t know what’s gotten into me. I totally forgot where we were. If you hadn’t stopped me, you probably would’ve ended up on my desk…” He shook his head to clear the steamy image and get himself under control. “Sorry. You deserve better than this.”

She placed her palms on either side of his face, forcing him to meet her eyes. “Listen, Dylan. It’s not your fault this happened. It’s the cookies.”

He blinked several times and then laughed, but she didn’t drop her hands.

“I know it sounds ludicrous, but they’re from this old family recipe, and legend has it that when measured with the right hands, it’s supposed to melt the hardest of hearts. I guess it meant literal hands for measuring and this was the first time I used mine. Or maybe it was when you touched the bag of sugar to pick it up. I don’t know, but the recipe has never worked for me before, yet today for some reason, it’s working.” She bit her adorable lower lip then added, “Maybe a little too well.”

His brain was still foggy with passion as he processed her sentences. But his mind couldn’t get past one. “You think I have a hard heart?”

“No,” she said, using her thumbs to trace along his jawline. “But do you have another explanation for this sudden need to kiss me no matter who’s outside that open door?”

He returned his hands to her waist. “It wasn’t exactly sudden. I’ve been thinking about it for a while. I’m a grown man, Robin, and I refuse to believe that some love potion is calling the shots here. I wanted to kiss you. I still want to kiss you."

Robin, who had yet to respond to his most forward advances, finally pulled his face closer to hers and then boldly said, "So what's stopping you?"

CHAPTER THIRTEEN

ROBIN DIDN'T KNOW how they got out of the dealership so quickly without anyone noticing them, but they had. Of course, by the time they'd left, most of the crowd was already gone anyway. Only the party rental company packing up their equipment and Dylan's staff, who he said were working on double commission for the event, remained.

Dylan pulled her through a secret door in the service garage, leading her to the back alley where he'd parked his truck. He gave her another deep kiss as soon as they were safely inside the cab and Robin was floating with excitement. This was what she had wanted that first day she'd walked into the dealership. It was the entire reason she'd entered the bake-off. She'd wanted Dylan to notice her.

When they walked into his empty apartment a few minutes later, she realized he was about to notice all of her. It wasn't that she was self-conscious of her body. She'd always been athletic and in relatively good shape. It was just that she'd never been fully naked with a man before when it wasn't completely dark outside.

The sun hadn't even set, yet Dylan had her pressed up against the door, his mouth trailing kisses along her throat and his hands making quick work of her sweater.

"Should we close the curtains?" she whispered.

"Probably," he said, but instead of walking across the small living room to do so, he continued to make love to her mouth as he expertly backed her down a hallway and into a bedroom. The vertical blinds on the window were closed, but still allowed for a decent amount of light. Robin once thought she'd be a trembling mass of nerves and anxiety if she'd ever successfully made it this far with Dylan, but her fingers didn't so much as quiver as she steadily undid each of the buttons on his shirt. When she pushed the fabric from his shoulders, she was rewarded with the sight she'd been fantasizing about for weeks. His tan skin was smooth and warm with a scattering of dark hair across his well-defined chest. The ridges of his ab muscles made a perfect pattern as his waist narrowed, the dark hair tapering to a thin trail along his belly button and lower into his pants.

She didn't get enough time to explore him, because as soon as his shirt hit the ground, he was reaching behind her to unclasp her bra. She returned the favor by undoing the fly of his pants. He clasped her hands. "Hold that thought. I have to go grab something."

She quickly shed her jeans and was trying to figure out the sexiest way to position herself on his bed when he returned with an unopened box of condoms. He froze as he seemed to be drinking in the sight of her. For the first time in Robin's life, her body actually hummed with the awareness of her own sexuality.

Leaning back on her elbows, wearing nothing but her panties and a smile, she relished the sound of his exhaled groan as he strode confidently toward her. As she looked up at him expectantly, he said, "You are the most beautiful woman I've ever seen."

And it was so easy to allow herself to believe that.

He set the condoms on the nightstand and finished unzipping his pants. When his arousal sprang free, Robin gulped. Was there anything about this man that wasn't perfect?

He eased himself onto the bed beside her and resumed

kissing her slowly, making his way from her lips down to her breasts. When he took one of her aching nipples into his mouth, Robin arched against him, moaning his name. She needed this. She needed him. And she told him so.

"You're sure," he asked.

"Now please," she replied, sliding her panties down her hips as he reached for a foil packet.

When he entered her, he whispered her name and it was the most erotic sound she'd ever heard. She lifted her knees to take him deeper inside and nearly shattered at the intense pleasure of his first full thrust.

She had been trying to play it cool, but there was no way she was going to last. It had been too long and she'd been wanting him so badly. She rocked her hips against him, and the friction was too much for her to bear. Robin threw back her head as waves of pleasure shuddered through her body.

Dylan held himself perfectly still as her inner muscles clenched around him. When her climax was over, she blinked up at him, her lips open as she gasped, her lungs only able to draw in small amounts of air at a time. She panted when she said, "I'm sorry I didn't wait for you."

He grasped her hips and deftly rolled them over so that Robin was on top. His hands slid up to her waist and, as she sat up straighter, he moaned. "There. Now you can make it up to me."

And she did just that.

DYLAN WATCHED THE woman sleeping beside him and wondered why last night had been so great. He'd slept with plenty of women in the past, but with Robin, it had been different. This time, he hadn't wanted to leave in the morning. Of course, he also didn't usually bring anyone back to his place so it wasn't as though he could make a swift exit. At least not politely.

But with Robin, there was no urgency to get away. No sense that she was going to wake up beside him and expect a ring on her finger. Listening to her breathe as she curled against him, he realized things felt different because this was the first time he'd slept with someone who understood his goals and shared his determination. Someone who was his friend first. Someone who would hopefully be his friend afterward.

When she stirred awake, he kissed her forehead softly.

His bedding was clean, but basic, and his apartment sparsely furnished since Dante had fully moved out. He could only imagine the plush decor of the bedroom where Robin normally slept. But since she still lived on her family's property and the house on his ranch was currently missing a roof, this had been the only place where he could bring her.

She stretched against him as she opened her eyes, taking in her surroundings. If she was disappointed by the inexpensive apartment, she was too polite to say so. Instead, she said, "Those sure were some cookies, huh?"

He laughed, causing her hand to move up and down as his chest vibrated. "They were good, but I'm telling you it wasn't the cookies."

She had to push the hair out of her eyes. "How do you know?"

"Because if they contained any traces of a love potion, it'd clearly be out of my system now. And yet, I still want to do this."

She yelped as he flipped her onto her back, but her giggles soon became moans as his head moved lower to her small, rounded breasts, and then lower still.

Thirty minutes later, he was in the shower and she came padding into the bathroom barefoot and wearing one of his University of Montana T's. "Dylan, I can't find your coffeepot."

"That's because I took it out to the ranch so the construction crew could use it."

"Well, that was thoughtful of you. But then what do you drink in the mornings?"

"I'm usually not home long enough." She hadn't asked, but she'd probably seen the meager supplies in his kitchen as well as the single recliner in the living room. He knew from experience that it would be best to explain now. "This apartment is just a place for me to sleep. A temporary home until the house on the ranch is habitable and I can finally move in."

Although, the truth was that when he said *temporary*, he left off the part where it had been that way for the past several years. But even when he and Dante had signed the original lease, Dylan had known he would end up in a bigger place eventually. He just needed to live somewhere cheap enough while he was saving his money. Once the ranch was done, it still might not be quite as extravagant as Robin was already used to, but it would be his.

"So no coffee. No breakfast." Robin leaned against the bathroom counter. "What do you usually offer the morning after...you know?"

"I guess we're about to find out." He ducked his head back under the water to rinse the shampoo. When he shut off the faucet, he said, "We could go grab some breakfast. The Gemstone Diner has the best hashbrowns in town."

"Dylan, we can't go out in public for a sit-down breakfast the morning after Valentine's Day with me wearing the same clothes I had on yesterday." Robin had left her truck parked back at the dealership and was completely at his mercy. "Everyone will know."

"Know what?" He wiggled his eyebrows. She threw his

towel at him but he easily caught it. "Just wear something of mine. I might have some smaller sweatpants."

"Yeah, everything you own that would fit me has some sort of college or sports logo on it. Pretty sure that would be a dead giveaway, as well."

"Keep staring at me like that and you won't be wearing anything soon," he said as he dried off.

This time she was the one who wiggled her eyebrows. But she didn't take him up on either of his invitations. "I should probably get home and take a shower."

"You took one last night," he reminded her.

"I know and now I smell like..." She picked up the bottle of shower gel sitting on the edge of his tub and read, "'Endurance, Speed and Cedarwood.' Plus, I need to pick up my truck, which is parked right in front of Bronco Motors with the Bonnie B logo right there on the door."

Dylan almost suggested that people would likely think that the truck was getting dropped off for service. But she was already shooting down every idea he could come up with to get her to hang out longer. Old insecurities he thought he'd overcome long ago threatened to surface again. No. He wasn't going to compare Robin to his ex.

The Abernathys were an established and well-respected family in the community and Robin had more than her own reputation to consider. It was one thing for the gossips to think they were dating. It was another to think that this was... Dylan wasn't exactly sure what this was between them.

"So then how about we hit a drive-through for some coffee and a breakfast sandwich and then go grab your truck?"

Robin nodded. "That works. What time do you plan to be at Broken Road Ranch today?"

"Probably not until the afternoon. I'm going to be buried processing registration tags all morning and running inventory reports. Trust me, it's just as boring as it sounds, but it also means that yesterday's event was a major success."

"Good," she said then rose on her tiptoes to kiss his cheek. "Because people will probably expect another bake-off next year."

"It'll be worth it if you make more of those Heartmelters for me."

"Sadly, I'm retiring my red apron after last night." Robin shook her head. "No more contests for me. They're too stressful."

"Then I'm retiring my microphone duties for the same reason. You'll still make me the cookies, though, right? Like a custom order?"

"I'm not committing to anything until I get some coffee," she said as she walked out of the bathroom and retreated down the hall.

DYLAN KISSED HER goodbye when he dropped her off at her truck and they made plans to meet at his ranch that afternoon. The demo would be done by then and they needed to bring the cows back to the barn before the weather decided to shift gears and dump a few more inches of snow.

When he walked into his office, he whistled at the sales numbers from the previous day, which Mickie had been keeping a tally of on a whiteboard in the break room. He was even more thrilled to see that there were still a few cookies on the plate he'd left on his desk.

As predicted, he was up to his elbows in paperwork and sent Robin a text telling her he might be a little late meeting her at the ranch. She responded that she already had Buttermilk and Maze Runner loaded in the trailer and had enlisted her brother Theo to go with her.

Still, Dylan didn't like the fact that it was yet another

job on his property that he wasn't doing himself. Unfortunately, the dealership was the only thing currently keeping the ranch afloat and his attention was also needed there.

It also didn't sit well with him that he was relying on Robin more than he should. What happened if she decided that she was done with this little project of hers? What happened when she was done with him? After the passion-filled night they'd just shared, Dylan wasn't ready to contemplate that. He fired off a text thanking her then added, Dinner tonight?

She didn't respond for a while and he told himself it was because she was driving. Then he told himself it was because the reception might not be the best on the ranch. Although, it had always been decent before. By four o'clock, he'd eaten way too many cookies and had been staring at way too many numbers. He grabbed his coat and headed toward the door. "I'm taking off, Mickie. I'll see you tomorrow."

His office manager was on the phone and waved him off. By the time he got to the ranch, he was amazed to see that the dumpster full of rotted roof shingles had been hauled away and there was a fresh layer of new ones on the roof. Dylan was also relieved to see the cows in the pasture adjacent to the barn and Robin and Theo walking their horses toward the trailer.

"Dylan?" Robin lifted her brows in surprise, but smiled. "I thought you were stuck at the office."

"How's it going, Theo?" he said to her brother.

Theo had a podcast talking about everything ranching, but Dylan was usually too busy listening to sports radio to catch many of the episodes. He should probably start making more of an effort. He might learn something.

"Hey, man. I heard Trail Boss here came in second at the bake-off."

"She did. I finished off the rest of the cookies she made before noon."

"Never thought I'd see the day." Theo shook his head then took Maze Runner's reins from his sister's hand and continued on to the trailer. That was an odd response.

Robin walked toward Dylan. "Is something wrong?"

"I texted and you didn't respond."

She patted her back pockets. "I must've left my phone in the truck. Did you need something?"

"Dinner. I was hungry and thought you might be, too."

"I could use a bite," Theo said from inside the trailer. Apparently the window had been open.

Dylan hadn't meant to include her brother, but he certainly owed the guy for helping herd cattle today. "You guys want to do Pastabilities?"

"I was kidding, man," Theo said through the open window. "I would only be a third wheel. And besides, I need to get the horses back. Just give Robin a ride home, okay?"

"Sure," Dylan said.

Robin raised her hand. "I can answer for myself, you guys." Then she asked Dylan, "Can you give me a ride home?"

Dylan did give her a ride home, but not until after midnight. They'd had dinner and then stopped by his apartment again to pick up where they'd left off that morning. He wanted Robin to sleep over again, but Dylan knew it wouldn't be a good look for him to drive her back to the Bonnie B when the entire ranch was awake and everyone was starting their work shifts.

And that's how it went for the next couple of days. They'd meet in the afternoons at the ranch before going to grab dinner and end the night back at his place. The only difference was she wouldn't leave until morning—in her own truck—when Dylan left for the dealership.

It was almost as though they were in a…relationship.

CHAPTER FOURTEEN

"WHY COULDN'T ROBIN make it?" Dylan's mom asked on Sunday evening as the Sanchez family gathered around the dining room at Sofia and Boone's house. His parents' kitchen remodel had finally been completed, but they'd already donated their old dining room table only to find out that the new one couldn't be delivered until tomorrow. Besides, they'd had dinner at Dylan's ranch last week and suddenly all the siblings wanted to take a turn hosting.

"I couldn't very well invite her to dinner at someone else's house," Dylan said.

There was a collective chorus of boos and at least two people muttered, "Give me a break."

His brother-in-law Boone said, "Don't be ridiculous. You know you can invite anyone you want over here."

Dylan tried to change the subject and asked Boone how his brother Shep was doing after their mom told everyone at the bake-off that her son was still single.

"He's probably feeling the exact same way you were at the mayor's anniversary party. You know, when you were getting grumpy about being the only single Sanchez at the table?"

"I wasn't grumpy." Dylan took a scoop of roasted red potatoes. "I was annoyed that I didn't have any elbow room."

"And do you have plenty of elbow room in your apartment when Robin stays the night?" Camilla asked.

He gave his sister a look of warning as he subtly jerked his chin toward their parents.

"Mom and Dad already know," Dante said, not very helpfully.

Their mom took a large gulp of wine then added, "So do all my clients who come into the salon. I'm not sure which topic is gossiped about more—Penny Smith's missing necklace or you and Robin Abernathy."

"What do you expect, Dylan?" Felix said. "How many people have a blue truck with the Bonnie B logo stenciled on the side that they park in front of your apartment?"

"At least twelve since her family just bought a few from Bronco Motors to add to their fleet. How do they know that truck doesn't belong to one of the ranch foremen?"

"Does it?" The question came from his brother-in-law Jordan.

"You know it doesn't," Dylan muttered. Then he cleared his throat. "I don't remember you guys talking about Eloise's car being parked in the same spot back when she and Dante started dating."

Eloise passed him the bowl of salad. "Actually, I'm pretty sure everyone in town did."

"Not that I was judging," Dylan said quickly. "I saw no problem with where you parked."

"I'd be careful if I were you, Dylan," Shari said. "Don't forget that Eloise and I are the ones deciding which one of our bridesmaids you're going to be walking down the aisle with."

Dylan's gut dropped.

"Have I told you about Drunk Patty, my roommate from boarding school?" Eloise asked a bit too sweetly.

"I thought Robin was one of your bridesmaids," Dylan's tone was almost accusatory. "Why can't I walk with her?"

And that's when everyone at the table started laughing. Camilla pointed her finger. "See, I knew it."

"Knew what?"

"That things were getting serious between you and Robin."

"No, they're not." Dylan helped himself to two pieces of chicken. "As far as I know, it's a casual relationship."

"Would Robin define it as casual?" his mother asked.

"I don't know because we haven't discussed it. I don't even think we've used the word *relationship* at this point."

"Don't you think you should ask her how she feels?" Dante asked.

"Maybe. Probably." Then Dylan shook his head at his brother. "Don't give me that look like you're some sort of expert at love. You met Eloise a few months before I met Robin."

"You know what you need?" Sofia tried to pass the salad back to him since he hadn't put any on his plate the first time around. "A grand gesture."

"Yes!" Camilla clapped her hands. "Something big that shows Robin exactly how you feel."

"Last time I let you guys plan a grand gesture for me, I ended up with over two hundred people and a news crew at my dealership."

"And generated a whole lot of sales from it." Jordan took the salad bowl from him. "At least that's what Mickie told her sister when she stopped by my office."

"It's not going to happen," Dylan said firmly to his family. There was no way he was going to put his heart out there only to get rejected again. Especially not publicly.

"If that's the case," his father said, chiming in for the first time, "if it *really* is only a casual relationship, then you should probably end it now before someone starts falling in love."

His father's words felt like a swift kick in the stomach. But with everyone voicing their disagreement, Dylan's head throbbed as though it had also been kicked.

"That's the worst advice I've ever heard, Dad," Camilla said, and Sofia nodded emphatically. But Dylan had completely lost his appetite and was tuning out the conversation.

"Excuse me, I'll be right back," he said to nobody in particular and stood to use the restroom.

But he kept on walking right out the front door.

Because he didn't want them to worry about him—or bug him—Dylan sent a text in the family group chat saying something came up and he'd talk to them tomorrow. Then he drove home with his dad's words echoing in his brain. Maybe his father was right. Dylan didn't want to be the one who fell in love only to have Robin end things. And the way things were going now, he was certainly at risk of doing exactly that.

Robin had once suggested that Dylan didn't put his foot down very often. But when it came to his heart, he had to draw a line somewhere. The longer he let things go on, the worse it was going to get.

He needed to ask her if he stood a chance.

ROBIN TRIED NOT to think about the fact that she had spent nearly every day with Dylan for the past two weeks. And yet, when Sunday rolled around, he hadn't said a word about bringing her with him to his family's weekly dinner. The only reason she'd dined with them last week was because they'd shown up on the ranch unannounced.

Was this Dylan's way of letting her know that things weren't serious between them? She could help him on his ranch. She could split the appetizer sampler platter with him at Doug's bar as she'd done last night. She could sleep in his bed. But she wasn't good enough to take home to his family.

It stung.

Yet, she would give him whatever space he needed. They hadn't defined their relationship, so if she'd been misreading the situation and expecting something he wasn't ready to give, then she only had herself to blame. The man had a reputation for a reason. He'd never pretended to be anything else.

Robin decided to distract herself by catching up on some emails and supply orders she needed to make. Up until now, she'd been outsourcing production of her braces and magnetic blankets to a manufacturing company in Kalispell. But maybe she should start looking into investing in a factory for Rein Rejuvenation here in Bronco.

When her phone rang at nine o'clock and she saw Dylan's name on the screen, she sighed a breath of relief—he hadn't forgotten about her—and then steeled her jaw in annoyance at the thought that he better not expect her to come running over now that he was available. She waited until the fourth ring to answer.

"Hey, Robin. How are you?"

This wasn't a good sign. He never began calls that way. At least not with her. Usually, he didn't waste time and launched straight into a familiar topic. "I'm fine. How are you?"

"I'm okay. I think." Yep, something was wrong. She was accustomed to him being way more chatty.

Robin's own nerves were already raw. Perhaps taking control of the conversation would help ground her. "Something on your mind, Dylan?"

"Actually, a lot is. I don't know where to start."

"This might be a first," Robin said, cringing at the cattiness in her tone. But sometimes you had to take the bull by the horns before it could knock you to the ground. "Dylan Sanchez, the smooth-talking salesman who always knows just what to say, suddenly doesn't know where to start."

"That's fair, I guess," he replied. "I wasn't even sure I could make this phone call, but I knew it would be worse if I didn't."

She clenched the phone harder in her hand and bit her trembling lip. This was it. He was about to break her heart. If there was any time to take control of a situation, this was it. She'd save them both the trouble.

"Look, Dylan, I think we both know that we were never meant to be together long term. You needed someone to help you on your ranch and I needed a project. It was fun while it lasted. Don't worry about it."

"Wow," was all he said before a long, excruciating pause. She could hear him take a ragged breath, which only made her heart ache more. Was he relieved that she'd made it so easy? He finally continued, "You seem to be totally fine with this."

"How else should I be?" she countered. It wasn't exactly like she had a choice. If the man wanted to call things off with her, she couldn't very well cry and beg him to stay. Not when she knew that deep down, he didn't want her. "Listen, I'm in the middle of researching some stuff for work so if we're good here, I need to wrap this up."

Her voice shook with the last two words because she also needed to wrap herself up in a giant blanket and have a good cry.

"Um, yeah. I guess we're good, then. Take care, Rob—"

"You, too," she cut him off, knowing she couldn't bear to hear her name on his lips. "Bye."

Robin disconnected the phone, ran a hot bath and then soaked all night in her tears.

She'd barely slept and was especially cranky the following morning when she went out to the stables and saw her brother Jace pointing out the horses to his son, Frankie. Her brother must have the day off from working at the fire station and wanted to let Tamara sleep in.

With everyone around her getting married and having babies, Robin felt as though she was falling behind and, at this rate, would never catch up. She almost went down the opposite row of stables to avoid the reminder that she was still alone. But at the last minute she decided she could use a happy distraction.

"There's my favorite seven-month-old," she cooed to her nephew as she approached.

"What's wrong with your eyes?" Jace shifted his baby to his other hip, farther away from her. "Do you have an infection or something?"

Robin did feel as though she was squinting more this morning. "Not that I know of. Why?"

"They're all red and swollen, like you're having an allergic reaction."

She sighed. "Yeah, it's called an allergic reaction to love."

"Wait." Jace's face filled with concern. "You were crying? But the Trail Boss never cries."

"Well, I guess there's a first time for everything."

"Was it Dylan?" Jace frowned. "Do I need to go have a talk with him?"

Robin rarely gave her brothers the opportunity to be protective over her since she usually handled everything herself. But it made her feel better to know that her family had her back.

Robin forced a smile but shook her head. "Remember that time when I was about twelve or so and we were out riding and came across that wild mustang with the injured hoof?"

"Yeah, I remember it took you about two hours to get it to trust you enough to get close. And then another three to slowly walk it back to the stables. You made that soft boot for it out of your favorite sweatshirt and nursed it back to health. I'm pretty sure that was when you first got the idea that you could make custom therapeutic devices for horses."

"It was. But it was also the first time I learned that just because I put enough energy into something and try to tame it, some animals are just meant to be free."

Frankie made a gurgling sound and Jace looked at his son. "Yeah, I'm confused, too, buddy. But I think Dylan is supposed to be the wild mustang in this analogy."

Robin would have rolled her eyes at her brother, but her lids were too swollen from crying to make it effective. "More than anything, I'm mad at myself for believing things with him could have ended any other way."

Jace's expression became more serious. "Who says it ended?"

"I did. Last night when he called me, I could tell in his voice that something was wrong. So I cut my losses."

"That might've been a bit premature, sis. I seriously doubt you and Dylan are done. There's too much heat between the two of you."

"What are you talking about?"

"More like what everyone in town is talking about. I only saw you guys together once at the bake-off."

"We weren't together. He was busy networking and selling cars."

"And you were too busy making those cookies that you couldn't see the way he rarely took his eyes off you all afternoon."

A seed of hope took root in her chest, but she wasn't about to let it blossom. "No, Dylan looks that way at everyone."

"Not at Bethany McCreery or that Gabrielle woman who's new to town. And definitely not at Mr. Brandt."

She didn't want to tell her brother that Dylan's interest was likely only due to the Heartmelters and the love potion effect they'd had on him. Although, he hadn't eaten any cookies until *after* the contest… Nope. Robin wasn't going to even consider it.

"Come on, Jace. You know as well as I do that the Sanchez brothers have a reputation for their charm and their flirtatious smiles."

"And now two of them are about to get married," Jace said. "So maybe their reputations should have been that they just hadn't found the right women yet."

"When has any man ever thought of me as the right woman?" Robin asked. "I've always been one of the guys."

"Or have you always acted like one of the guys just to fit in? You live on a ranch surrounded by cowboys. The men who want to earn their paychecks know better than to look at you the way Dylan Sanchez does."

Robin tried not to be swayed by Jace's assessment. She also tried not to be swayed by Brad's group text to her and Dylan later that morning about the height of the bathroom tiles. She wasn't going to respond because the Broken Road Ranch was no longer her concern. If she was going to survive this breakup, then she needed a clean break. She wasn't going to so much as think about the man.

And she didn't. Until Eloise stopped by the Bonnie B later in the week to show Robin some preliminary designs for Rein Rejuvenation's European marketing campaign.

Without any prompting by Robin, her friend blurted out, "So Dylan was a mess at the Sanchez family dinner last Sunday."

"Maybe his mind was preoccupied with replenishing

the stock of vehicles that seem to be flying off his lot since the bake-off." Not that Robin had purposely driven by the dealership in the hopes of catching a glimpse of him. Because that would've been stalkerish. Although, on Tuesday, she'd had an unexpected craving for a double bacon cheeseburger from Bronco Burgers and had inadvertently driven past there. But that was by accident and she went completely out of her way to take a different route home.

"He didn't even make it through dinner, Robin. He took off during the middle of the meal and left a plate full of food behind. And you know that guy never leaves food behind. Oh, and did I mention that he left right after I threatened to have him walk down the aisle at my wedding with my boarding school roommate Drunk Patty?"

"I met your former roommate in Rust Creek Falls when we were trying on bridesmaid dresses. She was lovely and very sober. Why would Dylan leave over that?"

"Because he wants *you*, Robin."

"That's not the impression he gave me on Sunday night when he called to end things."

Eloise gasped. "Oh no. I'm afraid his dad made a suggestion that evening and Dylan misinterpreted it. Did he really call to end things?"

"Well, he called. I was the one who had to end it."

"Just so I'm clear, he didn't actually break up with you?" Eloise asked. "Or tell you that he didn't want to see you anymore?"

"Not exactly." Robin flipped through the pages of Eloise's portfolio, refusing to glance up and risk having her friend give her any sort of sign of false hope. "But if he wants to see me, he knows where to find me. Besides, I already made the first move by going out of my comfort zone and entering that bake-off contest. It's his turn now."

"Good to know," Eloise said, then flipped the portfolio around so it was right side up and started talking about the ad images.

THE FACT THAT Robin had spoken those soul-crushing words so easily, so casually, only made Dylan feel more miserable. Before he could find the right words to ask her where they stood, she'd acted as though she were doing them both a favor. Proving that she hadn't seen their relationship as anything more than a good time.

And that had been what hurt the most.

Dylan looked up from the stack of hay bales he was hauling into the barn and saw his father's mail truck pulling into his driveway. He glanced down at his watch as his dad walked over. "Running a little late on your route today, huh, Dad?"

Normally, Aaron Sanchez delivered to this side of town in the morning and Dylan didn't get a chance to see him since he was only at the ranch later in the afternoons.

"I decided to switch things up today." His dad scanned the area where the construction crew was parked. "I haven't seen Robin's truck out here the past few mornings and thought I'd swing by and see if something happened."

"Yeah, something happened, Dad. I did what you said and called her to have the talk and...well, we broke up." No need to tell his father that Dylan hadn't been the one who'd officially said the words.

His dad smacked himself in the forehead and muttered a string of curses in Spanish. Then switched back to English as though his son hadn't been able to understand the bad words. "You were supposed to do the *opposite* of that, Dylan."

Dylan's eyebrows slammed together. "So you *didn't* want me to take your advice?"

"Of course not. Why would I want you to break up with Robin? She's the best thing that ever happened to you."

Closing his eyes, Dylan tried to take a steadying breath. "Then why would you tell me to call things off before someone got their heart broken?"

"Because, son, the thought of losing Robin was supposed to force you to make the right decision. It was reverse psychology."

Dylan groaned. "Then why didn't you just tell me how much my life would suck without her?"

It had only been a few days since he'd last spoken to Robin and he'd hated every single one of them. He missed her smile. He missed her bossiness. He missed the way she fit so perfectly tucked up against his side. He couldn't stop thinking of her. Or of ways to convince her to give him another chance.

"Look, Dylan. You've always been the type of person who wants more for himself. You were like that when you played T-ball, yet insisted on being the team pitcher. You were like that during high school when you bought that lifted 4x4 that looked cool but had a salvaged title and barely ran. You were certainly like that well before you ever met what's-her-name in college."

Dylan froze. He'd never told anyone in his family about his ex-girlfriend. "How did you know about Maribel?"

"Well, I didn't know for sure until right this minute. All I knew was that you were home for a visit, and I was on the side of the house trying to find a basketball Dante had overshot when a young gal pulled up to the house in a sleek, black convertible with a University of Montana bumper sticker."

He remembered that car well. It was flashy and expensive, just like its owner. It represented everything Dylan had thought he wanted in life.

"Back then," his dad continued, "it was no big deal for you kids to invite friends over for dinner. But that girl stared at our house for several long moments—as if trying to decide whether or not she should come inside—before finally driving away."

Dylan shoved his hands in his pockets and rocked back on his heels. He'd never been ashamed of his parents' modest home, but he was ashamed that he'd almost subjected his family to such a horrible snob.

"I'd been planning on introducing her to you guys that day. But she never showed." What he didn't tell his dad was that he returned that night to his dorm to find a letter under his door.

Maribel had written that she tried, but she just couldn't be with someone who came from such a different background. She needed to be with a guy who was "going places and could afford the type of lifestyle" she expected. Dylan had been devastated. But looking back, it was nothing compared to how his world had come crashing down when Robin told him it was fun while it lasted.

"I noticed a shift in your attitude right after that girl drove away," his dad said. "You switched majors from sports medicine to business and all of sudden, every time you came home for a visit, all you could talk about was being successful and making money."

Being dumped like that had been the driving force behind Dylan's desire to become whatever it was Maribel thought he couldn't be. He was proud of his roots and proud of being from Bronco, and he'd be damned if he was going to let some spoiled daddy's girl tell him he couldn't achieve financial success.

As if reading his mind, his father clapped a hand on his shoulder and said, "Surely, you've learned by now that success isn't measured by wealth or even skill. It's measured by happiness."

"Maybe that's the kind of advice you should give me next time, Dad, instead of the reverse psychology." Dylan leaned into his father's one-arm hug. "Not that I'm blaming you. Obviously, it was my pride that caused me to let the happiest thing in my life slip away because I was too afraid of taking a chance."

"You didn't think Robin would be like your ex, did you?" His dad made a tsking sound. "I mean, if the girl didn't take off running when she saw the condition of this place, then she clearly wanted to be with you because of who you are and not what you own. At least she *did* before you blew it."

"Thanks for the pep talk." Dylan didn't bother hiding his sarcasm. "Now, do you have any *helpful* words of wisdom for how I should win her back?"

Aaron Sanchez smiled, his knowing grin revealing the same dimples Dylan had inherited. "It just so happens that your mom and your sisters have an idea for a grand gesture."

CHAPTER FIFTEEN

THE LAST THING Robin wanted to do was attend the Heritage Rodeo at the Bronco Convention Center the last week of February. But Eloise had convinced her that with rodeo superstar Geoff Burris making his last appearance in the States before leaving for Europe with his fiancée, Stephanie Brandt, it would be a great opportunity for Rein Rejuvenation to get some exposure as a sponsor before launching its overseas ad campaign.

"I still don't know why I need to be here in person, though," Robin grumbled as she, Eloise and Stacy found their seats in the stands.

Stacy fluffed Robin's hair. "Because when they announce your company as a sponsor, it'd be nice for them to have a face to associate with the brand."

"I don't want to be on camera, though, Eloise," Robin told her friend. "You told the rodeo producers that, right?"

Except Eloise was talking to Dr. and Mrs. Burris, who were here to cheer on their sons, Geoff, Jack and Ross, who were all participating tonight.

"Here, put on some of my lipstick." Stacy already had the tube inches from Robin's face. Unless she wanted to risk looking like one of the rodeo clowns, she better hold still.

"I bet you're going to miss Geoff and Stephanie when they go to Europe," someone said to the Burrises from the row behind them. It was Deborah Dalton.

"We will," Jeanne Burris replied. "We're used to the kids doing so much traveling already on the rodeo circuit, but that doesn't make it any easier when they're gone. We're just lucky that Ross was able to be home in time for the event."

"Now tell me, is Ross still single?" Mrs. Dalton asked, and when Mrs. Burris nodded, she continued, "Because you know my Shep still hasn't settled down yet, either. I'd just really love for him to find a nice girl..."

"Maybe we should find somewhere else to sit," Robin whispered to her sister.

Stacy's face paled. "We can't. I mean, why would you want to do that?"

"Because we're both single and if you haven't noticed, Mrs. Dalton is right behind us and eager to play matchmaker."

The music stopped long enough for the announcer to welcome everyone, and Robin tried not to fidget in her seat as she remembered the last time she was in this building. She'd been convincing Birdsey Jones that she and Dylan were a couple so that he wouldn't bid on the bull Dylan wanted. Or rather the bull Robin had wanted for him. She almost reached for her phone to text Dylan and ask him if the sire had been delivered as scheduled.

In fact, this past week, she'd found herself doing the same thing. Thinking about something that needed to be done on Broken Road Ranch and then stopping herself before she reached out to him to ask. Although, when she ran into Manuel out at the Bonnie B, she'd asked the foreman if his nephew had ever met with Dylan. She'd found out that he had and, starting next week, Dylan would have someone else working with him out at the ranch and wouldn't need her help.

A familiar empty ache settled in her chest and she had

to remind herself to stop thinking of him and focus on the rodeo.

The barrel racing was first, which Robin always enjoyed since it had also been her specialty when she'd competed. Right after the last contestant rode out, her brother Theo walked up the steps past their aisle and winked at Stacy, who was sitting on the end.

"Why did Theo just wink at you?" Robin asked.

"I don't think it was at me. Maybe it was someone behind us. Hey, do you mind if we switch seats so I can talk to Eloise about something real quick?"

Robin didn't see why Stacy couldn't just lean forward and talk around her, but she stood. "Sure. I'm going to go get a drink anyway."

Stacy grabbed her arm and pulled her back down. "You can't leave yet."

"Why not? The barrel racing is over, and the breakaway roping won't start for a few more minutes."

"Because..." Stacy's eyes seemed to be searching for something in the distance. When the lights in the arena dimmed, she said, "Because it'll be too dark for you to see. Just wait until they announce...whatever they're going to announce."

Except it wasn't an announcement. The jumbotron suddenly lit up with the words "Bronco Motors Car Deals for Cowboys."

Great, now Robin was going to have to sit here and watch a commercial for Dylan's dealership because she couldn't very well get up to leave and risk having people think she was affected by the reminder of him.

Which she was. Her throat was already constricting.

When a spotlight shined into the arena entrance, though, something told her it was going to be much worse than a commercial. Suddenly, she saw Dylan himself and he was decked out in Western garb—including the hat she'd picked out for him at the livestock auction—and riding in a horse.

Robin's jaw fell open and she nearly slid out of her seat. What in the world was the man doing? He hated being the center of attention and yet here he was on a ridiculously big jumbotron in front of thousands of people doing some rendition of the cheesy car salesman commercial.

"You might've heard of Bronco Motors, home of the famous Valentine's Day Bake-Off." His smooth voice came through the speakers. "That's right, ladies and gentlemen, Bronco Motors is a one-stop shop for finding quality cars and quality baked goods."

"Hurry, let me talk to Eloise," Stacy whispered, trying to switch places again, but Robin was glued to her seat, her eyes in wide-open shock as she watched the live train wreck of a commercial taking place in front of her.

Had he lost a bet? She tried to tell herself that she shouldn't care. But as painful as it was to see him so soon after their break-up, it was even more heartwrenching to see someone she still cared about make a complete fool out of himself.

"We've got great deals every day of the week," he continued. "But tonight's special offer is a once-in-a-lifetime opportunity for just one lucky recipient in the stands."

Several spotlights weaved throughout the crowd as though searching for a person to land on. When the drumroll stopped, the light was directly over their area and Stacy's face was on the jumbotron screen.

Her sister squeaked and then pointed at Robin and yelled, "Not me. Her."

The camera pivoted to Robin and suddenly, it was her face with all of its slack-jawed confusion filling the screen.

"Smile." Eloise elbowed her as the crowd cheered. "Try to look natural."

Natural? Robin was naturally mortified. And possibly paralyzed with uncertainty. Yet, Dylan kept speaking. "Robin, you once made me an offer that you'd teach me something if I was willing to learn. Well, you held your end of the bargain and these past weeks I learned that I could actually feel the kind of love that I feel when I'm with you."

Nope, she wasn't paralyzed. Every nerve ending inside her body began tingling with anticipation as the audience broke out into oohs and awws when Dylan dismounted… was that Buttermilk? That was her horse. From the Bonnie B. That meant her family…

"Were you in on this?" Robin said as her head whipped to Stacy, only to find her sister standing with both their and Dylan's family a few steps behind her.

Eloise nudged her again and Robin turned back around in time to see Dylan coming up the steps toward her. She alternated between confusion and euphoria and the earlier tingling sensation was now generating enough warmth from inside her core that she was sure the radiating glow surrounding her was coming from inside her body and not the spotlight still shining on her. "It was you, and not your cookies, that melted this icy heart of mine, and I will never be the same. I love you, Robin Abernathy, and now I'm the one with a once-in-a-lifetime offer to make you."

Robin, needing to regain some sense of control, stood up, but her knees nearly gave out. Was this really happening?

When he was directly in front of her, she finally found her voice and asked, "What kind of offer? Because I already have a car."

"The kind of offer that involves this…" Dylan reached into his front shirt pocket and dropped down to one knee.

The crowd roared and nearly drowned out his voice as he opened a jewelry box that displayed a…key.

"Since we do so well picking out stuff together, I wanted to wait until you said yes before we go ring shopping. But this is for the front door at the Broken Road Ranch and represents all of my dreams that I want to keep sharing with you. I know you have plenty more to teach me and if you're willing, Robin, I'm ready to keep learning. What you see is what you get with me, but I will always try my best to be a man worthy of you. That is, if *you* want me. I can be pretty stubborn sometimes. I can—"

Robin put a finger on his lips. "Save the sales pitch and just kiss me."

The applause was nearly deafening when he stood and she flung herself into his arms, his mouth quickly claiming hers. When he pulled away, he held her face in his hands. "I'm sorry for not believing in you. For not believing in us. I was trying to save myself from getting my heart broken only to find out that it would hurt worse to not have you in my life."

Robin thought her chest was going to explode with how much love she felt for this man who hated making a scene and was currently embracing her on the biggest televised screen in Bronco.

"I'm sorry for jumping to conclusions and not sharing my feelings with you from the beginning," she told him. "I'd also say I'm sorry for pushing myself into your life by signing up for a baking contest I had no business entering and no shot of winning. But if I hadn't walked into your dealership that day, I'd have found some other way to get you to notice me."

"Oh, I'd have noticed you… Wait…" He paused, a crease forming between his brows. "You mean you don't bake?"

Robin shook her head, not the least bit apologetic.

"Nope. Does that mean you want to renegotiate your original offer?"

"Not a chance." He smiled and just like the first time Robin laid eyes on those dimples, she was lost.

"I love you, Dylan Sanchez, and I accept your offer for this once-in-a-lifetime opportunity."

"Good because while I was wasting a whole week without you, Brad was finishing our future master bathroom, and all I could think of was getting you out to the ranch so we could christen that new tub—"

Robin slapped her hand over his lapel and threw back her head in laughter. "Your mic is still on, cowboy."

"Then that's our cue to get out of here and go home." He kissed her again and then scooped her up into his arms.

Home. Robin couldn't wait to continue building theirs together.

* * * * *

Don't miss the stories in this mini series!

MONTANA MAVERICKS: THE ANNIVERSARY GIFT

Welcome to Big Sky Country, home of the Montana Mavericks! Where free-spirited men and women discover love on the range.

Sweet-Talkin' Maverick
CHRISTY JEFFRIES
January 2024

Maverick's Secret Daughter
CATHERINE MANN
February 2024

The Maverick's Marriage Deal
KAYLIE NEWELL
March 2024

MILLS & BOON

The Cowboy's Second Chance

Cheryl Harper

MILLS & BOON

Cheryl Harper discovered her love for books and words as a little girl, thanks to a mother who made countless library trips and an introduction to Laura Ingalls Wilder's Little House books. Whether the stories she reads are set in the prairie, the American West, Regency England or earth a hundred years in the future, Cheryl enjoys strong characters who make her laugh. Now Cheryl spends her days searching for the right words while she stares out the window and her dog, Jack, snoozes beside her. And she considers herself very lucky to do so.

For more information about Cheryl's books, visit her online at cherylharperbooks.com or follow her on Twitter, @cherylharperbks.

Dear Reader,

Starting over can be scary, can't it? When I write, I sometimes begin in the wrong place, too early or too late in the characters' stories. Only extensive rewriting powered by Diet Coke can fix this problem! Life presents us all with occasional blank pages—career changes, new relationships, empty nests—that require some hard work as we find our way, but they're also full of possibility.

In *The Cowboy's Second Chance*, Travis Armstrong and Dr. Keena Murphy are both caught in this mix of fear and anticipation of big change. Travis has retired from the army and returned to Prospect to fulfill his purpose in the Armstrong family—fostering teens who need a safe space as much as he did as a boy. Keena's in town to help a friend, but while she's there, she finds that her career and the life she's built around it could be so much bigger. Travis and Keena learn that leaping into their new beginnings, even if they're nervous at first, leads to a bigger and better story together.

I've enjoyed getting to know the Armstrongs and their neighbours. Thank you for joining me in Prospect. To find out more about my books and what's coming next, visit me at cherylharperbooks.com.

Cheryl

CHAPTER ONE

DR. KEENA MURPHY sat on the metal bench bisecting the long, narrow locker room and inhaled slowly. She held that breath for an exact count of ten. Tap by tap, one trembling finger at a time on her knees, she counted down. Exhaling lowered her racing pulse.

The paper gown covering her blue scrubs crinkled with each small movement. Whatever industrial cleaner the hospital's janitorial crew used on the floor smelled so familiar. Muffled chaos in Denver Medical Center's Emergency Department registered faintly, so Keena strained to differentiate the voices of her coworkers, the doctors and nurses still out on the floor.

Her sticky, dry mouth was a reminder that her twelve-hour shift had not included any time for food or water.

The doctor in her knew that was a terrible way to care for herself, even as she also understood how it continued to happen.

She'd met every single demand of the job tonight, and that was all that mattered.

"What a day." Angie Washington yanked the surgical cap off her head and balled it up in the gown she had crumpled in one hand. "You okay, Dr. Murphy? You don't look so good. Cheeks are pale." The bench jolted as she dropped down next to Keena and wrapped her fingers around Keena's wrist to take her pulse. "Bet you were hoping for a nice, quiet shift tonight, lots of time to make your goodbyes. That's the kind of shift *I* wanted tonight. We don't get too many of those, do we?"

Keena appreciated Angie's brisk delivery, as if there was nothing out of the ordinary about Keena's end-of-the-shift routine. The nurse was right. The shift had gone as most of them did, but this wasn't like her. She never let her ER team see her sweat. It had become Keena's way of life. The fact that she'd been counting down the minutes until she could slowly fall apart tonight worried her the most.

"What will I do without you, Angie?" she murmured and pulled her arm back. Whatever her pulse was doing, it was okay now.

This leave of absence was coming at exactly the right time. Keena's reputation as Steady Murphy, the nickname the nurses had given her early on for her calm response to pressure, was spotless. The fewer people who witnessed her control being as shaky as her grip as she opened her locker, the better.

"I was definitely not prepared to see a woman with multiple gunshot wounds." Keena dealt with trauma regularly but stabilizing the woman who'd been hurt by her angry ex-husband had required every bit of Keena's experience and most of the faith she possessed.

"What you did was amazing. She was lucky you were on duty." Angie waved a hand. "Any hesitation might have killed her."

Keena frowned as she studied her neatly folded jeans. "What *we* did, Angie. You didn't leave me alone for a second, and she needed all of us."

"She sure did and a few angels besides. The fact that she made it through surgery is proof miracles still happen around here. Honestly, that was plenty for one night." Angie sighed. "Following it up with the victims of a multicar accident on I-25 was…" Her voice trailed off as if it was impossible to find the right word.

"Yeah." Keena stood and pulled her clothes out of the locker. Tonight, a shower would absolutely be required before she could drive home. Fatigue made it too difficult to carry on polite conversation, so she gave up and started for the shower. When steam emerged, Keena gritted her teeth and stepped under the water. The fiery spray burned away the brain fog and made it easier to consider getting home. Her skin was a bright pink when she returned to her locker. No more pale cheeks.

Angie was still there, reapplying her lipstick.

"I'm leaving you in charge until I get back. Don't let anyone make a mess of my department." Keena was pleased at her stronger tone. Steady. That's what her team expected.

"Hope that wide spot in the road knows how lucky they are to get you, Dr. Murphy." Angie finished tying her shoes. "Three months and you'll be back? Is that what I heard?"

"That's the plan." Keena shoved her scrubs in the bin to be laundered. "Dr. Singh is traveling to Haiti to assist with the medical mission there, and Prospect…" Keena ran her hands through her wet hair and twisted it into a knot on top of her head. "That's the name of the wide spot. Prospect doesn't have another doctor, so Dr. Singh asked for help finding a temporary replacement." She'd been lucky enough to work with Dr. Singh while she was still a resident, before he'd left for the slower lane of small-town doctor.

"Think you'll be…bored? The head nurse here when I started told me that working Emergency changes a person. Rewires your brain. Tonight, we did the impossible. May have to do it all over again tomorrow, too." Angie raised her eyebrows. Her opinion was clear. Colds and vaccinations would be quite the change from shifts in Denver's only Level 1 trauma center. The worst cases were transferred here, and the challenge had been invigorating for most of Keena's career. Here she accomplished feats few people could manage. That had been what drew her to medicine all along, the chance to perform at a high level and stand out in the crowd. She had been lucky to work with the best of the best, from the administration on the corporate-level floor all the way down to the security guards who stood at the door each night.

If Keena and her team thought of themselves as braver than the rest, they had plenty of opportunity to prove that. Angie's question prodded one of Keena's own doubts about spending months away from her hospital. Being bored might sound lovely, but Keena wasn't convinced, either.

"Angie, when was the last time you took a vacation?"

The RN peered into the distance as she considered the question. "Well, my husband and I took the kids to Disneyland over the summer." She shook her head. "Honestly, getting two teenagers there and safely home was more stressful than some shifts here at the hospital. I don't know how two children can fight like cats in a gunny sack and still agree to conspire against their parents the way these two do. Next time I get a break, we're leaving those children with my husband's mother. A vacation sounds nice, Dr. Murphy. You deserve to rest a little."

Keena was hoping for just that. The wear and tear of Emergency added up. Slowing down in Prospect would be as nice as a vacation, leaving her refreshed and ready to take on nights like tonight without faltering. If the fear that she would lose her edge if she stepped out of the emergency department for too long floated through her mind now, Keena brushed it away.

It was a silly fear. Keena had been at her best under pressure before. That's all she wanted, a return to her old self. Her life was good; her work here had purpose. All she needed was a little R and R, and the adrenaline rush of shifts like this one would be exciting again.

"Boredom is going to be a blessing." Keena flexed her fingers, relieved to find them steady again. Returning to reality thanks to a mindfulness routine she'd learned out of self-preservation was good medicine, but only a bit of peace could restore her energy. That was the prescription she'd written for herself.

Keena double-checked the shelf in her locker to make sure she'd collected all the items she'd kept on hand to make hospital life more convenient—deodorant, toothpaste, toothbrush, floss, hairbrush—all the little things that could make difficult shifts bearable. Satisfied that everything was packed away in the box she'd been filling all week and her large bag, she was ready to leave.

"You know you aren't getting out of here without some kind of farewell from us, right?" Angie was leaning against the door to the hallway. "We're going to miss you too much around here for that."

Keena straightened her shoulders, determined to leave on a high note. "Since you've all been running this race right beside me tonight, I expect us all to keep this short and sweet."

Angie saluted.

"As a nurse, I try to never say 'the doctor knows best' too loudly. Bad for your egos." Angie held the door open. "But I hope you enjoy your break. When you're ready to come home, we'll be here." As Angie and Keena passed the large front desk, everyone seemed to be holding their breath.

A box of cookies sat on the nurses' station, decorated

and arranged to spell out *We will miss you!* in hot-pink letters. Angie handed her one. "Your favorite color."

Touched that Angie would remember something like that, Keena ate two cookies and read the comments on the enormous card signed by everyone in the department. Leaving was bittersweet.

She stopped to carefully survey all the faces, returning each person's smile with one of her own. "Thank you for all you've done tonight. I'll see you in a few months."

"See you soon" was much more accurate than "goodbye."

As she headed for the sliding doors, the security guard there tipped an imaginary hat, so Keena returned the favor before stepping out into the early-morning sunshine.

The reminder of the world outside the hospital and that it kept turning, no matter how frenetic the hours inside had been, was welcome. With each step she took, breathing became easier, and by the time she slid behind the steering wheel, Keena had evaluated her plans for the day and knew they were sound. In the heat of a crisis, Keena never hesitated. Decisions came easy.

Second-guessing herself was annoying and something she wanted to eliminate, especially since it had gotten worse as her mental energy flagged. Moving temporarily to Prospect, an old mining town way up in the mountains, presented an overwhelming list of unknowns, starting with whether or not Keena would excel at a family practice, especially without a partner nearby like Dr. Singh.

Having more time for her medical diagnoses didn't change the fact that people were depending on her to get them right.

"The answers to questions you haven't been asked yet aren't in this parking lot, Keena," she muttered to herself in the exasperated, pragmatic tone her mother always used.

It was the same voice that told her to get a grip in the middle of any new crisis. Growing up, Keena had learned her mother was more about practical solutions than nurturing care. Whenever she needed to check herself, her mother's voice was always there to help out. After she settled into her rental house in Prospect, she'd give her mother a call.

The short drive to her apartment took no time. Everything she'd need to take to Prospect was packed in two suitcases and a small stack of boxes near the door. Years of discipline kicked in, and Keena moved to her bedroom. No matter how alert she felt after the relief of successfully completing a busy shift at the hospital, the lack of sleep would eventually catch up to her. She didn't want that to occur on winding mountain roads and she'd arranged to meet Dr. Singh at his office that afternoon, leaving sufficient time for a nap.

Sleep came easily enough, but Keena was wide-awake before her alarm beeped and she hit the road.

Keena drove south out of Denver before turning west and starting to climb. The Iowa girl in her gripped the steering wheel tightly as each curve took her higher and closer to narrow shoulders. The signs of an urban community faded, replaced with scrubby grass, tall trees and even taller mountains in the distance, but following Dr. Singh's clear instructions was simple enough.

Eventually, a two-lane highway led straight into the middle of the historic district of Prospect. Keena studied the raised wood boardwalk that fronted the facades of the town's Old West businesses, including a livery stable, a barbershop and a bank. Other modern businesses had taken over some of the space. An old movie theater, the Prospect Picture Show, was showing *Rio Bravo*, and the large, two-story building called the Mercantile caught her attention.

That was Dr. Singh's landmark, the easy-to-see spot

marking the hard-to-see medical office nestled behind it. Making a quick turn on the small street on the other side of the Mercantile brought her right to Prospect Family Practice. This structure was smooth plaster with a large glass wall that made it easy to see the office's reception desk and seating area.

Parking was simple. Keena pulled into one of the empty spots lining the fence of a large park that covered the block behind the Mercantile. There were two kids chasing a ball right down the center of the grassy area while two women chatted at a picnic table. The playground at the opposite end was empty.

When Keena turned off the ignition, silence settled over the car immediately. There was no traffic noise, just sunshine, mature evergreens, a street giving way to an old neighborhood, and small-town quiet. The difference between where she'd been at sunrise and her present circumstances was overwhelming. Her temporary home presented a postcard-perfect image in the late-afternoon golden light.

Keena knew better than to romanticize the situation, but still, she wanted to savor the scene.

"It's as important to be in the present in good times as it is in bad," she reminded herself. Anxiety could still catch her off guard, even here in this setting, but she didn't have time to consider what that might look like because Dr. Singh stepped out of the medical office, waving wildly.

The familiar sight amused her. PJ Singh was a man who'd never met a stranger, and his friends received his wholehearted enthusiasm at all times. The residents who'd worked with him were lucky. But patients had always been his biggest fans. Keena had never met another doctor who connected with the patient, young or old, as well as he did.

He'd explained to her over and over how important that was when she was a young doctor. Keena learned quickly, had steady hands, and handled the rush of medicine well. She had been made for the ER. Family medicine required different skills and an understanding of how to treat the person, not only the injury.

That had been her biggest concern about this move to Prospect. Could she execute this type of medicine to the standards she'd set for herself and her emergency department?

Keena was determined to do good medicine here. Dr. Singh knew her and trusted her to take care of his town.

And Keena trusted herself not to let him down.

She might have her own doubts, but no one else would.

Steady Murphy was prepared to tackle the challenge of life in Prospect.

CHAPTER TWO

Travis Armstrong glanced at his watch as the sun dipped behind the ridge of the mountains that surrounded the valley leading up to Larkspur Pass. He'd been dispatched to Sharita Cooper's place by his brother half an hour ago to greet the new doctor who was scheduled to arrive since Wes was involved in something at the Majestic Prospect Lodge. Given every one of his four brothers had rearranged their lives to return home to the Rocking A at Travis's request, it was easy enough to make the short drive over from the ranch house and hunker down on the porch steps.

But the doctor was late.

And his nerves didn't handle waiting well.

Worse, he'd finished the book he left in the truck for times like this, so he didn't have anything to read while he waited.

He pulled out the house key Wes had sent him to deliver. His orders had been to make sure the doctor had all the necessities for the night, so that Wes could follow up in the morning. As the property manager for Sharita Cooper, their neighbor to the south who had turned a visit to Florida into a semipermanent lifestyle, Wes was responsible for renting the place to the new doctor in town. He had also been managing the Majestic, their neighbor to the north, but the Hearsts had decided to reopen the place instead of selling it. Wes was committed to helping them any way he could. As Prospect's only lawyer, Wes ended up with a lot of different responsibilities, so it was nice to have a chance to help him out. Travis was still fighting the urge to apologize for getting in Wes's way around the ranch since he'd retired and come home.

After years of having sole responsibility for the Rocking A's operations, Wes should have had a harder time adjusting to being crowded by the rest of them. Instead, as soon as Travis had mentioned the renovations needed to meet the foster home requirements, the Rocking A ranch house was bursting at the seams, filled with Armstrong men.

Hanging out in the silence of Sharita's empty house wasn't such a bad assignment after all.

Travis did a quick walk-through in the kitchen. Wes had brought in some staples, milk and bread, things like that. Electricity was on. Heat was running. November nights weren't terrible and the first snow was still weeks away, but the chill in the air would only grow sharper until springtime.

He propped his hands on his hips as he considered what else might be needed for immediate comfort. Utilities. Food. Toilet paper? He stuck his head into the bathroom to see that was also covered.

"Well, that took up ten minutes or so," he muttered as he moved over to the single, long window that looked out over the front yard. Nothing. No sign of the doctor. Sharita's house was comfortable, as lived-in as the Rocking A ranch house had been before their recent renovations, but there wasn't a lot of space to explore.

Travis pocketed the key and went outside. Nerves were always better handled outdoors.

The woodpile was low, so he grabbed the axe from his truck bed and moved toward the scrub of pines that formed a barrier between Sharita's house and the Rocking A fence line. Ever since the Rocking A's ambitious renovation and expansion had ramped up a month ago, Travis had escaped the noise and mess by riding the fence early in the morning. Was that necessary? Not really. Wes could do it all and had kept the whole place in good shape, but Travis insisted on taking the parts he could manage. If he recalled, there was a dead pine that needed to come down before it wrecked the fence.

Wes negotiated with the bank, talked to the accountant, buyers, suppliers and who knows who else.

Travis? He was all about the hard labor. Repairing fence. Putting out feed. Corralling stock.

Travis liked to work. Particularly jobs that required a strong back…that was his lane. The army had deployed him as an infantry soldier, a type of work that had been a challenge every single day. Coming home was a relief. He'd struggled to find his place in the Armstrong family in the early days, but staying in his lane now was fine.

He'd even found a way to broaden it and on the Rocking A, too. Thanks to him, there was a new crop of foster kids headed to the ranch. Why now?

Ever since the snowball of the foster home application process had started rolling down the hill, gathering speed, he'd been asking himself that.

"You pushed for this. Don't chicken out now," he snapped as he stepped up to the dying pine and swung with a satisfying whack. Each swing was accompanied by one of the thoughts he couldn't escape.

Why you?

Why would anyone entrust kids to you?

What makes you think you can do this?

What if they don't like where you came from?

What will happen to these kids when you mess up?

Travis shook his arms out as the pine fell. After dragging it near the chopping stump, he broke the tree down with more swings.

At this point, none of the doubts mattered. He'd started the process of becoming an approved foster home months ago, taking the lead, meeting with the caseworker and reviewing her comments on the improvements that would need to be done to the ranch to offer the best home possible for those teenage boys who might have nowhere else to go.

His brothers had pitched in to meet the caseworker's demands. They all understood. This place, Walt and Prue, had saved them all in one way or another. Continuing that was important.

Wes found the money.

Clay led the renovation.

Grant worked long days on any task necessary.

Even Matt was sleeping on a lumpy couch in town to make room for more kids who needed the Rocking A.

And Travis…

Well, he'd put in a full shift, day after day, but he'd also spent more time "checking fences" than strictly necessary.

The guilt receded a bit as he swung the axe.

When he noticed the shadows lengthening from the pines, he stopped to look at his watch. If the doctor didn't show soon, he was going to be late for the big celebration dinner his mother was preparing to mark the completion of the house renovations. Ducking the noisy, crowded event was tempting, but he knew it would cause an epic storm of disappointment.

Meeting his family's proud and expectant faces head-on opened up the dark gulf inside.

But disappointing his mother on purpose might kill him.

"Um, hi," a soft voice said from behind his left shoulder.

Travis twisted to see a petite redhead, one hand raised in an awkward wave. He made the connection from "beautiful woman" to "doctor he was waiting to meet" quickly but his mouth took a minute to catch up.

Speaking to beautiful women was one of the skills he'd always hoped to refine but never had.

"I didn't want to interrupt you midswing or startle you," she said as she took a hesitant step closer. "Are you Wes?"

Travis shook his head. "No."

When she glanced uneasily over her shoulder, Travis realized that might not have been the best answer. "I'm Travis. Armstrong. Wes is my brother." He set the axe down in case identifying himself wasn't enough to eliminate her concern. Facing a tall stranger with an axe might set him back on his heels, too.

She immediately clasped a hand over her chest. "Oh, good. No one warned me about any dangerous rugged lumberjacks and I was afraid it had slipped Dr. Singh's mind." Her smile was as bright as her long red hair as she moved forward. "I'm Keena."

Rugged.

Travis ran a hand over his beard as he contemplated that. Was rugged good?

Her hand was strong as they shook. Travis appreciated that.

"I'm Travis," he said before he could stop and closed his eyes at her amused smile. They both already knew his name. "And I'm very good in social situations."

Her amused laugh eased some of his disgust at his eternal awkwardness. "What a relief, as I am also wonderful with introductions, Travis."

Did he believe that? No way, but he appreciated the effort to make him comfortable.

"Wes was tied up with other business, so he asked me to bring your key over and make sure you were set up for the night." He pointed down at the axe as he picked it up. "I chop wood in my spare time."

He was relieved when she fell into step beside him.

Apparently it took more than a weird guy with a sharp tool to scare her away.

Then he realized that was definitely the kind of thought to keep locked up deep inside his own head.

"So, not a professional lumberjack." Keena shoved her hands in the puffy jacket she was wearing. It was bright pink instead of black or drab green. He liked that, too.

"Strictly amateur. Hobby. Part-time?" he asked in a weak attempt at a joke. Her bright smile was the payoff, so he kept talking. "Live next door. At the Rocking A. Wes also lives there. You can't see it from here." He motioned over his shoulder. "House is a couple miles that way, but you can see our cattle now and then."

Not the most exciting conversation, but he was proud of himself for stringing that many words together in succession. His family would be impressed.

"That may take some getting used to. In Denver, my next-door neighbors are so much closer." Her lips curled. "Still cows, though, thank goodness."

Travis frowned as he made sense of her answer. When her joke landed, his laugh sounded more like a grunt but that pleased her. Her giggles floated over their heads.

"I don't know what has come over me." Keena covered her cheeks with both hands. "I've never made a cow joke in my life." She touched his sleeve. "And I grew up in Iowa." Keena raised her eyebrows as if to communicate to him how long she'd successfully avoided making random cow jokes.

Since most women thought he was as dull as he was quiet, it was nice to be included in her amusement.

When they stepped up on the porch, Travis dropped the

axe against the wall. "Lean into it. You have come to the right place. A good cow joke always goes over well around here." Then he opened the door and waved her inside. "Take a look and then I'll help you carry your stuff inside."

"Oh, you don't have to do that. My packing was pretty minimal." Her voice trailed away as she inspected the kitchen, flipping the light switch on and off, before opening the refrigerator. "Oh, someone left groceries?" The question showed in her confused frown. "Was that you or Dr. Singh?"

Travis cleared his throat. "Not me. Wes was my first guess. He's good with this kind of stuff. Thinking ahead." He was good at everything.

Keena sniffed. "Not quite as impressive as chopping firewood though, right?" She pointed at him, then turned down the hallway toward the bedrooms and the bathroom.

Every step she took was determined, as if she couldn't waste the energy. Efficiency seemed important to her.

When Travis realized his hands were dangling like dead fish, he gripped them together in front of him and tried to relax his stance. Years in the army meant he stood at attention without even realizing it more often than not.

"This place is perfect. I saw the Homestead Market in town." Keena tugged off her coat. Jeans and an electric-blue sweater fit her and her surroundings perfectly. "Is that a grocery store?"

"Everything." Travis cleared his throat and tried again. "It's Prospect's one-stop shop. There's a hardware store in the Mercantile, but Homestead has groceries and an assortment of everything else under the sun."

She crossed her arms. "Can't wait to explore."

Travis met her stare. The silence stretched between them until he realized she was waiting for him to leave.

"Please let me help you unpack your car. My mother would be ashamed if she found out I didn't."

Keena nodded. "Okay, you're proving chivalry isn't dead." Then she led the way outside.

"More like being a good neighbor. She'd insist we unload the car, no matter age or weather. That may be a Prospect kind of thing." Travis tested the suitcases and boxes in her trunk before lifting both suitcases with one arm and the heaviest box with the other.

"Okay, Mr. Universe. Why didn't you make it easy on yourself and carry the whole car inside? We could have unpacked the trunk in the living room." Her teasing was warm, amused.

That made it easy for Travis to laugh.

"I'll try that next time." He waited for her to open the door and then set everything down in the living room. "Unpacking in the living room will still work."

She nodded. "Definitely. I have plenty of time to unpack this weekend before I start in Dr. Singh's clinic on Monday, but I'm going to need a good night's sleep before I tackle all this. Food, sleep, then settling in."

Travis shoved his empty hands in his pockets.

Keena smiled politely at him, waiting again.

"At least I can make toast for dinner. Where should I eat in town when I need a real meal?" she asked, shifting slightly toward the door. Was that a hint?

"No 'welcome to Prospect' dinner planned?" Travis asked. That surprised him.

"I was originally planning to drive to town tomorrow. Dr. Singh and his wife had agreed to meet friends for dinner in Fairplay tonight. I had a long shift at the hospital last night, so I thought I might wait until tomorrow but..." Keena sighed. "Obviously, I'm here now and that answer should have been much shorter. Good example of my own smooth social skills. I blame fatigue. I'm having dinner at their place tomorrow night."

Travis pursed his lips as he considered that. "I have good news and I have bad news."

She wrinkled her nose. "Hit me with the bad first."

"There's only one full-service restaurant in town, the Ace High."

She frowned. "That's a poker hand, right?"

"Kinda." Travis shrugged. "It's also the restaurant in the building that used to be the finest saloon in Prospect's old town, home of expensive poker games during the silver boom."

"Okay. One restaurant. That makes the decision easier, I guess?" she said slowly, confusion wrinkling her forehead as if she had no concept how any place could function with only one restaurant.

Travis understood that. He'd grown up in Prospect, but living all over the world had taught him the power of restaurant choices. It would be good to have more options.

He decided not to explain that the decision would be even more basic when she made it into the Ace. There was no menu. Her options were this meal or that meal. The end.

"Good news is that the food there is very good. All of it." Travis stepped closer to the door. The discussion of food reminded him that his mother was cooking and she would not appreciate it if he was too late. He might not get dessert.

The idea that sparked immediately...his mother would be ecstatic if he brought their new neighbor home.

Keena nodded. "That is excellent news. I can eat my own cooking sometimes, but no one wants to suffer that fate every night. I'll have some time to expand my skills now that I'm in Prospect for a bit."

This time, when their eyes met, they were both smiling.

As the awkward one in every group, Travis didn't experience that connection often. He realized he was having a hard time breaking it now.

Then, before he knew what he was doing, he said, "If you're up for it, I know a place a little closer where you can get a delicious meal. There's a celebration planned tonight. You won't even have to do dishes this time, since it will be your first visit."

She tilted her head to the side, waiting for more information.

"Come to the Rocking A. You need to know where the house is in case you have any emergencies. I'll introduce you to Wes, and my mother is making pasta." Travis realized that might not be the draw for Keena, but he loved his mother's red sauce.

"Come on. Being neighborly. That's a big thing in Prospect." Travis had never tried to wheedle a woman into coming to dinner in his life. He wasn't sure whether he was succeeding or failing until she smiled.

"Meeting the neighbors is important when you're new in town, right?" Keena picked up her coat. "Should I follow you? Are you sure your mother won't mind another person for dinner?"

"There'll be so many of us there, she likely won't notice another person at the table." Stuck, because he hadn't thought any of this through and he'd certainly never expected her to say yes, Travis stopped in the doorway. He wanted to sweep open his truck door in a courtly gesture, but he was sure the floorboard was littered with twine and wire and no telling what else he'd picked up working on the ranch, so he nodded. "Follow me. I want you to know how to find me."

The urge to smack his forehead was so strong that he almost followed through. Fighting it meant he missed the opportunity to stammer and stutter and explain that he'd intended to say that she needed to be able to find Wes just in case.

But that was a blessing, too.

Spending time with Keena Murphy was fast becoming exactly what he wanted to do.

CHAPTER THREE

KEENA WAS SURPRISED to be climbing up the ranch house steps behind Travis Armstrong on their way to meet his family for dinner. He'd seemed surprised to be issuing the invitation. How he'd frozen in place had been sweet and funny at the same time. She recognized the reaction even if she never let herself visibly hesitate under similar circumstances. Acting confident even when she didn't feel it had been critical to success in the ER.

It had also gotten her through countless confusing, loud family gatherings when her divorced parents' always changing "yours, mine, and ours" had threatened to swamp Keena growing up.

Faking it until she made it had become Keena's chief coping mechanism. It never failed.

Her plans for the night had been boring and entirely sensible: unpack, investigate her new place, and sleep until she couldn't sleep any longer.

But then Travis had invited her to dinner, his boots shuffling as nervously as a boy asking a girl he admired out on a first date. She'd been too charmed to say no, so now she had no choice but to make her best first impression on the Armstrongs.

She'd taken half a minute to smooth her hair and run her fingers under her eyes to eliminate any mascara smudges before getting out of the car, but there was no way she was prepared to wow her first new acquaintances in her temporary hometown.

Travis stopped before opening the door and glanced over his shoulder at her. "I can't decide if it's kinder to warn you about my family or let you experience them naturally." Since he appeared more apologetic than honestly concerned, she had a feeling Travis was trying for humor again.

She got the idea that he didn't show that to many people.

Keena pursed her lips. "Do I need weaponry? Can I borrow your axe?"

His shoulders eased a fraction. "Nah. They're more likely to smother you with affection than make you fight your way out."

"The axe might still come in handy." Keena put her hand on his arm and squeezed. That was one of the tips Dr. Singh had passed along to her to deal with anxious patients. Touching them got their attention, broke the cycle of anxious thoughts, and provided more comfort than words alone.

This time, it helped her, too.

Also, his arm was…hard. Muscle-y. Covered in plaid flannel. All in all, pleasant.

Then Travis reached for her hand and tangled their fingers together. "I'm glad you're here. You're helping me, causing a diversion, and I…" He closed his mouth firmly, obviously reconsidering whatever it was that followed. Keena was immediately interested in whatever required a distraction but now was not the time to dig for more info. "Let me walk you out when you go."

Keena blinked. "Urging me back to my house already?" She had so many questions. That was true always, but she was doing her best to contain them here.

He sighed. "Nope, but this will be the last time we speak

together without interruptions and curious glances for the rest of the night. Gotta make it count." Then he squeezed her hand, pushed open the door and led her inside.

Keena craned her head side to side as she followed him, curious about how her new ranch neighbors lived. The hall opened into a spacious living room. She could smell fresh paint and varnish, so the current-but-still-classic style made perfect sense. Comfortable, old furniture lined the walls, but the place was modern without being trendy. Everything was clean and bright.

Then an older woman popped her head through an open doorway ahead. "My boy brought a friend!" she exclaimed. "I never thought I'd see this day." Her emphasis on *friend* suggested she was more interested in romantic friendships than run-of-the-mill neighborly kinds.

"I texted my mother to warn her I had a guest. I regret that decision," Travis murmured next to her ear. "I don't know if you've ever been measured for a wedding dress by a stranger, but..." He shook his head.

Keena stretched up on her toes so he could hear her. "If we were in Iowa right now, my father would be staring you down just like at all first-time introductions to possible boyfriends. I like your mother's way better."

Travis's eyes were warm. "Big family?"

Keena shrugged. "When you add in all the half-this and step-that, yes. My dad doesn't discriminate, though. Any girl who brings in a boy gets to see the same show."

They'd argued enough over that when she was still at home that she'd had time to perfect it.

"Everyone is welcome here," Travis said, "but my mother might give your father a run for his money." He squeezed her shoulder. "She doesn't do double standards, though. If she's ever lucky enough to have daughters-in-law, she'll be as ready to protect them as she is her sons."

Keena liked that. Having a father who treated his daughters differently than his sons was wrong and annoying, but a protective mother who would battle for all of her family equally was sweet.

When they were quiet, they could hear the rumble of hushed conversation coming from the kitchen.

His lips thinned. "I could make you a to-go plate and some excuse about being worn out by the day if you'd rather."

Keena tilted her head to the side. This was her best "patiently waiting" pose.

Travis sighed. "Okay, would you make one for me, then?"

Keena moved around him and pulled him along to the kitchen where she halted, surprised by the sheer number of people watching her. She hadn't expected the size of the crowd.

"Trav, make introductions," his mother said as she stirred an enormous pot on the stove. If the living room had been comfortably updated, the kitchen had been fully modernized. It was still beautiful, in a modified farmhouse style, but the enormous stainless steel refrigerator was impressive, the center island gleamed with some shiny stone surface, and the cook was moving as if she was orchestrating a symphony of pots on a large stovetop. Wood floors and the butcher-block countertop lining three walls added warmth.

"At the table, we have," Travis said as he pointed and each person waved, "Wes, Matt and Grant." They were seated next to each other on a long bench at the large table. "On this end, we have Clay and his friend, Jordan Hearst." Keena smiled at the other woman, glad to see her. "Jordan and her sisters are reopening the Majestic Prospect Lodge, our neighbors on the other side. Jordan and Sarah are moving here from LA. Keep on going past the turnoff for the Rocking A and you'll see the sign."

Travis studied her face and waited for her to nod.

He understood how interested she was in getting to know another woman who was also new in town. The way Jordan patted the seat next to her made Keena think she was just as anxious.

"Sarah's still in LA, but she'll be here before Thanksgiving," Wes added.

"And then we'll all be hearing wedding bells, no doubt," Grant muttered under his breath.

"Now, now, you'll find a lady who can overlook that attitude someday," Matt said as he clapped a hand on Grant's back. "Maybe start looking across the street? Trav, Wes and Clay seem to have a lock on the neighbors to the right and left." Then he stood and took Keena's hand. "It's nice to meet you, Keena. You're a brave woman."

Keena smiled into his deep brown eyes, immediately caught by how warm they were.

"With Dr. Singh's leave of absence, I sure am happy to have another doctor in town." Matt pressed his hands to his chest. "I don't like treating humans. Cows and horses complain so much less than people."

She couldn't look away from his face, but eventually she realized he must be a veterinarian and smiled at his joke. Travis waved his hand in front of her to break Matt's hold on her as his brothers laughed. Keena expected she'd see a dazed expression if she glanced in a mirror now, but it was the correct reaction. Five men, all handsome, all wearing some version of a plaid button-down and jeans, but she couldn't decide where Travis fell in the lineup. Who was the oldest? Youngest?

"My dad, Walt, and my mom, Prue."

Keena shook his father's hand first and realized it might

be the first time she'd ever actually seen a twinkle in anyone's eye. Walt's lopsided grin was welcoming and she understood that whatever it was that charmed her in Travis could also be found in Walt.

When she turned to offer Prue her hand, the older woman surprised her by hugging her tightly. Since none of her family had been big huggers, it took a minute to adjust but she eventually squeezed lightly and stepped back. Seeing how stylish Prue Armstrong was in her beautiful sweater with some kind of diagonal hem and large pin on the shoulder made Keena wish she had taken more time to put herself together before she'd walked in.

It was too late to worry about that now, so Keena moved to sit in the chair Travis pulled out next to Jordan. Comforted a bit that Jordan was wearing a sweatshirt that appeared to have sawdust on the shoulder, Keena told herself to pretend she was confident and completely comfortable there.

Eventually it might come true.

"Where are the eatin' irons, Prue? Let's get this party started." Walt clapped his hands.

"Soon as you come get the *silverware* to finish setting the table like you were supposed to, we'll be ready." Prue's sweet smile didn't quite reach her eyes. "We're eating family style, so everyone bring your plates over to the stove and fill them up while your father finishes setting the table." Prue and Walt held a silent staring competition in front of the stove before he winked and her lips curled. Keena wanted to know what that was all about.

Travis led Keena to the stove first, an obvious honor reserved for the guest.

"Your parents are cute. How long have they been married?" Keena asked as she dished out spaghetti from the large pot.

"Forever, but they're divorced, have been for years. They never quite split up for good." Travis shook his head. Now she had more questions. She'd ask later.

"Make sure you get some of that garlic bread. I made it from scratch for the occasion," Prue Armstrong said as she hovered near the stove, like a proud mama bird over her nest. "Keena, look at this backsplash." She motioned regally at the gray-and-white tiles. "Didn't my sons do excellent work?"

Keena nodded. "And this pot filler. I've only seen them on TV shows. I can tell you love to cook, Ms. Armstrong. It must be wonderful to have all this space to do it." It was an impressive setup for someone who enjoyed cooking.

"Oh, call me Prue, but yes, ma'am, that pot filler was my special surprise from my ex-husband. Turns out, he was listening all those years when I thought I was talking to myself." Prue grinned. "Were there easier ways to get my attention rather than ignoring me, refusing to do any updates until we were divorced and living in separate houses, and then surprising me with a somewhat impractical but sweet gift like this in the kitchen in a house I don't even live in?"

Keena assumed the question was rhetorical and waited.

Prue scooped a large helping of salad onto Keena's plate. "Absolutely, but with an Armstrong man, you can count on hardheadedness."

Walt grunted. "Only way to love a woman who holds a grudge for decades." He dodged the dish towel Prue lobbed at his head before winking at Keena.

Keena bit her lip and turned to Travis for help.

"Step away from the stove," Clay said, "you're scaring the visitor, Mama."

The rest of the table cleared their throats and made conversation about the weather to fill in the silence.

Travis leaned over her shoulder to say, "Should I have warned you? They love each other...we think. They'll get back together...we hope, but..."

"Starting to believe arguing is their love language and one disagreement got too far out of hand," Wes murmured from across the table as they sat down. "Eventually the fireworks stop, Keena."

Clay cupped his hand over his mouth. "We need a matchmaker to take control of the situation."

"Only problem is finding one better than our mother. She'll be a tough cookie to crumble," Grant added.

"They never actually stop sparking, Keena, but both parties retreat for breathing room." Jordan patted her hand. "I'll give you the whole scoop."

Surprised and pleased at how easily the entire family had rolled her into the fold, Keena nodded. "I'd love that."

Keena made friends for life, but she'd never made easy friendships or acquaintances.

That might be because she was always working and work was serious business.

Finding immediate welcome here was sweet.

The rest of the dinner was filled with typical family conversation. How the day had been. What they were going to do about a herd in some pasture. How the repairs were going at the fishing lodge next door. When Matt was going to hold the next planning meeting for the town's big spring festival.

"Now then, for this special occasion, I made Clay's favorite dessert in honor of all the hard work he's put in, keeping this renovation going and finishing up the development of his big subdivision in Colorado Springs." Prue held up a ceramic pie keeper with a flourish. Then she frowned. "Applause, please."

Travis bumped her shoulder as he laughed.

"I hope that's for display purposes," Clay said. "We're going to need more than one coconut cream pie to feed this crowd and send some home with me." Then he picked up his fork as if he was ready to dig in.

Prue rolled her eyes. "Of course I made more than one. You know I like to show off my pie keeper. It's one of Sadie's, from her first line of kitchenware." Then she removed the top of the keeper. Keena could see toasted coconut and was immediately intrigued. "Walt, start serving, please and I'll get the others." She handed him a stack of plates.

"Sadie Hearst, the Colorado Cookie Queen. Heard of her?" Walt peered down the table at Keena.

"I have. I loved her Christmas specials when I was a kid. She always had my favorite celebrities in the kitchen with her," Keena said.

"She was my aunt," Jordan said. "Great-aunt, actually, but she helped raise me and my sisters. When she died, she left the lodge next door to us, along with enough memorabilia for several museums."

Ten different questions immediately popped into Keena's brain about the Hearst sisters, the museum and plans for the lodge, but Keena knew she had a habit of overwhelming people with conversation that could transition to interrogation. That was how she made the correct medical diagnosis, but it wasn't great at the dinner table. Instead of launching into her first question, Keena took her first bite of coconut cream pie.

"Oh, my, where has this pie been all my life," Keena murmured. "Maybe I'll learn how to make it while I'm taking a break from emergency medicine."

"Tell us about that, Keena," Prue said brightly.

When Travis shifted in his seat, she wondered if he was preparing to divert the conversation away from her. As if he understood her discomfort at being center stage. For some reason, her usual jitters were quiet here.

Direct communication was her favorite kind. But what could she say that they would understand?

"Long shifts. Sometimes it's straightforward. Pretty standard admissions. Chest pain. Broken bones. Home accidents. Things that are serious but routine." She shook her head. "Then there are the nights when every decision is life or death. Those are the toughest, obviously. Can the bleeding be stopped. Can the person get to surgery in time." She cleared her throat. "You never know what will walk through the door."

Now the jitters rolled in, so she focused on breathing through it. "Sorry. That might have been more information than you wanted. It's hard work but also rewarding." Kenna had learned the polite answer early in her career. Often when people asked about her job, they only wanted the short, sweet answer, not the truth. The size of her next bite precluded any more talking for a while.

Travis ran his hand across her back. It was the same kind of touch Clay and Jordan shared, she noticed.

As everyone finished their pie, Prue asked, "Everything ready for the caseworker's return, Trav?"

The tension that swept through Travis's body was easy to feel as Keena's arm brushed his.

He put down his fork and tangled his hands together in his lap. "Believe so. This place is light-years different from what she saw on the first tour. The rooms are ready to go, thanks to Grant and his bunk bed design."

Keena noted how the pink spread across Grant's cheeks before he frowned at his plate. "Just built what I wanted when I had to share a room with Mr. Neat."

"It's a nice setup, lots of privacy, which even Mr. Neat would have loved to have had." Clay sipped his wine. "Still won't help if one of the boys never learns how to use a laundry hamper."

Keena ate the last of her pie as she watched Grant scowl at Clay. This back-and-forth reminded her of family dinners at her dad's house, but it felt less awkward to sit back and watch these brothers bicker.

Maybe that was because it was okay to feel like an outsider here, which made sense being at the Armstrong table. But there was also the sensation that the family was opening its ranks to draw her in. That was new.

"The caseworker is scheduled to finish the home study by the end of next week." Travis ran his fingers over his nape before clutching his hands together again. "I've done CPR, first aid, classes about working with children with special needs." He shrugged. "If we aren't ready now, I don't know that I ever will be."

Silence settled over the table. Without understanding the background or what the problem might be, Keena knew this was important to Travis, to all of them, but she could tell that he felt the pressure. She'd noticed his change from "we" to "I." In their first meeting, she'd discovered he was a man of few words. Being put on the spot probably made it harder to find the right ones.

She tried her trick with making physical contact again and reached under the table to squeeze his hand tightly. Something shifted on his face and his shoulders relaxed.

Then he turned to her. "We're trying to get the ranch set up as a foster home for boys. We were all fostered and then adopted by Prue and Walt when we were teenagers."

Keena glanced around the table to find everyone staring. Now she was on the spot.

"Wow, that is…amazing." Keena squeezed his hand again. The only thing she knew about the foster care system was how heartbreaking it was to see caseworkers called in to care for children in her emergency department, the ones who had no one else to protect them. It was easy to imagine Travis and his family being a safe space for those kids. "That you found the family you needed and that you're all going to do the same thing for more kids, it's… Impressive. There's one question I still have. Who's oldest and who's youngest?"

When Grant groaned loudly, Prue scowled at him. "Matt's my baby, but they're all close in age, Keena." She patted Matt's cheek. "And Wes is the 'oldest.'" Prue made air quotes with her fingers. "He arrived first, but they're all one of a kind, let me tell you."

"Like an irregular shirt, one of a kind," Jordan drawled. Everyone laughed but Keena watched the way Clay's arm slid over Jordan's back to squeeze her close. So casually. It was sweet.

To shrug off the melancholy that flared at seeing such a simple sign of their connection, Keena shook her head. "I need a couple of hours to draw my family tree to make sure I know exactly how many brothers and sisters I have because my parents have each been married three times, so the branches get confusing. I think I'm the oldest, but I'm not certain anymore."

When everyone laughed as she'd intended, Keena ran her thumb across the back of Travis's hand. "But a good family is a blessing, so I try to focus on that instead of the number of Christmas gift cards I send out in the mail every year."

"That is some wisdom right there, Keena. Thank you for contributing to this scattershot dinner conversation," Prue said as she pointed at Keena. "Consider yourself welcome at my table here or in town whenever you like. I've got the cutest little apartment not too far from the clinic and I can tell I need to know more about you."

When Travis turned to glance her way, she batted her eyelashes innocently and sipped her glass of wine.

The way all the men at the table shook their heads at Travis would have made Keena laugh if she didn't know she was the reason for the commiseration.

"Thank you, Prue. Three months in Prospect should be enough time to enjoy a meal or two, I'm guessing." Keena wanted to make it very clear that she was temporary. "I don't get a lot of home cooking working the night shift in Denver."

Prue nodded. "I will do my best to rectify that, you sweetheart." Then she raised her glass. "And you never know, time in Prospect moves differently than it does in other places. Three months might turn out to be a whole lot more before it's all over."

It was impossible to miss that she'd met an expert strategist in Prue Armstrong. She'd taken Keena's warning and lobbed it back in a friendly but firm return.

Was Prue right? Could Prospect turn out to be more than a momentary rest?

Into the charged silence that fell while Keena tried to find an answer, Travis said, "Mom, do you have time to help me pick out bedding tomorrow? Be nice to have some personality in the rooms, show we're ready for a foster right now."

She immediately said, "I do not." Keena was busy scraping the last of the coconut cream off her plate when Prue added, "Sorry, hon. Patrick, Rose and I have plans in the store tomorrow, and then Sunday I have to go to Denver." She sighed. "Rose insists she needs me to go with her to the radio station to pick up her Broncos tickets. She knew I wouldn't be able to claim the store as my excuse to get out of going. Little did she know I talked Patrick into coming along." Prue's broad grin convinced Keena that she was pretty proud of herself for doing it, too. "We know Patrick and Rose share a love of football. Fingers crossed that some time together fans that tiny flame. We're going to do a trial run of a Friday night Sip and Paint at Handmade before the holidays gear up. Jordan and Keena will both be there, I'm sure."

Keena realized she was nodding before she was perfectly clear about what she was agreeing to. Sip and Paint? Were they painting walls or canvases? Either way, she didn't have much experience.

"Patrick is my father. Rose runs Bell House," Jordan said quietly to Keena before adding loudly, "I can't do it, either. Sorry, Travis. I'm too busy tomorrow." Then she took a bite of pie.

When she didn't offer anything else, Clay laughed as if he knew exactly what was going on before saying in a stilted, formal voice, "Oh, if only there was someone else who could help my dear brother create welcoming bedrooms for our new family members."

Keena finally realized everyone at the table was staring at her. She put her spoon down and coughed. "What? I'm sorry. I was in too deep with my pie."

Prue's lips were twitching as she said, "Dear, would you be able to help Travis with his shopping tomorrow? He could also show you around Prospect and you can pick up anything you might have left at home by accident."

"Um," Keena said as she looped hair behind her ear, "okay? I'm not sure I'm an interior designer, but I could help?" That uncertain tone would have sent everyone in the hospital into a panic, but here, the Armstrongs accepted it easily.

"Let me show you the rooms," Travis said. His tone was resigned but she didn't think he was unhappy with the way everything had turned out. He motioned her ahead of him toward the hallway.

They had almost made it all the way to freedom when Prue called, "Oh, Keena? One quick question for you."

Keena glanced over her shoulder.

"How do you feel about horses?" Prue asked sweetly.

Keena frowned, confused. It was clear that she was missing the part of the conversation taking place among the rolled eyes of those around the table.

"I don't really know anything about them. I grew up in the suburbs of Des Moines. We had dogs. I like dogs?" Keena turned to Travis for guidance but he shrugged.

Prue pursed her lips as she considered that. "It's not the end of the world, I guess. I've adjusted my views on the necessity of loving horses lately."

At the end of the table, Jordan straightened in her chair. "There are good people everywhere who'd rather drive than ride, Prue."

"Well, while you're in Prospect," Grant drawled, "it's an opportunity to add that skill to your résumé, Doc. If you'd like to go for a ride, I'll be happy to teach you. I've been working with a couple of horses that have the perfect personality for new and inexperienced riders."

"My son is a rodeo star, Keena." Prue tapped his shoulder as Grant squirmed under her proud stare. "You couldn't ask for a better teacher."

Keena wasn't convinced she needed riding lessons, but she took the phone he offered and entered her phone number quickly before sending herself a text. "I'll think about it. That's kind, Grant. Thank you."

Grant grinned as he dropped his phone into his shirt pocket.

"Let's go." Travis frowned at his brother. Keena noticed

the rest of the table was busy scooting crumbs around on their plates.

Keena waved and then followed as Travis towed her away.

"Hey, are you mad?" Keena asked as she dragged her feet to slow his march.

Travis shook his head as he stepped inside a spacious room and flipped on the light switch. "Not at you."

"Whoa, these are more than bunk beds." She stood on her tiptoes to stare through the rails at the bed. "This is more like a tiny, tiny home. You know, how everything has multiple functions."

Instead of a ladder, each bed had a shallow staircase that also held books. A floor-to-ceiling wardrobe formed one side of the bed, complete with doors that locked. The other end was a cube with a built-in desk. Under the bed, they'd put in a bench and a place for a small TV. Curtains could be closed for privacy.

"I saw a news story about these bunk bed pods, spaces commuters could rent in the big cities where the rent is out of control. The spots were basically a bed and a TV, a rack for some clothes." Travis paused. "No way would I want to live like that, but for these kids..." He shrugged. "Grant and I agreed we would have thought it was perfect."

Keena trailed behind him as he showed off both rooms and the bathroom they'd installed between, impressed at everything the Armstrongs had done. She'd lost track of all the things she wanted to ask about the renovation and the foster process and the ranch itself.

If she agreed to help him shop, no way would those questions remain contained. "If we go shopping, you know I'm going to be asking about...all this." He deserved fair warning.

Travis propped one hand on the doorframe. "If you'll

tell me how you can read my mind, how you know when the nerves are tying up my words, I'll consider replying to these questions."

She narrowed her eyes at him.

He waited.

"I guess we'll see how this shopping trip goes, won't we?" she murmured.

When she moved ahead of him on her way back to the kitchen, he said, "I guess *we'll see*."

Keena hoped Travis had missed the stutter in her step when his words registered. Something about his voice, the gravelly low tone, landed and stole her breath.

His family was painfully polite as Keena said goodbye and thanked his mother for dinner. Everyone was silent as Travis walked Keena to her car.

"I'll pick you up? Homestead Market opens at ten." Travis crossed his arms over his chest.

"It's a date." Keena instantly realized what she'd said, but no easy way out came to mind, so she moved on. "Your family is lovely. I'll see you tomorrow."

Keena didn't look back as she drove home. It had been a great opportunity to meet her neighbors. She'd help Travis and then she'd keep her distance. She'd come to Prospect, sure, but she would return to Denver and the career she loved better than ever. Disappointing Travis and his mother might be inevitable, but she could take care to make it as painless as could be. Maintaining enough distance between herself and the quiet cowboy to ensure that would be her goal.

CHAPTER FOUR

AFTER A LONG, sleepless night, Keena was relieved to watch the sunrise through the crack in the curtains over her unfamiliar bed. She'd learned some important lessons when her usual ability to sleep whenever and wherever failed.

First, she was not made for country life. She'd grown up in the suburbs and her apartment in Denver had plenty of comfortable white noise at all hours of the day and night. Traffic created a *shoosh* that she could pretend was the ocean. Her neighbors on all sides had conversations and televisions and radios to fill in any silence. She was never truly alone. Here? It was only Keena, her own breathing and whatever wildlife might be lurking in the dark outside.

Without sleep, her imagination filled that darkness easily.

No matter how often she'd told herself nothing was roaming around this tiny, comfortable house, the fact that she couldn't peer out the crack in the curtain and see a well-lit sidewalk to satisfy those doubts meant she was never convinced, either.

Here, the moon was bright, but that was the only light available.

Second, having her fears confirmed by yipping coyotes that sounded too close for comfort had pumped more adrenaline through her body than watching an ambulance screech to a halt outside the hospital.

Instead of investigating the noise, Keena had yanked the quilt over her head and pretended she couldn't hear them.

Altogether, it had been a long night.

"You'll get used to it. No one sleeps well the first night in a new place." Keena pictured her mother's pragmatic frown as she tossed back the quilt, slid her feet into warm slippers, and headed for the tiny bathroom. The floors creaked with each step. Those moans and groans didn't bother her in the daylight. But at night, she'd had to settle her racing heart back down every time something in the house settled.

After brushing her teeth and tidying up the messy bun that had unraveled as she tossed and turned, Keena decided her first order of business that morning would be unpacking the clothes she'd brought with her. If she was going to help Travis Armstrong decorate the room for his foster kids today, she was going to need something presentable for her introduction to her new neighbors in town. The mismatched sweatpants and T-shirt she'd slept in would not make a great first impression.

Keena studied the ancient drip coffeemaker and pulled some fragments of how-to from her memory to brew an incredibly dark, strong pot of coffee before moving into the living room to study her belongings. Sharita Cooper's house was warm, and all the basics were there, but Keena hadn't found a single radio in her hunt the previous night. That would have to change.

Spending too much time with only her thoughts for company would be a problem.

"Start a list, then." Keena pulled up the notes app on her phone and put down a wireless speaker that she could connect to her phone, and a single-cup coffeemaker. After she took a few sips of the brew she'd managed in the existing appliance, she removed that from the list. It was strong and dark and perfect as it was.

After dragging the largest suitcase into the bedroom, Keena unpacked everything quickly into the large wardrobe that stood next to the window. "A house with no closets may take some getting used to." Keena ran her hand down the smooth surface of the beautiful cedar wardrobe and thought it might be the simplest adjustment of them all. A shower, an exciting hunt for a hair dryer which ended at her growing list of things to purchase, and a bright red sweater to go with comfortable jeans made everything better.

Keena flicked the curtains wide open and studied the broad yard that stretched out in front of the window.

Sun rose over the ring of mountains that formed the backdrop in the distance.

Wide-open pasture dotted with a few cows stretched out between the window and those mountains. Whatever creatures she'd been imagining the night before were absent after sunrise. Would that be a comfort the next time she tried to sleep?

"Howdy, neighbors." Was she talking to herself more often in Prospect? It seemed so. Keena tried to loosen her neck and shoulder muscles as she walked into the kitchen. Breakfast would help. "The fresh air might not be good for your nerves after all."

She pulled out the loaf of bread and the butter from the refrigerator to make toast. The toaster was adorably retro, but she had the feeling that it was not a reproduction, but an actual appliance that had been in use in this house since the style was new. It might also be a fire hazard at this point, but the toaster worked.

A little trial and error was all it took to get the charred edges she preferred on her toast. Slathering the slices with butter had her mouth watering. Then she noticed the long line of cookbooks that filled a shelf next to the sink. A tiny window was framed above the sink. The view from this side of the house covered the stump where she'd met Travis the day before.

The handsome, awkward lumberjack that she was somehow shopping with that day.

Keena hummed loudly, grateful to have the opportunity to purchase something that would allow her to have someone else singing soon, since her voice was nothing to brag about. She studied the titles on the cookbooks.

The thought that it might be a nice move to take treats into Dr. Singh's practice on Monday popped up. She'd never done that before. Since it didn't sound like Prospect had much in the way of a handy donut shop to swing by before work, maybe she should try her hand at making something? There was an entire library of cookbooks to choose from, most of them by the Colorado Cookie Queen.

"*Gimme Some Sugar* sounds like a likely place to start," she murmured before she finished off her first slice of toast and pulled the cookbook down from the shelf.

Keena immediately recognized Sadie Hearst's smiling face on the cover. *Fifty easy-as-pie recipes to share* was the tagline under the title. Sadie in her smart white cowboy hat was holding a decorative plate with a selection of cookies. "Ooh, this is what I need."

She refreshed her coffee and took her toast to the kitchen table as she thumbed through the recipes, studying the bright photos that accompanied each. Sadie was scattered throughout the book, along with "Sadie's Yarns," notes from the Colorado Cookie Queen herself about the best occasions for each recipe.

"Is there one for 'hi, I'm your temporary coworker and kinda sorta boss but I know almost nothing about what you do here and I want to be your friend-slash-neighbor so take this cookie as a sign of my respect' occasion?" Keena flipped to the beginning of the book to study the table of contents. When the last bite of toast was gone, she ran a finger down each line until she landed on "First-Place First Impressions."

Keena was surprised that in a collection of "So-Easy-It's-Cheating Christmas Cookie Exchange" suggestions, "Better Last-Minute-than-Never Potluck" winners, "Sorry, I Lost Your Lawn Mower" apologies, and other funny and sweet notes, there was one that fit what she was looking for.

Sadie was posed in a kitchen, wearing a red-and-white gingham apron. There was a little girl turned away in the photo, so that her face was hidden. "The first day of school can rattle even the bravest cowpokes, am I right? Send them off with two dozen of these and be ready to hear about six new best friends. Just don't send your good container, hon. Better than even chance you'll never see that again."

Keena pursed her lips as she considered that. Her last first day of school had been more than a decade ago but the nerves fluttering in her stomach as she considered finding her way around Dr. Singh's clinic were familiar. "That's not very Steady Murphy of you, Doctor."

Keena read the short list of ingredients for "Chock-full Cowboy Cookies" and checked her refrigerator before adding to her list of items to pick up in town. Then she scanned the recipes to see if there was a "thank you for inviting a stranger to dinner" suggestion because the Midwesterner in her felt the urge to return the kindness the Armstrongs had shown her. Her mother would have some good ideas on what to deliver as a thank-you gift, but she would also have so many questions.

Keena had always had a plan for her career. Her parents had been big supporters of that plan.

They didn't understand this need for a detour when everything was going the way she wanted it to in Denver, not even when she mentioned that she'd be helping out an old friend.

If the Armstrongs were big on helping neighbors, Keena knew her Midwestern parents would be the same. Neighbors helped neighbors, friends helped friends, but her mother had made it clear that Keena putting her own career on hold to help was a mistake and doing too much by her mother's measurement.

Keena hadn't explained the toll Emergency had taken on her lately.

If the staff at the hospital viewed her as unflappable, her parents had a whole lifetime of moments to rest that judgment on. They'd trained this self-sufficiency and keen focus into her in the first place, whether they'd intended to or not. Years of split custody and new stepparents and ex-stepparents and different formations around the family table meant that Keena had learned early on to take care of herself.

The anxiety that came along with it had required that she also learn to cope by herself. It didn't matter what her parents thought they knew about her and what she could handle or what she deserved. She was in charge of her decisions, as always.

Keena was going to make Prospect work, Dr. Singh would have the help he needed, and by the time she went back home, the whole town would know that she was a good doctor. They would miss her when they left.

And if she managed to make these amazing cookies, they would believe she'd been baking her whole life.

She'd added walnuts to her list of groceries when a grating scrape loud enough to be the roof sliding right off the house scared her out of her chair.

It was followed by another loud rip, the sound fabric makes when it's torn in a rush.

Was it coming from outside?

Keena rushed to the kitchen window, but she didn't see anything out of the ordinary. Nothing was amiss on the road or the small yard in front of the house, so she ran into the bedroom and shrieked in surprise.

Keena clamped one hand over her heart as she stared at the cow who was staring right back at her.

Through the window. Only the pane of glass separated them.

Grass was dangling out of the cow's steadily chewing mouth. With an audible gulp, the grass disappeared. So did the cow's head. Then there was another loud tear before the cow returned to face Keena, more grass being digested slowly.

"Was that you?" Keena demanded before she shook her head. Did she expect the cow to answer?

If the cow answered, she was getting in her car and driving back to Denver immediately. Forget her clothes. Forget Dr. Singh and forget Prospect.

When the cow blinked, seemingly unperturbed at the turn of events, Keena realized only one of them was acting unusual at this point.

Steady Murphy was not so steady this morning.

Then the cow showed how little she cared about the situation by meandering past the window.

Toward the road.

A vision of Bessie wandering out onto the asphalt and pondering life while straddling the double yellow line as a packed school bus hurtled around a curve and headed right for her popped into Keena's head.

"Why do you always have to go right for the worst-case scenario?" Keena asked, annoyed at her brain and the cow and country life in general. Racing through the small house took no time, and Bessie didn't know there was a finish line so she'd stopped to rip up more landscaping near the corner of the house. The slam of the door caught the cow's attention, and Keena realized she was half a second from actually chasing the cow out into traffic.

Not that there was another car on the two-lane road at this time, but there might be.

"Don't run, beautiful," Keena said in her best patient-soothing voice. "We're friends here. I don't care anything about those flowers that have probably been there for a century. The homeowner? Huh! It will be our little secret." As she spoke softly, Keena moved closer, ignoring the frosty crunch of dying grass under her slippers.

When Bessie glanced over at her, Keena hoped she was considering returning the way she'd come and shifted to cut off the route to the road. If the cow couldn't go forward, she would go back, right?

Bessie didn't do either.

She also didn't return to her breakfast.

Instead, she and Keena were locked in a staring contest while Keena inched even closer.

The sound of a car on the road behind her confirmed Keena's fears. "Do you hear that? You could have been the world's largest roadkill this morning. No one wants that. Go back through whatever hole you walked through, and we'll forget about the damages, okay? Come on, Bessie. Doesn't that sound like a plan?"

"Are you bargaining with livestock?" Travis asked. Keena craned her head over her shoulder to see that he had parked his truck between Bessie and the road. He shut the door. Bessie huffed out a breath at the noise. "And that is Chuck. Not Bessie."

Keena turned back. "Is that why you've been ignoring my courteous request? Because you're a bull and not a cow?"

Travis's chuckle assured her he was approaching them. Surely he would take charge of this situation. "Better watch out. If Chuck holds a grudge, you might be in danger. He's a steer, not a bull."

Chuck was wary, obviously, but he'd stopped destroying the flower bed.

"What's the difference?" Keena asked.

When Travis didn't immediately answer, she hazarded taking her eyes off Chuck to see that Travis was biting his lip. He said, "Castration?"

Keena blinked and willed the color she could feel racing up her body to flood her cheeks to just...not. She was a doctor. Embarrassment was unacceptable. "Sorry, Chuck."

"We're all very sorry, Chuck." Travis's laughter drifted behind him as he stepped around the steer to open a wide gate in the fence. Chuck considered it before returning to his buffet.

"Move over to close the gap up by the house, Keena," Travis said, "and if he decides to come your direction, get out of the way."

Keena froze, midstep.

"I don't think he will," Travis added.

Did she know Travis Armstrong well enough to follow his instructions here?

Since he was the only one of them with any hope of getting Chuck on the right side of the fence, Keena moved into place and held her arms out to make herself bigger.

Travis tilted his head to the side as he considered her stance before nodding. "All right. Head on home, Chuck."

He moved cautiously toward the steer and clapped his hands. Chuck ripped one last bite out of the flower bed and moseyed toward the open gate. Travis continued the loud claps while Chuck took his own sweet time, but once he was in the field, Travis pulled the gate shut again.

Relieved, Keena dropped her arms. "Thank you."

"Good news, Chuck is contained." Travis stopped in front of her. "Bad news, he's going to show up again when you least expect it. He's an escape artist."

Keena exhaled, listening to the sounds of the morning, as she tapped her fingers against her thighs. She concentrated on the texture of the denim and counted her breaths. When her heart rate returned to normal, she realized Travis was watching her mindfulness routine. "Sorry. Old habit."

He shook his head. "No apology necessary."

"No time to panic when you're working in the hospital, right?" Keena brushed her hair over her shoulder, relieved Chuck had chosen a breakfast time after she'd had a chance to shower and fix her appearance. Travis would not have been impressed by her bedhead or sweatpants.

Not that it mattered whether Travis was impressed.

Obviously.

"Intellectually, I know there was no reason for that fight-or-flight reaction here, but my body never got the memo."

Making excuses for an over-the-top reaction to a placid steer named Chuck was not how she wanted her encounter with Travis to go today, but life had other plans apparently.

"Stress reactions. I get it. Decades in the army showed me all kinds of ways to deal with that. Your way is probably the best. Everything else leads to trouble or heartache at some point." He crossed his arms over his chest.

Did he suffer from post-traumatic stress or was he thinking of a friend? Someone he knew? Keena knew the doctor in her was fighting to rise to the surface but she had learned that not everyone welcomed an on-the-spot diagnosis.

"Nice footwear. Are you wearing those into town?" Travis's lips curled in amusement as he pointed at her feet.

Keena glanced down at her slippers. They were shaped like hamburgers, complete with drooping lettuce and bright red tomatoes under a sesame seed bun. "I was chasing a cow around the yard with hamburgers on my feet."

Travis's grin was contagious, so Keena giggled as they stared at each other. She'd never seen someone so open; the amusement filling his eyes and lighting up his face were unforgettable. Thanks to that moment, she now recognized his eyes were blue.

Since blue eyes were her weakness, that was a game changer.

"You're lucky to have survived this, Keena." Travis chuckled and covered his heart with his hand. "I don't believe I've laughed this hard in… I can't even remember."

"Good. I'm glad my fright and overwhelming embarrassment has some silver lining," Keena drawled and coughed as giggles threatened again. "Are you ready to go into Prospect? I believe I will change my footwear in case we encounter any other cattle today."

"Ready when you are, but we can take a look at the fence before we go, see if we can find Chuck's point of entry." Travis stepped up on the porch and followed her to the screen door. She opened it and stepped inside, while he hovered in the doorway. Was he afraid to come in?

"Did you want some coffee before we go? It's so strong you'll be able to hear colors but I'm not sure that's a downside."

He shook his head. "No, I don't drink coffee. Don't need the caffeine jitters most days."

Keena didn't spin around with her prescription pad in hand, but his comment filtered into her brain as she changed into boots. Whether or not it was PTSD, Travis was on guard for the physical components of stress.

Keena grabbed her phone from the table and her puffy jacket. "Now that I've recovered from the shock of meeting Chuck this morning, I wonder if he was one of the critters I imagined walking around the yard last night. You'd think the coyotes would have every creature smaller than Chuck cuddled up safe and sound somewhere to avoid being dinner."

"Most of the critters around are more of the cute, mostly harmless type, and the coyotes always sound like they're standing under the window, but they could be miles away." Travis trotted across the yard to dig around in the bed of the truck before he pulled out a roll of wire and…a hammer. That she recognized. What was the other pointy tool? Her reminder to herself that no one liked interrogations floated through her brain. She could ask some other time.

Instead, she said, "I don't know anything about repairing fences."

He shrugged. "I'll say 'hold this' and then you'll hold it. I know enough for both of us."

Since he was the fence expert, Keena trailed behind Travis as he walked the edge of the yard lined by barbed wire fence. When he stopped, Keena nearly ran into his shoulder. She'd been so focused on watching where she was stepping that she missed the cue.

Travis slipped a heavy glove on. "Likely spot."

Keena studied the easy give of the barbed wire. Along most of the rest of the fence, it was stretched tightly. This section waved a bit in the breeze. "How do you know this is the spot? Because it's loose?"

He nodded. "Loose and…" He pointed at the wire.

When she looked closer, she could see strands of hair stuck on the fence. "It's a sign Chuck got a little bit of hair trimmed when he went through."

She wrinkled her nose. "Doesn't it hurt? Why would a cow do that more than once?"

Travis cleared his throat. "Steers aren't known for being smart, Doc. It's a real problem that anyone who works with livestock has encountered. They are stubborn. They are almost always hungry." He shrugged. "They defy explanation sometimes, except to say they were on one side of the fence when they wanted to be on the other, so they do whatever it takes to go through it, even if it might hurt."

Keena took the hammer he held out and inched closer to watch him snip wire off the roll in his hand. Then she held the roll, too. Travis stepped up to the sagging middle line of barbed wire and wrapped the small piece he'd cut off around it. Then he wrapped the unnamed tool around the new wire and twisted it. There was no strain showing on his face, but the way his shoulders and arms bulged was...impressive. If she hadn't watched him chop wood already, she might have been caught by surprise.

But she hadn't yet forgotten the way those muscles had worked. She was grateful to see this show, too.

When he'd twisted as far as he could, he handed her the twister-thing to dig in his pocket for a small bar thing. She had to lean in to see what he did, but he continued wrapping the loose ends of the new wire until the sharp points were tight against the fence.

Travis stepped back and tapped the wire. Instead of sagging loosely, it twanged. That was more like what she expected of the wire, so Keena was impressed again.

"Nice." She carefully poked the wire and watched it slide up and down the metal post. "But you aren't done, right?"

He shook his head, took the wire roll and the scary tool

out of her hands. She watched him snip a length of wire, wrap it around the metal post and under the barbed wire and do the wrapping thing again with the little bar thing.

This time when he stepped back, he said, "Now I'm done."

Keena handed him the hammer, disappointed that the project had taken so little time. She was happy to watch Travis do that at least one more time.

"Imagine doing that a few million times a year." Travis sighed. "All because of hardheaded animals like Chuck."

His smile was so sweet, it made her happy to see it in this instant.

"You never get tired of it?" she asked.

"Oh, I get tired of fences, for sure, but never of this place." He walked farther down the line. "When I was stationed overseas, it took forever to get back home and I noticed this kind of ache. I never knew there were levels of homesickness." He glanced at her over the shoulder. "Did you, Doc?"

She huffed out a laugh. "I'm not sure there's an official diagnosis for homesickness, but I understand your point. Maybe it's tied to how much it feels like home in the first place. I haven't been home for the holidays in years, but I don't miss Iowa, you know?"

"What about your family?" Travis tipped his head to the side.

Keena studied his face as she drew up alongside him. Trying to talk to Travis was a challenge. He didn't say anything more than he had to.

Somehow that made her so much more interested in everything he shared.

"My parents…" Keena wondered if she was going to get into this. "Those families where there are multiple remarriages on both sides and you have half siblings and step-siblings and you're the oldest on this side and the black sheep if you only talk about this group of kids but the golden child if you're considering those only from your dad's side..." She sighed. "It's not easy figuring out who you really are while you're in the middle of all that. Getting away from it made things much clearer. I love them, but when I go home, everything gets cloudy again. Talking on the phone one-on-one is much easier."

She wasn't sure she wanted to see his reaction to that. It wasn't easy to confess that family wasn't "everything" to her. She'd heard so many people talk about the sacrifices they made to stay connected in this modern world. For Keena, it was better to get snapshots instead of a running narrative.

"I might not get how all those connections change things, but I definitely understand needing to get away to figure out who you are." Travis took the wire from her and snipped off another piece. He repeated the steps to tighten the top wire near the corner of the lot that met the Rocking A fence line. "Becoming an Armstrong was a real process for me."

Keena bit her lip. He was talking. She didn't want him to stop.

"I can honestly see the question marks in your eyes, but you aren't letting any of them fly," Travis said as he led the way back to his truck. "Why is that?"

Keena hurried to follow him across the yard. Travis's easy amble had picked up speed.

"I've been on good behavior because I know unleashing a blizzard of questions isn't the best way to make friends." Keena frowned because she hadn't intended to be that honest.

Travis grunted. "With us, might be exactly what I need."

Keena crossed her arms over her chest at the relief that

spread through her. He was giving her permission to be herself with this. How considerate that would be.

"What are these tools called?" Keena pointed at the items in the truck bed.

He nodded. "Ah, an easy one. You've heard of a hammer?" His lips twitched as he watched her face. Keena scowled in response. "The others are fence pliers, really good for cutting wire and protecting your fingers when you need to pull or twist. And the little bar thing is called a wire-twisty thing. I'll need to do some research to get the scientific name for you. My dad taught us to repair fences with lots of pointing and waving when we offered him the wrong tool. Repeat that by process of elimination until we guessed the right tool."

"It worked for you. Someday you'll teach it to your own son the same way, huh?" Keena watched him as he processed that and knew the instant something inside him changed. His face relaxed.

"Thanks. I hadn't gotten to that, the fun part, of what I could share with any of the kids coming through here. I was stuck on the responsibility." He tugged his hat up and rolled his shoulders. "Talking to you is good, Doc. You might have cured some of what ails me."

Keena laughed. "Yeah? I am very good at my job."

The warm gleam in his expression as he smiled at her did something to Keena's heart, as if it lit up in response.

His lopsided smile was almost as attractive as his ready laughter.

As she slid into his truck, Keena was warning herself not to fall for blue eyes in a nice face. Her career was in Denver. Nothing was going to distract her from that.

When Travis pulled out onto the road, he asked, "What made you decide to face off against Chuck anyway? Eventually he would have returned home with no intervention. He always does."

Keena pursed her lips, wishing she'd known that Chuck was a homing cow. "I was afraid he'd cause an accident in the road." Was that silly?

Travis looked thoughtfully at her. She didn't want to know that she'd made a fool of herself for no reason, so she didn't ask.

"And what about holding your arms out like that?" he asked. "What did that do?"

"Make me seem bigger? More threatening?" Keena couldn't keep the question marks out of her answer.

"Hmm, I don't think that would have fooled him." Travis smiled slowly. "You've been reading up on how to escape bears, haven't you?"

Keena narrowed her eyes to try for her best steely glare before the chuckles spilled out. "Maybe I have." Then she gripped his arm. "Do not tell anyone about this encounter ever, do you hear me? The arms, the difference between steers and bulls, the hamburger slippers…all of that better be locked away or else."

She waited for him to ask, "Or else what, city girl?"

But instead, he met her stare. "I would never. This stays between you and me." Then he winked and she felt it all the way down deep in her soul.

Keena had tried to prepare herself for all the challenges of small-town life and medicine, but keeping her distance from this blue-eyed cowboy was going to be the real test.

CHAPTER FIVE

BY THE TIME Travis followed Keena back to the truck in the Homestead Market's parking lot, he was worn out, had spent twice what he'd intended, and had learned a lot about his new neighbor.

She was curious. He'd lost track of the number of questions that he'd answered. In no particular order, he'd shared: they had included space for four boys, many foster kids needed a temporary spot until family could be located, Prospect had originally been called Sullivan's Post, saying the store was "doing land-office business" meant it was a busy Saturday at Homestead Market in Western-speak, his favorite color was blue, there was no color he hated, his only decorating rule was no camouflage anything, and he hadn't set a budget for this shopping trip. Her brain moved quickly and he was almost certain it moved in a straight line somehow, but what came out of her mouth often seemed routed through left field.

Since he preferred listening to talking, catching up had been a struggle in the beginning, but her pleasure over each new fact she learned was a nice reward. He'd pushed the shopping cart in her wake, always alert for sudden stops at this cute thing or that important item she'd left off her list.

They'd only had two serious disagreements. Discussions, really.

Keena had argued passionately that the kids who came to stay needed some fun stuff, in addition to the bedding, toiletries and school supplies already picked out. Her choices: big puffy house slippers in the shape of cowboy boots or high-top sneakers, and small wireless speakers shaped like soccer balls, basketballs and footballs.

He'd given in on the speakers. They were fairly inexpensive, and he would have thought something like that was cool when he was a kid. She'd given up on the slippers but the firm set of her chin made him think she wasn't finished with the conversation.

He'd had more fun walking every aisle of the home goods section of the store than he'd expected. He'd have time to wash the denim-colored comforters, white sheets and pillowcases with red or green stripes depending on the set, and get the rooms set up before the social worker came. Keena's reasoning about her choices was sound; everything was comfortable, washable and easy to personalize when they knew who would be staying with them.

"Livery stables rented horses? Is that right?" she asked as she hefted one of the bags they'd crammed into the shopping cart after checking out.

"Horses, wagons and stalls sometimes. The blacksmith worked out of this livery stable, too." Travis handed her the next bag and watched her meticulously arrange it in the back seat of his truck. That care would come in handy since he wasn't exactly sure their haul would fit inside the cab. "Prospect was a boomtown and the livery was big business. Travelers would need fresh horses or repairs to their rigs if they made it this far before heading off on the next stage of their journey."

"I can't believe the building has been standing all this time. That's a testament to human ingenuity and the materials they chose, for sure." Keena waved a hand at Prospect's version of the big-box store housed in the large space behind the old building's facade. "This is amazing." She took her smaller bags of groceries and settled them in the tight space behind her seat. "I can't wait to see what other surprises this town has."

That was the second thing he'd learned about Keena: she was enthusiastic. Instead of hanging back on their shopping trip, she'd taken the lead and made her selections confidently.

What he'd remember most was how generous she was. When she wedged the corkboards that she'd chosen carefully to be her housewarming gift for each boy against the seat, he said, "You didn't have to buy anything for my new family but thank you for doing that and taking so much time with me today. For everything."

She paused and met his stare over the shopping cart. "Every kid needs a corkboard, Travis. They can hold calendars and important assignments and mementos. Very useful. And if I'm here when you meet your kids, I will also personally arrange a welcome message for each one on these boards."

"And if you aren't here?" Travis asked. At some point in the hour-plus he'd spent trailing behind Keena, he'd realized he was going to miss having her nearby. Had anyone ever made such an impact in such a short time? Maybe Prue and Walt, but he couldn't name anyone else.

"Once I go back to Denver, you'll have to do the best you can to carry on my legacy," Keena said and shook her finger. "I bought plenty of extra cards and things to keep you in business for a while." She picked up the small bag that was filled with greeting cards, streamers and balloons and whatever she thought might add a touch of celebration for each new boy.

He hadn't had the heart to explain to her that few of these kids would be ready for a party when they arrived. There wouldn't be anything to celebrate for some time.

"You're thinking hard now." Keena arranged the cards against the corkboard. "Probably because I have no idea what the situation will be when these kids get here." She waited for his nod before doing the same. "You're right. I was never a foster kid, so I can't relate, but I have spent time with kids who have been through trauma." She shifted the bags around to make sure they were packed correctly. "There is a point in the emergency room when something normal, something that shows care and concern and that life goes on, makes a difference for that kid. Am I wrong that it's the same for kids in foster care?"

Travis braced his foot on the cart as he considered that. "No. You are not wrong." He sighed. "I'll never forget when Prue took me fabric shopping the first time. She was making me a quilt of my own, something she did for every one of her boys. My colors. My pattern. Mine to keep no matter where I went next." He still had it, rolled up carefully and stored in the top of his closet. Years of use had left the seams weak, but he could never give it up.

She had made something for him. He didn't exactly understand what went into making that quilt, but he had seen the time Prue had invested in a gift for him. That made it valuable then and priceless now.

"What did you choose?" Keena asked as she took the cart and walked it around into the cart corral.

"The pattern is a star, I can't remember the name, but the colors are bright blue and purple. She added in some black, and it might be the loudest quilt ever assembled but I love it." His grin matched hers as they stared at each other over the bed of the truck. "My biggest worry is that so many fosters don't even have suitcases. I didn't. If I was lucky, I had a heavy-duty trash bag to throw all my stuff in when it came time to go. Other times I had to make hard decisions on what to leave behind." Travis wanted her to realize this but he didn't want to reopen old wounds. "It can hurt when the 'normal' from one place doesn't make the cut when you have to move on. That's all I'm saying. The speakers will fit in tight spaces. Great idea."

Keena bit her bottom lip as she studied his face. "Okay, I understand." She held up both hands in surrender. "We did good work today."

"And," Travis said as he motioned over his shoulder, "we missed the lunch rush. If we head for the Ace High now, we may have the run of the place. I'm buying." He wanted the opportunity to talk to Keena without an audience, although Faye would be there. She ran the place for her grandparents and tried to do it singlehandedly as waitress, hostess and sometimes cook. She would spread the word back to his mother, but Faye was always at the restaurant. There was no way to avoid that exposure. She'd been his first friend in Prospect, not counting his brothers, so Travis expected her to share just enough gossip to appease his mother and no more.

"We could walk and take a look at the buildings as we go." Keena covered her eyes with one hand as she tried to avoid the late-afternoon sun. "Let's do that."

Before he could agree, he heard, "Hey, Keena, wait up."

They both turned to see Jordan trotting through the parking lot. "I want to introduce you to my sister Sarah. She surprised us all by coming into town earlier than we thought."

He knew Wes would be over the moon when he found out Sarah was back.

Sarah brushed her hair back into her ponytail before holding her hand out. "If I'd known my sister was going to drag me through the grocery store on the way home instead of taking the direct route, I might have put on some makeup before we were introduced." Sarah glared at Jordan before smiling pleasantly at Keena. "I'm Sarah Hearst. I think we're going to be neighbors."

Keena shook her hand enthusiastically. It reminded him a bit of the way Dr. Singh greeted visitors. Was that something they taught in medical school?

"Yes, I'm looking forward to seeing this lodge." Keena pointed at the bags in the back seat. "I found a whole collection of Cookie Queen cookbooks in the kitchen, so I'm going to try my hand at one of the recipes as a way of making sure my new coworkers are predisposed to like me."

Sarah clasped her hands together. "Oh, nice, you've heard all about our history, I guess? That will leave lots of time for us to find out all about you."

Keena shrugged. "No famous relatives on my side."

"But I bet you have plenty of wild stories to tell about working in the emergency room." Jordan held up a hand as if to stop her protest. "Let's make plans for lunch after Handmade's first Sip and Paint night on Friday." She pointed to Sarah. "This one's the marketing genius, so the name for Dad's painting event is still being brainstormed."

Travis was interested to see Keena wrinkle her nose. "I have zero artistic talent."

Jordan snorted. "Hasn't stopped my dad from trying to teach me everything he knows. The only real requirement for this is whether you drink wine." She waited for Keena to nod. "And do you like gossip?"

Keena glanced at him before nodding sheepishly. He was learning Keena liked information of any kind.

"Who doesn't?" Sarah drawled. "Friday night, join us at the Mercantile. You'll love Prue."

"Oh, I do." Keena smiled at Travis before returning her focus to Sarah. "She makes a wonderful red sauce."

Sarah's mouth formed a perfect O, which Travis took to

mean that Jordan hadn't had a chance to update her sister on the dinner with the Armstrongs.

"We're about to head over to lunch. Should we save you a spot?" he asked Jordan. "I'm interested to find out what happened to all the plans you had today that kept you from helping me with choosing stuff for the new bedrooms."

Jordan blinked her eyes oh-so innocently. "No, no, no lunch for us, Sarah's in a hurry to get back to the lodge and her boyfriend." Jordan said the last word in the same obnoxious younger-sister tone she always used to give her sister and Wes a hard time. Travis appreciated anyone who kept his "older" brother on his toes. "I wanted to get Sarah's expert opinion on some dishes I was thinking of picking up for a continental breakfast at the lodge."

"Do we have anyone staying at the lodge? No. Do we have a plan for this breakfast? Not really. Have I been driving for hours and hours and hours to get from California to Colorado? Yes," Sarah said with a hiss as Jordan took her hand to drag her into the store.

"Whose fault is that?" Jordan asked brightly. "And you'll want your special drinks to be in the lodge's refrigerator this afternoon. Guess where we have to go to get those?" Jordan turned to wave over her shoulder at them, her eye roll very familiar.

"Sisters are pretty much the same everywhere you go, I guess," Keena murmured. "Arguing as a way of showing love."

Travis was skeptical. "I wouldn't know if that's true, but would you believe there's a third one? She lives in New York. We haven't had the pleasure of meeting her yet. Patrick Hearst, their dad, is a real nice guy. Quiet."

Keena smiled at him. "Can you blame him?"

Travis grinned. "Let's tour, shall we?"

They walked and talked. Keena asked him about the

wood boardwalk, what the buildings were framed in, how much money would have been stored in Prospect's bank during the boom, and why the hair salon and barbershop had split the floors of the old bathhouse the way they had.

Luckily, she never got tired of his variations on "I don't know."

"What I'm hearing is that I need to take this tour again with Clay," Keena said and pulled open the door to the Ace High.

"If you want to know about old construction, yes. If you're interested in the history of the town, see if you can get Rose Bell, who runs the Bell House Bed-and-Breakfast," Travis said and motioned over his shoulder at the blue Victorian that took pride of place in Prospect's downtown. "Her family has been here a long time. She might be able to answer questions, too."

As they sat down in a booth, Keena said, "Thank you for being patient with all my questions. I get the impression that I've forced you to talk more than usual today. Have you used up your quota of words for the rest of the year?"

Travis grunted. "Not yet, but I am going to sit in silence this afternoon."

When she laughed as he'd hoped she would, he relaxed. Teasing her was a gamble.

Keena reached across the table to squeeze his hand and he knew for certain the gamble had paid off. "I have had a lovely day. I can't imagine a better way to get used to the town."

He wanted to ask why that was so. What had made the difference? Was it knowing that she could find whatever she needed, even in a place as small as Prospect? Or the way her curiosity was fired up in a new place with all these questions to be answered? Or was it the people she'd met?

Why did he hope his company was somewhere in the answer?

Instead of asking any of his own questions, Travis waved at Faye so she'd know they were ready to order.

"Tell me what's good here," Keena said as she moved the ketchup bottle and saltshaker around. "I need to study the menu."

Before he could reply, Faye slid to a stop next to their table. "I see Trav hasn't explained how the Ace works." She slipped her pen behind her ear. "Two choices. You can have whatever you want as long as it's one or the other of those options. Today, we have meat loaf and pot roast for dinner. Lunch is long gone at this point. The fixin's include fluffy mashed potatoes, charred brussels sprouts, glazed carrots, and rolls or corn bread muffins." Faye pointed at Travis. "He's having meat loaf, hold the sprouts. No sprouts will ever touch his lips voluntarily." The way she shook her head sadly reminded Travis that he and Faye would never see eye to eye on some of her vegetable offerings.

Faye pulled out her pen and said, "Now what can I get you, Dr. Murphy?"

Travis snorted at the way Keena's mouth dropped open in surprise. "How did you know? Pot roast and I'll have his brussels sprouts, too. With coffee."

"Oh, honey," Faye said as she patted her shoulder, "first time in a small town?" Then she was gone before Keena could comment on that. Faye didn't need to waste time standing around, especially with a large family entering the restaurant.

Keena raised her eyebrows at him, the question in her eyes.

"Is that your way of asking..." Travis watched her hold

both hands out as if she meant to encompass Faye, the menu, their table and how Faye knew who she was. "Well, you understand there's no menu now. This place is named after the saloon that used to be here, the Ace High, fanciest one in town. Faye is your neighbor on the other side, unlucky owner of Chuck, and..."

"We've been friends ever since Travis landed in Prospect." Faye plopped a glass of water in front of Travis before sliding the bread basket and Keena's cup of coffee across the table. "Sometimes more, if you include three weeks one summer where I convinced him to be my boyfriend." Faye put a hand over her mouth to cover her chuckle. "No one counts that, though."

Faye dropped her bombshell and then hustled back to the kitchen.

Keena raised her eyebrows again.

"Does that look mean you're not going to ask all your questions?" Travis sipped his water as he watched her stir the coffee in front of her.

"I mean, I wouldn't know where to start. Did you break Faye's heart? Did she break yours?" Keena asked as she inched closer as if she couldn't wait to hear more.

"No hearts were involved. Lips possibly, but no other body parts were included that summer." Travis relaxed in the seat and watched as the information filtered through Keena's brain. Her face was so expressive. He read amusement, interest, and then he could see the questions start to build.

Sort of how steam escapes before a volcano erupts.

Luckily, Faye deposited two plates on the table and Keena's mouth dropped open again.

Faye laughed. "That's the reaction I like to see."

"Keena already met your favorite steer this morning, Faye. I patched a couple of spots on the fence, but I warned her he couldn't be contained by any fence built by man." Travis met Keena's stare. Was she afraid he was going to tell more about that encounter? He never would. He'd learned how to keep confidences early on.

"I swear, that troublemaker. He don't know where the grass is really greener, which is where I put it out for him every morning about dawn." Faye slapped the table. "I'll ask Gramps to keep a closer eye on that section of fence, Keena."

Since Gramps was almost ninety, Travis tried to help as much as he could. "Should be good for a bit."

Faye squeezed his shoulder. Travis understood the thank-you that she couldn't put into words. "The Armstrongs make fine neighbors but stop by without an Armstrong and I'll give you all the juicy gossip you need, Dr. Murphy. And I'll see you at this painting thing the Hearsts are putting together. Not sure the restaurant will be left standing if I leave for a couple of hours on Friday night, but it's time to find out."

Keena didn't have a chance to respond because Faye was already trotting across the dining room to answer the ringing phone. "Does she run this whole place by herself?"

Travis glanced at Faye over his shoulder. "Tries to. If a painting class will convince her to take some help, it'll be a good thing. And if you ever need to know anything about anything that is happening in this town, Faye should have the information. Somehow, the time she spends here, the people who come and go, she always knows things first." She was also the kind of friend who knew when to spread the story and when to sit on it. For that, she was one of his favorite people in town. "Her grandparents have had the smaller operation on the other side of the house you're renting for as long as I can remember. They're older now, and Faye is doing her best to run the place and keep the whole town fed here."

"So you fix the fence when you can." Keena smiled slowly.

Travis felt the color rising in his nape. Something about the sparkle in her eyes felt like approval.

Or admiration?

Whatever it was, he was more comfortable with rapid-fire questions that put him on the spot. The way she stared at him now made him wonder how much she could read on his face. He worked hard to contain everything, but this pressure of stepping up to lead the family in fostering a new generation, something that mattered to all of them and that he was most likely the least qualified to do, was causing weak spots in his defense. Was Keena going to be the one to slip through the gaps?

CHAPTER SIX

BY MIDMORNING OF Keena's first day of shadowing Dr. Singh at Prospect Family Practice, she'd discovered how the rhythm of her work life had changed.

The most obvious difference was the daylight. She'd spent so much time working the night shifts in Emergency, that she'd forgotten how cheerful morning people could be. Dr. Singh's office manager, Reginald, was possibly the purest ray of early sunshine Keena had ever met. He managed to hold on to that positivity even in the face of near-overwhelming obstacles, which included a jammed copier and the long-suffering stares of both Kim, Dr. Singh's physician's assistant, and Emily, who took care of billing and appointments.

Reginald was unperturbed by this. He called them Thunder and Lightning to their faces as he poured their coffee mugs to the brim.

She and Dr. Singh were in the exam room with Sam Walker, midseventies, retired rural postal carrier who appeared as healthy as could be to Keena but who seemed to have a monthly standing meeting with Dr. Singh. They could hear Reginald singing and whistling while he worked.

"Sam, Dr. Murphy here has made a rookie mistake." Dr. Singh dropped the stethoscope he'd been using to listen to Sam's heart and lungs. "Reg can be annoyingly chipper on cloudy days. With sunshine and the cowboy cookies

Keena brought in, we may need to sedate him for his own safety. If we don't, the rest of the office will be ready to commit mayhem."

Sam sipped from the coffee cup Dr. Singh had passed him as soon as they'd walked into the exam room. "They're good cookies, ma'am. I almost want to sing, too, but it ain't nearly as pleasant as all that joyful noise." He finished the last bite of the cookie he'd taken the second time Dr. Singh insisted he try them.

"I wanted to make friends. Food seemed a good start. I like food." Keena rested her elbow on the counter, curious as to what was going on here, but nonetheless happy to watch Dr. Singh work.

In the pause of conversation, they could hear someone singing show tunes.

"Is that *Oklahoma*?" Keena whispered. Movie musicals were one of her nerdy hobbies. Listening to Reginald sing made her wish she'd packed some of her favorites to bring along.

"That's usually a Friday song. When the good news that the weekend is coming sparks a joy that cannot be contained, you will hear about the surrey with the fringe on top so often that you will wish fringe had never been invented." Dr. Singh slid down into the chair beside Sam and picked up his own cup. "Did you check on volunteering at the library, Sam? The sign I saw for part-time help was gone the last time I went in."

Since Dr. Singh seemed to be prepared to make endless small talk and the list of appointments Emily had shown her was long, Keena wondered if she was supposed to take the lead in this exam, to get them on track.

Before she could start asking medical questions, someone rapped on the door. "We've got an emergency in Exam Two, doc. Most likely needs stitches."

Keena immediately set her cup down and found Kim and their new patient in the exam room next door. When someone was bleeding, no one waited for backup in the emergency room.

She listened to the young woman, whose name was Lucky Garcia it turned out, tell Kim about the accident she'd had the night before while she was working on a car that she was restoring. She'd been wrenching at a carburetor when the tool in her hand slipped, leaving a gash in her palm. Two little girls were hanging on either side of their mother while she tried to explain how silly she felt about the clumsy accident.

"Looks like stitches to me. What do you think, Dr. Murphy?" Kim asked but was marching toward the door, already on a mission to grab everything they'd need to sew up the wound on Lucky's hand, she guessed.

Keena pulled the rolling stool closer to Lucky. "Since you are still bleeding, Ms. Garcia, I think so. Bring me..."

The door closed behind Kim before Keena had finished her sentence. Annoyance bubbled up because if the nurse had waited one more minute to listen to her instructions, they might have saved time. Instead they'd waste it when she returned, and Keena would have to make corrections. When the tense silence in the room registered, Keena focused on the kids. "And who are these young ladies?"

"Meet Eliana and Selena." Lucky ran a hand over each little girl's head. "Most commonly known as the Garcia twins around town. They are always in motion, so they create a blur that makes it even more difficult to distinguish who is who."

Keena laughed. "Must be tough to keep up with them."

"You have no idea." Lucky sighed. "I couldn't leave them with Dante at the garage because he's shorthanded today and you do not want to see what these two can get up to without constant vigilance."

Kim returned with the tray. "I know 3-0 sutures are pretty standard, but Dr. Singh would go with smaller based on the wound, so I also brought 4-0." She passed Keena the tray and moved over to enter notes in Lucky's file. Keena mentally ran through the usual checklist: nylon sutures in the smaller size, which Keena also preferred, needle driver, tissue forceps… Kim had gathered everything.

Keena's worry eased. Dr. Singh had built a strong team. She had help when he left.

Just as Keena dabbed the antiseptic along the edges of the wound, Dr. Singh stuck his head in the open doorway. "Oh, thank goodness. I was afraid I was too late!"

Keena turned to face him, prepared to state that she had the situation in hand, but he was holding out two cookies and making "come hither" motions toward the girls. "I was afraid I would have to eat these treats myself."

"Oh, no, we wouldn't want that." Lucky's voice was dramatic. She was committed to the bit.

"We'll go eat these in my office. Join us when you get all this taken care of," Dr. Singh called as he led the twins out of the exam room.

Lucky immediately relaxed. "I've been pretending this didn't bother me all day long. It bothers me."

Keena added more antiseptic around the wound. "This will feel better any minute now. You should have had this done last night. This must be pretty painful," Keena said calmly as she made the first stitch, hoping to get this started and finished before Lucky caught on to what was happening. Making conversation while she worked had always been a simple but effective way to distract a patient from the worst.

"I had it stopped last night, but this morning, I noticed I

bled through my bandage almost as soon as I got to work." Lucky rolled her other hand into a fist. "And I tried to find a babysitter, but Dr. Singh is so good with the girls, I knew it would be fine."

Keena bit her lip as she made quick work of five more stitches and then pressed gauze to the wound to stop the bleeding. Would she have thought to also distract the little girls while she worked? Keena wasn't so sure.

"No hospital around. Even the after-hours medical office is almost an hour away." Lucky glanced down and smiled when she realized Keena had finished. "Hey. That's amazing."

"I wondered about after-hours emergencies. Dr. Singh mentioned he sometimes gets calls, but they're filtered through an answering service. Why didn't you try to get him?" Keena scooted back on the stool and moved the tray to the counter behind her. She would have been available to help with something like this, too.

"Dr. Singh deserves to be off of work when he can, you know?" Lucky pressed her fingers lightly to the stitches. "I thought it was under control until this morning."

Being the only doctor in town was going to take some getting used to. In her estimation, this should have been an emergency call, but Lucky had made a different decision.

"Think you'll like small-town life, Dr. Murphy?" Lucky asked as she waved at Keena's scrubs and white coat. Dr. Singh preferred a simple shirt, jeans and running shoes. "We don't often see Dr. Singh in his medical duds, but I imagine you're facing even bigger differences than the dress code."

Keena stood to wash her hands. "Scrubs are comfortable. I don't know why everyone doesn't wear them. And apparently, cookies are dangerous to morning people. They inspire show tunes and excessive high spirits which can annoy their coworkers. I've been on the night shift so long I didn't know that." She tilted her head. Reginald was singing something else now. "Is that 'Happy' or..."

Lucky nodded. "I think so. He loves positive vibes. If you're still around for Western Days in the spring, be sure to catch Reginald onstage. He does the most amazing song impersonations. You're standing there, looking right at a cowboy, as if he'd just jumped off a bucking bronco, dusted off his hat, and picked up a microphone, but what you're hearing sounds like Frank Sinatra or Billy Joel or David Bowie. His range is wild."

Keena rested a hip against the counter as she tried to imagine the middle-aged father who coached his son's flag football team performing "Uptown Girl." It was easier than she expected.

Lucky was grinning when Dr. Singh swung by to drop off the twin girls. "If you're like Jordan and Sarah Hearst, Doctor Keena, they were both worried that life in Prospect would be boring." She managed to hide a grimace as her little girls hit her at full speed. "But one thing you can count on around here is that this town comes up with its own entertainment."

Dr. Singh nodded proudly. "Oh, yes, Keena, you missed the Halloween contest in the park. I enter every year but my costume hasn't won yet. And when the snow starts to fall, Prospect is a beautiful place. My wife and I will be sorry to miss winter this year."

Reginald groaned from outside in the hallway. "Winter, schminter. Give me sunshine."

Keena thought she and Reginald could agree on that as well as the best playlist, but she hadn't had a chance to experience snowy mountains. Maybe she'd like it? Blizzards in Iowa had been zero fun.

"Guess I better get back to the garage." Lucky stood

and took the wrapped cookies Dr. Singh held out. "First-rate medical care with cookies to go? No way you can get that in Denver."

Keena nodded at Kim who was hovering. "If you see any signs of infection, come back in and let me take a look. We'll remove the stitches next week."

Lucky and her little girls were a happy, noisy parade down the hall when Dr. Singh clapped her on the shoulder. "Good work, Keena. I hope you see how easy it is to settle into Prospect."

Keena made a few notes on Lucky's chart and asked Kim to schedule a follow-up phone call for the next day so she could make sure there was no further breakthrough bleeding before she returned to her coffee mug.

"Reg, do we have time for a break?" Dr. Singh asked.

"Yep, next appointment isn't for half an hour," Reginald said as he juggled the ringing phone, waving goodbye to the Garcias, and topping off Keena's coffee cup.

"Keena, let's go sit in my office. I want to show you my files." Dr. Singh motioned for her to follow him, but when they were both settled, he stretched his arms with a happy sigh. "It's nice not to run from one emergency to the next, isn't it? Time to catch your breath, regroup. It has a positive effect on my well-being, you know?"

Surprised at the conversation opener, Keena sipped her coffee to take a moment to consider her answer. "It's only day one, Dr. Singh, but I don't believe I'll have any trouble settling in." She smiled. "Can't get too comfortable, though. You know I need my running shoes when I go back to Denver. Very few coffee breaks and breathing has to be worked in on an as-needed basis." She bit into the cookie and mentally patted herself on the back. Following the Cookie Queen's recipe had been simple.

She'd enjoyed the process so much that she'd ended

up trying a second and a third recipe, so now Keena had a whole collection of cookies to deliver after work. The pharmacy inside the Homestead Market would get a container, for sure.

She wasn't sure it was important to have a good working relationship with the town's pharmacist, but it couldn't hurt.

Not as much as eating two dozen cookies all by herself, anyway.

"Do you think you can work on calling me PJ before you go back to your regular life?" he asked with his broad smile and twinkling eyes. When they'd first met, Keena had trusted him instantly. That was a rare reaction to have as a resident at the mercy of whatever attending physician was on duty that day, but Dr. Singh had been all about education and compassion. Some of the other doctors who'd taught her had been as good with teaching technical stuff, but none had been as thoughtful or encouraging as Dr. Singh.

"I'll try. PJ." Keena wrinkled her nose. "Sounds funny to my ears."

"But to mine, exactly right." He held a finger up. "I've mentioned how grateful I am for you stepping in here. Prospect has become my home and I worried about leaving my new family without someone to care for them. I don't worry anymore."

Keena chewed her cookie and swallowed carefully. It would not do to choke when he'd said such a nice thing. "I needed the break. This is going to work out very well for both of us."

"How is the house?" Dr. Singh asked.

"Sleeping is not easy. Yet. The change in schedule and the absolute lack of any noise has taken some getting used to, but otherwise, the place is great." Keena was prudently avoiding any mention of Chuck or her rescue from the beast thanks to Travis Armstrong. That story would go with her to the grave.

"It was nice to have Lucky mention how we make our own entertainment here." Dr. Singh motioned at Reginald who had transitioned to whistling. Keena couldn't identify the tune. "While you are here, maybe you could give some thought to how it would be to live here. Permanently."

Keena crossed her legs and braced her elbows on the arms of the comfortable chair as she tried to understand his point. Prospect was a lovely town, but she had no plans to exchange it for the career she'd built in Denver.

"Why did you need a break?" he asked softly. When Dr. Singh got serious, his expression transitioning from friendly smile to patient understanding, it made everyone around him nervous. He was very good at his job. This expression was a sign that things had gotten real.

This was what he meant by treating the whole patient.

"You remember how I was in the early days." Keena pinched a pleat in her pants and forced herself to meet his stare squarely. Convincing them both that she was in control and recognized her own limitations was important here. "Working Emergency requires steady hands, right?" He nodded in agreement. "And I always had steady hands when I needed them."

"You did. No one was calmer in the face of the unknowns that arrived at our door." He pushed his glasses up. "But as I recall, it still took a toll on you. Running on zero sleep. Very little food that counts as nutrition. Constant adrenaline. It builds up. Was that the first time you and I discussed how important sleep was, even for medical residents?"

It had been. She'd had to learn how to turn off her brain when it was time to rest.

She nodded. "You kept dropping notes and cards with the same website written on it in my coat pocket." Eventually, she'd surrendered and visited the site, and learned so many of the mindfulness exercises that she depended on today to siphon off the anxiety.

"Because being present is important." Dr. Singh said the words she knew by heart. He'd said them often enough.

"I haven't forgotten any of that. I needed to learn it and I still use it." Keena forced her fingers to relax. Something about this conversation was making her more tense than she'd been on her first day at a new place of work. That hadn't happened in years, so she'd had the jitters.

"There came a time for me," Dr. Singh said slowly as he stared at her over his glasses, "where my coping skills were failing me. I added exercise and cut out caffeine, but I still reached the point where sleep was impossible to come by. The time adds up and creates these memories that are easy to file away during the shift but harder to store when you should be free to think of other things." He braced his hands over his chest, covering the word *Vail* in the center of his sweatshirt.

"Right. So we take a break, we regroup, and then we come back to work stronger." Keena smiled. "I don't know if a mission trip to Haiti is going to be much of a break for you, but you will be so happy to see your small town again, whether or not there's a lot of nightlife to keep you busy."

He pursed his lips. "But of course. I know what Prospect means to me, my career and my life. I don't want to sacrifice one for the other, you understand. Here, I can have everything, do whatever it is I dream of. My question for you is..."

Keena braced herself. This had been the whole point of the conversation, of course.

She trusted Dr. Singh. If he had been diagnosing her, would she be able to ignore his judgment?

"What if you enjoy your time here so much that it's even harder to absorb the demands of Emergency when you go back?" Dr. Singh reached across the desk to grip her hand. "Just because there is only one doctor in Prospect now doesn't mean that this is how it has to be."

Keena gripped his hand tightly. "What are you saying?"

"Life and careers and medicine and family are all about timing." Dr. Singh smiled. "What if this is the perfect time for a break and for you to consider if you'd like to be a partner with an old friend in a small-town family practice?"

Keena laughed. "PJ," she said carefully, her lips forming the letters awkwardly, "I've built something in Denver. I could have left and gone to bigger hospitals and cities, but it's my emergency department. How could I leave it?"

He shrugged. "You wouldn't be the first to determine you've gone as high as you could go there."

"Then why would I..." *Leave it for a place like this?* Keena didn't finish the question because she didn't want to insult him, but it floated in the air between them.

She could do more, for sure. Leaving Denver to come to Prospect would mean doing less.

Wouldn't it?

He shrugged. "Let's say the situation this morning had been reversed." He clasped his hands together on the desk. "Lucky and her girls came in first and I started the sutures. What would you have done?"

Keena shifted in her seat. She knew where this was headed. "Offered to take over the sutures so you could..."

His sly smile confirmed she was falling into his trap. "Instead of offering to babysit for a few minutes to give mom a break..." He held up a finger. "Or volunteering to have my monthly sit-down with Sam, you would have done only what you think you're good at."

Keena wanted to argue because this was going to turn into Dr. Singh teaching her something but… "Right. That's right. I couldn't tell that there was anything wrong with Sam."

He shook his head. "Nothing but loneliness. He retired and lost his wife in the past couple of years. She had a heart attack, so his initial visits were out of concern over his health, but he's fine."

Keena rubbed her forehead. "I should have paid better attention in my psych rotation."

His huff of amusement reassured her. "No real psychology needed. Empathy, compassion, curiosity, those are way more important here. Sam and I talk about current events, drink coffee and after twenty or thirty minutes, we both feel better and go on about our days. Next month, that will be you. What are you going to do?"

What a scary question.

"I was thinking about how different the rhythms were between Denver and here this morning. I don't have any idea what's in store for me yet, do I?" Keena asked.

"You have accomplished everything you can in Denver, Keena. You know it. I know it. What if, instead of a bigger city with a bigger hospital with bigger trauma…" He waited for her to meet his eyes. "What if you need to try bigger medicine? To learn new ways to heal people that might require more than technique?"

Keena sipped her coffee. "You are so sneaky."

He laughed until he had to wipe tears from his eyes. "I really am. Almost everyone loves me too much to point that out, but you are not like everyone else." He exhaled. "I wanted a new challenge when I arrived in Prospect. I found it."

"But you were always so good with patients, PJ." The nickname was a bit less weird this time.

He grimaced. "I wasn't so different from you when I started. Excellent medical skills but the struggle to slow down and connect with people took time. That requires maturity and confidence that you know what you know, I believe. I made myself do it and look at me now." He held out his arms to encompass his office. "On top of the world."

In a tiny town in the Colorado Rockies when he could have been running metropolitan departments anywhere.

But with the time to follow his interests, his passions, and be with a wife, granddaughters, a whole town who loved him.

"The good news is you don't have to figure it all out today, Keena." PJ stood and pointed at the door. "And you won't have to do it the way I did. This team? They're really, really good. Getting them here to Prospect wasn't easy, but it was worth the trouble."

Keena followed him out of his office to go check on the next patients. Reginald was singing. Kim was unboxing supplies and putting them in the ruthlessly organized supply cabinet PJ had discussed so proudly. Emily was loading paper back into the copy machine. Prospect Family Practice ran efficiently. All it needed was a doctor who could continue to treat patients well.

For the first time in a long time, her job had changed. This was a different kind of medicine, one built on relationships.

Keena had three months to find out if she was capable of being that kind of doctor. Dr. Singh had given her a shot at something new.

Whether she was ready or able to take on that challenge was up to her.

CHAPTER SEVEN

THE WAY ELLEN MONTOYA, the caseworker assigned to review Travis's application to foster children, surveyed the crowded kitchen table upon her arrival had him second-guessing his request for his whole family to be present for the final home study. Travis knew it was important to introduce Ellen to everyone, because they were his support system, but when all the Armstrongs were gathered in one place, it was too much. Jordan and Sarah Hearst were on the periphery, too, hovering near the refrigerator.

In case.

That's what Sarah had said. They had wanted to be nearby in case they were needed.

Travis hadn't had time to consider what sort of event might require nine adults in total, but regardless, they were prepared for it.

Ellen cleared her throat. "Well, thank you for the introductions. It is lovely to meet you all. I know Prue and Walt by reputation, of course. They served on the board of the foster support foundation. Every now and then, Bridget Williams mentions how much they have contributed over the years." She smiled at Travis. "And I hope you know that we take every home study seriously. This is our chance to make sure you've considered the impact adding a foster child, even temporarily, will have on your home and family.

"When we meet someone who has even loftier goals

like yours, to take on the older kids who may have reached the end of our ability to help, it's critical to take enough time to make the right decision." She patted his hand and Travis had to focus hard not to grip hers too tightly. As scared as he was of failing, he wanted this. It was almost impossible to put into words how important this was, but he was getting so close. They had already come so far.

"Wes, Clay, Grant and Matt..." Ellen made sure to look at each man directly as she addressed him. "You understand the impact of what we're doing here, and the work you've all done to create a comfortable, spacious place is obvious. The difference between the house I first saw and today is impressive."

"It's easy to get stuck in the past. The old house was bogged down, but these boys are the future, Miss Montoya." Walt nodded. "Took a minute for us old-timers to catch up." There was a sharp knock under the table and he winced but carried on. Travis thought his mother had shifted in her seat. Was she giving his father nonverbal signals under the table? "We'll be here to support but this is Travis's show to run. Nobody will do better for these boys who need the Rocking A."

No one? Travis wasn't sure he agreed, but he appreciated the vote of confidence.

Ellen nodded. "Then it's time to finish up this interview with Travis. Alone. Thank you all for coming."

When they started to drift away, Travis fought the urge to beg someone, anyone to stay with him. If he couldn't find the words he wanted, he could always count on Wes to step in and smooth out the awkward spots. If Wes didn't do it quickly enough, Matt would flirt with the nearest lampshade to lighten any tension. Clay and Grant weren't as skilled at the tough conversations, but both would do something, do anything they could to help.

Jordan squeezed his shoulder as she passed by, breaking into the runaway train of his thoughts. That helped.

Ellen was right.

This was his thing.

He needed to prove himself ready to take this on without them.

When the last clump of boots cleared the kitchen and the front door slammed behind the crowd, Ellen inhaled and exhaled loudly. "You ever have so many people watching you that you're convinced something is wrong? Your shirt's on inside out or your hair is being weird all of a sudden?" She fanned a hand in front of her face. "Not sure how you manage that much attention all the time."

"Ever since I told them I started this application process, that's been every family dinner and conversation. Out of the blue, everyone's watching me and waiting for something." Travis slumped in his chair with relief at hearing someone else say what he'd been feeling for too long.

He'd never have expected it to be her, but he would take any gift he could get right about now.

"And try walking into the house all by yourself at fourteen. Prue and Walt seemed the perfect parents, you know?" Travis scrubbed a hand over his forehead as he remembered how awkward he'd felt that day. "It was like my shoes were too small and I couldn't remember how to work my mouth correctly. For that matter, I still have the problem with my mouth."

She grinned. "But your feet fit your boots now?"

He nodded. "Yes, ma'am. Any trouble I have walking cannot be blamed on the fit of my shoes."

She laughed at his weak joke, and Travis attempted to relax his shoulders.

"I can tell you're nervous about this, but I only want to be sure you're ready. This kitchen will serve up good meals and, around this dinner table, you will rebuild lives that have been shattered." She rested her elbow on the table and propped her chin on her hand. "I don't know everyone's story before becoming an Armstrong. What is yours like, Travis?"

The itch of the tag in his shirt made him shift in his chair as he tried to come up with a good answer, one that was the truth without being too true. "I was one of those kids. Shattered. Runaway. Picked up by the police finally and bounced from one home to the next." For fighting. He wasn't going to say that, though. He'd had his reasons and they hadn't mattered a bit since Prue Armstrong had wrapped her arms around his bruised shoulders and welcomed him home. "When I got here, I had a hard time trusting that any of this was real. But it was. It is. Those people will help me take care of any kids who need a place."

The lump in his throat almost choked him, but Travis gulped in air.

"Prue was a big part of that, wasn't she?" Ellen asked. "It's too bad about their divorce."

"Yeah, there have been signs of..." How would he categorize this? "Re-acquaintance?" That was vague and modestly old-fashioned enough to fit his parents' relationship.

Even if his father had spent the night in town at his mother's apartment while they were all struggling to get the renovation of the ranch house finished. Neither one of them had much of anything to say about it to their sons.

Their sons appreciated the small bit of discretion.

Ellen made a note on her file, but he couldn't read it upside down. "They both made it clear that this is your thing. I wanted to talk to you about what it was like in this home with two parents, Travis. Kids are naturally drawn to some personalities, some styles. You understand? I bet the five of you boys each connected to Prue or Walt in different ways."

That much was true. He'd feared Walt was convinced he'd gotten a dud when Travis showed up. "I couldn't stay on a horse for the first three years I lived here. That put some strain on my ability to connect with Walt." Since his father had worked dawn to dusk, most of it in a saddle, Travis had missed out on some of the bonding the others had immediately. "I spent too much time with my nose in a book to be easily understood at first."

Ellen leaned back. "That must have been hard. The odd guy out, I guess?"

It had been.

There were still whispers of it, even though he knew his family loved him.

"Maybe. I believe it will also help me if I should run into a boy who doesn't quite fit the Rocking A at first glance." That was his hope. Foster care had a certain reputation. News stories covered the homes where bad things happened, but for every one of those, there were others like the Rocking A where lives were saved.

Travis had experienced one of those unhappy foster care stories first, so he knew exactly how wide the gap could be. If there was any way to build a bridge, he'd do it.

Ellen's lips curled. "You very well may be right. Have you considered how hard doing this will be on your own?"

Travis started to motion over his shoulder at the parade of people who had just left.

"I know. You have support." Ellen dipped her head down. "But Prue and Walt did this together. The fact is you don't have a partner, someone who's ready to make the hard decisions with you. Are you worried about that?"

Travis studied his hands on the table. There were a lot of answers here, but the only one he could trust was the truth. "Of course I am, but there's no guarantee I'll ever have that person in my life. I refuse to miss out on my purpose because I have a hard time asking a pretty woman out to dinner."

Ellen chuckled. "That is a fair answer, Travis Armstrong. Very fair."

She flipped through the certificates of completion for all the training he'd done. "I can't think of any other concerns I have. I expect this to be an easy approval. I'll meet with the review board and I'll let you know as soon as I have the final decision. I expect it to be quick."

"Our house tour was pretty quick. Want to see the boys' rooms again before you go?" Travis asked as he stood, ready to walk some of the nerves off. "We're pretty proud of all the work we did."

She nodded and trailed behind him as he marched toward the addition. "So we've got the two rooms, four beds total. Pretty sweet setup. We all wished we'd had something like this."

Ellen followed him inside the first room. He'd made the beds with the comfy bedding Keena had picked out, set up the corkboards she'd insisted on, and placed one of the wireless speakers he'd bought under duress on each desk. It was impossible to miss how much warmer these rooms were, thanks to Keena's input.

He sort of regretted not having the silly slippers to put on each bed, but there was time to fix that.

"A Broncos football," Ellen said as she picked up the speaker. "Interesting touch. Are you a big football fan?" Curiosity made her eyes bright behind her glasses. Why did the answer to this feel significant?

Travis cleared his throat. "Uh, no, not really, but we wanted to have something everyday, you know…something useful and fun. For little kids, stuffed animals make sense, but for older kids...speakers that they can connect to a phone or tablet seemed a good choice."

"What if they don't have a phone or tablet?" Ellen asked but waved her hand before he could stumble through an answer. "Never mind. That's a problem for later, right?" Then she crossed her arms over her chest. "Who is we? Did you and Prue pick all this out?"

"We..." Travis wished he'd been more careful there, but this seemed like another significant answer. "Keena Murphy helped. She lives next door." He pointed over his shoulder as if that was in any way helpful.

Ellen opened her file. "Keena. Someone I haven't been introduced to yet."

Before he could explain that there was no reason for an introduction as she was only visiting and not involved in this plan any further than this single step, he heard the front door open. "Travis? Are you here? Your mom waved me inside as she and Walt were leaving."

Before Travis could determine how to answer Ellen or head off Keena's arrival, they heard her coming down the hallway. It sounded like she was rolling something in front of her. What could that be? When she stuck her head around the doorway, Keena's cheeks immediately flooded with color. "Oh, I'm so sorry. I didn't mean to interrupt. I'll leave this here and go. Travis, call me later, okay?"

He'd wanted a rescue, but he hadn't imagined it this way—Keena appearing like a gift out of nowhere. Instead of allowing her to slide the wheeled suitcase his direction and scurry away, Travis quickly wrapped his hand around her wrist. He noted how she reacted to his touch. Her pulse sped up to match the pale flush in her cheeks. She brushed a loose strand of hair back into her ponytail before tangling her fingers through his.

Ellen held out her hand. "I thought I'd met all of the

Armstrongs, but you're a new face. I'm Ellen. I'm the caseworker who will be working with Travis through the learning curve as a foster parent. You are?"

Keena nodded and shook her hand. "I'm Keena. I live next door."

Since Ellen knew that part, Travis added, "Dr. Keena Murphy."

"The decorator." Ellen patted the denim comforter. "What type of medicine do you practice?" Her pen was poised to make more notes.

Keena shifted back and forth on her feet, clearly uncomfortable at being the focus here. Travis had never seen her in scrubs. They helped him understand a different side of Keena. "General medicine for now, but my background is in trauma, running the emergency department in Denver's only Level 1 trauma center."

Keena must have realized she was giving more information than required. Her mouth snapped shut.

Ellen was thoughtful as she studied the suitcase Keena had rolled in. "Are you moving in?"

Keena frowned and then seemed to notice the way Ellen pointed at the suitcase. The pink in her cheeks turned to red. "Uh, no, this is for... Travis."

Ellen raised her eyebrows. "Is he moving out?"

Keena cleared her throat. "No." She stepped back as if she'd like to make a quick exit but stopped instead. "When we were shopping to finish out these bedrooms, Travis explained that we couldn't buy too many personal items because the kids might have to leave them behind. Because they don't have a way to carry everything." She brushed the hair behind her ear again, and Travis took a chance on touching her back. The way she'd broken through his anxiety when he'd been forced to talk to his family about all this that night at dinner had stayed with him. A simple touch had reset his brain, made it easier to put his thoughts in order.

Ellen pursed her lips. "I saw the speaker. That's a nice touch, too." Her eyes darted to meet his, but he wasn't sure what that meant.

"I wanted to do funny slippers, too, but Travis talked me out of it." Keena shrugged and grimaced as she met his stare. "One thing you will learn about me, though, is that it's not that easy to get ideas out of my head once they're there, so..."

Travis watched her bend down to unzip the suitcase. Stuffed inside were a few pairs of the boot-shaped slippers and a duffel bag. "I couldn't decide if a suitcase or a duffel was better, so now you have both. Your foster kid won't have to use a trash bag when it's time to leave here. That didn't seem right to me."

Her face was bright red at this point.

And Travis was speechless. Touched. Amused. But also aware of their audience.

Ellen studied them both silently for entirely too long. "Well." She brushed off her hands. "I'll do some research, check the references you've listed, verify all the trainings are complete, and give you a call when I have the final approval from the board." She motioned between the two of them. "I'll leave you to the rest of your evening."

Confused, Travis glanced at Keena. She was staring at his hand wrapped around hers, and he understood what Ellen thought she saw: a romance between her prospective single foster dad and the beautiful doctor next door.

Exactly what she'd been in the process of suggesting before Keena had rolled in.

Keena was half a second ahead of him and determined to set everything straight. "Oh, we didn't have..."

"We didn't have any special plans for tonight, Ellen. Just

the usual." He pulled Keena to stand next to him without letting go of her hand. "There's no need to leave."

Ellen huffed out a breath. "Third wheel? No way. Besides, it's a long drive back home to be in the office bright and early tomorrow." She picked up her file and notebook and patted Keena's shoulder. "Lovely to meet you, Keena."

Travis locked his eyes with Keena's to keep her from trying to explain any further as they followed Ellen back outside to her car. The social worker was happily driving away when Keena unwrapped her fingers with a yank. "What did we do? Why didn't you set her straight?"

Travis propped his hands on his hips and stared up at the darkening night sky. "I believe we just passed my home study." The relief that settled over his shoulders was light, comfortable. For the first time in the months since he'd gotten his first negative report about the dissatisfactory, cramped, out-of-date conditions of the house, Travis was truly relieved.

And a little weak in the knees to be over that hurdle. Some of the happiness he'd been waiting for bloomed in his chest.

"By lying to your foster approver. Great start, Travis." Keena shook her head. "Your motives might have been pure, but you dragged me into lying to her, too. And I don't think lying to the people charged with keeping children safe in this world is anything to celebrate."

She huffed out a breath. "Adults who care for children should tell the truth."

The anger was easy to see in her posture.

And she was absolutely right, except… "I didn't tell her we were a couple." She'd assumed it.

"You also didn't tell the whole truth about us when it was right there. Half-truths to make your life simpler are beneath both of us." Keena's lips were a tight line. "That's disappointing."

After she'd slammed her car door and backed out of the yard, Travis crossed his arms over his chest and came to terms with how the night had gone.

His home study was complete.

All signs pointed to success there. The whole evening would have been satisfying, really, except for Keena's reaction. What she said was technically true. He had dragged her into the chaos.

But what he'd said was also technically true. He hadn't made any false claims to his social worker. If she was happier to believe he was in a relationship, what was the harm in letting the misunderstanding continue?

Even if his logic was sound, Travis knew he'd have a hard time forgetting what disappointment looked like on Keena's face.

CHAPTER EIGHT

ON FRIDAY AFTERNOON, Keena stood at the back of the group as Dr. Singh said goodbye to his staff. Comparing her own politely restrained last night in Denver to this emotional going-away celebration illustrated the differences in her and Dr. Singh's styles. This group hugged. They took pictures in pairs and then a big group photo. They had given him a small camera and orders to update them weekly on how he was doing. There were tears, both sad and happy.

It was a lot to absorb. Keena did so from the outer edge of the party while she tried to ignore the increasing anxiety building in the pit of her stomach.

How had she ever imagined anyone would accept her in place of Dr. Singh? Even Keena would rather have him in charge. No way was her rudimentary bedside manner up to earning this kind of affection.

"Keena, I'm leaving you in the best hands." Dr. Singh smiled at her warmly. "I know you'll do well here."

She smiled in agreement and hoped they were both right.

Keena wanted Dr. Singh to feel confident he was leaving his practice in good hands even if she had her own doubts. It was important to her that he trust her.

Reginald picked up Dr. Singh's bag. "Let's lock up. Doc has an early drive to the airport in the morning." The whole group moved together to turn off lights and double-check that all the computers were shut down. Keena slung her purse over her shoulder and took one last glance around Dr. Singh's office. For the next three months, it would be hers. Alone.

Just like every bit of responsibility for the health of the entire population of Prospect.

No pressure.

"You'll do well, Keena," Dr. Singh said from behind her. "I understand your concerns. Just remember that this kind of medicine is about understanding the patient more than the problem quite often and you'll do fine."

She nodded. He thought he was helping her, but he was actually speaking her biggest fear aloud.

"If you have the opportunity, please send emails and photos." Keena trailed behind Dr. Singh and tried to shove the anxiety down. Following along behind him like a lost child begging for comfort was a bad look. Her mother would have tsked if she'd seen it. "We all want to know how the mission is going." If she wasn't good at this, it might also help her count down the days until he returned.

He surprised her by wrapping his arms around her in a hug. "You're going to be fine. Thank you for doing this. My staff? They're pros. Don't hesitate to rely on them and ask for help when you need it." He raised his eyebrows and waited for her to meet his stare. They both laughed because they knew asking for help could be the sticking point.

Then he waved, slid into the driver's seat and drove off without looking back.

Just like that, she was responsible. For all of it. Everything. The weight of the world settled on her shoulders.

And specifically the future of Prospect Family Practice. Reginald, Kim and Emily were all watching her carefully. The brilliant smiles had transitioned to polite expressions.

"Big plans for the evening?" Reginald asked after receiving pointed glances from Kim and Emily. He'd obviously been elected spokesperson for the group.

Keena knew it was time to fake a little confidence until she made it. "I was considering going to the Sip and Paint at the Mercantile?" Her answer had a hint of a question at the end that she hadn't intended but it made perfect sense. She'd been wavering all week about going. In some moments, she was completely committed to jumping into the Prospect social scene and making new friends, even though she knew being the outsider at first could be uncomfortable. Then she'd remember she had no artistic talent and lacked the ability to make small talk easily when she was nervous and decide it was better to have people think her unlikable than *know* it.

Also, this divide between her and Travis made her uneasy about stepping into the room with his mother who he'd already told her would go to war for her sons. She expected Prue to be polite, but if any of the warmth of her welcome was missing, Keena would regret that.

Kim clasped her hands together. "Faye mentioned the class when I was over at the Ace yesterday. Apparently this is a trial run, only open by invitation, before Prue rolls it out for everyone to sign up. Patrick Hearst is going to be teaching everyone simple projects. Sounds like so much fun!" Her tone suggested she would have jumped at the opportunity to go if anyone had thought to invite her.

And newcomer Keena was lucky enough to have an invitation somehow.

All because she'd crashed a dinner party at the Armstrongs'.

That had worked because she'd done it without overthinking it.

Knowing the Armstrongs had improved her connections

in Prospect by leaps and bounds, but she hadn't known that going in.

It had also indirectly gotten her wrapped up in Travis's half-truth to the social worker.

She'd been thinking about that night and him all week. Keeping her distance was the smart thing to do, but she'd enjoyed every minute she'd spent with Travis. Her mind had wandered his direction way more often than she was okay with.

Was spending her Friday night with his mother and friends smart?

Keena realized it didn't matter. She was definitely going to need something to discuss with her coworkers on Monday morning. Sip and Paint filled that need perfectly.

Once the decision was made, Keena didn't waver. "I'll let you know all about it on Monday. Maybe there will be cookies, too." After the rest of the staff left, Keena decided to have dinner in town at the Ace High instead of going home before Sip and Paint started. Otherwise, the temptation to stay on the sofa at home might kick in.

Since the sun hadn't completely set, Keena left her car parked behind the Mercantile. She could stretch her legs on the way to the Ace. The Prospect Picture Show drew her attention. Windows along the front of the building showed a two-story lobby that made her think of black-and-white movie classics. Framed photos of movie star cowboys lined the walls, and the carpet was a deep, rich red. The marquee displayed movie times for *Stagecoach* that weekend.

Next to the theater was a small furniture store featuring handmade wooden items. Keena studied the exterior, interested in what kind of business had been there during the early days, but she could only make out a name, Legrand. Then she noticed a small plaque.

She read, "Legrand Millinery was once Prospect's most

exclusive milliner. Pierre Legrand created fabulous hats and other accessories that only the most successful could afford. When townspeople discovered the artist Pierre was actually Arthur Lee from Chicago, they called the sheriff in. After public discourse and trial, Arthur Lee continued to run Legrand Millinery until his death in 1924."

Keena shook her head as she crossed the street, aiming for the Ace High. "Arthur was able to fake it until *he* made it in Prospect. Good for him." The town offered opportunity and a pinch of forgiveness for him. If she stumbled in Dr. Singh's practice, maybe Prospect would do the same for her.

This time, Keena was prepared for the innovative non-menu at the Ace. Settling back to enjoy her pork chop with apple cinnamon glaze, roasted new potatoes and caramelized broccoli, Keena observed the crowd and chatted with Faye who zoomed by as she worked to feed the dinner crowd.

"Last call for pie," Faye said as she pulled off her apron. "We've got about thirty minutes until Sip and Paint starts. Want to walk over together?" The way she pointed vaguely toward the Mercantile and shifted on her feet made Keena wonder if they were going to run all the way there. Then she realized she had the conditioning to keep up after nights in the hospital, so she agreed.

"Great, I'm going to go grab a bite and make sure the kitchen is all set. Pie?" She pointed at Keena, eyebrows raised.

"Better not. No room," Keena said but realized Faye had somehow read the answer in her eyes because she was already halfway to the kitchen. She smiled and slid out of the booth to go pay for her dinner. Another benefit to the simplified "this or that" menu meant no one needed bills to say what had been ordered. She simply told the host, who was also running the cash register, she'd chosen the pork chop, offered her credit card, and was ready to go as soon as Faye finished her meal. Instead of going back to her table, she paused in front of the community bulletin board. There were flyers about upcoming holiday shows at the various schools, a garage sale hosted by the Methodist church the first Saturday of every month, and three babysitters looking for more work.

The cozy, small-town charm of the place settled over Keena as she scanned the board. She liked it. She liked all of it. The warm feeling about her new surroundings returned. Her neighbors were watching old movies, attending their kids' events and hiring babysitters they'd known since they were born for the occasional night on the town. Prospect was the kind of place people always imagined or dreamt of but here was the real thing.

"Ready?" Faye asked as she slipped on her coat. "Let's go before someone stops me, wanting intel on someone or something."

Keena followed in her wake.

Outside, Faye's pace was quick but not "busy restaurant server" level, so it felt permissible to ask questions. "Does Prospect have a newspaper?" In her head, the front-page story would be about who took first place in the spelling bee.

"No, not anymore. It closed down…" Faye paused as she considered. "Five years ago? Lucky Garcia runs a community page on social media and she tries to highlight all the big news around town." She got out her phone to pull up the website and show Keena. "You need to follow her. When the weather improves, she sets up food truck nights at the garage."

Keena favorited the site on her own phone. "Are you

encouraging me to eat somewhere else, Faye? What about the Ace?"

Faye sighed. "Honestly, one night a month? I'll take the break, thank you. When you're the only one in town, the demand turns to pressure and I feel that." She wrinkled her nose. "You may, too, now that you're the only doctor around."

When they walked inside Handmade for their trial Sip and Paint, Prue hustled them upstairs. "Finally! I'm so excited about this night I can hardly stand it!" She then swept past them in the large open room. "Keena, I saved you a seat right by me. Faye, you're down there with Lucky."

Someone had arranged small easels and canvases on a circular table. There were eight seats arranged in a semicircle, all facing a man seated on a stool at the front of the room.

"Dad, this is Keena. I think she's the only one here you haven't met tonight," Jordan called as she patted the seat next to her. Her sister Sarah waved from the other side. "This is Patrick. You have officially met all the Hearsts now."

"The ones in Prospect." Sarah bent forward. "There is another."

Jordan rolled her eyes. "The most Hearst of them all, our baby sister is still in New York but we're working on her to come visit."

Patrick waved at Keena. "If you need me to separate them at any time, you let me know, Keena. They're trouble separately, but when they're together..." He shook his head slowly. "Prue, did you want to get this event started or should I?"

"You can," Prue said magnanimously, but before he could speak, she added, "though I would like to welcome everyone to our trial run at this Sip and Paint night. Patrick and I are making plans to build out the paint section downstairs, however, we're going to need to plant the seeds and get some painters in this town to make it all worthwhile. He had some concerns about teaching short classes and beginners like this, so I'm expecting you all to make him comfortable tonight." Then she picked up the wine bottle and started to pour. "I'll get us all started with a drink, how's that?"

Everyone turned back to Patrick and he cleared his throat. The bemusement on his face matched Keena's internal reaction whenever she got swept up by Prue so she connected with him immediately.

"Tonight, we're going to do a simple landscape. Since I've been back in town, I've spent a lot of time studying Key Lake, so we're going to paint a Key Lake sunset. There are individual containers of paint in front of you and three different sizes of brush. I want to start with a hazy sky, so we'll use the number 8 brush and the darkest blue." He held up the brush and waited for everyone to do the same. He pointed at the completed painting that was hanging behind him. "Here's the inspiration, but each landscape will be different and that's how you know it's art. Pick up some paint on your brush and move it to the palette, then we're going to add a few drops of water like this." He demonstrated, stirring lightly. "Watering down acrylic paint lightens the saturation and gives you a kind of watercolor effect. That will work beautifully with this sunset."

Keena anxiously watched her neighbors before attempting her first stroke.

"Keena, drink your wine. That will help." Patrick smiled encouragingly at her. "Some of us get stuck because we're afraid. Wine smooths all that out."

The laughter around the table made Keena realize she had a tight knot of tension between her shoulders, so she followed his direction. When the first glass was low, Prue topped her off. Then Keena picked up her brush and followed Patrick's lead.

"Don't worry, Keena. You will never paint as badly as Sarah and I do and our father has yet to give up teaching us," Jordan murmured as they cleaned their brushes to work on the darker foreground.

As the evening went on, Keena relaxed and started to enjoy the chatter and laughter. Sarah and Jordan bickered. Prue tossed outrageous zingers when things got quiet. Rose Bell, who she hadn't met yet but ran the lovely historic bed-and-breakfast, didn't say much, but the intense stares she traded between her canvas and the teacher convinced Keena that she was going to be good at this. Faye and Lucky were laughing together on their side of the table.

"Nice, isn't it? Having a chance to be silly and forget all the rest for a minute?" Prue asked. "I don't think the wine is strictly necessary but when in doubt, I always say 'do,' you know?"

Keena had no trouble believing that. Prue struck her as someone who lived full speed ahead.

"How was the first week at the clinic?" Prue craned her neck to see Patrick's example better before picking up some red on her brush.

The group turned its attention to her and Keena understood Prue wasn't the only one curious about how she was fitting in. "Good. It was really good. I've always loved working with Dr. Singh, and the rest of his office is so professional. Almost every concern I have, they deal with it before I can voice it." She glanced at Lucky.

"Stitches are healing as expected, Dr. Murphy." Then she toasted Keena with her wineglass and Faye motioned for the rest of the table to pass the wine bottle her direction.

"Everyone, please, it's Keena. In the office, out of the

office, Keena. I'd appreciate that." As she said it, it felt right. She didn't want there to be any distance between these ladies at the table and her. "And seriously, if you have an after-hours emergency, do not hesitate to call me. I don't want anyone to suffer needlessly because it's after five o'clock. I'll never be as popular as Dr. Singh." Keena paused and studied her wineglass. How many times had Prue filled it? That was too much honesty. "But I'm a very good doctor."

Prue squeezed her shoulder. "Well, now, we sure are glad to have you here for as long as possible." Then she leaned in close. "Travis told me the two of you got a little sideways, but he didn't give me any details."

Keena glanced around the table. Every other woman was suspiciously engrossed with her painting, but she had no doubt their ears were straining to make sure they didn't miss Keena's answer. "Oh, it's nothing serious, Prue."

She sniffed. "There are two things you should know about Travis."

"Better be careful. Nobody likes to have their secrets spread around town," Rose murmured.

Keena appreciated Rose's words of wisdom at the same time that she regretted that Rose had said them. Why did she desperately want to know whatever Prue had been about to share?

Prue settled back in her chair as she considered that. "She makes a solid point." Then she perked up. "If you were to ask questions, I might be able to answer them."

Rose frowned, but Prue patted Keena's hand. "Go ahead."

Confused, Keena glanced at Jordan, the only person she'd actually experienced the Armstrong dinner with. Sarah caught her eye. "You might as well, Keena. You're in the middle of—" she pointed around them vaguely "—

all this now. Becoming an Armstrong leads you to some unexpected places."

But she wasn't an Armstrong. For that matter, neither were any of the other women at the table except Prue.

"What did Travis say?" Keena focused on the frame of trees around the edges of the canvas.

"I went out to the ranch to fill up the fridge with some leftovers I had this week, and Travis mentioned you two had opposing views. Has to do with the social worker's visit, I believe," Prue said.

Keena finished the trees and decided to add more light yellow in the sun's reflection on the lake. If that's all Travis said, Keena knew it was in her best interest to keep the details to herself.

But she was even sorrier for Rose's well-meant words of caution. It would be nice to get some clues about Travis without spilling what had set them at odds.

Keena wasn't ready to admit that her biggest concern was how disappointed she'd been that he let the social worker leave with the romantic misunderstanding in place. She'd started to build this ideal man in her head based on his patience and humor, the care he had for the kids he hadn't even met yet.

No way was she confessing any of that to his mother. There was not enough wine in the world to loosen her lips that much.

"Well, I hesitate to interrupt the conversation," Patrick said as he finished the slow stroll he'd made around the table, "but it looks like most of you have completed your paintings. All that's left is to let the paint dry and show off your work. One at a time, we're going to turn the easels to face the center of the table. I love this part. It's where you see how many different ways there are to see something. Sarah, let's start with you."

"He's going from worst to first, everybody," Jordan said as she scooted back in her chair. "You will see proof that artistic talent can skip entire generations in three, two..."

Sarah sighed. "She's right. I want to argue, but she's right." After carefully turning her easel, Sarah flopped down behind it. "It's like if an alien was describing the scene to his dog and the dog tried to paint it."

Laughter swept the table as Jordan clapped her hands. "I love it." Then she spun hers around. "I was going to say that mine was like if you'd painted the scene and left it out in the sun to melt, but Sarah's description fits mine, too."

Both Hearsts had the suggestion of a lake in the golds, but they were surrounded by...blobs. So many dark blobs.

Patrick sighed and turned to Keena. "Moving on. Keep my hopes up, Keena."

She bit her lip, nervous as she turned her own easel. "Is this better?"

"There's no way to be worse," Patrick said dryly as his daughters giggled and clinked their glasses. "It's nice. I love the way you've worked in the shadow on the lake to show space and perspective."

Relieved, Keena relaxed into her chair to finish her wine. Being anything better than terrible was winning in her book, especially since she couldn't land in last place behind Sarah or Jordan.

Prue spun her painting around proudly. "I embellished mine a bit."

Keena leaned forward to see that Prue had added a couple sitting in a boat, facing each other.

"Are they wearing ball caps?" Patrick asked slowly.

"Broncos caps. Both of them. Cute, right?" Prue grinned. "I love adding romance to the scene."

Rose Bell grunted as she tugged down her own Broncos cap, her lips a firm line. "Faye, Lucky, you go next. I need to add some finishing touches."

Jordan moved closer. "My dad is single. Rose is single. They're both big Broncos fans. Prue is matchmaking."

"She's not subtle about it, either," Sarah chimed in. "Prue is always pulling these strings, making couples where she wants."

Prue whispered, "Not true. I don't run around making matches. Sarah and Jordan made their own matches, Keena. I only encouraged them. That's my gift."

Sarah and Jordan communicated silently in head tilts, eyebrow raises and shoulder rolls, before Sarah said, "That's fair."

Faye cleared her throat. "Can I have your attention?" She displayed her painting.

"Beautiful strokes showing the individual leaves, Faye. That's nice attention to detail," Patrick said. "I'd expect nothing less from you."

Faye immediately started gathering up her brushes and paints to clean up her station.

"We aren't quite finished, Faye," Patrick said softly. "Besides, you let me take care of all that tonight, okay?"

Keena wasn't sure Faye agreed with his comment, but she settled back in her chair.

"That leaves me," Lucky said as she waved a hand at her own.

Patrick pursed his lips. "The way you've worked with the colors tells me you're making this scene your own, Lucky. That's something that's hard to teach. I like it."

Keena would have put herself solidly in the middle of the crowd as far as painting ability went. She might not have untapped talent, but it was something she could practice and improve on if she wanted to.

That might be something to pursue while she was in Prospect and had the time.

"Rose," Patrick said, his lips twitching, "you're up."

She sniffed haughtily and turned her easel around. Of them all, Rose had most closely followed the inspiration. Her painting was good.

It also featured what appeared to be a woman in a wedding dress and a man in a cowboy hat faced off in front of the sunset.

"Lovely. Very romantic. Two people no one in this room recognizes getting married in front of the lake." Prue patted Rose on the back.

"It's you. And Walt. See the hat?" Rose said baldly. "I can add in more details if you need them, but you should get your eyes checked. The whole world can see you two headed for the altar again sooner or later."

She and Prue glared at each other.

Sarah and Jordan perched on the edges of their seats, waiting for whatever came next.

Eventually, Patrick spoke up. "I hope you ladies have arranged rides home tonight. We might need to limit the number of wine refills when we do this for the real world."

Prue nodded. "Good point. Rose and I'll just be walking a couple of blocks. I figure Faye is headed back to close down the Ace."

Faye nodded.

Sarah waved her phone. "I already texted Wes to come get us. We can give Keena a ride and drop her off."

Prue beamed at her. "Sarah, I knew I liked you from the minute I met you." She was bustling away to help clean up the paints and easels when Sarah moved Keena out of the way.

"That is not true. I got the coldest of shoulders from Prue Armstrong when I introduced myself the first time.

Her attitude about the Hearsts returning to Prospect has greatly improved." Sarah shoved her hands in her pockets. "Want to tell us how it's really going? We can talk about this town, the Armstrongs, Travis and any number of things without spreading tales. We don't know too many secrets to tell at this point!"

Keena laughed. "Everything has been so easy. Travis and I..." What could she say? "I had this daydream of who he was, you know? The cowboy hero, the white hat who lived for doing the right thing or whatever, and he's just a person. He didn't exactly lie but I expected more. Which is absurd. He's a neighbor, a maybe-friend, nothing else. There's no reason to feel let down about a little ol' bitty lie that doesn't change the outcome of anything after all." Keena closed her eyes. "I've had too much wine."

Jordan slung her arm over Keena's shoulders. "Proceed with caution, my new friend." She and Sarah exchanged a speaking glance. What was it saying? "Sarah was going to make a quick stop and get the lodge ready to sell. She's half a second from settling down here permanently to raise more Armstrongs."

"And Jordan never stayed a second past when things got hard...until Prospect and Clay Armstrong showed her what staying could mean, like love and family, and community," Sarah added. "There's something about the men from the Rocking A in particular that makes you believe in old-fashioned goodness. It's like it goes all the way to their bones." She shrugged. "And it makes it hard to walk away from them. If that's not what you want, it makes sense to keep some distance between you and Travis. Whatever you thought you'd found in Travis, it's there. Maybe he messed up, but that thing you were starting to believe in, they have it, every single one of them."

"And Prue," Jordan added under her voice. "She's just hard to resist."

They all laughed.

"What's the story with the wedding couple Rose added?" Keena asked while no one was paying any attention to them.

"You saw how Prue and Walt are. They should not be a divorced couple, but the same stubbornness that makes them loyal and dedicated to the town and their family also makes it impossible for either one to give in and let go their small grievances." Sarah covered her heart with her hand. "That's my judgment but if either of you tells Prue I said any of that, I will deny, deny, deny."

Jordan pointed out the window at a truck parked below. "Wes is downstairs. Keena, ride with us. You may be fine to drive, but everyone will feel better if we see you home."

The urge to argue was strong, but she'd seen so many late-night accidents caused by drivers who would have sworn they were okay to drive that Keena agreed. She went to thank Patrick and Prue for including her.

To her surprise, Prue wrapped her arms tightly around her for a hug. Keena hesitated before returning it. "Do not be a stranger, Keena. Travis will eventually figure out the right way to fix all this, I promise."

She wanted to explain that there was really nothing to fix.

No hard feelings, even.

They were just neighbors anyway.

Weren't they?

Instead, she asked, "What makes you believe Travis is the one who needs to make a change?" Prue barely knew her. By the laws of family loyalty, wouldn't that make her the bad guy in any argument with Prue's son?

Prue smoothed Keena's hair back. "Hmm, I suppose

it's possible that *you* made a mistake, but I can't see Travis holding on to that. Of all my boys, he's the one who understood best how easy it was to do that when I messed up. His forgiveness for honest mistakes by the people he loves comes easy. I don't believe that has changed about him." Prue held a finger over her lips as if she was sharing secrets. "Don't tell Rose I let that slip. Travis has a real soft heart under all that muscle. That also means his own mess-ups bother him until he makes them right. He'll do it again this time. I think you're already on the inside, pretty close to that soft heart."

When she realized Rose was watching them closely, Prue mimed turning the key to lock her lips and moved away. None of the questions Keena needed to ask were right for the occasion, so she locked them away, too.

Keena clattered down the stairs behind the Hearsts and out onto the wooden sidewalk, but she stopped as she realized Travis and Wes were both resting against the bumper of the truck in front of the door.

"Hey," he said softly. "I heard you might need a taxi ride home."

Keena glanced at Jordan. She had the offer to ride with them, but Travis's hopeful expression was impossible to refuse. "Are you going my way, driver?" Prue's secret was fresh on her mind and she wouldn't mind the chance to clear the air between them.

His slow grin landed in her abdomen, butterflies flitting and flapping wings.

Then he stepped around to the passenger side of the truck parked next to Wes's and opened the door. After she slid in, he shut it. Keena held Jordan's stare as Travis backed out of the parking spot. Whatever happened next, Jordan seemed to believe it was going to be big. Her warning about how the Armstrongs had changed everything was flashing across her face in the woman's wicked grin.

Maybe it was the wine.

Or it could have been the way she'd thought about Travis every day since she'd seen him last, even if she was irritated with him.

But Keena knew letting Travis drive her home was the right choice. She wanted to know what came next.

CHAPTER NINE

BEFORE TRAVIS HAD followed Wes into town Friday night, he'd been at loose ends.

Late that afternoon, Travis, Grant and Wes had finished moving the cattle, grazing up in Larkspur Pass through the summer, into one of the lower pastures closer to the house.

They'd gotten a late start because Ellen Montoya had called to deliver her good news while they'd been working in the barn. Travis's application to foster had been approved. As soon as they matched a child who needed a place like the Rocking A, she'd give him a call. Telling his brothers that had been a relief. One weight rolled off his shoulders as another, a heavier one, settled in.

Now he'd have to provide a safe space for a kid he hadn't even met yet. He'd have to be a father, one good enough that no one worried about the missing mother in the equation. He'd spent some time remembering how much Prue had smoothed the way for him in the early days. Ellen Montoya's concern about him doing this alone had landed on top of all his other questions.

So much pressure.

The happiness he had expected to experience once everything was arranged had been elusive so far.

Travis had also confessed to the caseworker that he'd allowed her to leave with the wrong impression of his relationship with the beautiful doctor next door. Ellen had reassured him that his relationship or lack thereof had had zero impact on the decision to grant him fostering duties.

So he'd put that disappointed look on Keena's face for no good reason.

And then Ellen had advised him he might want to explore why he'd seized the chance to suggest there was more in the first place. Her chuckle as she'd hung up was what stuck in his brain, though.

He couldn't get that out of his head.

"This winter, we sure are gonna be glad we scraped together enough for the down payment on Sadie's undeveloped land in front of the Majestic," Grant had reminded the three of them in the barn. The sun had sunk below the ridge of the mountains. Now that the days were short, night came quickly. "You remember that year that the first snow fell before we got the herd moved?"

They all remembered. It had been a long December that year, waiting for the snow and ice to melt, so they could get the herd closer to the barn. Feeding and watering had been a struggle.

"It was a good lesson," Wes had immediately said. "When Dad asks why I'm bringing them in so early now, all I have to do is remind him of Matt's frostbitten toes and the way Mama threatened to move him into the barn permanently, and he stops singing that tune."

Travis had removed Sonny's saddle before filling his water and feed buckets. He'd had no clue his brothers were getting ready to corner him in the barn for a discussion about his emotions. He might have headed for Mexico, if so.

Instead, when he finally noticed Grant had propped one arm against the stall and was wearing that annoying half smile of his that always warned of trouble, Travis had yanked his hat off and prayed for patience.

"Am I going to need a whistle to referee this...whatever is coming." Wes's horse, Arrow, bumped Grant's shoulder as Wes led him into the stall next to Sonny, but Grant and Arrow spoke the same language, so neither one was upset by the contact.

Their mother liked to say that Grant was part horse himself.

When she wasn't around, Travis enjoyed identifying exactly which part of the horse Grant was.

"I've been good. For so long." Grant held out both hands, pleading. "I have bent over backwards, brother, to ignore your black cloud ever since I came home."

Travis straightened and stepped closer to Grant. He was partially right. They hadn't had a knockdown argument since he'd come home, but Travis's good behavior and long patrols of the fence line had more to do with that than any small amount of holding back on Grant's part.

Wes braced his hand in the center of Travis's chest. "I realize you might have something to say about exactly how 'good' Grant has been. We all do." Wes raised a brow at Grant. "But if there's a bruise on either one of your faces, I'll be the one to hear about it from Mama. I've got plans tonight and no time to paper over your shenanigans, so let's rip a couple of bandages here and now."

Travis was braced to be the first to do the ripping, but Wes turned to face Grant. "You go first. What's your deal?"

Grant's eyes grew round as his mouth dropped open. "What do you mean? I've been on my best behavior ever since I got back." Travis couldn't see Wes's face, but Grant could. There must have been something there to convince him to readjust his answer. "Listen, I..." He tipped his cowboy hat up. The frustration they sensed seething under the surface was right there, close to boiling over. "I retired. I came home. I pitched in on this renovation thing. I'm all good now."

"Retired?" Travis repeated. If he'd had to place bets on when Grant would leave the rodeo circuit, where he'd been a star, it would have been decades in the future.

Probably after some broken something kept him out of the saddle and not a second before. His whole life, Grant had been the star, the one who could do anything from the back of a horse. Clay and Wes and Matt were smart. They'd gone to college, finished their professional degrees.

And then there was Travis.

"Yeah, retired. What you do at the end of your career, so you can finally take it easy," Grant had said slowly, enunciating every word. "Like you did, Travis. Ending up here with Mom and Dad suited you just fine though, didn't it."

Wes grimaced, still with his arm out, a hard bar across Travis's chest.

Travis heard the insult in Grant's tone, if not the words, but Wes replied first. "Is this taking it easy? Ranching isn't what anyone dreams of for their golden years, is it?" Wes asked, disbelief clearly resonating in his voice. "Remind me you said that in February when every bit of water on this place is frozen solid and at least one calf comes early."

Grant rolled his eyes. "We don't do anything like other people, do we? Instead of picking up basket making and staring at the walls, we build houses and sleep in bunk beds. Why do we do that?"

At this question, both of his brothers focused on Travis. They'd done it for him.

"And I've said thank you." Travis propped his hands on his hips. "Why is this back to me now?"

Wes grunted. "Honestly, both of you are real burrs under my saddle."

Grant inhaled and exhaled slowly. “I get that, big brother. By now, you should be better at handling us misfits.”

Growing up, he and Grant had been poles apart in terms of their personalities, and yet they’d also been closer than any of the other three. They’d done this quite often: switched sides in the middle of an argument to keep Wes and Clay on their toes.

Why? Hard to say for sure, but it was fun.

“You ever wonder what would have happened if Prue and Walt hadn’t adopted all five of us?” Grant sat on one of the hay bales across the aisle. “Wes would have a lot less gray hair, I’m guessing.”

Wes sighed as he took one of the other bales. “We’ll never know.”

Travis huffed out a breath, amused at Wes’s long-suffering face.

“You’ve been stewing all week long. I expected some of this…” Wes gestured toward Travis “…this cloud to clear up once we met the renovation deadline. Nothing’s holding you back now. Surely you know that. It’s a matter of time, could be days even, until we have kids in the house. So what’s your deal?”

Travis scratched his chin as he considered how to answer the question. None of the Armstrong men were overly open with their emotions, and he’d done his best to keep his own under tight wraps.

“Come on. We’ve shown you our support.” Grant propped his legs up on the hay bale, Wes beside him. “I’m one hundred percent serious. This is a safe space.”

Wes scowled at him. “You almost had it, but you had to keep pushing.”

Grant covered his chest with both hands. “We all play our roles. You’re the good one. Clay is the smart one. Travis is the heroic one. Matt is the cute one. I’m the problem." His smirk was the expression Travis expected to see, but he wasn't sure Grant thought it was as amusing as he was trying to pretend.

Wes shoved his boots off the hay bale. "Problem? Maybe, but only because you work so hard at it." He pleaded, "Travis, go. Talk. Now."

"The heroic one." Travis paced in a slow circle in the open air of the barn. He could see the house, the neat yard with all their trucks lined up in front.

Grant made the continue motion with his hand.

"I'm guessing Travis doesn't agree with your list of our roles, Grant. I know I don't," Wes said.

Wes and Grant let the silence stretch whisper-thin, and finally, Travis said, "When we were kids, we talked a little bit about where we came from." He propped his shoulder against the barn door, staring out into the yard. "Wes and Clay both had pretty good homes, not their real family, but people who cared for them before things changed and they had to move to Prospect. Grant and Matt had never been in foster care before, so they had no idea what to expect."

"You never talked any more than you had to for the first five years of your life here on the ranch," Grant said. "Unless I made you."

Wes rolled his eyes. "True. Didn't have to talk much with you around."

When their smiles faded, Wes asked, "So tell us now. Was it bad?"

Travis nodded. "Sad news story at five, six and ten o'clock bad." Was he going to tell the truth? What was the point? He was so far away from that now that it might as well have happened to someone else. "Criminal tendencies. Juvenile detention. 'This is your last shot, kid.' That bad."

Grant sat up and braced his elbows on his knees. "Okay,

so were you worried that would pop up on a background check or something?"

Wes shrugged. "The army's moral character enlistment standards would have flagged any criminal history on a background check, and I can't believe you've had any run-ins since then, so that can't be it."

"Prue and Walt refused to let me waste my last chance," Travis said, "but the things I did to survive… I just hoped either the good one, the smart one, or the cute one would decide they wanted to be a foster dad and let me fade into the background. Everyone would be happier, and the kids would be better off."

Grant frowned. "I'm going to ignore the fact that I didn't make the list of potential foster dads and say I understand."

"The worry makes me do things like let the social worker believe someone like Dr. Murphy would be stepping up to co-parent in the near future." Travis scrubbed his hand over his face. No matter how many times he replayed it, he couldn't get the image of Keena's disappointed gaze out of his head. "I'm afraid I'm not enough."

Travis wasn't sure they heard him. He hadn't wanted to say the words aloud, but it was a relief to finally let them loose.

He expected Wes to give him a pep talk. He took his role as "oldest" seriously and could usually be counted on to coach as needed, whether that was delivering the truth or a helping hand. Instead, Grant said, "Yeah." Rather than poking and prodding, Grant was completely serious.

As if he knew what that felt like.

"If you think you're alone in that, you aren't," Wes said softly. "I wish I had the solution, but it's not pretending. With us or the social worker. Or Keena." His emphasis on her first name signaled Wes was aware that the thing with Keena was more than incidental to his current mood.

"Fix what you can fix, Trav." Grant frowned, his gaze locked on the floor between his boots. "Everything else will have to work itself out in due time."

Wes raised his eyebrow at Travis. "It's solid advice. And from the problem," Wes murmured, "I didn't expect that."

"When it's right to hold him down and force answers about whatever happened to spur this retirement," Travis drawled, "please include me."

Wes laughed. "May take all of us to get it done."

Grant let out a fake laugh, slapped his hands on his thighs and stood. "On that note, I believe it's quittin' time."

"Hot date?" Travis asked as Grant left the barn.

"Something like that," Grant muttered before he slid inside his truck.

"Think we should be worried?" Travis asked Wes as Grant drove away.

Wes slung his arm over Travis's shoulder. "About Grant? Yes. But we have bigger issues at hand."

Travis hummed in agreement because that much was true. He hadn't seen Keena in days and he missed her. Finding a way to apologize and close this gap between them had him preoccupied.

"Our first crisis tonight is that it's your turn to cook dinner." Wes was laughing as he trotted up the steps to the ranch house.

Wes might not like it, but Travis only had one good go-to meal: hamburgers and hand-cut fries. So the decision was easy. Wes must have been satisfied because they were quiet as they ate and cleaned up the kitchen. Then they sat in front of the TV. Travis was bored with whatever movie Wes had chosen to watch but unmotivated to find any better way to occupy his time. And the replay of their serious conversation played on a loop in his head.

If Grant were here, this would have been prime time

to start an argument purely for entertainment, at least on Grant's part.

Instead, Travis had stared straight ahead while his "older" brother cut concerned glances at him when he thought he wasn't paying attention.

Travis was ready for a distraction when Wes had snatched up his phone and exhaled loudly. "Finally!"

"Finally, what?" Travis asked as he dodged the ragged throw pillow Wes tossed at his head.

"Finally Sip and Paint is over and I can find better company." Wes pointed at him. "All you've done all night is grumble under your breath like an old bear with a sore paw. I understand worrying. I do. This is more than that." He shook his head as he tugged on his boots.

Travis grunted but it was hard to argue the point.

"Thinking about something Ellen Montoya said," Travis mumbled.

"Nah, you're thinking about Keena Murphy. I know that look." Wes snagged his key off the long line of hooks by the door. "I've seen that hangdog look in the mirror more than once."

"Both things could be true, Wes." Uncomfortable that Wes had landed so near the real problem, Travis had said, "I guess Sarah's over at the lodge."

When Wes had paused with his hand on the door, Travis had been reaching for the remote. There was probably nothing better on, but it was something to do.

"Actually, she and Jordan had quite a bit of wine, so they're calling for a ride home," Wes said.

Travis nodded and watched the channels flicker by as he pressed buttons.

"Keena's with them." Wes had crossed his arms over his chest. "I could drop her at her home or..."

Travis had rolled up off the couch before he realized

how quickly he was succumbing to Wes's plotting. "Your truck will be too crowded. I'll be happy to pick up Keena instead."

"I figured you wouldn't mind awfully much," Wes said dryly as he led the way out the door.

Travis had followed Wes and stood beside him outside the Mercantile to wait for everyone to come down.

It was one thing to understand how he'd come to be standing outside the Mercantile like he was picking up his prom date. But it was a whole different thing to realize he had no solid plan or clue about how to start the conversation after Keena was buckled in beside him and they were halfway back to the ranch.

Before he could find the right words to break the ice, Keena said, "Thank you." She faced him. "For picking me up. I appreciate it."

"Happy to help a neighbor." The awkward shoulder shrug was what convinced Travis he needed some kind of training session on how to adult correctly in public. He was a mess. "And I've been trying to find a way to talk to you this week."

She hadn't responded to that by the time he pulled into the front yard at Sharita's place. When he parked the truck, Travis inhaled slowly. "I'm sorry."

Keena sighed. "You don't really have anything to apologize for, Travis. I shouldn't have dropped in that way, and this thing with being a foster… What do I know about it? Nothing."

He stretched his arm out along the back of the seat. "I told Ellen today there wasn't anything between us, and she said it had nothing to do with getting approval anyway, so…it was a weird thing I did in the moment. That definitely deserves an apology."

Travis thought Keena was smiling but the cab was dark there in the front yard.

"You got the okay? Congratulations, that's wonderful." Keena squeezed his arm, and the glow of happiness he'd expected ever since he'd hung up the phone that afternoon finally spread through him.

Had he just needed to share the news with someone?

Travis replayed the reactions he'd gotten from Wes, Grant and his parents and realized he'd been waiting on her response. He'd wanted to talk to Keena about it.

Ellen Montoya's chuckle echoed in his head.

"I wish there was more light in the front yard." Keena snorted. "What am I saying? I wish there was any light in this yard at all."

"The front porch light isn't good enough?" Travis asked, determined to keep the conversation alive even if they had to talk outdoor lighting.

"For the three feet it lights up?" Keena wagged her head side to side. "Chuck avoids that circle, yes, but I'm afraid I'll step on something small and furry on my way to safety."

Travis relaxed in his seat. She was easing back into their normal pattern. If she hadn't forgiven him yet, she would. On his second unexamined impulse of the night, Travis got out and hurried around to the passenger side to open her door. Then he held out his arms.

"What? You're going to carry me?" Keena asked, giggles rolling out of her mouth even as he did his best to gallantly scoop her up. Gallantry lost to reality and Keena ended up braced over his shoulder instead. Carrying her the twelve or fifteen feet up to the porch would have been easier if she hadn't gripped one of his ears for safety while she laughed until she lost her breath.

"That's one way to avoid meeting the things that go

bump in the night." Keena held her sides as she gasped for breath and fiddled with the house key. "Are you on call anytime I need safe passage through the dark yard?"

"Anytime you need anything. I'll answer." Travis wanted to keep their night alive. "If you'll let me, I'll show you how I learned to love the night here in the middle of nowhere. Took some adjustment when I first arrived at the Rocking A. Most of the foster homes I moved through were in places where it's never really dark, thanks to streetlights and people all around."

Keena narrowed her eyes. "Will I have to go back out into the dark? Or can you teach me from this three-foot circle?" She motioned to the edges of the porch light.

"Either way, I'll be with you. You can trust me." Travis wished he'd planned this better. Or at all. He was going with the flow at this point. He was not that kind of guy.

"What do I need? A flashlight? A bat or something clublike for defense?" Keena asked.

"Quilts." Travis ran a hand over his nape and waited for Keena's reaction.

First, she studied his face. Then she shrugged and went inside the house. When she came out with a stack of quilts and two pillows, Travis didn't even hesitate to carry her back across the yard, laughing as she clung to his shoulder.

"We aren't going to get any points for style, but we're getting better at that." Keena fumbled with the latch on the tailgate and tossed the quilts down when it finally opened.

"At least my ear is still attached. I was afraid you were going to take it as a souvenir the first time." Travis set her gently down on the tailgate. "Your feet aren't touching the scary dark ground, are they?"

Keena shook her head. "No, but I'm pretty sure raccoons can jump. Or is that squirrels?"

Probably both, but he wasn't going to say that.

Travis spread out one quilt for them to sit on, gave Keena another for their legs, and wrapped the third one around their shoulders. “Are you warm enough?”

“Warm enough for what?” she asked suspiciously.

Travis chuckled. “Good question. Okay, when I first arrived on the Rocking A, Wes and Clay were here. Grant came in a week or two after I did, and the space was so much smaller. I’d spent a lot of time…on my own.” On the streets. Running away or hiding when he needed things to cool off before he went back home. “So to be surrounded by all these people and the noise…it was too much. Before, I would have hit the streets. They weren’t scary, right? I knew them, day or night. Here, I couldn’t see what was coming.”

Keena studied his face. Since he’d spent time with her, he knew there were questions bubbling beneath the surface. Tonight, she held on to them.

“Yeah. I understand that.” She rested her head against his shoulder. “Although I can’t imagine being scared of anything when I have an amateur lumberjack at my side.”

“Not even jumping possums or whatever?” Travis asked as he lifted her legs out of the danger zone to drape them over his lap. The way her giggles floated away in the night was sweet and satisfying. He took a second to commit them to memory.

“Straining to see the threat in the darkness made me miss so much.” Travis watched her face. “What can you see?”

Keena tilted her head back. “So many stars. I wish I knew more about the constellations. A brilliant slice of the moon. The warm glow of the lights in the house. The outline of the mountains rising up. There are a lot of shades of dark out here, I guess.”

"And what do you hear?" Travis asked as she relaxed next to him.

"Rustles that may or may not be steers intent on revenge," Keena said with a smile in her voice, "but they aren't nearby. If it makes sense, I can hear the silence. I can hear your breaths."

Travis was certain she could also hear the way his breath caught when she said that, but he didn't have any control over that.

"Once you taught yourself how to see in the dark, where did you escape to?" Keena asked.

"Took a while to find my spot, but eventually, I made a place in the hayloft. I could swing my legs out through the opening and see…forever." Travis hoped it didn't occur to Keena to imagine what kinds of creatures he might have spotted. That could undo everything she'd embraced there with him in the dark.

"This reminds me of my end-of-shift routine at the hospital," she said quietly.

Travis wanted to know more, but on the other hand he didn't want to break the spell between them. He waited to see if she would volunteer more.

"Working Emergency is a little like what you were saying about trying to see the threat before the attack happens. Your brain never stops running scenarios, you know? Always assessing the patients needing help and figuring out which ones should be at the top of the critical list and which ones could wait and how long they could wait, not to mention what was coming in with the next ambulance, whether you had the right staff, equipment, knowledge, experience available for this case or that one." She exhaled softly. "It could be hard to see what was really happening because you were thinking of what the next crisis might be. I had all these mindfulness techniques. You've seen them.

The counting down, centering myself, because my brain would run away and take everything I needed with it."

Travis stared at the top of her head, still resting against his shoulder, and realized the two of them understood each other in a way he would have never been able to put into words before meeting Keena.

"When you left the house that night, that look of disappointment on your face..." Travis concentrated on the night sky. "That's the kind of expression I am so scared of finding on my family's faces if I fail at this fostering thing. Seeing it on your face was like a punch to the gut."

Keena eased back. "I'm sorry. I do that. I build this outline of people in my head, one they can never live up to, and then..." She sighed. "My mother always said my unrealistic expectations would only lead to disappointment, usually when I was already disappointed because she or my father had missed something important in my life or broken a promise due to...whatever. It's too much pressure, so I usually stand on the outside. It's easier to be an observer than be involved, you know? I can get hurt if I'm involved. Being an observer builds in some safe distance from others. Being shuffled from one parent to the other, and the houses and siblings and schedules... I learned to do that to protect myself, I guess, but there's something about you and the way you...get me, that I fell into these old patterns. You and I, we're...different."

Relieved to hear her say some of what he'd been thinking, Travis tangled his fingers through hers. "We are different. I agree. Not sure exactly how we ended up here, but I feel that difference, too. Disappointing you felt wrong. I don't want to do that again."

Keena raised her head and looked at him. "Were you going to ask me what I can feel, next?"

Travis chuckled. "Why am I afraid of that answer?"

"Oh? Maybe you should be." Keena's teasing voice was too cute for his heart. He was in serious trouble. "My nose is very cold, but the rest of me is comfortable. Relaxed in the deep, dark night because I'm safe with you." Keena wiggled closer. "I also feel that kissing you would make me happy, secure."

When she pressed her lips against his, Travis closed his eyes. The relief and pleasure and over-the-top joy he felt with her in his arms, sitting in the darkness, on the tailgate of his truck on a cold November night didn't make a lot of practical sense. Their first kiss was shy and sweet. Keena smiled at him. "I'm usually right, Travis."

He was amused and thrilled at how his non-plan plan had turned out, when Keena pressed her hand to his cheek to kiss him again. This time, they were more confident, as if this was the kiss they were each made for.

"Do you feel better about the darkness, Keena?" Travis asked, hopeful.

"Yes," Keena said, "but I'm still going to need you to carry me up to the porch before you leave. I don't want to press my luck the first night out with the woodland creatures."

They were both giggling as he swung her over his shoulder.

CHAPTER TEN

AT THE ACE HIGH on Sunday, Keena happily slid across the seat to let Sarah into the booth and nodded acknowledgment to Jordan who slid in across from her. Keena was pleased to have the chance to talk to the Hearst sisters again. When she'd considered taking over the clinic for Dr. Singh temporarily, she'd worried how she would make acquaintances in a new town.

Keena hadn't counted on Sarah and Jordan.

"I hope this late lunch isn't too much of an inconvenience, Keena," Sarah said as she handed over one of the glasses of tea Faye deposited as she buzzed by. "We were hoping that we would miss the lunch crowd and have a chance to snag Faye for a minute. Jordan has been cooking up a plan." Sarah bent forward to say in a stage whisper, "And when Jordie has a plan, she drags everyone along with her."

"You say that like it's a bad thing, Sarah." Jordan was waiting for Faye to venture closer. Just as Faye did, Jordan whipped out a hand, wrapped it around Faye's wrist, and reeled her into the booth seat next to her. Then she crowed, "Look at that! I caught a Faye!"

Faye's deadpan stare at Keena surprised a giggle from her.

"About twenty percent of the time, I can catch her. I've been practicing." Jordan clapped her hands gleefully.

"I needed a break. You could have just asked me to sit

down." Faye waved over her shoulder at the young woman behind the host stand. "But if you want food, someone is going to have to bring it to you. See how that works?"

Jordan pursed her lips. "A flaw in my strategy." Then she stretched across the table to say in her own stage whisper, "That is also one of Jordie's things. I never quite nail the plan the first time around."

When the young woman from the host stand delivered their late lunch, beautiful golden-brown fried chicken with coleslaw, green beans and baked macaroni and cheese, Faye said, "Now, what's the topic?"

Sarah held out a hand before Jordan could launch into whatever it was she was so excited to share. "First, family business. Jordan knows, but Travis met his first foster last night. His name is Damon. He's fourteen and he needed an emergency placement because of something that happened with his current foster family."

Keena put her fork down. She didn't want to miss any of this.

"The social worker called around eight o'clock or so last night to see if Travis could help. Apparently, she's hoping the issue can be worked out with Damon's first family." Sarah shrugged. "We haven't met Damon yet, but Travis wants to introduce us all, maybe tonight but maybe not, depending on how it's going."

"Any idea what kind of emergency it could be?" Faye asked as she glanced around the table.

"Wes said Travis was very quiet last night and even this morning," Sarah said softly.

When everyone turned to look at her, Keena wasn't sure what she was expected to say. "I know he's worried about being a good foster parent, but I think he's prepared." For anything. Travis was the kind of steady that convinced Keena he could weather any storm and come out the other side stronger. "If this is only a short stay, Travis can build some confidence, and if it's longer, we all know how great the Rocking A and the Armstrongs will be for Damon."

She picked up her fork, mainly to have something to do with her hands.

Because everyone was still watching her.

"Did the two of you iron out whatever it was that Prue was buzzing about at the Sip and Paint?" Faye asked. She made a "so sue me" face as Sarah glared at her. "What? That's what you wanted to know. You were trying to send her psychic waves. I've discovered that actual words are a lot more effective." She took one of the rolls from the basket and slathered it with butter. "If Keena doesn't want to answer, she doesn't have to. Okay, so usually my manners are better than that." Then she muttered, "Sometimes."

Keena put her fork back down. Now she had a decision to make. She could gloss over the details, keep the ladies at arm's length and remain a pleasant acquaintance. That was her usual choice.

Or she could risk telling a bit more than the bare minimum, trust the women that far and see what happened next.

"Travis and I had a disagreement on allowing the caseworker to believe we were a couple. I think..." She sipped her tea as she fumbled for a way to sum up years of learning how important the truth was to her. "I'm like Faye. I want people to say what they mean. I don't expect most people to stick to the whole truth, but Travis had changed my mind about him, so when he let a trivial lie go, I...fell back to what I knew. I pulled back because that's safer. It hurt to be disappointed, but we've talked it over. I understand him better. I get it. We're friends."

Keena could feel the color filling her cheeks as she carefully avoided thinking about kissing him under the stars.

"Uh-huh," Faye drawled. "Friends. I believe that."

Sarah was obviously the peacemaker in the group because she immediately said, "Oh, good, I'm glad you worked it out. He didn't need to be weighed down by that, too, not now."

Keena nodded. She absolutely agreed.

She took a bite of the macaroni and cheese on her plate and decided the others might have to carry the conversation without her for a bit. Her lunch needed more attention.

"Let's come back to the newest budding romance in Prospect," Jordan said and raised her hand. "I want to talk about my plan."

Sarah nodded. "The floor is yours."

"Good." Jordan bounced in her seat. "You haven't been to our lodge yet, Keena, but we're going to fix that soon. The place was empty for years, but we've been cleaning it up."

"Mainly Jordan has been cleaning. She never stops," Sarah murmured and smiled brightly at her sister. "She's very dedicated. A hard worker."

Jordan cleared her throat. "Anyway, we have this restaurant that's attached. I'm not cooking. Sarah shouldn't, either. And so it's kind of just...there, for now."

Sarah jumped in. "Though, Michael and I have been kicking around an idea for it, in maybe early spring before the Western Days festival. Our cousin Michael is the new head of Sadie's Cookie Queen Corporation. Jordan and I were certain he would be a soulless number cruncher, but he has shown a streak of Hearst daring. He liked my museum suggestion, even agreed to bankroll it here in Prospect in exchange for a little help from me." Sarah clapped gleefully. "Wouldn't a cooking show, maybe a short competition of some kind, be fantastic? They could tape it at the lodge. The Cookie Queen Corporation would be the sponsor and have a TV crew here. We could offer to partner with one of the food channels or maybe stream it on our website or something." Sarah clapped some more. "We'll figure out the details later, but..."

Jordan had narrowed her eyes into a mean glare.

Faye laughed and pointed at Keena. "Sarah will also be roping us all into the plan. That is the Hearst way. From what I remember, their great-aunt Sadie was better at it than even these two, but what you are seeing is the cart before the horse. Whatever Jordan wants us to do for her will come before the TV show. Hearsts have a real eye for long-term strategy, but they also like the spotlight."

Keena smothered a grin as both sisters directed their scowls at Faye. Eventually, Jordan shrugged. "I mean, she's not wrong about any of that. Before Sarah's big, grand idea, I was thinking..." Jordan tapped her chest. "What if we host a community Thanksgiving potluck at the Majestic? You've seen the sheer number of Armstrongs crammed into the ranch house kitchen for a simple family dinner. If you add Sarah and my dad and Rose Bell and you, who will all be included in that number for a big holiday celebration, anyway, it's going to be elbow to elbow in there. A bigger, grander space is needed."

Sarah touched Keena's shoulder. "This is not to put any expectations on you to join us, of course. If you have other plans, like going home for the holidays, we won't kidnap you and force-feed you turkey, I promise. I won't let Jordan out of my sight, so you can make a safe getaway."

Keena couldn't contain the giggles at that. "Thank you for the invitation. Going home to Iowa is more stress than celebration for me, so I normally volunteer to work the holidays at the hospital so others can be with their families. I'd love to be included in your Thanksgiving crowd. Let me know what I can bring."

Jordan cleared her throat. "Okay, so let us return to the

plan. We'll open up the lodge's restaurant kitchen. We'll provide the turkey, and everyone can bring their family's favorite holiday side dish. Since the Ace is closed for the day, we'll invite anyone who'd like to share a community Thanksgiving potluck out at the Majestic."

Keena nodded. "That's generous."

Faye pursed her lips. "Why do I feel there might be a catch here?"

"Because you know Jordan at this point," Sarah said under her breath.

"No catch!" Jordan batted her eyes innocently. "But, if anyone wants to come early or stay after to help us with refinishing the floors or painting or, depending on the weather, clearing flower beds or…what have you," she said airily, "we would be very thankful for that, too."

Keena waited for Faye's reaction. In the big Thanksgiving scheme of things, she didn't have much at stake. It sounded sort of genius to her.

"I'm in. I always enjoy a day away from the restaurant. Yes, please. My grandparents have been dying to see the Majestic since it reopened. I'll set Gram up in the kitchen to oversee the operation, arranging the dishes and directing all the volunteers with setup and cleanup. Making one dish instead of an entire meal? I love it. Hey, if we work this right, I might even fit in a nap somewhere." Faye grinned. "That's a winning plan, my friends."

"I like it, too." Keena rested against the seat, pleased with her lunch and the way the conversation was flowing. Driving into town, she'd been nervous. At Sip and Paint, she'd enjoyed herself, but Prue Armstrong was such a strong personality that she'd kept the event moving in the right direction. There was no space for awkward silence when Prue was nearby.

Here, the discussion might have lagged, but she was

convinced that the Hearsts were born with something special, personalities or characters that made it easy to connect to them. Sadie had made it from this small town in the Rockies to become a famous TV chef, after all.

"Since I am next door, if I can also help get the restaurant ready beforehand, I'll be happy to roll up my sleeves and..." Keena wasn't sure where she was going with that. She knew nothing about what might need to be done to open up a restaurant. "Mop or something."

Sarah groaned as if defeated.

Jordan's smile should have made Keena nervous.

"Thank you, Keena. I know we can find something for you to do before the big day rolls around," she said sweetly.

Faye groaned in commiseration. "If I've picked up all the news, I need to go check on Gram in the kitchen. She wanted to scrap the week's menu the last time I talked to her, and we don't have time or money for that kind of artistic temperament."

"Her grandmother is the cook?" Keena asked.

"Never met her," Jordan said, "but I get the impression she's more like the 'executive chef' in that she tells people to jump and they ask how high. Runs the kitchen with a firm hand, but it's impossible to argue with success. They have this amazing apple pie that comes from one of Sadie's special recipes and it's worth all kinds of personality quirks and weird goings-on."

The three of them were all full and happy when they stepped back out on the sidewalk. Jordan hugged Keena before she knew what was happening. "Lunch was great. Can't wait to show you around the Majestic."

Keena returned the hug and then gave Sarah one. "Thank you for inviting me today and for Thanksgiving. Maybe next weekend I can come over and you can put me to work."

"Oh, dear," Sarah murmured as Jordan lit up.

They were bickering when they got into the car and drove away. Keena knew the smile on her face might seem silly, but she'd had a blast.

The weekend had flown by. She'd spent it doing so many things she enjoyed, it was a new sensation. Resting. Painting. Hanging out with friends. Getting ready to go back to work on Monday after not spending time putting her apartment back together or preparing for the next crisis in the ER.

If Dr. Singh could see her smile, he might believe she was inching closer to accepting the offer he'd made out of the blue. Keena wasn't sure if she was or not, but it was difficult to argue with this bubble of contentment.

Prospect's pace left her plenty of time to relax and even explore new hobbies. Adjusting to that was easier than she'd anticipated.

A quick trip through Homestead Market to pick up the groceries on her list and several cute plastic containers that could be used as gifts if this baking thing overwhelmed her, and she was back in her cozy rental house.

One of the biggest problems she'd discovered with her rental was the lack of internet access. Like most people, she spent entirely too much time online shopping for this, researching that, and generally wasting time. Here, Keena would have loved to pull up music and bake, but until she got the okay from Sharita through Wes to add service, she had to rely on the songs she'd stored on her phone…over and over. Sharita's aged collection of DVDs ended around 2012, so whatever was there was "classic."

Luckily, Sharita had an extensive collection of Colorado Cookie Queen shows on DVD to work through, thus the never-ending grocery list.

But Keena had an occasion to plan for and apple pie

was on her mind. If it was good enough to smooth over personality quirks, Keena needed the recipe. She hit Play on one of Sadie's earliest Christmas specials and settled on the couch with a stack of cookbooks.

Sadie was cooking with celebrities. It was a cookie exchange–themed show, so she tried a new recipe with each guest. When Sadie and one of Keena's earliest and hardest crushes stepped onto the TV stage amid wild applause to make "Cute as a Button Butter Cookies," she sipped her cup of coffee and tried not to cringe. Was it embarrassing to remember the way she and her next-door neighbor had choreographed dances to his Top 40 hits? A little bit, but it helped that there was no way anyone in Prospect, Colorado, would be able to find any footage of preteen Keena dancing to lyrics she most definitely had not understood at the time.

Watching Sadie now, it was so easy to see her warmth in Sarah's and Jordan's personalities. Even Patrick had displayed the kindness Sadie showed when Keena's heartthrob tried to drop a hard glob of cold butter in the dry ingredients bowl. Sadie explained why that was a bad move, made a funny joke that had the whole audience laughing along, and then resumed her easy demonstration of the best method to make treats for Santa or "your favorite neighbor down the street. Do not waste these on a rascal, you hear?" The twinkle in Sadie's eyes convinced Keena that even the rascals in Sadie's life enjoyed pretty good cookies.

After the holiday special ended, a new show started. Sadie returned but she'd moved out of the studio. "Well, now, I was hoping we'd meet again." Sadie's grin and tone suggested this was how she always started her intros. She held out a graceful hand. "Here I am, in my favorite kitchen, back of the Majestic Prospect Lodge before the lunch rush starts. Got my trusty apron and my favorite hat." Keena scooted forward, immediately curious about the kitchen she had just been discussing with Sarah and Jordan. Sadie tapped the white cowboy hat before tipping it up. The sparkle of joy was easy to see in her eyes. "I'm a thinking today is a good day to make some molasses cookies. You ever had a perfect, soft molasses cookie? My mama used to make these, and you could never hold on to a bad day or a rotten attitude when these were around. That's powerful, right there."

She leaned forward as if she was about to share something top secret. "If I tell you how to make these, you gotta promise to use 'em for good in this world. That's one thing we ain't ever got too much of, good in this world."

As she listed the ingredients she'd be using, Sadie dropped little tidbits about the best kind of molasses to use for different applications. Blackstrap was too intense for these cookies and light molasses too mild. Dark molasses was the "Goldilocks choice" here. Her enthusiasm was contagious, so Keena started a new grocery list.

Sadie mixed the wet ingredients and then the dry. She talked about refrigerating the dough and then pulled out a fully prepped bowl from the large stainless steel refrigerator behind her.

"We're going to roll out some balls, about yea big," Sadie said as she held one up to the camera, "and scatter 'em across the cookie sheets. Now, getting them the same size is more important than what size they are. Leave breathing room for these beauties to bake."

"Better make sure I put 'dark molasses,'" Keena muttered as she pulled out her phone. "None of that bitter blackstrap molasses for me." She hadn't meant to say it the way Sadie did, but that's how the words came out. Did it seem right at the beginning? No, but she could see how easy it was to slip into.

Just like she'd slipped right into the flow in Prospect.

A text from Travis flashed on the phone screen before she set it back down.

Are you up for a visit?

Keena read it three times before she convinced herself that she understood it correctly.

Of course, she typed and bit her lip as she tried to decide whether it needed an exclamation mark or not.

Before she could commit, she heard a car in the front yard and went to check who exactly had arrived.

Travis waved from the driver's seat. She'd forgotten that Sarah had mentioned he was taking his new foster around to show him the town and make introductions.

Then she realized she'd somehow made the list of important people who deserved an introduction and wished she had a mirror hanging beside the door. What was her hair doing?

Didn't matter. He was sliding out of the truck before she could decide whether she had time to address it or not.

A tall, thin boy got out of the passenger side and stopped halfway to the door. His hair was long, hiding his eyes, but the way he held his left arm made it clear that Travis was stopping to introduce his foster to the doctor instead of the neighbor next door.

Which was fine.

Keena was both, so she was getting an early intro, even if she knew this was practical more than personal.

And honestly, she was too personally involved already.

"Hi, I'm Keena," she said as she stopped on the bottom porch step. "Please come in."

The kid eased closer and took the hand she offered but he didn't move to climb the steps.

"Nice to meet you." The kid glanced at Travis and away. Keena wondered if Travis knew anything pertinent to his injury.

"This is Damon." Travis moved to touch the kid's shoulder but stopped when he shifted away. "He's going to be staying for a bit. Thought he'd like to know who was living next door."

"I'm glad you did. I was going to make cookies. Do you have time to sit and wait for them?" Keena asked as she stepped down in the yard, moving slowly to give Damon plenty of warning.

"We better not. We've got a big day planned tomorrow, headed into town to visit the school." Travis frowned as Keena gently took Damon's hand and pulled on his sleeve.

"Can I take a look at your arm?" she asked Damon softly. "Dr. Keena is my whole name, but I want you to stick with Keena."

Damon licked his lips but let her remove his jacket sleeve. Through the neck of the thin T-shirt he was wearing, she could see a bruise. "Looks like you took a fall. Is it only bruising or…" Keena waited. If he had other injuries, she wanted him to share them without worrying about possible trouble later.

"Yes. No broken bones. I was climbing a fence and misjudged the height. Landed hard on the ground, but that's all." Damon shyly met her stare.

Keena whistled. "Oh, no, did you learn anything from that?"

One corner of the boy's mouth curled up. "Stop climbing fences?"

Delighted, Keena pointed at him. "Good one. I like it better than mine. I was going to say use the gate instead because you could have broken more than your arm from that height, but you're even smarter than I am." She took a chance and offered him her fist. His hesitation confirmed for Keena that fist bumps were no longer cool, if they ever were, but Damon humored her and returned it anyway. That successful interaction boosted Keena's confidence.

"If it's okay, I'll wait in the truck." Damon was pulling on the jacket as he walked away. "I like your hamburger shoes."

Keena stared at her house slippers and wondered if she'd ever get the hang of having the proper footwear for Prospect.

Travis watched him before turning back to Keena. "His record for words spoken. I'm glad we stopped."

Keena squeezed his arm. "You doing okay?"

He nodded. "Yeah, I just…wish I was better at talking, too. I might have broken my own record today, for that matter, filling in silence."

"I'm sorry for turning into a doctor." She smiled brightly. "Try some ibuprofen, but make sure he eats first. We don't want his stomach upset, just in case."

"Kid needs to eat around the clock for a month as it is." Travis rubbed his hand over his lips; the concern was clear on his face.

"Have you called in your mother to address the problem?" Keena asked, determined to lighten some of his load.

"Yep, she's headed our way with biscuits on her mind. I've also warned every adult Armstrong connected to the Rocking A that the kid doesn't need to be climbing fences. Ever." He relaxed. "And you don't have to apologize for trying to help. I appreciate it."

Keena sighed. "I have this weird compulsion. I see a problem or something I don't understand and I immediately launch into discovery mode. Sometimes people want to…just be and not answer twenty questions. Also, a fist bump? I don't know what came over me."

Travis laughed. "No apologies for that either. I understand compulsions. I have at least one myself."

"What?" Keena asked, reminded of Travis's comments about caffeine. Was that a sensitivity or did he have another trait that compounded an introvert's need for quiet?

Then he slid his warm hand around the nape of her neck, under the fall of her hair, and brushed his thumb over her cheek.

"Oh," Keena whispered as he bent closer, moving slowly, giving her plenty of time to decide about this kiss.

Then his lips were on hers. This kiss was different from their teasing kisses in the dark. They knew more about each other, what could be between them. This kiss was about missing each other for a couple of days and being uncertain when they'd be together again and warmth and need.

There was also a teenage boy in the front yard watching this kiss.

"Gotta go." Travis risked an injury of his own by backing down the steps and across the yard, his eyes locked on her face.

Keena collapsed against the door when she made it back inside, shaken by how much she missed him already. Had she known Travis Armstrong long enough to feel like this whenever he drove away?

Whether she had or not, the feelings were there.

What would it be like to leave Prospect to go home where she belonged when Dr. Singh returned?

Keena rubbed the ache in her chest before standing solidly on her own two feet.

That was a problem for later.

Today, she was going to watch Sadie Hearst finish these molasses cookies and then she was going to find the perfect recipe for the too-skinny boy next door and the man determined to keep him safe.

CHAPTER ELEVEN

TRAVIS REALIZED HE was humming to himself as he mucked out Sonny's stall and wondered how long he'd been doing it. It had been a busy few days since he'd taken Damon for the sightseeing tour of Prospect, and so far, everything was going…fine.

They weren't about to win any awards for most exciting dinner conversation, but Damon had agreed to attend school. He'd been doing his homework, too. And he and Travis had been learning their way around each other as Travis had shown the kid how to care for a horse. They'd covered how to saddle Sonny, how much the horse ate and drank every day, the places he liked to be scratched and places that would provoke a whiffle of disgust.

The kid was a lot like he'd been when he'd landed at the Rocking A, a complete novice when it came to horses, but Damon had one characteristic Travis hadn't. The horses didn't scare him.

That was a good sign.

This afternoon, Grant had offered to give Damon actual riding lessons, so Travis had jumped on the chance to get some work done in the barn. He enjoyed watching Damon learn, because the kid took everything so seriously, a little wrinkle appearing between his eyebrows as he listened intently.

That made it easy to imagine working with him around the ranch.

Grant was the best rider out of all of them, and Travis wanted Damon to know the rest of his family, so he'd stepped back and got busy with the chores he'd left undone that week.

While humming apparently.

When he moved the wheelbarrow back to its normal spot along the wall, he realized it was later than he expected. Dinner should have been ready half an hour ago, but no one had raised an alarm. Darkness outside suggested Grant and Damon had gone in for food and left him there entertaining himself in the horse stalls.

If they were getting along that well, it was hard to be mad.

Annoyed? Sure, that was normal.

He switched off the overhead light and pulled closed the barn door as his phone rang.

When he saw Keena's name, his mood did a one-eighty.

"Hey, neighbor, how are you?" he asked. He winced at the over-the-top excited tone. Keena would think she'd gotten the wrong number. It wasn't like him.

In fact, this whole…lightness wasn't like him. It might take a minute, but he'd like to have the chance to get comfortable with it.

"I'm okay. Have you seen Damon lately?" she asked quickly.

Travis hurried toward the house. "No, why?"

"I was walking through the living room and saw something out the window, along the road. I think it was Damon. He was walking toward town. I didn't think walking along a dark road in the dark night with all the creatures of the darkness waiting to pounce was a good plan?" Her tone rose at the end as if she was trying to be calm about everything. "I'll grab my coat and check if you'll stay on the phone with me."

Travis gripped his phone tightly as he stuck his head inside the house. Grant was standing at the stove. "Dinner's almost ready if you want to get Damon."

Travis listened as Keena's front door opened and closed. "Damon's supposed to be with you."

Grant pointed with a spatula. "He said he had a spelling test to study for."

"Spelling?" Travis and Keena both asked.

"Do teenagers take spelling tests?" Keena posed the question, although it sounded like she already had the answer. Travis could hear her quick breathing, as if she was hurrying across the yard.

"I don't think so. I'm headed for my truck, but don't hang up." Travis slammed the door shut and trotted through the yard, while he dug his keys out of his pocket. "Five minutes or less, Keena. I'll be there."

"No worries. I can see him from here. He's fast, but I've worked the night shift for years. I can catch him." Keena was quiet but Travis could hear her footfalls as she hurried down the highway. "Damon, wait up! I'll walk with you. I love the moonlight."

No way would the kid believe that, even if Travis appreciated her attempt to tell her own harmless lie to stop the kid from getting hurt.

Travis couldn't make out what Damon said, but Keena answered, "I can't let you walk all the way into town by yourself. I'll keep you company."

Damon's response was muffled. "Yeah, it's Travis on the other end. I was worried about you."

Travis could hear a bit of apology in her voice.

"Want to come back to my house and wait where it's warm?" Keena sighed. "Nope, we're going to keep walking. I have cookies. Want one?"

Travis couldn't tell if Damon had accepted the offer or not.

"I'm close now. You should see my headlights coming around the curve." Travis slowed down. Speeding around the curve would put them in more danger than walking along the shoulder at night, even though that was so dangerous it made his stomach clench to think about it. Two city slickers wandering country roads in the darkness… that was how horror movies started.

As soon as he saw the bright pink back of Keena's jacket, Travis exhaled. He passed them and then eased over on the narrow shoulder ahead of them. Damon stopped and turned back toward the ranch, as if he was trying to decide if it was better to strike off in that direction on foot.

Keena was clutching a plastic container to her stomach and appeared to be ready to run behind Damon, no matter which direction he went in.

"Nobody is taking off into the dark tonight." Travis took his time as he picked through the right words. "We're going to talk. We can do that at home or in the truck or on Keena's porch or right here in the middle of the road, but we're going to discuss how running away is not going to work for me. Or you."

Travis leaned against the truck and crossed his arms over his chest. "Keena is freezing, kid. Let's get this conversation over with."

"I could go back myself." She sniffed. "It's probably safe. I might have heard Bigfoot in the trees over there before we rounded the curve, but I bet he's gone now."

Damon groaned loudly. "I have to go home. I don't want either of you out here. You both go back. I'll go on to town. Everyone will be happy."

Keena popped the top off the container and took a cookie out. "I'm not a parent, Damon, but even I can see the flaws in your plan. Were you going to hitchhike all the way back to Denver? Do you know how dangerous that is?" She offered him the container. "They're Cookie Queen Chocolate Chip and I've already eaten six. Please take one."

Travis wasn't surprised when Damon took the container she offered. He hadn't had dinner. At fourteen, Travis would have been ready to chew bark off the trees if he'd missed dinner.

"And when you did get to Denver, if you ever made it at all, then what?" Travis asked. What could convince the kid to take such a dangerous step? He'd just been humming happily to himself about how well things were going.

"I'll convince the Smiths to take me back. I'll promise to never get in trouble again and things will be the way they were." Damon shoved half of the cookie in his mouth.

Travis could see how that might be something to daydream about, and if the kid had been happy there, maybe that was the best answer. But there was a piece of the story missing. How had a fall from a fence resulted in an emergency placement if everything had been going so well with Damon's foster family?

Keena was obviously on the same track because she said, "Spill the rest of the story, please. If it was that easy, why didn't you promise not to get in any more trouble before you landed here?"

Damon shrugged. "I did."

"Why would it work this time, if it didn't work then?" Travis asked as he intercepted the container and took one cookie for himself.

"I'll convince them." Damon scuffed his sneaker on the road. "I'm not a country kid, Travis. That's all. I need to be in the city. Don't worry about me. I'll be okay." He shifted the backpack over his shoulder. "I have some money and food. I'm all set."

"You loved every minute we spent in the barn with Sonny. No way were you faking that, kid." Travis held his hand out. Eventually, Damon slid the backpack off his shoulder and passed it over.

Travis unzipped it. "Jeans, good. Two sweatshirts, good. What about underwear?"

Damon didn't answer.

"Not so good. And the food appears to be..." Travis felt the crumpled wrapper of the chip bags he'd been sending for lunch. "Chips. I respect the choice but it won't provide much energy." He felt a hard something at the bottom of the bag. "And one wireless speaker in the shape of a football."

Travis couldn't read Keena's eyes in the darkness, but the way she snapped to attention told him she was pretty proud of the purchase she'd forced him to make.

"You can have it back. I don't need it." Damon's voice was firm, but he was still young enough that it was easy to hear the disappointment, too. He'd give up the speaker because it was the right thing to do in his mind, but he didn't have to enjoy it.

"It's yours. You can take it with you when you go," Travis said, "but that's not going to happen tonight." When Damon moved to go around him, with or without the helpful items in his backpack, Travis held up his hand. "Because I'll make you a deal. Tomorrow, in the bright sunshine, I'll drive you down to Denver. We'll meet with Ellen Montoya to talk about you not being a country kid even though you have horse fever now and we'll see if she has a better match for you. You aren't a prisoner here, but I have to keep you safe, Damon. Hitchhiking is dangerous. And life on the streets..." Travis cleared his throat. "Believe me, I know it's not safe. I don't want that for you."

Then he offered the kid his hand to shake. "Tomorrow, we'll go and we'll find a better solution."

The boy hesitated. He'd probably had more than one adult make him a promise only to break it as soon as it benefited them. Damon might understand how Keena had felt about Travis slipping into his lie about them with Ellen Montoya. They both deserved to be surrounded by people they could trust.

Travis was resolved to keep every promise. That meant he had to be careful when making them.

Damon shook his hand and Travis relaxed. "We'll take Keena home and then go eat dinner. After that, I'll text Ellen that we need to talk with her tomorrow and the Smiths, too. How's that?"

"Okay." Damon took the backpack from Travis. "Thank you."

Travis opened the door for Keena. "Everyone in the truck." After Damon slid in the passenger side, Travis backed up around the curve and into Keena's front yard. "Need me to carry you across the grass?" He slid out and held her hand as she followed.

"Nah, I'm a big girl." Then she pressed the cookie container into his stomach. "Take these away from me or I'll eat the rest." She squeezed his hand. "You gonna be okay? I know this is a challenge." Her voice was low. He wasn't sure if Damon would be able to hear what they said to each other.

"I'm okay because of you. Thank you for calling. I would have lost my mind when I found his room empty. After I murder Grant for believing the kid was taking a spelling test, I'll feel better," Travis said.

Damon's muffled chuckle answered the question about what he could hear.

"Good night. Call me and tell me how everything turns

out, okay?" Keena hurried across the grass to the safety of her porch and stepped inside.

"The doctor's really pretty," Damon said. He was crammed up against the passenger side door as if he'd rather be riding on the outside of the truck if he could figure out a way to do it.

"Yeah, she is." Travis wasn't sure how to open up the conversation that needed to take place.

"You'll have more time for flirting when I go back to Denver," Damon said.

Travis grunted. "You were going to be my secret weapon. Keena's a sucker for kids."

Damon didn't answer and Travis wondered what Keena would think about that particular half-truth. Or maybe it was the whole truth. He didn't know. They hadn't discussed kids, but she was good with Damon. He still would have sworn in a court of law it was right to make Damon think twice about leaving.

Back at the Rocking A, Travis said to Damon, "Head on inside and get some dinner. Then, if you have any homework other than an imaginary spelling test, get started on it."

Damon stopped in the middle of the yard. "You aren't coming in?"

"Not yet." Travis needed a few minutes to himself first.

Travis now faced the same problem he'd had when he'd first arrived at the Rocking A. There was nowhere to go to have the time that he needed to work through his feelings. The house had his dad, Damon and most of his brothers, so he headed for the barn. He skipped the light switch because that would be the only clue any of his family would need to track him down. He climbed the sturdy ladder up to the hayloft that extended along one long side of the barn.

He didn't worry much about the darkness there because this was his spot.

Had been for a long time.

The first thing he'd done when he returned home for good was make sure the ladder was strong, the flooring of the loft was solid, and the path to his favorite spot was clear. He'd plopped down on the quilt he kept up there for nights when he couldn't sleep and needed to stare out the opening at the stars. Now, he heard boots on the ladder.

He didn't have to check to see who had followed him.

When Walt dropped down next to him with a grunt, Travis sighed. "Everything's okay, Dad. I needed to get my head straight before I try to unravel this thing with Damon."

His father didn't answer for a minute. They both stared out into the night as if the answer was outside.

"How many times did you run away before we ironed out an accord?" Walt asked. "Four? Five? All I know for sure was you scared Prue Armstrong to tears that last time, and I was almost certain that was a feat beyond mortal men, much less skinny boys with chips on their shoulders."

Travis's lips twitched but he contained the smile. That would not please Walt, a smile at the reminder of the way Prue had panicked the night he never came home. That wasn't the amusing part. It was that Walt had always been the voice of reason for Travis and he was happy to have his father nearby for this.

Even if it was going to try his patience.

And Walt's for that matter.

"I wasn't running away, though. That's the difference." Travis had needed space. That's all. He'd had no destination to hitchhike to in mind, no place called "home" that he wanted to return to the way Damon did.

"Maybe you knew that then. Maybe you only learned

later, but your mama and I were in the dark." Walt wrapped his arms around his legs. "Thing we learned real quick about you boys was that each one of you was a 5,000-piece puzzle. Every piece had weird edges and only trial and error put them together."

Travis closed his eyes. "I'm not good with puzzles. We should have had this conversation before I upended the ranch to bring in more pieces."

Travis rested his head against the rough wood and wondered how his father had gotten him to admit his biggest fear that easily. There was almost no hope that Walt had missed it, either.

"You think we were good with puzzles in the beginning?" Walt snorted. "Prue was good. She's always had this knack of understanding all kinds of people, even young ones who'd rather hide away than argue or fight. Me? I had to turn every single new piece thisaway and thataway until something clicked. Nobody explained to me how much flying by the seat of your pants is required in parenthood, but I'm doing you the favor of warning you now."

"Could be too late," Travis said. "What if I've already messed up my first chance?"

Walt yanked his cowboy hat off and tossed it on the hay. "By getting these nice rooms ready and filling them with special things and curving your world to fit these kids you haven't met yet. How can you mess that up?"

Travis shrugged.

"Use your words, Travis," Walt grumbled. "Can't believe you've got me talking to you the way Prue does me, but in this case, we need to have some words between us. What are you afraid of here?"

Something about the darkness and the open space around them made it seem possible to say the scary things out loud and survive it, so Travis said, "I've never been a parent. I wasn't even a child for long, you know? Until I got here, I only had me and I did things to survive. You know I was half a step from jail the night the social worker left me here and raced away. What if I can't learn what I need to in order to figure out these puzzles?"

What if I fail at this one thing that I've wanted more than anything?

What if I'm too broken to do this?

That was what Travis held close to his chest. If he failed at this, who was he going to be?

"You remember the first time I put you on a horse?" Walt asked. "Thought you might cry, you were so scared."

Travis scowled. "You were supposed to forget that and never bring it up again."

Walt chuckled. "Can't forget it. I think it was my moment, like the one you're having now. I only knew what I knew, Travis. My daddy never taught me how to deal with emotions like fear except to pretend they aren't there. Pretend you don't have emotions, period. Took me a while to learn how bad a lesson that was. Five boys and a wife, all learning that lesson alongside me, too. Wouldn't recommend that. Sure am grateful that Prue made it clear that you boys would feel the way you felt and that would be the end of it. Your mama made you all who you are today." Walt clapped a hand on his shoulder. "That's my biggest worry about this new family we're all building. You need a Prue to balance you out. Not a wife, I don't guess, but someone who can work alongside you to sort all the pieces. Wes is good at that, but the rest of us are about as good at puzzles as you are."

His father's grim tone wasn't intended to be funny, but something about the way he said it amused Travis.

That eased some of his panic and made it easier to think.

"All right. Call Wes. That's what you're telling me?" Travis asked. "Not surprising. That's often the answer to any problem."

Walt shrugged. "This particular question? We can figure this one out. Put Wes in your back pocket for real emergencies."

Travis turned back to stare out at the night. "Tomorrow I'll take Damon to talk to his caseworker one-on-one. If it's better for him to leave us, that's what will happen. It's not some commentary on what I've done here." Eventually, he'd get that through his head and he'd move on.

"Or you can talk to the kid tonight, spread all the puzzle pieces out, and get a better look at what needs to be assembled," Walt said as he stood. "That's the correct answer. You wait here."

Walt was gone before Travis could argue.

He'd needed a minute to get control of his own emotions before he worked through the problem with Damon. His father knew it, too.

Moments later, the overhead light switched on and Damon walked down the wide aisle in the barn. "Hey."

Travis held up his hand. "Hey yourself, I know you have strict orders not to climb fences. Are you able to climb ladders safely or..."

Damon shrugged. "Guess we won't know until I give it a shot."

Travis was relieved that the kid didn't seem afraid of him or the barn. "The first few weeks I was here at the Rocking A, I didn't step foot in the barn unless Walt was with me."

"Why?" Damon asked as he followed Travis over to the open door in the gable. He sat on the quilt when Travis pointed at it.

"Scared. I knew there were critters in here. Mice.

Worse. Horses were intimidating, and I had to hide all that because none of my brothers had the same reaction. Grant would have slept in a stall with his horse if he could have. Then there was me, jumping at shadows."

Travis sat in Walt's spot and braced his arm on his knee.

"I was pretty sure Walt would have dropped me off on any other family's doorstep because I was never going to fit in here at the Rocking A. Spent a lot of time sneaking out of the house, too. Eventually, he made me a deal. I could leave whenever I wanted. He knew I needed the space sometimes to breathe, but I had to come here. No one else would know this was my spot, but he could find me when it mattered." Travis pointed at Damon. "Don't you spill my secrets."

"I won't." Damon shook his head. "You can trust me."

Good. That's what he'd wanted to hear.

"Trust me with your secret, Damon. I'll keep it. I promise. I need to know why you've got to get back to Denver. Did you leave something behind? We'll go pick it up. Our agreement still stands. I'll take you to meet with your social worker and we'll find whatever works the best, but I only want what's good for you. That's my only goal. I'd rather have the whole story going in, so I know how to help."

"It's… For some reason, I think you might understand this. The Smiths have another foster kid, a little guy named Micah." Damon glanced at him. "I'm worried about leaving him there alone. He needs me."

Travis picked up hay and broke it into tiny pieces as he tried to formulate a tricky question.

"It's not the Smiths, if that's what you're about to ask me. They're…fine." Damon bent his knees, his lanky legs forming a shield. "But Micah's…sensitive. Gets bullied on the bus. My bus usually dropped me off before his did, so I've been waiting at his stop to walk him home. Last week, my bus was late and these kids had Micah cornered."

"So you jumped in to defend him. How many kids?" Travis asked. This was a familiar story. He'd fought a few of these fights growing up, too.

"I don't know, four or five. Micah got free and I was losing." Damon grimaced. "Turns out watching karate movies doesn't teach you much karate, so I took off running, hit the fence to climb, made it to the top but they grabbed my leg and yanked me down. When I landed with a crunch, they took off running. The shop owner carrying out the trash got a big shock when he found me gasping for breath, since the fall had knocked it out of me. He called the cops, and the ambulance, and…everything escalated."

"Why were you in trouble? Seems like the bullies should have been the ones in trouble with the police," Travis said, offended at unfair treatment in general and for Damon specifically.

"I get in trouble for fighting. A lot. I mean, I've been on my best behavior because Micah was scared to death we'd get split up if he complained about the bullies or whatever, and there's something about the kid that makes me want to look out for him." Damon shrugged. "He still believes in happy endings, families that belong together and all that."

If Travis knew anything, it was that Damon wanted to believe those things, too.

He and his brothers had held on to that until they'd made it to Prue and Walt.

Damon met his stare directly. "Do I think that could happen here? Maybe. You and the Armstrongs seem nice, but I can't leave Micah. He's like my brother now."

Now that Travis understood Damon had been determined to return for a "who" instead of a "what," everything made sense. But he wasn't clear on the right answer.

Was he ready to add a second foster, one younger than he'd expected to take charge of? If not, how easy would it be to say goodbye to Damon? He'd been imagining the kid riding in the Western Days parade with his family.

Before Travis could test the waters to see if Damon was receptive to bringing Micah here, his phone rang. He pulled it out to stop the ringing and noticed Ellen Montoya's name on the display. "Hello? I was about to text you to request a meeting for tomorrow."

"Oh? What's going on?"

Travis was very aware that the subject of the conversation was watching him from across the quilt. "We want to discuss some concerns Damon has about his brother, Micah." He would have explained in more detail, but he hoped Ellen Montoya could remember enough about the boys to understand what he meant.

"Funny you mention Micah," she said. "The Smiths caught him sneaking out of his bedroom window tonight with a backpack filled with what he thought would be enough clothes and food to make it to Prospect. The kid's not even ten years old, Travis. Is it any wonder the Smiths were alarmed?"

"But Micah is okay," he said before he realized how that would sound to someone else. Damon scrambled across the hay to land next to him, his ear pressed hard against the phone in Travis's hand.

"He is. The Smiths made a promise they'd talk to me about bringing Damon back here, to rejoin their family," Ellen said, "so this is me talking to you about it. I'll be honest. I've got concerns. Damon's influence might not be what Micah needs. This running away is new behavior. I wonder how much of that has to do with Damon."

Travis pulled the phone away from Damon's grasping hands. The kid was desperate to defend himself. That made sense. This was important to him. "Did Micah tell the Smiths or you about the bullying he's been experiencing? That's part of what I heard from Damon tonight when I stopped him from running away."

"Oh, no, him, too? This is a mess." She sighed. "And no, I don't believe the Smiths have that information, No one has shared it with me."

"The boys were afraid that would be what split them up. Damon's been watching out for Micah." Travis didn't want to give too many details. Damon's trust was new. It was important to treat the information carefully that he'd shared.

"We're coming to the office tomorrow. Could the Smiths meet us there with Micah?" Travis asked. Should he volunteer to move Micah to Prospect? That would get him away from the bullies, both kids would stop running away from home, and all he had to do was...open up the door and tell him to jump in the truck.

It seemed simple but it was another huge step.

"Come down. I want to talk to both boys, for sure, but I can hear the unspoken words, Travis. Micah is younger than you're prepared for. He's also got some trauma in his background that made finding a couple like the Smiths important. He's extremely cautious of men. I wasn't sure Ian Smith would make the cut."

Travis realized this whole time, even with Damon, he'd been worried about his own reaction, what he would do right or wrong, but he was dealing with kids who had their own histories. Had he even considered that piece?

The question reminded him of his father's analogy of the jigsaw puzzle.

"Okay, Damon and I will get a good night's rest and travel down tomorrow. We'll meet and then we'll all make a decision together. There's no sense in getting too far along in our heads tonight." Travis held Damon's stare as he spoke, hoping the kid was catching on to what he was saying.

"Yes. That's what we'll do. I'll see you tomorrow around…eleven?" Ellen asked.

"Perfect. We'll be there." Travis ended the call and slipped his phone back in his pocket.

Damon was quiet, his hands balled tightly into fists in his lap.

His fears were written on his face, but Travis wasn't sure what the right words might be.

"Thank you for listening," Damon said softly. "Is it okay if I sit here a bit longer?"

Travis nodded and stood. That had to be his cue to leave. "Thank you for telling me. Don't know what will happen tomorrow, but I'll go ahead and make a promise that you can tell me anything and trust me to keep it. Tomorrow, next week, next year, or beyond."

Damon nodded. Travis wasn't certain the kid believed him. Some things had to be proven first, but if he got the chance, Travis would keep his promise.

When he went into the house, his father and brothers were seated around the kitchen table.

Before he could speak, Grant said, "Sorry. I know better. I was the kid who had a story for every occasion. Gonna have to step up my game."

Surprised and touched, Travis waved it off. "Not sure any of us are truly prepared for this. I thought I had all the questions and none of the answers. Turns out, I don't even know all the questions yet." He rubbed his forehead, exhausted but certain he'd never sleep. "Tomorrow we'll get together with the other foster parents and the foster brother he left behind and come up with a plan."

Walt shifted his stance. "Ah, he wanted to get back to

family. Makes more sense. Looks like we'll either be losing a Damon or gaining a…"

"Micah. He's almost ten. Not comfortable with men." Travis watched them trade stares around the table, all obviously reaching the same conclusion he had. The Rocking A was nothing but men at this point, which didn't fit Micah at all.

"Damon's taking over the hayloft. It's his spot now, for however long he stays." Travis squeezed his father's shoulder.

"Where are you going to hide out?" Wes asked.

Travis wasn't surprised that everyone knew about his hideaway. Walt had probably told them the same night he'd told Travis it was his and warned them all to let him have his space. It was a sign of respect that they'd followed Walt's direction.

"We may have to share it now and then," Travis said.

"You want company tomorrow? I'll be happy to tag along," Grant offered.

"Or a lawyer? I can go, too." Wes shrugged. "We could be backup."

Relieved that he had them to talk to, Travis tilted his head back. "Might need you more when I get home if Damon goes back. I'd already fitted him for his own horse and tack for Western Days." When he thought of the people he wanted by his side to navigate this conversation with the social worker and the Smiths, Keena's face popped into his mind.

But that didn't make sense. This was his thing anyway. He'd be fine on his own.

Walt slipped an arm around his shoulder. "We'll be here no matter what."

TRAVIS HELD ON TO his father's promise all the way through to seating himself at the conference table in the cramped office space Ellen Montoya shared with the other social workers. He'd dressed in his best button-down. Damon was seated next to him, one leg tapping out a nervous rhythm, and a small, well-dressed couple walked in behind Ellen Montoya. As she made the introductions, Travis caught sight of Micah for the first time. He stood carefully between Ellen Montoya and his foster mother until Damon said, "You aren't gonna hug me? Rude."

Then the boy walked quickly around the table, and threw his arms around Damon's neck. The hug went longer than Damon expected because he patted Micah's back and sent Travis a silent plea for help.

"Micah, why don't you sit there with Damon, okay?" Ellen suggested. Instead of moving to the next chair, Micah climbed into Damon's seat, made him scooch over, and crammed himself into the too-small space. Then he turned suspicious eyes on Travis.

Travis pretended not to feel the weight of that stare while Ellen did a recap of the situation. The Smiths admitted they had no idea what Micah was experiencing on the bus.

Ellen asked Damon questions about the ranch, Travis and his family, and school.

All in all, Travis thought the Rocking A came out pretty well in the telling.

Damon said, "Micah and I should try Prospect together. There's plenty of room. We'll go to the same school so I can watch out for him. Maybe until the end of the school year. Then we can decide which home would be better for us. That's what I think."

Ellen's eyebrows shot up, but no one at the table argued with him, so the solution had merit. She asked, "Micah, what do you think about living in Prospect? Travis and his brothers run a ranch."

The way the kid looked immediately at his foster mother

confirmed Travis's suspicion. The ranch wouldn't be the best place for him. Micah needed a mother.

Then Micah turned back to him. "Do you have dogs?"

His foster mother laughed. "He loves dogs. When they walk down the sidewalk in front of the house, he stops whatever he's doing to watch."

Did that mean they didn't have dogs themselves?

Because Travis would add a whole pack of dogs at the ranch if that sealed the deal. He wanted this to work out in a way he had never expected.

"I don't right now, but I have horses. What do you think about horses?" he asked.

Micah tilted his head back. "Do I like horses, Damon?"

Damon laughed. "Yeah, kid, horses are good."

Micah nodded as if that was enough confirmation for him. "I'd like to meet your horses. We should circle back around to dogs at some point."

Travis bit his lip to maintain his serious expression, but wondered who this kid was, given he was talking like a corporate manager in his midforties.

Ian Smith's brow was raised. "That's what I say every time he asks if we can get a dog. We'll circle back around when he's older."

All the adults in the room smiled and relaxed because Damon had offered them a workable solution. If they tried it and it failed, they'd come back to the table and try something else. Travis shook the Smiths' hands, relieved and so pleased to meet the couple who were as committed to these boys' happiness as he wanted all foster families to be.

Then he noticed the way Micah continued to watch him closely and wondered how long he'd have to convince the boy he could be trusted. Even if all the running away stopped, Travis had a hunch he hadn't cleared all the obstacles yet.

CHAPTER TWELVE

ON SATURDAY MORNING, Keena made a mental note that she had to schedule the phone company to provide her an internet connection as soon as possible. She'd been busy at the clinic all week, but she missed her distractions now that the weekend had rolled around again. Finding a hobby had reached the top of her to-do list.

"Or else I really will do it," she muttered as she dropped the hank of hair she'd been measuring for bangs. Whenever the urge to cut her own hair arose, Keena started to worry. That was the sign of a desperate woman. Since her choices were limited, it was an easy decision that what she needed that morning was a shopping trip. She hadn't had a good opportunity to explore Prue's craft store. If Patrick was there, he could give her some tips on an inexpensive way to explore painting. "Or even expensive if that will keep you from cutting your own hair." The first time she'd chosen impulsive bangs had been in high school. Keena still couldn't look at her yearbook pictures from her junior year.

Not long after, she parked in front of the craft store and gave herself a lecture about walking into new places and trying new things and how other people managed to do it all the time and so could she. Tourist traffic was light on the wooden sidewalks in town. This was the perfect opportunity to go into the store because she would have space to shop and ask for help. For someone who had endless questions, the concept of being a beginner and having to start at the *beginning* was stressful. Tapping her fingers in her usual rhythm slowed her heart rate and Keena realized she couldn't remember the last time she'd done that.

Had she worked all week at Prospect Family Practice without once fighting back the rush of anxiety that had become routine for every hospital shift?

KEENA WIPED HER palms on her jeans as she stepped into the building with space divided for Prue's craft shop and a hardware store. She needed to ask Travis sometime about how this came about.

"You were going to cut your bangs to keep from thinking about Travis, Keena," she muttered to herself. "Don't make me give you another lecture." As much as she felt the flutter of nerves before walking into any new situation, she usually managed to stop talking to herself before she committed.

Keena straightened her shoulders and stepped into Handmade.

Walt Armstrong had propped his elbows on the checkout counter with the cash register while Prue was staring down into his eyes. The way they immediately moved away from each other convinced Keena she was interrupting something...important? Or...

Prue recovered first. "Keena! My favorite doctor. I was wondering if I was ever gonna get you back in my store."

Walt waited for Prue to finish before tipping his hat at Prue. "Let's continue this conversation. Over dinner. Your choice."

Prue pursed her lips. "I'll think about it, cowboy."

Keena turned to study stacks of quilt patterns for a design called the Rocky Meadow. Keena knew nothing about quilting but the blocks were different kinds of flowers with embroidery details.

"We've got a small model hanging above the stairs if you're interested in seeing that pattern worked up," Prue said as she walked past Keena. She held the door open for Walt and then offered him her cheek for a kiss. Keena knew he accepted the offer because of the loud, playful buss and the way Prue giggled and said, "Oh, you."

Keena moved across the store to the section labeled Paint and prayed for the color in her cheeks to recede quickly.

"Patrick's gone back to LA for a week or so to pack up his house and talk to a real estate agent, but I'll do my best to help if you're interested in picking up things to give painting a shot," Prue called as she pulled a chair out from the large worktable. "He put together a beginner kit if you think you might be that interested. Has acrylic paints, two small canvases, a collection of brushes… The basics to get you started. There's also a couple of books for beginners over there in the stand next to the easels." Prue crossed her arms and rested them on the table in front of her. "I expect he'll have more to choose from when he gets back."

Keena pulled out one of the books. "I never realized how much the hospital took out of me. Days off were about errands and getting reset for hospital shifts. Here? I've baked so many cookies I'm starting to dread the idea of eating cookies."

She glanced over her shoulder at Prue to make sure the other woman understood that she was making a joke.

"Dire situation you got yourself there." Prue shook her head sadly. "If only I knew of a house filled with men and two growing boys that might be able to assist with your situation."

Keena paged through the book. Even though it said beginner, she wasn't sure she had enough experience yet to attempt any of the projects. "Two boys?"

Prue nodded. "Yep, Travis took one down the mountain and brought two back. It happens that way sometimes, I guess."

Keena moved over to where Prue was sitting. She needed more details. "I asked Travis to let me know what happened. I guess he's happy with this solution? I know he was already attached to Damon, making plans for the future. Letting him go wouldn't have been easy."

Prue smiled. It wasn't exactly a "gotcha" grin but it was in that family. She was pleased Keena was asking questions about her son. "He is, but he will enjoy telling you about that. I was surprised he didn't ask you to meet with the social worker. I tell you, every single time we were introduced to a new boy who might be ours and heard parts of his story, it took me and Walt some time to absorb the details and carry all the emotion. Travis is strong, but I'm not convinced anyone can be strong enough to do all that alone."

Determined to ignore the message being shouted clearly between the lines there and stuff down the confusion about why Travis would choose her for support over his concerned parents or any of his brothers who had lived the experience from the other side, Keena waited impatiently for more hints. Was Prue not going to tell her what happened?

Then Prue pointed at Keena's purse. "You have your phone, don't you?"

Keena frowned. Of course she had her phone. She never left home without it, especially now that she was the only medical care available in town. When it started ringing, she watched Prue's grin grow wider. What was that called? She'd passed right through "Gotcha" to…gloating?

Keena plucked her phone from her bag. "Hey, Travis."

"Good morning. You answered fast. Were you expecting a call?" he asked.

"No, but your mother was. How she knew it was coming to my phone is still a mystery." She laughed reluctantly at the way Prue brushed off her shoulders as if she was just that good.

"Let me solve that one. I called to beg for her help. She said she was swamped at the store today and she couldn't get free, so I should try calling you." Travis's dry tone convinced Keena he was aware of what was happening here, too. "Are you in Handmade this morning?"

"Yeah, I thought it would save me from cutting my own hair." Keena smiled at the sharp inhale Prue made in reaction to hearing that.

Travis obviously didn't understand the threat. "So you're busy, too?"

Keena laughed. "I am so unbusy I'm about to make serious hair care mistakes. What can I help you with? I'm going over to the Majestic to see if Jordan and Sarah can put me to good use this afternoon, but I have time now if you need me."

Maybe "need me" wasn't exactly the correct choice of words, but she had no way to remove them from the conversation now. *Want me?* Was that any better? Not really.

"Your mother did mention you now have two boys to care for. I guess things worked out with Damon." Keena returned to the Paint section and studied the kit for beginners Patrick Hearst had put together. Did she have enough talent to justify spending the money on that? Not really, but at this point she had more money than she'd ever have talent, so there wasn't much stopping her. She stacked the book for beginners on top of the kit. Optimism had swept aside reason with Travis's call.

"Yeah, turns out the 'what' Damon was desperate enough to hitchhike for was a 'who' named Micah who has some trust issues when it comes to men. Nothing too intense, but he's more comfortable with women present. He's also desperate to ride a horse. I wanted my mother to come out and take Lady for a ride, but she's busy at Handmade."

Keena took a long survey of the completely empty store before landing on Prue's pleased expression as she cut fabric at the table.

"You know I don't know anything about horses, right?" Keena asked.

"I wasn't sure, but I suspected. That's okay. I'm going to ask Grant to come along, so he can help with a lesson at the same time. Micah will be more relaxed. That will make Damon happy. And it's a nice warm day in November, so we should all get outside. Not sure how many more warm sunny days there will be before winter arrives."

Keena waited for Travis to wind down his sales pitch and wondered if he was as aware of how easy their conversations were now compared to that day they'd met over the tree chopping.

"What do you say?" Travis asked.

"I'm in. Give me twenty minutes or so, and I'll meet you at the barn." He whooped with satisfaction, so Keena hung up.

"Just absolutely swamped here," Keena murmured as she carried her stack of purchases to the cash register.

Prue sniffed. "Well, now that you're here, this is turning into a good sales day."

Keena had to agree. Prue's sales had taken a big jump, thanks to her maybe-someday hobby.

"My boys accuse me of being a matchmaker, but I'd say they're all lucky. Coincidences like this one, you needing something to keep you out of haircut trouble and Trav looking for help, always work for the Armstrongs." She slipped a receipt into the cloth tote stamped with her store's name and slid it across to Keena. "Born under lucky stars every one of those boys."

Keena shook her head. "Can't argue with success."

"Well, they try. They got too much of their daddy in them not to just take the win." Prue leaned against the counter. "I do not like to interfere in my sons' business..." Prue paused to see if there was any reaction and Keena wondered if the well-meaning woman uttered that whopper of a tale often. "They're grown, after all, but I would like to give you some advice. I appreciate that you have this career that you've invested your life into. It's an important job and Denver is lucky to have you, I have no doubt. Heck, I guess the whole state might need your expertise in an emergency."

Keena gripped her new tote bag with both hands as she waited for the "but." If Prue was building a case for a match with Travis, there had to be more coming.

"And I hope you remember what's important when it comes time to make a decision about what you do next," Prue said with a smile.

Keena stood there until it was clear Prue had finished her thought, although there was nothing else behind it.

Confused, Keena asked, "Aren't you going to make the case about how well I can do that right here in Prospect? With Travis? At the Rocking A?" All signs pointed to that being the logical next part of the dialogue.

Prue shook her head. "Honestly, Travis and his boys will take care of that for me. I'm gonna look out for you."

Did she need someone on her side?

Why were there sides at all?

Prue's smile was softer, a little bittersweet. "I am warning you that love becomes something else when it's for a man and his children. I swear, men will test your patience at every turn, so often that a smart woman begins to question her own intelligence some days. It ain't easy to walk away, but when you got all these other tiny connections, the memories of when this boy ran away from home or that one broke three fingers playing like he was a bank robber in a ghost town he shoulda never been in the first place and you and your husband have to make a flying trip together to the emergency room or when a boy you loved has the opportunity to go back home to his parents and you have to settle for occasional updates to know he's okay for the rest of both your lives..." Prue sighed. "Those are ties that never come undone, and that cowboy you'd like to erase from your life comes back around and you can see in his face how well he loved those kids...and you've got yourself a real dilemma." She held up her hands. "So I'm on your side, no matter what."

Prue didn't meet her stare. Was the emotion in her honesty overwhelming her? Keena understood how that could happen, so she held up the tote. "Thank you for your suggestion and the advice, Prue."

"Oh, now, this whole visit was definitely my pleasure." Prue waved goodbye.

Keena mulled over Prue's words on the drive and realized that her caution made sense. What had Prue given up to build this family with Walt? Were the regrets what kept them apart? And if she left behind the career she'd made in Denver for a possible new life in Prospect, with Travis and his boys, what kind of regrets might she have?

It was too much for a Saturday morning, even if Keena appreciated Prue's concern.

All this heavy thinking because she refused to cut her own hair.

Keena could see Travis and Damon leaning against the fence, watching as Grant worked with a young boy in the paddock. Both had one foot propped on the lowest rail.

"Good morning," she said, "good to see you again, neighbors." She waited for Damon to face her before smiling brightly. "Beautiful day to learn to ride a horse, I'm guessing."

"There's already a forecast for snow flurries at the end of the week." Travis gave a friendly wave and Damon's face immediately brightened. Kids loving snow must be a universal thing. Even in Iowa, they'd celebrated the first few snows every season. By March, they were ready to be done. "Will it amount to much? No, but it's a signal that our time outdoors on the ranch is drawing short. Once the snow arrives in full, we'll be locked inside together, and playing hockey in your socks across the living room floor can only burn off so much energy."

That was an oddly specific example. How often had Travis and his brothers done that? Prue must have been very laid-back or on the edge of desperation to survive the winters to allow that.

What would it be like to be snowed in at the Rocking A? That was another big question to consider, but she was tired of those. She wanted activity.

Keena crossed her arms over her chest. "This is my waiting patiently pose."

Travis couldn't contain the grin. "What comes next? Or should I not ask?"

She narrowed her eyes. "You don't want to know."

He immediately surrendered. "Let's get this lesson started." Travis waved Grant and his student closer to the fence. "Micah, this is Keena. She lives next door. I was thinking about taking her out for a horse ride. What do you think about that?"

An actual horse ride? Keena tried not to overreact. She'd intended to watch Micah and Damon have a lesson, not attempt climbing on a horse herself. Still, she'd been asked to help, so she shielded her eyes from the brilliant sun as she smiled up at Micah. "I don't know much about horses. Do you think it's a good idea?"

He nodded. "Only you might need some lessons before we go."

The kid was obviously smart, too.

"Good suggestion," Grant said as he moved toward the barn. "Let's go saddle up some horses. You can show Keena how it's done."

Grant and the boys headed off. Keena stepped closer to Travis. "You're going to saddle my horse for me, aren't you?"

He laughed and draped his arm over her shoulder. "Yes, ma'am. We've been trying to convince Grant that he ought to be offering riding lessons out here, but he's not falling for it. I'm hoping working with you might change his mind, but he's not off to the best start, picking the kids over the beautiful woman."

Keena raised her eyebrows. "Wow, you're different today. Must be having some of the weight off your mind?" The first time they'd met, he'd been awkward enough to be charming and set her own social anxiety at ease. Today he was flirting?

"Could be. I'm also glad to see you. I'm excited to show off the ranch." Travis paused midstep. "I'm happy." He frowned as if the word tasted funny in his mouth.

Keena laughed. "Don't celebrate too soon. This ride can still go awry. I'm whatever stage of rider comes before beginner." She bit her bottom lip as if she was admitting a horrible secret. "I don't want you to judge me harshly."

Travis took her hand in his and smoothed out the fist. "If you'll agree to give it a shot, I'll tell you a story so that you will understand why I would never judge your horse riding ability."

She huffed. "But only if I agree to go with you all over to the Majestic. What is that, twenty miles?"

He blinked. "More like three or four miles. This is not a weeklong trek. We'll saddle my mother's horse, Lady. She is the easiest ride we have. All you'll have to do is keep your feet in the stirrups and your…self in the saddle. Lady and I can do the rest."

"My…self in the saddle, you say?" Keena's lips twitched in amusement. "They have trail ride companies who take city slickers up on the mountains for rides like this. If they can do it, I can, too. Right?" Some reassurance would be nice.

Travis nodded. "There are kindergartners who manage to do more than stay in the saddle during the parade for Western Days. That was one of the things I got excited about with Damon and Micah. They're going to love it."

"Kindergartners?" She straightened her shoulders. "Surely I can keep up with them. You sold me with the comment about the snow. I've been in Prospect long enough to know that Sharita's house is comfortable, but the cabin fever will be intense when I'm shut up inside it for days at a time. I want to hear about playing hockey in the living room, too." Keena pointed at the jacket she was wearing. "How does Lady feel about hot pink?"

"She's pretty stylish. My mother wouldn't have it any other way. I bet she'll love that color for you," Travis answered, his lips curved in amusement.

Keena watched as Travis saddled up two horses, both beautiful and extremely large. He was going to ride Arrow, Wes's horse, while she was going to cling to the saddle of Lady, and theoretically, this was going to be a lovely afternoon excursion. Damon had been learning to saddle and ride Travis's horse, Sonny, and to Keena's inexperienced eye, he seemed comfortable as he waited for everyone else.

"Micah, you want to ride with Grant or me?" Travis asked as he paused in front of the smaller boy. "Your choice. Next time, we'll put you up on your own mount if you feel up to it."

Keena held Lady's reins and tried to send her horse friendly brain waves, while they waited for Micah to make his decision.

"Come on, squirt. You can ride with me, the rodeo star, or with that guy." Grant held his hands out as if he was displaying his charms better. "It shouldn't be this difficult. Only one of us will never tell you to eat your vegetables or go to bed before you're ready."

Travis huffed out a breath when Micah pointed at Grant's horse, Bandit. Grant picked the boy up and dumped him like a sack of potatoes in the saddle, and Micah laughed with his whole body. Grant swung up behind him, tipped his hat at Keena with a roguish grin, and walked the horse out into the sunlight.

"I would have handled him like spun glass. Grant tosses him like a football," Travis muttered under his breath. "I should take a page out of his book."

"Are you familiar with the term 'fun uncle'?" Keena asked while she watched him check the saddles. "I have a stepbrother, single, no kids, who likes to give out hundred-dollar bills to all the kids in the family every Christmas. He's not going to teach them right from wrong, necessarily, and they love him for it. I think we know which one of your brothers is the fun uncle."

Travis considered that. "They haven't even met Matt yet. These kids are going to have choices to make if there can only be one fun uncle."

Keena realized that the closer she got to physically climbing onto the horse, the more her nerves fired up. The longer she stood there, watching him do things she didn't know how to do, inhaling unfamiliar odors of the barn, and picturing in her head how awkward she was going to look attempting this for the first time, the faster her heart pounded. Breathing became something she had to concentrate on. And the funny little comments Travis threw out now and then had stopped blocking the alarms in her head. Eventually, Keena leaned against one of the stalls and started working through the exercises that pushed away the panic.

She counted each inhale, held it for five beats, and exhaled slowly until her lungs were crying out for air. She tapped each finger against her thumb and did her best to clear her brain of any images depicting her embarrassing fall from a saddle.

"You okay?" Travis asked, his voice a low rumble next to her ear.

As if he'd been patiently waiting for her to grab control of her runaway brain.

"Sorry. I'd almost gotten used to not having this panic take over here in Prospect." She flexed her fingers. "Glad to know it's still with me, like a ratty old blanket I've been dragging behind me."

He bumped her shoulder this time. "You don't have to ride, you know. This is completely optional. No reason to put yourself through it if you don't want to. Micah seems to be overcoming his own fears quickly."

"I want to try this." She licked her lips. "If you'd asked me a month ago if I ever dreamed of going horseback riding, my answer would have been a dumbfounded no. But even as I know I'm going to be terrible at this and I, as a hard-and-fast rule, do not do things I am terrible at, I still followed you into this barn." She glanced over at Lady who was definitely judging her, even if Travis wasn't. "She's beautiful. I understand why your mother loves her so much."

"Yes, Lady's the daughter she never had until Sarah Hearst popped up next door."

Keena raised her eyebrows.

"Daughter-in-law? In my family, they're blood relatives. We haven't had one yet, but I'm certain of it." Travis shifted his hat back. "Why don't you head on inside? I'll unsaddle the horses and we'll go with four wheels instead of legs."

"Eight." Keena pointed as he tilted his head to consider that. "Eight legs. Two horses. If my math is correct, that's eight legs."

"Good to know you can still do multiplication, Doc." Travis stood slowly.

"Wait." Keena wrapped her hand around his arm. "I want to try, but this is definitely one of the stories that go with us to the grave. You don't tell anyone whatever Lady says to you behind my back when this is all over."

His slow grin eased some of the anxiety. "I swear. Nobody will hear about it from me." Then he grasped her hand. "I'm going to take you over to the mounting block. That will make the whole thing easier."

Keena's mouth was suddenly dry so she nodded her agreement. When they were back out in the sunshine and Lady was calmly waiting, Keena stepped up and slid lightly into the saddle. Travis murmured softly to Lady as he adjusted the length of the stirrups and made sure the saddle was secure. Keena couldn't understand what he was saying to the horse, but his tone had a positive effect on her nerves, too. She realized she was breathing better. The pounding of her heart in her ears had receded.

As long as Travis was close by, she knew everything would be okay.

She watched him put a foot in the stirrup and swing up in the saddle and immediately knew she would never be able to do that. Her horse riding life would depend on having a tall something to climb up and step off of.

Before she could ask a million questions about their plans at the Majestic and the setup or proximity of a nice step stool, Travis took the reins she'd been holding on to for dear life and forced her cramping fingers to loosen. Keena relaxed a fraction when she saw that Grant plus Micah, and Damon had already moved out into the pasture. She didn't have an audience for this first attempt at being on a horse.

"We're going in a slow circle here in the paddock to get a feel for Lady's gait and to make sure the saddle feels right," he said in a low voice. "I've got the reins. You concentrate on the saddle part."

"And staying upright in it," Keena muttered as she clutched the saddle horn so hard her fingers turned white.

Travis hummed an agreement and he kept up the steady stream of encouragement to the horses, an indistinct murmur that Keena could feel more than hear. Eventually her spine relaxed a fraction and she could settle into the rock of Lady's gait.

"Okay, what do you think?" Travis asked.

Keena forced her eyelids open. She hadn't even realized she'd squeezed them shut, but the whole experience improved with sunshine, open space, Lady's placid brown eyes blinking back at her, and Travis's amusement. "Part of the challenge of horseback riding is that you have to keep your eyes open. The horse can see, but she doesn't know where you want to go, so you have to give directions."

Keena let go of the saddle and shook her hands to send blood back into her fingertips as she smiled. "Fine. I'll try it your way. Let's see if we can go in a line. Lady's tired of walking in circles."

"Sure. First, tell Lady she's doing a good job. Run your hand down her neck, give her some scratches if she wants them."

Keena froze, midreach. "How will I know if she doesn't want them?"

"You will know. She'll shake her head or most likely give you a death stare. Lady might be mostly human at this point. She and my mother have been together for years." Travis pointed with his chin. "Try it and see."

Nervous, Keena did as he directed, running her hand down Lady's neck, surprised and charmed at how warm and soft the horse was. Lady tipped her head to the side in a broad clue on where to scratch, so Keena followed her and was rewarded when the horse huffed a happy breath.

How Keena could tell the difference between a happy horse and a mad horse at this point, she wasn't sure, but something in her gut told her she and Lady were building a connection.

"Okay, let's work with the reins. Hold these loosely but don't drop them. Lady will follow Sonny, so you aren't going to need to give her much prompting." Travis urged Sonny a few steps forward. "Squeeze lightly with your legs to tell her to move forward. Since you're both learning here, you can also say 'go.'" Travis held up a hand. "And for stop? You pull lightly on the reins. Never tug. Never yank. That will hurt the horse and my mother will kill us both without waiting for a trial or a judge to render us guilty. Light pressure and say 'Whoa, Lady.' That's all it will take. Try both."

Keena wanted to call it quits again, but Travis was watching her proudly.

Even Lady seemed to be urging her on, so she followed

his instructions. Her shout of terror and elation, all tangled together, instantly died in her throat as the image of a startled Lady rearing and dumping her in the dirt flashed in her brain. Keena held her breath as Lady moved in the same lazy circle they'd been working on in the paddock and stopped immediately at Keena's signal.

"Why do I know in my heart it won't always be that easy?" Keena said under her breath.

"Could be because you've got the heart of a cowgirl and you know animals have their own minds," Travis answered. "Either way, I think you're ready to give the open pasture a try. Do you?"

Keena wasn't convinced she was ready, but his steady regard made her want to give it a shot. "Lady's ready, for sure. I'll hold on." When she realized her jaw was aching from gritting her teeth, Keena took a deep breath. "This is so much fun."

His low laugh improved her mood a fraction. "Give it a chance. Follow me."

More than anything, Keena wanted to do this well, and by the time they made it to the fence that separated the Rocking A from the Majestic Prospect Lodge property, she had managed to yank her stare from her white-knuckled grip on the loose reins to how the land rolled gently before rising sharply into the mountains.

"Travis, I understand your homesickness. This place is gorgeous." She could see in the distance how the shadows changed on the mountainside as clouds interrupted the sunshine and then moved away. The dying grass was dull now, but in the springtime, she could imagine a rich green. And the autumn colors would be so intense that a person might never forget them. When she realized that was a season she wouldn't see in Prospect, Keena felt a pinch of regret.

"Larkspur Pass." Travis nodded to the valley between the mountains. There was a faint trail worn that disappeared over the edge. Grant and Damon had reached the gate between the ranch and the lodge next door. "We moved the cattle we graze up there down closer for the winter. Once the snow comes, it's a tough ride." He shrugged. "If we get a chance, we'll go for another ride before that happens. You need to see how pretty it is then, too."

Keena nodded enthusiastically, grateful that her less-than-natural ability to ride Lady hadn't convinced him she never needed to slip into the saddle again.

After a few hundred trips, she might be able to do this without any trouble.

Keena followed Travis through the gate Grant had left open.

"We bought this part from the Hearsts, used to belong to Sadie." Travis and Sonny closed the gate behind them. "Normally, we'd leave this open, but I don't have the energy to chase down one rogue Chuck that would pick my first ride with a pretty lady to make a fool of me."

"Are you calling them all Chuck now? My Chuck isn't special?"

He pointed toward the lodge on the hill. It faded so well into the surroundings that she might not have seen it without hunting for it. "I like the name."

"I guess they aren't pets," Keena said as she followed behind him. Lady was quite content with their speed and distance so far. Keena couldn't imagine a better partner for her maiden ride.

"No, not pets, although Chuck the first has been over at Faye's for long enough to meet the pet criteria. Since her grandparents have slowed down, she's got her hands full with the restaurant and the farm. She doesn't have a lot of time for buying and selling livestock right now."

"She was telling me about the food truck nights that Lucky arranges like they're such a relief to her. But I wondered if she ever got a break. She ran out of the Ace High for the Sip and Paint like she expected the dinner crowd to stop her."

"She works too hard, but it's next to impossible to convince someone who loves what they're doing that they deserve time to do other things, too." Travis led the way up a faded trail. "Letting go of the small farm they have would be a big help, but it also might break her grandfather's heart, so she's stuck doing what she can."

Keena watched him sway easily in the saddle as she considered his words.

Maybe it should have been harder for her to walk away from the hospital, even for a temporary reprieve.

She'd understood immediately the way Faye spoke about the restaurant. She was proud of it, enjoyed what she was doing, and at the same time it was sucking every bit of life out of her. At that point, anyone would be desperate for a break.

Even a doctor who had built the emergency department she dreamed of and couldn't imagine herself anywhere else.

Those people, like Faye and Keena, who loved what they did but sacrificed so much to do it, might gamble on something new, just to have a chance to breathe again.

Keena wondered what Prue might say to that. In Handmade, she'd considered what Prue had given up to make the Armstrong family work. What if life on the Rocking A, where winter might mean so much snow that five growing boys played hockey in the living room when they weren't struggling to keep livestock fed and watered, had been her emergency department? Had this divorce been Prue's way to get breathing room, some space for herself?

If so, that made Prue's promise that she was watching out for Keena sweeter and so much easier to understand.

"I'd love to meet Faye's Gram. The food she sends out at the restaurant is amazing."

"She's...intense." Travis wrinkled his nose. "Has a firm opinion on everything related to the Ace and keeps Faye running. Prospect could easily support another restaurant which would lighten some of Faye's load. I'm hoping that when the lodge reopens, they'll follow up with redoing the restaurant, too. This place used to be for special occasions, the date-night destination for Prospect and other little towns around. When Sadie shut it, it was a big blow."

"Whoa, Lady," Keena said and did a mental high five for herself when Lady smoothly halted next to Sonny. They were in front of the lodge, a large open space that was... rustic. That was the kindest adjective Keena could come up with. A bridge from the parking lot crossed over a stream that flowed into the lake, and on the other side was the lodge. The lodge's siding was dull and graying, but it was clear someone had been doing improvements.

"Is that a new roof?" she asked.

He was surprised as he turned to her. "Good eye. It's a repaired roof. There was an episode with bats. In the attic. They had to be remediated immediately, so while the crew was working on that and the improvements needed to keep any bats from returning home, they got the roof fixed. Jordan and Sarah are pushing hard to get the place reopened in time for the spring Western Days weekend." Travis slid out of the saddle and looped Sonny's reins over a low branch there at the edge of the parking lot. A few hardy sprigs of grass survived in the sunshine around it. Travis did the same with Lady's reins. "After the first of the year, if you see my mother headed in your direction, turn and go the other way. Right now, the push for Western Days volunteers is low-key, but she will turn up the heat once the preparations get serious. She's determined to make this anniversary weekend bigger and better than ever." He moved to stand next to her. "How are the legs?"

Keena wrinkled her nose. "I forgot I had legs somewhere around the gate. I can't feel them."

He whistled. "You will." He offered her his hand. "Good news is, that gets better the more often you try this. The bad news is, they are going to remind you of this ride for days."

Keena sighed. "I figured. Lucky for me I know a good doctor who can tell me how to cope."

"Yeah?" Travis said as she slipped her hand in his and tried to swing her leg down. It was so much harder than it should have been. "What will the prescription be?" he asked.

"Water. Ibuprofen. Lots of both. That's a start on a lot of the things that I treat." Keena held on to the saddle tightly, afraid to trust her legs, until he touched her hips and guided her to the ground.

When both feet were planted, Travis said, "You let me know when I can let go." She nodded and took a step, relieved that her legs responded as requested. Maybe she would be sorry when she woke up tomorrow, but she wasn't going to make a fool out of herself now.

Not yet, anyway. Keena refused to worry about how she was going to make it back into the saddle when their visit was over.

Instead of warning him that he might need to get a strong team to help hoist her back into the saddle, Keena turned as the door to the lodge opened and Jordan stepped out. "Keena! Travis! I'm so glad you're here. Doc, you are so brave."

Keena blinked and looked to Travis for more information. "Jordan doesn't like horses."

Jordan shivered as if she'd felt someone walk across her grave. Keena laughed. "I'm not sure horses like me, but after today, I feel better about them."

Travis's smile felt like something only the two of them understood and shared.

And that was nice.

"Let me show you the lodge." Jordan clasped Keena's arm tightly and pulled it through hers, the woman a force of nature towing her along. Inside the lobby, Keena understood why Jordan was excited to show the place off. On the outside, the lodge showed some wear and tear, but inside, the beautiful wood floors were lit with golden sunshine streaming through large windows. There was a bright rag rug in yellow and orange and a few pieces of charming rustic furniture that seemed to fit the place perfectly.

"You've been doing some hard work here," Travis said. He propped his hands on his hips as he did a slow circle. "It's nice to see the painting hanging where it belongs."

He had to mean the large landscape positioned over the check-in desk that lined one long wall. It was of the mountains, snow covering the tops, and lots of lush evergreens. It was striking and seemed as if it had been made to hang there.

"My dad. He painted that for Sadie." Jordan smiled. "You see why he despairs any time Sarah and I pick up a paintbrush."

Keena laughed and followed as Jordan urged her down the hallway to show off more of the hard work they'd been doing. Most of the guest rooms were empty except for bed frames and mattresses, but they were spotless. She listened to the plan for a "soft launch" to give the sisters a little practical experience running a lodge, since none of them had ever done so. Jordan explained how Sadie had grown up here before her career and her family took her to LA.

It was a sweet tour of a place that was going to be fantastic someday, because the Hearst sisters were determined, and it was clear that they loved the Majestic and Sadie Hearst a lot.

Along the way, Keena was aware of two things.

At all times, she knew where Travis was. If he was trailing behind them or he'd stepped away to study something more closely, Keena was aware of it without watching it happen.

And there was the faintest scent of vanilla that wafted along with them.

"Have you already fired up the oven?" Keena asked as Jordan and Sarah led her back through the lobby to the restaurant. "Something smells good."

The glance the sisters exchanged immediately caught Keena's attention.

"Oh, yeah? What do you smell?" Jordan asked.

Travis sniffed the air. "Sweet. Are you baking cookies? A cake?"

Sarah's smile was kind as she hugged Keena's arm closer. "Vanilla. I can't smell it right now, but is that it?"

Keena nodded. She'd been baking enough cookies since she'd gotten to town that she knew Sarah had nailed it.

Jordan wrinkled her nose. "We have a small ghost story to tell you. Not a scary one. It's a friendly ghost and seems to be living in our kitchen."

"It pops up now and then, almost like Sadie would if she were here, so we aren't too bothered by it," Sarah added. "It doesn't surprise me a bit she'd want to welcome you to the Majestic herself."

Keena turned her head to catch Travis's eye. He

shrugged as if to say he had no response. They were going to have to go along with the ghost story.

"Well, I've been watching all of Sadie's old shows since I got to town. I'm happy to have the chance to tell her I'm a big fan." Keena would examine later whether she believed in ghosts or not, but it was hard to deny that the smell of vanilla intensified after her statement and stuck with her while she was in the Majestic.

CHAPTER THIRTEEN

TRAVIS RESTED ONE shoulder against the doorframe as he watched Grant, Damon and Micah work as an efficient team to sand the floor of one of the lodge's guest rooms. Damon was guiding the floor sander while Micah vacuumed up dust along the sanded edge. Grant was hands-on, offering advice and correcting techniques when needed. His brother saw him and said, "Wouldn't have guessed learning how to use one of these things on the living room floor of the Rocking A would be put to use again so soon."

"Are you using the experience, or are they?" Travis drawled.

Grant pursed his lips. "I am a teacher. You told me that. I taught them how to saddle their horses and ride, giving you and your doctor some privacy. Now I am passing along another valuable skill here. Are you making good use of the time I've bought you is the real question. It's hard to court after the kids come along, dontcha know?"

Travis nodded. He could understand how that might be true. "I'm glad you put them in safety equipment." He pointed at Damon's and Micah's eye and ear protection.

Grant nodded. "Soon as we finish this room, I think we ought to call it a day. The horses have been tethered outside awhile. They've got water and sunshine, but Lady will be ready to get back to her comfy stall."

Travis had headed in this direction to suggest they start wrapping up. He hated to leave because it was clear everyone was bonding over their work. Damon and Micah exchanged a high five. The younger boy had pointed out something on the floor and Damon moved to hit it with the sander.

"I'll have to drag Keena down from the ladder. She's painting the restaurant wall that has all the windows." Travis wasn't going to add that she'd made such painstaking progress that it would take her three full days at the rate she was going.

"I bet she's a perfectionist, isn't she?" Grant asked. "I'll help Keena paint if you want to take the kids back to the ranch." His tone clearly said, "If I have to," and Travis knew that Grant was poking and prodding him to admit he wanted to spend more time with Keena.

"Or Wes and I could take the horses and you can bring my car over," Sarah said from behind them. "Jordan is pushing my buttons with all her orders. If I don't take a break, I will make a break…possibly all the way back to California."

Grant held his hands up. "Easy, Sarah. No need for more folks to start running away. Travis is such a gentleman that he will be happy to meet your terms. You and Wes take their horses home, and then we'll all invade the Rocking A kitchen to find something to feed these hungry boys. How does that sound?"

Sarah said, "Why do I get the feeling that you won't be the one doing the cooking?"

Grant pretended shock. "Now that you mention it, it's Wes's turn and he mentioned a pot of chili, I think." Then he blinked innocently.

"What do you want to do, Trav?" Wes asked as he joined the group. "We'll be happy to watch the boys, including this troublemaker, if you want to take Keena to town for dinner or..." He shrugged. "Yeah, that's about all I've got to offer. I'm not exactly known for my romantic sensibility."

Sarah squeezed the hand he'd extended to her. "If you'd find a place to hang up a porch swing around here, we'd have plenty of places for...romance."

Grant and Travis exchanged smirks while Wes cleared his throat. "We'll be riding off with the kids. You figure out your own romantic moves, brother."

Grant went to fetch Damon and Micah and when he explained it was dinnertime, both boys perked up. Travis realized he was going to have to pay more attention to when it was time to eat. They weren't ready to make demands yet, so he needed to watch these things closely.

"You guys okay to go back with Grant and Wes? Keena's in the middle of a project. When she finishes, I'll bring her over to the house."

Micah nodded. "Can we ride by the lake? I didn't get to see it."

Travis noticed he'd asked Grant instead of him. That wasn't a problem.

"It's cold and the sun's setting. Let's save that for our next ride, okay? We'll get back and let Uncle Wes feed us. Then I want to show you the wonders of my collection of video games." Grant's smile showed he knew he had both boys.

Damon watched Micah trot down the hallway behind Grant, Wes and Sarah. "I can stay behind with you. I like doing this. I like helping."

Travis took a chance and squeezed his shoulder. Instead of shifting away, Damon watched him curiously. Then he smiled and Travis felt it direct in the center of his chest. The emotion of that tentative smile, the first one, left a mark. He wasn't sure he'd ever recover.

"There's so much to be done here, we'll drive back over

tomorrow. I know Jordan will be happy to have your help. How's that?" Travis asked, proud and excited at how the single afternoon had shifted things between these boys and his family.

"All right. It's a deal." Damon followed the group toward the lobby.

Travis called out, "Hey, Damon, will you watch out for Micah? Grant will keep him safe but he's a horrible influence." Damon's lopsided grin wasn't a big reaction but it was new and Travis felt stronger because of it.

Keena was still at the top of the ladder, still holding her tiny paintbrush because it was "better for cutting in" though it would take years to finish the job, and waving at Damon and Micah as they said their goodbyes. Jordan hit them both with high fives and clapped when Damon told her he wanted to return to help with the sanding.

Sarah ushered Damon out the door ahead of her before Jordan could promote him to operations manager, while Travis wandered back over to Keena. She immediately glanced down at him. "Thank you for saving me. I wasn't sure I had it in me to climb back in the saddle for the ride home. I was trying to decide if walking all the way might be easier."

"Is that why you're channeling Michelangelo with the interior latex paint? You were avoiding the ride home for as long as possible?" Travis pointed to the lobby. "They probably have a bed here you can use if you want to stay the night."

"Nope, I want my comfy couch, thank you." Keena handed him the tiny brush. "I took my assignment seriously. That's all. I finished cutting in. Tomorrow I'll work on the rest." Then she moved slowly down the ladder.

"Muscles stiffening up?" Jordan asked as she plopped the top back on the can of paint. "I wasn't sure you were even moving there for a minute. Were you actually waiting for the paint to dry between each brushstroke? Interesting technique."

Keena narrowed her eyes at Jordan. "Are you saying I'm a slow painter?" She cupped her hand to her ear. "Surely you aren't complaining about free labor." Travis loved watching her tease Jordan. It was as if they'd been friends forever or at least long enough to give each other a hard time now and then.

He liked how Jordan and Sarah and now Keena had become parts of Prospect and the Armstrong family.

Jordan held up a finger. "Excellent point. Free labor is my favorite kind of labor. I am so impressed with your attention to detail and appreciate you being here. How is that?"

Keena turned to him. "Reading between the lines, I'm still getting that I'm not good at painting walls, either."

"Or you're entirely too good," he murmured and brushed a drop of paint off her forehead.

Her sweet smile matched the glow that lit in his chest as they stood there.

"Gross," Jordan groaned. "If it's not Wes and Sarah, it's you two." Her awful grimace suggested she was about to revolt.

"When is Clay coming home from Colorado Springs?" Travis asked.

"Sometime this week," she responded sadly. "Then I can make my own lovey-dovey faces."

"I have Sarah's keys. Want to go for a joyride through Prospect?" Travis jingled the key ring at her.

Jordan snorted. "Nah, my baby sister, Brooke, wrecked her car once when we were teenagers, and Sarah's revenge was cold. Brooke did all the laundry for five years after that."

"You okay here on your own?" The sun was setting quickly now that the days were short. Travis knew Clay had his concerns about Jordan staying at the lodge alone, but he'd heard enough of the debate to understand Jordan was confident in taking care of herself.

Also, there was a ghost on duty.

"Yes, I'm going to throw a frozen pizza in the oven and watch trash TV. Sarah hates all the reality dating shows. Want to join me?" Jordan's sly grin was proof she knew the answer was no even as she asked the question.

Keena sighed. "TV. That reminds me to call the phone company on Monday. I need to stream something besides the Colorado Cookie Queen. I do love internet cat videos."

They were all laughing as Travis and Keena left the lobby. He noticed she'd braced her hands on her low back as if the muscles there hurt.

"Regrets over the horse ride?" Travis asked as he stopped her.

She shook her head immediately. "None. I want to do it again…whenever my legs have forgiven me for this lesson." Her bright grin reassured him that she meant every word. "You aren't going to believe this, but I don't like to do things I'm not great at. Trying this…it was a huge step. I also expected to be good at painting walls. Imagine my surprise to hear that I am not."

Travis chuckled. "You might not know this, Doc, but you aren't alone. There are people all over the world who'd prefer to be good at everything right out of the gate."

Keena rolled her eyes. "That's not really what I meant."

Travis flexed his fingers. "I understand. I do. Is it okay if I rub the muscles in your shoulders? Might help." It would help.

She hesitated but eventually swept her hair over her shoulder. When he pressed his hands carefully on her shoulders, his thumbs working against knotted muscles, her head dropped forward and she moaned.

"I promised to tell you why I wouldn't judge you." Travis concentrated on the tender spots at the nape of her neck, glad she was turned away. Telling stories he wasn't particularly proud of was so much easier when he could do it without eyes on him. "After arriving at the Rocking A, I hid away because I was so terrible when it came to the horses. Just couldn't stand it with Wes and Clay being comfortable and Grant riding as if he'd been born in a saddle from day one. Then there was me. I hung on for dear life, and I had trouble sleeping at night because I knew Walt was going to need our help the next day. It's hard to settle in when you're aware you don't fit."

Keena tilted her head to the side, a silent clue on where the pain was centered. He smiled as he shifted to work on the tension there.

"You figured it out, though. Now you have something else to teach your sons, and you'll be able to do it with the understanding that not everyone gets it the first or second time, but you don't give up."

He was silent as he considered her words. There was something about Keena that led her to exactly what he needed to hear when he needed to hear it the most. "I guess so. That's a nice way to look at being absolutely terrified of horses. So much so that sleeping in the scary darkness seemed like a good way to handle it."

Keena grasped his hand as she turned to face him. "It's the only way to look at it. Maybe you didn't fit in at first, but of all the Armstrong sons, you're the one doing the big work now, opening the ranch up to fosters again. You picked up on a character trait of Walt and Prue that makes them rare in this world."

He studied her face. "I don't know how you do what you

do. You must be an amazing doctor. Patients must come just to pour out their troubles."

Keena squeezed her eyes shut. "Funny you should mention that. I'm good with the technique, but I never trusted my bedside manner. Turns out, that will get you pretty far in the emergency room, where you patch together patients and then send them on to others who heal them, but in Prospect?" She sighed. "Dr. Singh leaves enormous shoes to fill, you know? He was always the only doctor I could talk to as a resident. You've seen it, too. That's been my worst worry, that I'll connect with patients as well as I ride a horse."

Her mouth dropped open, as if she was inviting him to laugh along with her.

He shook his head. It wasn't funny because it wasn't really a joke. He understood admitting his fears and pretending it wasn't all that serious to keep others from comforting him, or worse, reassuring him, which only made him feel less capable in the end.

"Thing is, as long as you can overcome the fear, you can practice and get better." He tilted his head back. "I'm strictly speaking about riding here, you know. I am not a doctor so..."

He waited for her to meet his stare. "Right. Only a cowboy, not a doctor...even if that advice sounds more like something Dr. Singh would say to encourage me." She smiled. "Thank you. I was worried how I'd do without him. I'll come back to you when I need pep talks."

He nodded. "I like this arrangement. For you, I've got encouragement."

"And I believe you're going to be an amazing foster parent, even without a make-believe girlfriend waiting in the wings to lend a hand." Keena blinked innocently up at him.

"I guess, although I would put you and me against all odds, no matter how hard the job was."

Her eyebrows shot up in surprise.

He knew the feeling. "I didn't mean to say that out loud."

And it was clear she didn't have a clear response. "I like you, Travis..."

"But not like that." He'd heard that more than once, so the sting didn't register anymore. "I get that."

"No, I like you like that, too." Keena laughed. "Any woman who watched the way you chopped wood, the muscles in your back and arms rippling like waves..." Her words trailed off. Travis waited.

"Where'd you go?" he asked when he was convinced she wanted to stay exactly where she was in her mind.

"You're very good-looking. You know that." She said it so matter-of-factly that Travis wanted to believe her. "A man who is reshaping his comfortable world to help kids who need a safe place. That's hero stuff, Travis. You should have a line of the best women waiting for a turn to be your real-life girlfriend. The fact that you don't see it makes you that much sweeter."

Grant had said something similar, calling him the hero in their lineup, but he hadn't spent much time considering it.

Keena's opinion shifted something inside of him.

She wasn't family.

Keena hadn't watched him grow and change and mature in Prospect, either.

With her, he was only a man.

A good man.

Keena Murphy had the power to take a look at the wounds he hid from almost everyone else and say the words he needed to begin the healing. How did he convince her to spend more time with him?

"I have a babysitter tonight. Didn't even know I was going to need one, but I'm glad the fun uncle showed up right on time." Travis ran his hands down Keena's arms. "Would you be interested in exploring Prospect's nightlife with me?"

She frowned. "Are we back to joyriding in Sarah's SUV? I don't enjoy doing my own laundry, much less someone else's."

"Maybe after. I was thinking first you might like to eat junk for dinner and watch whatever old Western is playing at the Prospect Picture Show." Travis shook his head when her eyes lit up. "Let me make something very clear before you say yes. If we go, we might be the only ones in the theater watching the movie. The rest of the audience will be watching us, and the story of our outing will sweep through the town like the wildfire that destroyed Sullivan's Post the first time. It was fast, if you don't know how that went."

Keena bit her lip as she weighed the pros and cons. "I want to see the movie. Will you kiss me during the show?"

His mouth dropped open and she shrugged. "If we're to be the story going around on Monday, we should at least make it good."

Travis opened the door to the SUV and waited for Keena to slide in. He wasn't sure why his whole life had suddenly turned into a romantic comedy but he was excited to see where it would lead next.

CHAPTER FOURTEEN

ON THURSDAY AFTERNOON, Keena was resting against the main counter at Prospect Family Practice, blearily staring at the computer screen in front of her.

She was entering notes about the fourteenth student from Prospect Middle School who had come down with the flu. None of the cases were critical, but it was a lot of miserably sick kids to see and absorb over the period of four days.

As always happened, adults were also trickling in with flu-like symptoms, and most of them handled it with a lot less grace than the students did. She and Kim had worked out a steady routine to diagnose each and prescribe antiviral medication if they were within the effective window.

Keena was glad that folks in Dr. Singh's office knew their jobs as well as they did. It was easy enough to figure out her part of the process. After work each evening, she'd been spending time with Sarah and Jordan as they focused on improving the lodge's restaurant, so she was busy. She liked busy. Her worries about how she'd spend her time in Prospect seemed silly now, but after a long week, she needed a boost of energy stat.

A water bottle suddenly blocked her view of the screen and it took Keena longer than she liked to realize what had happened.

After she opened the bottle and drained half the contents, she smiled at Reg. He was shaking his head in disapproval. "We can't have the doctor getting dehydrated or sick, Dr. M. You realize how much trouble we'd all be in then?"

She nodded her agreement.

"I get it. I used to do this every night, where I got so overwhelmed with work that little things like food and water got lost in the shuffle." Keena realized how much better she'd been feeling now that days like this were by far the exception instead of the rule. "Thank you for watching out for me."

Reginald sniffed to make sure she understood she was pressing her luck. He pointed at her. "Always will. The difference between those nights and these days? You're all we've got. This is definitely a situation where, if the airplane is losing cabin pressure, you put your own oxygen mask on first before assisting others." His stern expression convinced Keena that he was a successful flag football coach, too. Keena didn't want to disappoint Reginald.

Emily hung up the phone. "That was the school. The principal thinks we've made it through the worst. They didn't have any new absences today." She picked up her notepad where she'd checked off a note on her to-do list. "And the pharmacy supply of the meds is holding up. The pharmacist placed a special order after you asked me to let him know about the first case we had on Monday. That was good thinking, Dr. M."

Keena exhaled slowly. The praise meant more to her than it should have, but when she'd seen the first flu case walk in, she'd been afraid of how bad it could get in the close confines of the Prospect schools. During heavy years, her entire emergency waiting room would fill with people, some of whom had reached the critical stage before they forced themselves to get medical attention. Getting overwhelmed at the hospital was one thing. The resources they'd need to call in for assistance—more staff, more meds—were close at hand. Here? Reginald was correct. Looking out for herself and her team was the smartest thing she could do to take care of the rest of the town.

They all needed a boost at this point.

"I wish I had a cookie," Reginald muttered under his breath.

Keena nodded. "Yeah, I was thinking the same thing."

"I'll run over to the Ace for pie. We all need a slice," Kim said and hurried out the door before Keena could stop her.

When Kim walked back in with an entire pie held in victory over her head, Keena said, "I wasn't hinting that we needed pie!" And if she had been, she certainly would have walked over to pick it up and pay for it. She was the leader here, after all.

Sort of. In name only?

"Faye sent it over, no charge. She's been hearing all week long about the sick kids so she knew it was important to the health of this town that we get a sugar boost." Kim cut the pieces and handed them out while Reginald poured coffee. The first bite of apple pie hit like it should have been accompanied by an angelic choir. Keena's energy rose, her eyesight cleared up, and she was almost certain she could make it through the rest of the day.

Kim laughed. "Sometimes the doctor needs someone else writing the prescription."

Keena nodded. "I've been searching Sadie's cookbooks for this recipe. I didn't understand it was the same thing as finding hidden treasure. I need to take off the rest of the afternoon because I must find the gold."

Emily tipped her head to the side. "Nope. Not this afternoon, Dr. M. We've got a well-baby checkup and then two patients who need physicals for insurance purposes."

"Good thing you got this pie, then," Keena said with her mouth full.

They laughed at her garbled words and Keena realized everything about that moment was right. She had been successful running Dr. Singh's practice. His staff liked her enough to volunteer to go on emergency pie runs. And she still had plans for a life after work and on the weekend and in the future.

If Dr. Singh could see her now, he would be celebrating, no doubt. She should send him a message.

"I was thinking of sending Dr. Singh an email today," Reginald said causally. "Anybody have any updates they want to include? Tidbits of town news?"

He didn't glance at Keena but she was almost certain the words were aimed at her. Instead of answering, she sipped her coffee and waited.

Kim wrinkled her nose. "I'm sure he's missing the gossip, Reg. I heard the most interesting story."

Keena braced her elbow nonchalantly on the corner of the desk. She loved gossip but she wasn't sure she should let them know that, so pretending to be a bystander was the way to go.

"Oh," Reg said as he spun in his chair. "I wonder if it's the same story I heard. Did it happen at the Picture Show this weekend?"

Keena closed her eyes because now she understood what was coming next. Travis had warned her, but the flu epidemic in the schools had delayed the story's spread. It had taken a couple of extra days to make it around to Keena. Watching a movie at the Prospect Picture Show while she and Travis had split an enormous tub of popcorn and a family-size box of M&M's was more fun than she expected.

Kissing him in front of that audience made her feel young and silly in love.

That was something she'd never regret, even if she must face the consequences today.

The idea of falling for Travis Armstrong flitted around in her brain. If she tried to examine it too closely, it flew away but that didn't mean Keena could forget about it.

"There was a couple making out, right in the middle of the theater. All lips and hands, there in front of everyone." Kim held her hand over her heart as if the scandal was too much for her. "Can you even imagine?"

Keena sighed. "We... The couple wasn't making out. There were lips but no hands. It was a kiss. That's all."

Reg inched his glasses down. "Were *you* there, Dr. M?" His tone was so innocent, as if he would never imagine such a thing happening.

Keena cleared her throat. "I was."

"Who was the couple, Dr. M?" Emily leaned forward as if she was desperate for the answer. Keena hadn't learned to read Emily as well as the other two. Had the admin really not heard the story yet?

"One of them had red hair. That's what I heard." Reginald's grin was slow and sly.

Emily straightened immediately, her eyes locked on Keena's casual updo.

"Who was she kissing?" Kim drawled.

Reginald shrugged and stared at Keena.

"Dr. Singh doesn't need to know about any redhead kissing any cowboy at the Picture Show. And that's all it was, a kiss." Keena stepped back from the desk with her best severe frown. It would have been more powerful if she could have kept her lips from twitching in amusement before she walked toward her office. "Let me know when the next patient gets here."

Whatever they said to each other didn't make it to Keena's ears, but the stage whispered "Travis Armstrong" was loud and clear. She covered her hot cheeks with both hands before she forced herself to get back to business. Keena checked her email first. Every now and then, she considered sending a message to Angie Washington to make sure that things were running smoothly in the ER, but she knew there was no way she could step back in to help if they weren't. Right now, her priority had to be Prospect.

The rest of the afternoon was quiet and easy, so Keena was relieved as they locked up the clinic. She considered driving home to make a healthy salad for dinner, nixed that almost immediately because this string of work days required something stronger, and headed over to the Ace to see what Faye was serving.

She'd taken the first bite of a warm corn bread muffin while she waited for her steak to cook just as Faye trotted out from the kitchen, her eyes locked on Keena. There was something about her expression that told Keena her friend's urgency wasn't to do with the usual dinner rush. "What's up?" she asked and put her muffin down. She realized she'd forgotten to turn her cell phone ringer back on after leaving the office. She had two missed calls from Grant Armstrong. "Is there an emergency?"

"Yes, Grant needs you to meet him at the ranch. There's been an accident. They're out searching for Damon right now, but they want you to be nearby, in case..." Faye left the sentence unfinished. Based on that, Keena understood the Armstrongs were afraid the outcome was going to be bad.

Keena stood and pointed at the table. "I'll pay up next time." Faye waved her off as she hit the door at a run. Keena dashed into the clinic and grabbed anything she could think of that might help with an accident at the ranch and then sprinted to her car. Traffic was light so she pressed the gas pedal hard on her way out of town. She wasn't sure how long the trip was taking, but it felt like forever because she knew Damon needed her now.

Grant was waiting for her at the barn, horses saddled. "We'll go slow, Doc, but this is the best route to reach Damon and Travis. You trust me?"

Keena nodded and accepted his help to get into the saddle. She handed him her bag, gripped the reins and said, "Let's go."

Keena had never wondered how smart horses were, but it was clear that Lady was aware this was an emergency. She followed Grant without urging and matched his speed without waiting for her clueless rider to give the commands. All Keena had to do was hold on and pray.

Grant handed her a flashlight as they neared the first ridge that led over toward Key Lake. She'd never seen the lake this close in person, but it was a dark shadow. The moody tone wasn't reassuring.

Then she saw Travis and Walt on their knees next to the edge of some kind of bank or drop-off. "Hurry, Grant." When she was close enough to spot Micah clinging to Travis's shoulder, she slid out of the saddle and caught herself against Lady. "Thank you, Lady." She was running before Grant could catch up and managed to brace herself in time to catch Micah as he launched himself at her. Tears were silently streaming down his cheeks, but he didn't say a word. Fearing the worst, Keena pressed Micah's head against her shoulder and inched closer to Travis.

From here, she could see over the edge. There were two large bright lights pointed down to an outcropping where Damon was lying on his back. At first she thought his eyes were closed. "Has he been conscious?"

Travis seemed to realize then that she was there and

he grasped her hand. "He's awake, raises his hand or answers when we ask a question. I've been waiting for Grant to show up with you and the rope. I'll climb down and lift him out of there. Just needed more hands." He ruffled Micah's hair, the worry clear in the tension on Travis's face.

"Have you called in the emergency? Is an ambulance coming?" Keena asked as she took the bag Grant offered.

"Yeah," Travis replied. "Wes is waiting for the sheriff at the closest gate over at the lodge." He paced. Keena slipped her arm around his. "Dispatch said they'd request an air ambulance and would connect them with the sheriff when they were nearby." He held his hand out for the rope that Grant had. "Let's get Damon ready for when they arrive. No time to waste."

Keena tugged at him to get his attention. "Wait, Travis. If he was unconscious when you got here, he could have a head injury, a spine injury. We need to make sure it's safe to move him before we do anything else." She knew he wanted to argue, so she spoke first. "I can do that. I can go down and see if it's okay to pull him out or if we need to stabilize him first. That will help the EMTs when they get here." She held up her bag. "I'm ready. I have everything Damon might need and emergency blankets to make the waiting easier. Send me down, then we'll figure out the next step." They had to know Damon's condition before anything else happened.

"I don't want to lower you down there. It's too dangerous," Travis said.

"So make the climbing part as safe as you can. I need to be with Damon. Now." Her firm tone must have convinced him, since he took the rope Grant brought and tied one end over her puffy coat, wrapping and knotting, wrapping and knotting until Keena had no idea how she'd ever get herself free. She wasn't worried about falling. Travis would keep her safe.

That was the thought she kept repeating to herself as she inched down the side of the steep drop toward the lake. Travis had her. She was safe. All she had to do was be a doctor and that was what she did best.

When her feet touched down next to Damon, he said, "How did they talk you into this, Doc?"

The relief that swamped Keena at hearing his strong voice made her weak in the knees. Carefully, she sat next to him. "We arm wrestled and I won." His lips curved in a grin that got Keena's heart pounding again. She immediately unwrapped the emergency blankets she'd shoved in her bag and covered him. Damon's skin was pale and clammy and his pulse was racing, classic signs that shock was going to be their initial problem. "How is the head? Any pain?"

Damon licked his lips before speaking. "No, not really. I don't think so."

Keena lifted the blanket up and gently ran her hands over his arms and legs. "Tell me what hurts."

"Back. Pretty sure it's torn up from the slide." Damon closed his eyes. "Leg."

Keena paused. "Which leg?"

"Left. Can't feel my left foot, either." Damon blinked. "That's a bad sign, right?"

As she resumed her examination, Keena analyzed all the possibilities. "Could definitely be worse, young man. I hope you're prepared to be literally grounded for years and years. They won't even let you sit in a chair until you go to college… Too high. You might fall off." She smiled down at him, relieved that he was with her and she could speak to him like this.

He gripped her hand. Another good sign. "As long as

this doesn't convince Travis to close up the Armstrong foster home I will be happy to stay off any elevated surfaces."

Keena realized he'd had enough time to imagine more than the worst-case scenario. Poor kid.

"Keena, talk to me." Travis was angling the light over them so she could see better. Micah was still clinging tightly to him.

"He's making jokes, Travis. That's a good sign. See how far away the air ambulance is, okay?" Keena yelled and then whispered, "Damon, can you wave at Micah? He's a little frightened."

Damon let go of her hand and held his own hand close to his face before wiggling his fingers. Keena couldn't tell if that had any positive effect on Micah, but it helped steady her. "We'd be better off waiting for the EMTs to lift you out of here. You gonna be okay with my company for a few more minutes?"

He nodded.

She took his hand in hers. "No way Travis is going to change his mind about you. You better decide you like being a cowboy. He has big plans for both of you boys. I hear there's a parade. Matching outfits. That kind of thing."

"I like it here. Micah's getting better. Hope we can stay." Damon blinked rapidly. "Think I'm paralyzed or anything, Doc?"

These were the questions that had always stopped her in her tracks in the emergency room. Patients and their families desperately wanted to hear the best scenario, but as a medical professional, she knew how often the worst came true. She couldn't lie about this. "Honestly? I don't know if there's some kind of injury causing numbness or if it's shock or what, but we'll figure it out together. You and me and Travis and Micah and about a million Armstrongs for backup, okay?"

He nodded again.

She knew she had to come up with a diversion, but what?

She couldn't tell if her brain was playing tricks on her, but she wanted the faint noise she could hear to be the air ambulance. That would mean the sheriff was nearby and help was coming. "Have you ever ridden in a helicopter, Damon?"

The kid huffed out a breath. "Of course. On the way back and forth to the bank to deposit my lottery winnings."

Keena narrowed her eyes. "Sarcasm. In this case, I'll allow it." She smiled at him. "What color do you think the one you're about to ride in will be?"

Keena might not be able to lie to comfort the patient. She might not know exactly the right words for every situation. But she could ask questions. As soon as Damon answered this one, she'd fire another one at him. Keeping him alert and talking would be the best thing for both of them.

"I'm going with blue. What color do you think?" he asked.

Keena pursed her lips. "Blue would have been my pick, too, but it's no fun if we choose the same color, so how about...green? I'll go with green."

He shifted slightly. "What does the winner get?"

Keena whistled. "Oh, he wants to run a bet while we're waiting. Okay..." She brushed his dark hair off his forehead. The sound of the helicopter was becoming much clearer now. The struggle to get him back up to the top would take a lot out of everyone, but most especially Damon. "Loser bakes the winner her favorite cookie."

He rolled his eyes. "Or *his* favorite cookie."

She laughed. "Fair enough." This time when she tilted her head back to see what was happening, Travis and

Micah were still there but they'd been joined by sheriff's deputies and one paramedic wearing a dark blue uniform.

"Good news, Damon. It looks like you are about to take a ride in a blue helicopter, my friend," Keena said, keeping an eye on the growing group above them. "We've got a fourteen-year-old male with possible spinal injury or compression, temporary loss of consciousness, and pain in his left leg which may indicate a break."

The paramedic nodded. "Are you able to assist with loading the patient up for extraction if we lower the board?"

Keena straightened her shoulders. This was a new part of trauma medicine that she hadn't experienced before but she knew she could handle it. "Lower the board and give me clear instructions. This boy is ready for his helicopter ride."

CHAPTER FIFTEEN

THE RESCUE CREW that gathered at the edge of the steep bank pulled Keena up right behind Damon. Travis's knees turned too weak to hold him up any longer. He settled on the ground next to Damon and gasped for air. His lungs burned as if he'd been holding his breath ever since he'd looked up from the tack he'd been mending in the barn to see Micah clinging to Sonny's back with no Damon behind him.

"I'm really sorry, Travis," Damon said softly. "What a mess."

Travis rubbed his eyes hard and realized they were leaking tears of relief. He couldn't remember ever being as scared as he had been staring down at this boy who needed help.

"I knew I shouldn't take Micah to see the lake, but he kept going on about snow coming and missing his chance for months and months and months." Damon closed his eyes. "It's a lake, you know. It would still be there, even if it did snow, but it should have been simple enough."

Travis realized he didn't have much time to fall apart. Micah was around there somewhere, and the kid hadn't been able to speak as they'd ridden out to find Damon. After watching all this, he might never speak again.

Damon tried another apology, and Travis put his hand on the kid's arm. "Listen, this was an accident. Taking off on your own wasn't smart, but you know that already.

Everything else could have happened whether I was with you or not. Let that go. Help me reassure Micah and we can discuss what sort of boring chore you'd like to do for the rest of your natural life as a reminder that poor judgment has consequences, when we're all safe back home." He waited for the kid to nod before smiling at him. "We aren't done yet, but everything is going to be okay. You will be fine. We'll all be fine."

Travis took a chance that his knees would hold him and stood to peer over the crowd. He needed to check on Micah before the EMTs got Damon on the helicopter.

When he spotted Keena's bright red hair, he realized Micah was glued to her side. Keena pointed at Travis and asked Micah something. Her frown made Travis think that Micah's trauma still had a hold on him, but she pasted on a brave smile when they stopped next to Damon. "Look who I found." Micah immediately knelt beside Damon and pressed his face to Damon's chest.

Micah's sobs took every bit of tension inside Travis and twisted hard. Keena reached out to comfort him, but before she could say anything, Travis wrapped his arms around her and pulled her close. "I was so scared."

The weight of her hands on his back eased some of his trembling. "I knew I would be fine, Travis. This is what I was meant to do. Painting? No. Herding loose cows? Also no, but I am good in a crisis." She squeezed him tight. "You found him. You saved him. Now talk to Micah. You don't have much time before the EMTs will be ready to leave."

Travis knew she was right, but he didn't want to let go of her. Or Damon. Or Micah. He clutched her hand but squatted down to run the other one over Micah's back. "Hey, bud, we're all okay. Damon's going to ride in this cool helicopter while you have to go home and when you're ready, go to bed, because life is totally unfair. But he'll be home soon to tell you all about it."

Micah still didn't speak but he pressed himself tightly against Travis's chest, his arms gripping tightly. Travis rubbed a hand up and down the boy's back and nodded at the EMT who stepped up. "We're going to load Damon now. You'll be coming with us, correct? We need a family member."

Travis nodded and squeezed Micah. "You hear that? I get to ride along. I'll make sure Damon doesn't make any stories up about flying to Denver, okay?" When tears started streaming down Micah's cheeks again, Travis broke. Then the bigger pieces splintered until Walt came forward.

His father squeezed his shoulder and helped loosen Micah's grip. "Micah and I have a big job, taking care of all these horses while you're gone. We'll be countin' the hours until you get back."

Micah stepped back to take Walt's hand and some of Travis's panic receded. The boy who didn't trust men more than he had to trusted Travis's father. Walt met his stare. "I will call Prue, tell her everything. She'll stay at the ranch with us tonight. Wes and Sarah will be driving down to Denver to meet you in the hospital."

Travis inhaled a ragged breath, grateful they'd already come up with a solid plan. What would he have done without this family behind him? This was the kind of emergency he'd never planned for, one son headed to the hospital while the other was shattered at home.

But his parents were there for Micah. His brothers would step up to help him.

And then there was Keena who was pointing at Damon and saying something forcefully to the EMT.

"Ma'am, I can't give you permission to ride along. You

aren't a family member, that's up to the family." The EMT held up his hands at whatever expression Keena flashed at him.

"His father is giving permission for me to accompany Damon to the hospital, although I am his personal physician and that should count for something." Then Keena raised her eyebrows at Travis in a clear "Tell them I can come along or else" look.

Travis nodded. "Yeah, she's coming with us." Then he wrapped his arm around her shoulders and the EMT crew lifted Damon into the helicopter. "I'll never be able to thank you for this. Ever."

She jerked back. "Thank me? No thanks needed. This is my job. This is my calling, Travis. Your purpose is to help these kids. I can heal them..." She tilted her head to the side. "Or I can find the right doctor if I can't."

He wasn't going to argue with her, not here and not over this, so Travis bent down to squeeze Micah tightly one more time and sent a silent thank-you to his father before he and Keena followed Damon into the helicopter. They were buckling themselves in when the EMT asked, "Closest hospital, right?"

Keena immediately bent forward. "The best hospital. Take us to Denver Medical Center."

Travis wasn't sure when the power had shifted but the EMT didn't turn and ask for confirmation or permission this time. The blades got louder and the weird sensation of the earth falling away caught all three of them by surprise. Damon was the only one who managed to speak. "Whoa. They need to warn me before they do that."

Keena smiled at him, then at Travis and reached for his hand. At this point, he was going purely by instinct. Grabbing her hand, following her lead, made perfect sense, and in no time, they were landing at the hospital. A team raced out to meet them, and Keena started shouting Damon's condition as they hurried inside. "Fourteen-year-old male, his pulse is still fast but steady, lost consciousness briefly but has been able to provide updates on his condition since. No blood or bruising to the head, but signs of abraded flesh on his back and left side. Pain in the left leg and some numbness in that extremity. We'll need to check for concussion and run the usual tests to see what may be causing an impingement in the nerves of his..."

Travis glanced away from Damon as Keena's words halted.

Another doctor had met them at the sliding doors to the ER. "And I am not in charge here so we will need to see what Dr. Shane orders to diagnose further treatment."

Keena put her hand to her forehead. "Sorry, Dr. Shane. Old habits die hard?"

The older man who was already listening to Damon's chest nodded. "That they do, Dr. Murphy. I'm happy to have the chance to shake your hand." He did so quickly before sending a nurse scrambling to make a call to find out how quickly they could get Damon in for scans. "The tales I have heard of the amazing Steady Murphy. Your night shift crew talks about you like you're a myth. It's a pleasure to meet a legend in the flesh. I believe this whole team is counting down the days until you return to take charge of Emergency again."

Keena's pink cheeks could be the result of the adrenaline rush from this rescue.

Or it could be embarrassment at being treated like the conquering hero by her successor.

Either way, Travis finally completely understood that Keena wasn't just a good doctor. She was a superhero to the people in this hospital. And she'd been hanging out in

Prospect all this time without anyone knowing what she was capable of.

How would it make sense that someone who was capable of doing this, who could without hesitation climb down to Damon, keep him calm and evaluate his health, then hop in a helicopter for emergency transit, and impress the coolly confident doctor on call at the time…how would she leave this for small-town life?

Her insistence that she was only a temporary neighbor made perfect sense.

"I'll find a place to sit in the waiting room. Travis is going along with Damon for his tests." She said the words firmly as if there was a possibility the doctor would argue with her decision.

Dr. Shane held up his hands in surrender and said, "Travis, if you'll go with this nurse, we'll make sure Damon's not suffering from a concussion first, and then evaluate from there."

Travis stared at Keena until the doors between them closed and then he focused on Damon. He spent what felt like hours waiting while Damon was checked over, but eventually, they returned together to an open room in the emergency department. Keena was already there, and Travis was happy to see that Wes and Sarah had arrived. And Grant, too. Travis hadn't expected that, but it was a welcome surprise. When they all turned to face him, he said, "And now we wait."

Grant took up a spot next to the bed. "Well, this is not looking good for your career in the rodeo, kid. A little fall from a horse and sliding a hundred feet or so? Even the clowns would tease you about that."

Travis gripped Keena's shoulders before she launched in to defend Damon and waited for the kid to plead his own case. "I've decided not to waste my time with the rodeo.

Going straight to Hollywood stunt man." Damon's voice was weak but steady.

"A man with a plan," Grant said and offered the boy a wide smile.

Sarah shook her head. "Boys are weird, but these two are okay, if you guys want to take a walk? Keena, you and Travis could find some coffee. It's been a long night." She pointed at the small window on the opposite wall. "Or night and morning." The pink sky of sunrise filled the window.

"Good idea." Keena took Travis's hand. "Let's go to the cafeteria for coffee." They were silent as they rode the elevator down to the cafeteria on the lobby level. Travis managed to keep it all together as they got through the cafeteria line and Keena greeted coworkers. He poured too much sugar and creamer into his cup and stirred it while the coffee turned pale.

They chose the closest table and sat down. Before either of them could say anything, he put his head in his hands and waited for the emotional fallout.

Keena came around the table, wrapped her arm around his shoulders and waited silently. When someone walked by, she said, "Hey, Frances, can you grab a cold bottle of water for me?"

She put one hand on his back and moved it in steady circles, and then said, "Thank you. Yeah, we'll be okay. Thanks." She unscrewed the lid and offered the water to him. "I forgot you don't drink coffee. I'm sorry. This will be better for you anyway."

Travis pressed the cold bottle to his forehead. "I'm okay. I was afraid I was losing it there for a minute."

Her hand never stopped rubbing and eventually he felt like himself again.

"You're a rock star, Dr. Murphy." He sipped the water

before adding, "Or should I call you Steady Murphy. That is what Dr. Shane said, isn't it?"

Keena huffed out a breath. "If you knew how unsteady I was the last time I worked the night shift, you would understand how a nickname can weigh on a person. Every single night, I was holding on tightly to make it back to the locker room where I could fall apart in private. People depended on Steady Murphy. They told each other stories about her as if she was different." Keena clutched her cooling coffee cup with both hands. "I was so scared to let anyone down."

Travis was solemn as he studied her face. "I can't believe how lucky we've been to have you next door all these weeks without understanding who you are." Travis hadn't had a moment to dig down to the problem he was having with the revelation, either. It was a good thing that the best at anything was in town, right?

"It was the hamburger slippers, wasn't it? You have no faith in a woman who wears shoes like that, I bet." Keena wrinkled her nose as she teased him. "I was afraid I'd lose my edge in Prospect."

"But you haven't." What a relief she'd been nearby for Damon.

How many other emergencies was she missing while she'd stepped off the beaten path, Travis wondered.

"No," Keena agreed with a beautiful smile, "I haven't. I don't think I will, either, which I'm kind of glad to say out loud. It's a bit of a revelation, that this emergency response mode, this ability to think in the middle of a crisis, is really who I am. I love medicine and the rewards are so sweet when I can make a difference like I did tonight, or last night? You know what I mean."

Listening to her talk illuminated the unease he'd been feeling since they walked through the hospital doors. He'd been imagining a future with Keena next door to the Rocking A. His off-the-cuff decision to pretend she was his girlfriend in front of the social worker had been wishful thinking and he'd never recovered from that.

No matter how often she made sure to mention that she was only in Prospect for the short term, he'd been doing his best to change that in his own mind.

Seeing her here, though, there was no way to avoid how far she was out of his and Prospect's league.

It was going to hurt when the inevitable happened and she returned to her calling here. But he was someone who understood fulfilling a purpose. Damon and Micah had confirmed his.

And this rescue had clearly proven Keena's.

He'd been doing his best to weave her into his plans for Damon and Micah and whoever came next. Keena made every bit of this up-and-down foster process feel better.

Depending on her was easy.

Loving her was even easier.

But that didn't change who she was or what she was meant to do and losing her would sting. When she clapped a hand to her forehead, he eased back.

"I better call Reginald to see what we do about the clinic until I'm there." She got out her phone. "I'm still struggling with being the only doctor on call and letting people know how to get ahold of me."

Travis listened to her one-sided conversation where Keena and Reginald decided to move all of her appointments for that day to the following Monday. They were closing the clinic early on Wednesday, and then all day on Thursday and Friday for the holiday, but they'd fit everyone in who had an appointment before then.

Travis wasn't sure how to return to their conversation, so he was happy to see Grant walk up. "I drove your truck down so you'd have it if you need to stay over." He offered Travis the keys and they watched Keena move over to another table to make conversation with someone in scrubs. "Your doctor has been amazing."

"I told her." Travis sipped his water and wondered if he had any gas left in the tank for another deep conversation at this point.

"I expected a lot more to come with that answer." Grant pulled a chair out and sat. "You okay? For a man who has to be deep in love at this point, you sure are playing it cool."

Travis nodded. "Just realizing how much I've been depending on Keena." He motioned around the cafeteria. "And here's this whole place that could be benefiting from her amazing-ness."

He rubbed his forehead, aware that he was on the verge of making no sense.

Grant said, "Uh-huh, but there are other doctors here, too. They deserve a chance to show off their own talents. Prospect only has Keena. Let's keep her."

Travis grunted. "She's been clear all along that keeping her wasn't on the table. Seeing her in action here makes it crystal clear why."

Grant opened his mouth, so Travis braced himself for something annoying. Instead, his brother simply shook his head. "There's time to figure that out after Damon comes home, right?"

"Yeah." Travis would spend a lot of time thinking about it in the meantime, but Grant had a point.

"Let's go upstairs and check on Damon. Mom was in a panic when she found out all she'd missed, so she and Dad are planning to come later today." Grant rubbed his eyes. "Wes and Sarah are going to head back now to stay with Micah and I'll ride with them. We all needed to see that Damon was okay for ourselves."

Travis could understand that. Seeing everything in full color made some things so much clearer. For now, Keena was the only person available to help in an emergency in Prospect. He'd make sure she went back with Grant. Then he'd figure out how to keep the distance he'd failed to maintain between them in the first place for the rest of her stay.

Keena was coming back to Denver.

A smart man would take care to remember that.

For himself and his kids.

CHAPTER SIXTEEN

KEENA REALIZED THAT something had changed when she returned to the table in the cafeteria and Travis was gone. On the way up to Damon's room, she replayed their conversation in her head, but the only thing that stuck with her was the fact that he'd called her a rock star.

At the time, she'd thought he was teasing. That was their thing, trading funny things back and forth. If Travis seemed out of it, he had good reason. They'd been up all night, most of it spent in the windy cold. Damon was going to be fine, Keena was certain, but they'd burned through tons of energy to get to this point. If she counted the busy days at the clinic and lack of food for hours and hours, it was a miracle she was still putting one foot in front of the other herself.

But the fact that Travis had left without telling her was a bad sign. Ever since she and Travis met over the woodpile, they'd had this invisible link. Walking away from her like this seemed a deliberate move to cut that tie.

As she stepped off the elevator, she was having the usual internal debate, where one side convinced her to shut down, step back and accept the distance he was putting between them because it was the safest option here. She would be fine. Everything would be fine.

The other half? That half of Keena was angry.

Since she needed to think clearly, Keena stopped to stare out the window overlooking the hospital parking lot.

Bright sunshine warmed her face as she inhaled slowly and then exhaled.

Was Travis putting space between them here? That might have worked if they'd never rescued Damon together, but it didn't work for Keena anymore.

The long night had shown her that she'd already tumbled too far into… What? Not love.

If she left Prospect, she would worry about Damon and Micah.

And whether Prue and Walt would ever figure things out.

Then there was the lodge and the Hearsts and this friendship that she didn't want to lose.

She might never find Sadie Hearst's treasure of an apple pie recipe and learn to make it or paint mediocre mountain landscapes.

Her panicked ride to help Damon might be the last time she ever climbed in a saddle if she returned to Denver to step back into her old life.

Keena closed her eyes to focus on the quiet conversation at the nurses' desk and Dr. Singh's smile flitted through her mind.

PJ would welcome her to Prospect Family Practice with that smile every day.

If Travis had decided he wanted distance from her, they were going to have to learn to share Prospect.

Because Keena couldn't leave.

And love was definitely part of that equation, but she wasn't convinced she had the final solution regarding Travis.

Even if the anger simmered below the surface, she knew Damon's hospital room was not the place for an honest airing of feelings, so she pasted on a calm smile and joined the group gathered around Damon. He was awake. At some point, Dr. Shane had come in to say there was no evidence of head trauma. Damon was cleared to eat and drink, and he was doing his best to do both at the same time while Travis juggled a fork and his glass of juice.

"Looks like we got some good news," Keena said softly as Damon swallowed whatever it was he was chewing. He gave her a thumbs-up and then pointed at a piece of bacon on the tray in front of him.

Travis hmphed. "Seems like if you can point, you can pick up the bacon yourself, but I'll humor you this one time."

It burned, waiting to ask Travis what his problem was, but now was not the time to let everyone in the room know that he was being a total jerk to her. Everyone was focused on Damon as they should be.

The fact that Travis didn't face her or even acknowledge her arrival made it that much more difficult to hold on to the appropriate bedside manner. She had so much to say, but it was all for his ears only.

Wes turned to her. "Keena, Sarah and I are going to head back to Prospect. My parents are on their way. Do you want to ride back with us? Grant will also be with us, but I'll make him promise to be on his best behavior."

Grant sighed. "You never let me have any fun."

She shook her head immediately. She wanted to make sure that Damon got everything he needed. It wasn't time for her to go.

Before she could say that part, Travis interrupted. "That's a good suggestion." He didn't say her name but stared directly at her. What was that about? "I mean, Prospect doesn't have a doctor while you're here. We don't know what the next day or two looks like, but there will be plenty of family here with Damon and the hospital staff here won't want to let steady Dr. Murphy down. You've made it clear that Damon is your patient. You can go back to Prospect. We'll be okay."

Keena was vaguely aware of Wes and Sarah shooting glances at each other as if they were surprised by this comment. Grant muttered under his breath, but she couldn't make out what he was saying.

And Travis returned to staring at Damon's breakfast tray.

So she addressed Damon. "What do you think? You're my patient, not him. Want me to stay?"

Damon took the glass Travis held out and finished the juice before answering. "I'd feel better if you were in Prospect, since that's where Micah is. He was so pale when we left. What if he's sick and you aren't there?"

Keena studied Damon's dark eyes and some of the hot anger Travis had inspired drained away. Their reasoning was not that far apart, but the way Damon said it meant something. There was a person he cared about in Prospect, so he would make the sacrifice and send her back.

Whereas Travis had turned into some weird robot who appeared to care very little about where Keena was.

"Okay," Keena said reluctantly, "I'll take the offer of the ride. That will give me extra time to get home and start on those cookies I owe you, but don't you think for a minute I'll let anyone here forget they owe me big-time favors and I'm calling them all in for you. If they don't have you out of here by tomorrow, I'll come back and get you myself."

Damon solemnly nodded. "I doubt any of them will cross you, Steady Murphy."

His snort of laughter tickled Keena so she giggled in response. "I'm never going to live that nickname down now, am I? I had a shot of enjoying life as a free woman in Prospect where no one had ever heard it, but you're going to fix that."

Damon grinned. "No way, but I told Grant and you know how he is."

"Hey," Grant said before he shook his finger. "That's a valid critique of my character. I believe you may have fully integrated into the Armstrong fold, kid. That didn't take much time at all."

Wes sighed. "Damon, I sure hope you're on the side of good. We need all the help we can get with the other side as it relates to this family."

"We'll go pull the SUV up to the Emergency entrance downstairs, Keena," Sarah said. She hugged Damon and then gripped Travis's arm to pull him out in the hallway. Keena glanced at both of the Armstrong brothers left in the room to see if they knew what she might be saying. Both men shrugged.

So Keena squeezed Damon's hand.

Travis stepped back inside the room and she moved to leave but Damon said, "Hey, Keena, if I'm not home tonight, the three of us, you, me and Micah could have a video call. We can both make sure he's okay." She agreed. He added, "And I'd like chocolate chip. The ones you made before were really good."

"You got it." Keena locked eyes with Travis and said, "I'll be calling you for updates. I'll also be asking my friends to come through to check on Damon's progress. You can send me away, but I'll be following up on my patient." Then she leaned closer to say, "And don't think we're done with this conversation. When you get back to Prospect, you better have a good explanation or an excellent apology."

Grant whistled dramatically but Wes towed him down the hallway.

Proud of her exit line, Keena followed but stopped in the restroom to wash her face with cold water, a guaranteed wake-me-up. The woman staring back at her was worn out; her hair was tangled into one large knot, and her eyes were bright with anger still, but Keena wasn't giving up. She headed directly for the emergency department. Annoyance had her hitting top speed. It was like she'd never missed a night on duty. Angie Washington was coming in for her shift and they met at the nurses' station. "Dr. Murphy, what are you doing here? Are you back?"

Keena rubbed her forehead because she was so tired. The question stopped her in her tracks, but the answer was easier than she expected. "Honestly, Angie, I believe I'll be making the move to Prospect permanently. Dr. Singh offered me a partnership in his clinic, and I've never felt more at home any other place, but at this moment, I can't even explain why I feel that because cowboys are so annoying, you know?"

The nurse pursed her lips as she considered the question and laughed when Keena waved it away. "Don't answer that. I've been running on fumes for too long."

"Some things haven't changed, I see," Angie murmured. "What can I do, Dr. Murphy?"

"I came in with a friend…a patient, rather. His name is Damon. He's in an exam room waiting for test results after a fall. There's some concern about numbness and pain in his leg. Dr. Shane is aware he's a friend of mine. Could you check in on him and his dad now and then? I'd sure appreciate it."

Angie nodded. "I'll text you with any updates I get. How is that?"

Keena sagged against the desk. "Perfect. I don't know what I would have done without you, Angie."

She smiled. "You seem different, Dr. Murphy. Hard to put my finger on exactly what that is, but there's something more…alive? Is that the right word?" She tilted her head back. "Does this friend or his father have anything to do with that or your decision to change temporary to permanent?"

Keena returned the nurse's smile. "I'm afraid so and I don't know what to do about it." She suddenly remembered Wes and the others. "I'm sorry. It has been a long night and my ride is out front waiting. Hope it's an easy shift."

She was happy stepping out into the afternoon sunshine and sliding into the back seat next to Sarah. Wes and Grant turned around to stare at her when she slammed the door. "Everything okay?" Sarah asked.

"Yeah," Keena said before she leaned her head back against the seat and took a deep breath. "I finally figure out the answer to one important question and something else unravels right before my eyes, but I guess I should get used to that."

Sarah squeezed her arm and mouthed, "Hardheaded Armstrongs," so broadly that Keena had no trouble reading her lips. The laughter that escaped was a relief.

Wes and Grant seemed to realize this was something they weren't a part of so they turned around and faced the front. She waited until her traveling companions successfully agreed on a fast-food stop and they were soon on the road. "Could one of you help me with something?"

Grant turned to stare at her. "Anything. You know that. You're one of us now and you always will be, even if Travis is aiming to take over my claim to fame as the problem in this family." He frowned. "I guess I'll have to be the hero for the moment, at least."

Keena felt the sting of tears well up but she forced them back. "Give me your mother's phone number."

Grant reared back and looked to Wes for direction. He had not expected that.

Before reasonable Wes could try to dig around for more

information, Sarah pulled up Prue's number on her own phone and handed it to Keena. "Calling in the big guns is an interesting strategy." She smiled extra hard and extra bright at Wes and Grant as if to reassure them that everything in the back seat was fully under control. "In this case, I approve."

Keena quickly punched in the number before she could chicken out. When Prue answered, Keena blurted, "Prue, it's Keena. Do you remember telling me that you were on my side? We were standing in Handmade, talking about how falling in love with a man's children creates these ties that you can never be free of." She stared hard out the window. She didn't want to watch anyone's reaction to her admission, not yet. "Well, I messed up. I've gone and done it and Travis is being a..." She wanted a good word, one that Sadie Hearst might have tossed in there, but none would come to mind.

"Oh, hon, you don't have to fill in the blank. I've lived this conversation more often than I'd like. Sometimes these fellas can't tell skunks from house cats, and when they fall in love, all reason flies out the window." Whatever Walt said in response to that was shushed loudly by Prue. "Tell me, what can I do?"

Keena sighed. "I'm not sure, but I think Travis expects me to walk away from Prospect, so he started shoving me out the door."

"And you ain't goin'? Is that what you're sayin' here?" Prue asked.

Keena waited for panic to take over, for her pulse to race or some kind of physical reaction to betray her anticipated anxiety, but none came. "I believe that's exactly what I'm saying. Dr. Singh is looking for a partner. I know now how much I can bring to this practice. I'm going to accept."

Prue's victory yell made Keena pull the phone away from her ear. Everyone else in the car with her heard it, too.

"This is a challenge worthy of my skill, sweet girl. You give me today and tomorrow, and Travis will work all his confusion out. You can count on me." Prue's wicked laughter settled over Keena like a promise.

She knew where she belonged.

It was time Travis figured it out, too.

CHAPTER SEVENTEEN

WHEN HIS MOTHER and father arrived at the hospital, Travis had been cornered by an efficient nurse named Angie. Instead of asking him questions or introducing herself, she walked up to the bed and said, "Damon, we have a good friend in common. Her name is Keena and she asked me to make sure you get VIP treatment." Then she'd peered over her shoulder at Travis and sniffed. "You must be the cowboy."

He couldn't put his finger on why that sounded like an insult, but Angie was unimpressed with him. "And the father. Yeah."

She pursed her lips. "Dr. Shane's got a consult with a neurologist first thing." Her finger made determined taps as she paged through Damon's chart on the tablet in her hand. "It's just a precaution, but it looks like you'll be enjoying the dinner they serve in this fine establishment. I would apologize in advance, but it's chicken finger night in the cafeteria and those are pretty good." She picked up his cup and shook it. "He needs water." Then she handed it to Travis and pointed toward the hallway. "You'll find an ice and water machine next to the nurses' station, cowboy."

Travis was ready to stretch his legs anyway, so he held the cup up to his parents in the doorway. "Be right back."

His mother's disapproving expression made him wonder if he was somehow in trouble as he followed the nurse's orders, but then he realized he was a fully grown adult and straightened his shoulders before he walked in the room. His mother and the nurse stopped mid-whisper and shot him nearly identical looks of judgment.

Whatever Keena wanted to say to him, she'd already lined up her support group. Getting to his mother before he had a chance to get her on his side was smart.

He shouldn't have been surprised.

"Thanks, Travis," Damon said, taking the water and sipping it. "Angie says she's known Keena for years. Someday we'll have more funny stories about her to share, won't we?"

The three adults in the room turned to watch him closely.

He was beginning to understand that he'd messed up by assuming he knew what Keena was thinking.

"Since she told me she was about to become Dr. Singh's partner in the clinic, it would not surprise me a bit, Damon." Prue raised her eyebrows at Travis and hmphed when he sat down with a thump.

His phone rang and he saw Keena's name on the screen. She'd requested a video call so he swiped up and felt the wash of relief when she and Micah appeared together. It looked like they were in the kitchen at the Rocking A. "Hey, Travis," Micah said loudly as if he hadn't quite got the concept of the video call, "how is Damon?"

Travis did his best to memorize the way they looked before he said, "He's good. Talk to him."

After he handed the phone to Damon, he met his mother's stare and they stepped outside, his father trailing after them. "She turned my own mother against me. I admire that. I really do."

Prue rolled her eyes. "Get a grip, Travis. No one is against you. We are all for you. All of us. Me, your daddy, Wes, Clay, Grant, Matt, Sarah, Jordan and the entire town of Prospect. Have been since you first landed in our living room, scared of every shadow. You're brave enough to join the army, travel wherever they sent you and come back home alive, *and* take on fostering on your own, but you can't tell a woman how you feel?" His mother poked her finger in his father's chest. "Who does that remind me of?"

Then she stomped back inside and closed the door abruptly.

Walt scratched his head. "Now, when we left Prospect, I was on her good side. You've gone and messed that up for me, son."

Travis massaged his temples, critically aware of how little sleep he was running on at that point. "Got any advice on how to fix it?"

Walt shoved his hands in his pockets. "I've tried quite a few different things in my time. Fancy dinner invitations, flirting, arguing, agreeing with everything she says, and most recently finding the cash for a fancy pot filler in the kitchen she always dreamed of."

"None of them have worked with Mom," Travis said.

Walt grunted.

"Guess I could try the one thing I didn't hear on that list." Travis nodded. "An apology."

CHAPTER EIGHTEEN

ON THE SUNDAY before Thanksgiving, Prue and Keena finished arranging the Majestic Prospect Lodge's restaurant while they listened to Sarah and Jordan Hearst dissect each decision they'd made regarding the setup for the community's holiday dinner.

While the sisters bickered over whether or not to do full place settings or something more casual, Keena draped the last crisply pressed tablecloth over the table where she and Prue had been stacking the linens. The tiny red-and-white gingham check was cheerful yet smart enough to say this was an occasion.

"No one will miss Sadie Hearst's influence here," Prue said with clear satisfaction. "I love that Jordan is using so much of the stuff Sadie left in storage. It's a nice touch."

Keena agreed as she picked up the bouquet of silk mums in deep oranges and burgundies that Sarah and Jordan had bought yesterday. The duo had been struck with the floral inspiration as they were digging in the magic closet for anything they might use for centerpieces and "absolutely had to go" in search of the pretty decorations. Prue and Keena had been elbow-deep in soapy dishwater at the time, making sure all the plates, silverware and glasses were clean and ready to go.

"Do you think they do this to get out of work or..." Prue crossed her arms and frowned at Sarah and Jordan who were pacing off steps like they were about to turn and duel.

Keena laughed as she stared down at the bouquet. "I don't know if it's a choice they make, but it seems to happen that way."

Prue nodded and took the bouquet from Keena before she marched right between Sarah and Jordan and plopped the flowers down on the table. "Enough. It's a family dinner. Food will be served buffet-style. Put the plates down at the end, silverware on the table, and quit the yammering." She pointed at the mums. "Keena and I are out of here."

Keena didn't wait around to see what the reaction would be. Prue urged her to lead the way through the lobby and out the front door, so Keena managed to hold back her giggles until they were safely in the parking lot.

"Those girls will wear an old woman out, I tell you." Prue placed her hand dramatically on her brow as if she'd been through battle.

"Old woman?" Keena said doubtfully. "You were running rings around all of us, Prue." She'd been busy calling the shots, so she'd had to stay one step ahead. But Keena didn't see any value in saying that part aloud.

"I have five boys. My physical conditioning is superior." She pulled her phone out and sent a text. "Good thing yours is too, Doc." Then she raised her eyebrow. "Travis has been waiting on Damon hand and foot since they got home, but if he doesn't fix all this between you today, I'll do something drastic."

"Nothing drastic, Prue, please." Keena pulled her own phone out to check for texts but it was blank. "There is always the possibility that Travis is looking for someone else, even if I do plan to be right here in Prospect." She exhaled slowly. "And that's okay."

Prue's snort startled a crow from one of the pines at the edge of the parking lot. "No way. That man is gone, has been ever since he told that social worker that teeny little lie, remember?" She patted Keena's shoulder. "I've been working, never you doubt that. This is all under control."

"Prue, I..." Keena had been trying to find the right words for Prue Armstrong for days, but they wouldn't come. She would have to stumble her way through and hope Prue could hear her message. "Thank you. Whatever happens this week or next year or whenever, it's hard to find the right words to say how much I admire the way you make such a big, wonderful family wherever you go. I appreciate how everyone feels loved when they're around you."

Prue covered her mouth with her hand and blinked rapidly. "Well." She cleared her throat. "I don't have the right words, either." She squeezed Keena tight and held her there for a moment. "Keena, I spent a lot of time telling my boys they need to find good partners, but this ol' world has exceeded my expectations when it comes to you." Keena started to remind her the universe hadn't done anything in her case yet, but Prue spoke first. "I've always wanted some kind, smart, caring daughters to go with this mess of sons. And however I get 'em, I'm gonna keep 'em, you hear?"

That reminded her of how Travis had been certain Prue would go to war for all of her kids, not only her sons. It was sweet to be included in that number, no matter what.

Keena nodded. "All right. I'm going to head home and attempt my third apple pie. Faye's has some kind of secret ingredient I can't quite figure out." Something in the back of her mind made her wonder if she should try vanilla.

"If Jordan calls, ignore your phone. You know she wants those beams stained and I don't trust the girl not to get a wild notion in the middle of the night to go for it before the holiday. You can start answering the phone again in December. We will need to drop hints for extravagant gifts they can wrap up and leave us under the tree." Prue waved and Keena was still laughing as she drove onto the highway, headed for home.

It had been a good day. She was running through the list of dishes she was planning to master before Thursday when she stopped in her front yard and saw Travis sitting on her porch steps.

She got out and slowly crossed the yard, her hands in her back pockets.

"Hi," he said and stood. "My mother told me you were on your way here, so I decided to wait."

"The déjà vu is hitting. At least you don't have an axe this time." Keena scuffed her sneaker in the crunchy grass. "Thank you for the texts about Damon's prognosis. I'm glad the numbness is improving. Deep bruises like that can take a while to clear."

Travis took a small step forward. "Seems he's being tormented by being able to look at horses but not get on one. He's grounded anyway, but he and Micah have brushed every horse in the barn until they shine like show ponies."

Keena laughed. His tone was "overwhelmed single parent who wished his kids could be outdoors doing what they love."

"Sometimes the punishment is harder for you than it is for them."

Travis grinned. "That's what my father said."

Both of their phones dinged with incoming messages.

Travis held up his phone. "When my mother hears someone talk about how Dr. Murphy helped a student with the flu or rescued the newest Armstrong or toiled to resurrect the Majestic…that was from Jordan Hearst… My mother passes it along to me. Prospect's hero. How did I ever think I could let you go so easily?" He rubbed his forehead. "I tried to do it because… I love you. I want everything you dream of for yourself to come true."

Keena moved closer to him. "Your mother warned me about falling in love with a man and his children. It was already too late for me. Whether I'm in Prospect or Denver, my heart belongs at the Rocking A."

Travis tipped his head back, blinking rapidly, before he pulled her into his arms. "We aren't going to make the same mistakes my parents did, Keena. I promise."

Keena pressed her forehead to his chest, content to listen to his heart beating. "We won't. I don't think they'll let us."

His chuckle filled her with the bubbly certainty that she was absolutely where she belonged.

"My text is from your father." Keena's lips were twitching. "Would you know anything about that?"

Travis sighed. "When I realized how badly I'd messed up, my dad tried to help."

Keena read, "'One—make sure Travis apologizes. He means it. He knows he's lost without you.'" She paused to check that she had his attention. "'Two—ask him what he's learned. It's important.'"

He ran his finger over her brows and down her cheek. "We belong here. We belong together. Whatever else life throws at you or me, nothing comes between us."

Keena was certain Travis Armstrong was the only man who could make her believe those words. That bone-deep honor she'd put her faith in early on was so easy to see when she stood there in his arms.

He'd made her the promise she'd hoped for but never expected to find. As she repeated the words, Keena knew she was home. "I love you, Travis Armstrong. Nothing comes between us."

EPILOGUE

IT WAS THANKSGIVING. Travis settled his best hat firmly on his head and hopped out of the truck. He took the stack of containers Keena had handed him with firm orders to "Be careful. There's a pie in there," and moved around the truck to meet her in front. Micah was holding her hand and Damon was leaning heavily on the crutch that made it easier to walk on uneven ground. He'd only need the aid for a few more days.

"Which one are the cookies in, Keena?" Micah asked as he ran a finger down the stack of containers.

"Red. It's your favorite color. That makes it easier to remember," Keena said as she bent down and added, "but I saved you a few at home, too." Her wink and fist bump reassured Micah so he zoomed ahead of Damon to the front door of the lodge and yanked it open for them.

"First official outing. You ready for this, Steady Murphy?" Travis drawled. He loved to see the spark of annoyance that lit in her eyes, but she was onto him.

"That's it. The one time you get to say that today. You promised." She waggled her finger at him.

Travis was nodding as he dropped a quick kiss on her lips. "Yes, ma'am. You can trust me."

"I do." She slipped her arm through his and proceeded to the lodge. Inside, there was a crowd milling and Travis was impressed all over again at what the Hearsts had managed with some elbow grease and the assistance of their friends. The lobby was still sparsely decorated, but the restaurant appeared ready for business. After he set Keena's desserts down where his mother indicated, he stepped back to join the rest of the crowd. Everyone appeared to be forming a loose line in preparation for the ringing of the dinner bell.

Jordan Hearst raised her voice to get their attention. "I want to say a quick word..." She gestured to her sister. "Yes, Sarah, it'll be very quick, about how much we appreciate everyone coming here today. The Hearsts have so much to be grateful for, thanks to Prospect. We loved Sadie more than life, and we can't thank her enough for bringing us home, but we can thank you for making us family."

The sentiment captured exactly all the jumbled up words in his head as he stared at Keena. "I couldn't have said it any better."

When he realized everyone was staring at them, Travis cleared his throat.

"You were saying," Prue prompted him.

The happiness in Keena's eyes reassured him. From the very beginning, she'd understood him like no one ever had before. That hadn't changed. Somehow, they were connected and he knew in his heart that was only going to get stronger.

"Words aren't always easy for us," Keena whispered, "but you know what we're very good at?"

Travis traced his thumb over her cheek before he pressed his lips to hers. Their audience's wild whoops and applause confirmed that they were very good at kissing.

And with a lifetime ahead of them, they would only get better.

* * * * *

Keep reading for an excerpt of a new title
from the Intrigue series,
A STALKER'S PREY by K.D. Richards

Chapter One

Brianna Baker took a deep breath of crispy, New York morning air and picked up her pace along the Central Park path. There was probably another twenty-five to thirty minutes before dawn broke through the dark skies overhead and Bria wanted to be back at her Upper West Side townhouse before then. The morning air was invigorating and the forty-six-degree temperature was motivating, but the best thing about getting her morning jog in before the sun came up was that there was little chance that anyone would recognize her.

The brief snatches of time where she could be alone, unrecognized and just breathe and be herself, were what had kept her sane since her acting career had taken off and propelled her into celebrity status.

She wasn't complaining, at least not out loud. Acting had been her dream for as long as she could remember. And the fact that people, millions of people, thought she was good enough to spend their hard-earned dollars going to see her movies was thrilling and humbling in equal measure. But that fame had a price. The loss of her privacy for one. And lately, a nearly debilitating insecurity. The third movie in which she starred as Princess Kaleva, warrior princess, sent to Earth from an alien planet to retrieve the five elemental stones needed to save her people from certain death, had broken box office records in the US and overseas. She was officially an international superstar.

She was proud of the Princess Kaleva movies. They were showing little girls everywhere, especially little brown girls, that they were strong, powerful and smart and that they could be anything they wanted to be. But what she really wanted was to be taken seriously as an actress. But ever since she'd taken on the Princess Kaleva role, her agent had found it difficult to convince the Hollywood honchos that she could do the more serious roles.

Which was why she'd lobbied hard for the part of wife and mother, Elizabeth Stewart, in *Loss of Days*, a film about a family in crisis as a result of a child's drug addiction, when it had come up. It was a bonus that the majority of the filming, although on a tight six-week schedule, was going to be done in New York. In her heart, the city was still her hometown, even after fifteen years in California. It had taken some convincing and several auditions, but she'd won the part. And now she was weeks away from finishing the film she felt in her bones would prove to all of Hollywood that she could play serious, dramatic roles and not just be a busty superhero.

Princess Kaleva had pushed her into the ranks of celebrity, but *Loss of Days* was going to earn her the respect as an actress that she really coveted.

She picked up her pace. Although the sun had started to peek over the trees, the portion of the trail she was on remained deserted. She'd been jogging the same loop around the park since she'd come back to New York a little over a month ago to shoot the film. It totaled just over two miles and she wanted to make it the whole way before the park was packed with people.

She pushed through an uphill stretch of the path, her lungs burning. When she got to the top, she stopped, taking a moment to catch her breath.

Footsteps ricocheted off the trees behind her.

Bria glanced over her shoulder.

A figure jogged up the hill in her direction. From the size and gait, she pegged the person as male, but the shadows and a baseball cap pulled down low on the man's head obscured his face.

A bolt of unease shot through her. She began jogging again. She hadn't told anyone on her team about her morning jogs. Mika Reynolds, her agent, would have told her in no uncertain terms she was a fool for venturing out so early, and Eliot Sykes, her public relations manager, would have admonished her for jogging alone. But one thing she hadn't completely adapted to in terms of her recent celebrity was the complete and total lack of privacy that seemed to come along with it. And she wasn't sure she wanted to.

Bria shot another glance over her shoulder. The man was moving quickly, at more of a run than a jog, and with purpose.

She turned and began to sprint, less concerned with pacing herself than she was with getting to a more public space.

He's out for his morning run. He's not chasing you.

She tried convincing herself but survival instincts, honed over thirty-five years of being a woman in the world, pushed her forward.

She could hear the crunch of leaves indicating that the man was still behind her.

A level of fear she hadn't felt for a long time flooded her body, pushing her forward. She was still a bit of a distance from the entrance to the trail and she hadn't seen anyone other than the man behind her.

Without thinking, she plunged into the trees. Between the noise she was making crashing through the brush and the sound of her heart drumming in her chest, she couldn't tell if the man was still behind her.

She was probably overreacting. The man was most likely just another jogger out for a run, wondering why the weird lady had jumped into the woods.

But a voice inside her head screamed that that wasn't it at all.

She raced through the shadows, branches scraping against her arms and snagging her leggings. Darkness still clung to the dense woods, making her hasty decision seem ever more perilous.

She ran until her lungs threatened to burst, then crouched behind the thick trunk of a tree. She forced herself to listen past her own breathing for sounds that someone else was close.

She didn't hear anything she wouldn't have expected to hear in a thicket, but it was little comfort. If she stayed here and someone really was after her, had she just made it easier for them by darting into the trees? She had even less of a chance now of running into other people.

She couldn't stay cowering behind here forever. She pushed to her feet and plowed forward.

It seemed like it took forever, but finally, she saw the glow of streetlights.

Bria burst through trees, falling onto a walking path in front of a middle-aged man in a suit and carrying a briefcase. He started, freezing for a moment with wide eyes. She could only imagine what she looked like to him.

After a second, he rushed forward, concern plastered over his face for the wild woman who had literally just fallen at his feet. Thankfully, he didn't seem to recognize her. The last thing she needed was to have photos of herself online, leaves clinging to her leggings and twigs sticking out of her hair.

Bria assured the man that she was okay and didn't need an ambulance or the police.

He started away slowly, shooting a glance over his shoulder at her.

She attempted to smile, reassuringly only, but her eyes darted back into the darkness of the trees she'd just burst out of. She couldn't be sure, but it seemed as if the shadows shifted, taking the shape of a head and shoulders.

A car horn honked in the distance, tearing her gaze away from the trees for a moment. When she turned back, there was nothing to see but a solid wall of darkness.